THE BILLIONAIRE IN BOOTS

Center Point
Large Print

Also by Julia London and available from Center Point Large Print:

The Charmer in Chaps
The Devil in the Saddle

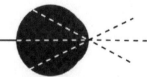

The BILLIONAIRE *in* BOOTS

A PRINCES OF TEXAS ROMANCE

JULIA LONDON

CENTER POINT LARGE PRINT
THORNDIKE, MAINE

Big families figure prominently in this book. I wouldn't be who I am had I not been born into a big Texas family. I was a middle kid and I soaked up what was happening with siblings, and aunts and uncles, and grandparents, and the many, many animals around us. This book is dedicated to my family, who may not realize how much they have influenced my writing of this particular series in ways both big and small. A special acknowledgment to my family's love of dogs—they've been part of my life since I was born.

The
BILLIONAIRE
in
BOOTS

SADDLEBUSH LAND AND CATTLE COMPANY, ESTABLISHED 1872 THREE RIVERS, TEXAS

From: Nick nickprince@saddlebushco.com
To: Charlotte charlotte@saddlebushco.com
Subject: Finance Reports

I need to see this month's finance reports. Thank you.

From: Charlotte charlotte@saddlebushco.com
To: Nick nickprince@saddlebushco.com
Subject: Re: Finance Reports

It's in your inbox. Finance is in the RED folders. ☺

From: Nick nickprince@saddlebushco.com
To: Charlotte charlotte@saddlebushco.com
Subject: Re: Finance Reports

Thanks, I found them. This seems like a good time to mention again that it's very hard for me to remember what color is for what topic. Just for the record, this is not the first time I've expressed my concerns about your filing system.

From: Charlotte charlotte@saddlebushco.com
To: Nick nickprince@saddlebushco.com
Subject: Re: Finance Reports

Which is why I made you a handy-dandy color chart and stuck it on your wall. Turn your head to the right. It's staring you in the face.

From: Nick nickprince@saddlebushco.com
To: Charlotte charlotte@saddlebushco.com
Subject: Re: Finance Reports

How was I supposed to know that was a handy-dandy chart? I don't generally look at the walls, and besides, there is so much "color" in the office that everything looks like your chart. This filing system is just not going to work for me, Charlotte. Frankly, it feels like things are a little off in the office right now. I think we should have a quick staff meeting.

From: Charlotte charlotte@saddlebushco.com
To: Nick nickprince@saddlebushco.com
Subject: Re: Finance Reports

Great idea! As long as we are having a quick staff meeting, I'd like to add a few things to the agenda. 1) It is the custom of civilized staffs all over the free world to provide some sort of snack at meetings to make tedious subjects bearable. See: Donuts. 2) I would like to discuss why every Monday when I ask you how your weekend was, you say the same thing: "It was a weekend." What does that even mean? I *know* it was a weekend, I'm asking how yours went. I don't think it would kill you to engage in a little chitchat, particularly as we are the only two people on this staff and in these offices. Oh, and 3) you ate my lunch TWICE. And for the record, quinoa is not pronounced KWIN-NO-AH, it is pronounced KEEN-WAH.

From: Nick nickprince@saddlebushco.com
To: Charlotte charlotte@saddlebushco.com
Subject: Re: Finance Reports

Well, it looks like the need for a staff meeting is greater than I understood. You really need to rethink this idea that donuts have magic qualities. But by all means, if you want a donut, you should bring one. Bring a dozen, I don't care. The more critical issue is that we need to be adults and mutually agree that your freaking rainbow filing system is not working for anyone but you, and you can put all the charts you want on my wall but I am never going to remember that red is for finance. My brain *does not work that way.* And while I'm at it, you should also know that I am acutely aware when you sign your emails with kissy-face emojis you're being a smart-ass, and furthermore, last week when you told me I should "plant kindness to gather love," I knew that came from a damn tea bag because I LIKE GREEN TEA TOO.

Come in the office, please. Let's get this over with.

From: Charlotte charlotte@saddlebushco.com
To: Nick nickprince@saddlebushco.com
Subject: Re: Finance Reports

Oh, I'm coming, all right, don't you worry, boss. But first, I am walking down the street to Jo's Java to get some damn donuts.

Chapter One

SUMMER
THREE RIVERS, TEXAS

In every family there are colorful stories that are often repeated, trotted out for newcomers at family gatherings, and thereby sealed into the family's collective memory. Like the story about Nick Prince's little brother, Luca, who rode out onto Three Rivers Ranch with his best friend when he was twelve and didn't come home for two days. The number of law enforcement who went out on the search grew with each telling. Nick was fourteen when Luca disappeared, and what he remembered was ranch hands along with a couple of sheriff's deputies riding out to look for the boys. Of course Luca and Brandon had no idea they were missing—to this day Luca maintained he'd been pretty clear with his mother that he'd gone camping. His mother remembered it differently.

And then there was the story about Nick's only sister and Luca's twin, Hallie. She'd been a promising ballerina and had danced in the Ballet San Antonio's production of *The Nutcracker* when she was a teen. The way the family liked to tell it was that Hallie had taken flight in a spectacular jump and crashed into a cardboard tree that was part of the set. That brought the house down, as the telling went. What Nick remembered was that she'd fallen off the pointe of her shoe and had stumbled a little, and that no one had noticed but the Princes. Hallie would roll her eyes every time this story was told and declare she'd never had harsher critics than her own family.

And Nick? Well, he was the one born with a broken heart.

Apparently, he was pretty colicky in the first months of his life and had cried so much that his maternal great-grandmother would hand him back to his mother and say, "I don't know what to do with a baby born with a broken heart."

His parents thought it was funny. Easter Sundays were the preferred time to bring the story out for guests. His dad would say, "Alberta was so convinced Nick over here was put on this earth to endure some great tragedy, and really, all he had was gas. Isn't that right, Nicky?" He would invariably clap a beefy hand on Nick's shoulder so hard as to make his eyes water.

"Grandmother couldn't look that old hound dog in the eye, either, remember?" his mother would say. "Said he looked so sad she couldn't bear to know the tragedy he'd suffered."

"The only tragedy that dog ever suffered

was how fat you let him get," his father would counter, and that would spark an argument between Nick's parents over their conflicting ideas about the care and feeding of family dogs.

To the rest of the family, the being-born-with-a-broken-heart theory was a great way to explain Nick's general sense of malaise. Yes, he could be a grump—he knew that about himself and would own it. He didn't like being a grump. But let anyone who criticized him spend one afternoon separating calves from their mothers and listening to them bawl. Oh, was that too hard for all the drugstore cowboys out there? Then try branding a cow with a red-hot iron.

Nick hated hurting animals, but unfortunately, that was part of ranch life. Electronic ear tags were easily removed by modern-day cattle rustlers, and on a spread the size of Three Rivers, the only way to keep the ranch's superior cattle from being stolen and sold at auction was to brand them. Once, when he was nine, he refused his father's direct order to get up and get ready to brand. His father had taken a layer of skin off his backside. He had not been given the choice of entering the ranching profession. As Nick was the firstborn son, his role was assumed and codified and probably chiseled onto a stone tablet somewhere.

Nick hated everything about ranching. He hated the grind of the work and the hours spent in a saddle riding around this massive ranch his forebears had built. It was a lonely profession. He hated hurting animals, hated hunting, hated stringing fence and worrying about water for the herd in the middle of a drought or worrying about the herd in the middle of the storms spawned by hurricanes in the Gulf or worrying about letters from PETA about their livestock management.

He didn't particularly like the oil business, either, in which his forebears had also begun to dabble just after the turn of the twentieth century when Spindletop gushed for nine days down near Beaumont.

What Nick liked, if anyone cared, which they did not, was flying. He'd earned his pilot's license years ago and had a Cessna he flew around the state. He had his instrument rating, his multi-engine certificate. Next up was his commercial pilot certificate, because Nick wanted to fly big planes. He wanted to fly big planes into big airports around the world and see something other than cactus and cows. He'd had it all set up, too, had paid to attend a flight school in Dallas where he would not only earn the commercial certificate, he would take aviation theory and get in the in-flight hours he needed to apply for a job at a major airline.

And then his dad had died.

Dropped dead of a massive coronary about a year and a half ago.

Nick missed his old man like crazy. But with his dad's death had come the revelation of some significant debt. Everyone knew that his dad had liked the high-stakes gambling in Las Vegas. But no one knew that he'd racked up debt that had left the family coffers reeling. In more ways than one, his father's death had been the quake that had shifted Nick's foundation.

That his father had expressly left the running of the ranch to him was the aftershock that just kept on giving. The more Nick ran this ranch, the worse things seemed to get. They were rich in property and poor in cash, and he was the one who had to make the hard decisions. They'd had to let some of the ranch hands go, which meant Nick was now in a saddle or truck more than he'd ever been. It had been nearly a month since he last flew. It was like the ranch was eating him up, one bite at a time.

So maybe he wasn't born with a broken heart, but he walked around most days feeling like the damn thing had indeed been broken somewhere along the way.

The sun was beating down but good as he drove to the offices of the Saddlebush Land and Cattle Company, the umbrella business that oversaw the various Prince enterprises. Pepper, his collie, rode shotgun. Nick was sweaty and covered in dirt, but he was running late for a meeting with the new banker from Frontier Bank and couldn't do much about it. He had found out a couple of days ago that the work of drilling some water wells his dad had ordered just before his death had not been paid. Nick suddenly needed forty thousand dollars the company didn't have. He'd have it in a month or two, when they took some of the herd to market, but in the meantime, he needed a loan.

He parked in front of the offices, took out a bandanna, and wiped his face.

His father had built the office in the middle of the town of Three Rivers, named after the family ranch. It was on one end of Main Street and fashioned to look like a repurposed old barn. This was another one of those deals that made Nick shake his head. His father had built an office building much larger than anything the company would ever need. He'd built it at the height of the construction bust when oil production moved west and people around here lost their jobs. He'd built it when perfectly good office space sat empty out on the San Antonio highway.

Then he'd gone and commissioned a fifteen-foot-tall bronze statue of a bronc rider that sat outside the offices. What he paid for that alone could have fueled Nick's plane for half a year.

The only other notable thing was on the porch. There were two rocking chairs, as if Grandma and Grandpa moseyed out here in the mornings to have their coffee. It was ridiculous. And tucked behind the rockers where no one ever sat was a blue bike with a basket.

Nick leaned across the truck and opened the passenger door. Pepper leapt out and trotted to the glass door entrance. Before Nick could get out of the truck and lock it, the glass door opened and Pepper slipped inside.

Nick walked briskly to the door. He stopped there to use the boot brush to knock off as much of the dried mud as he could, then stepped inside to the Saddlebush suite of offices, with its iron wagon-wheel chandeliers, hand-scraped wood floor, and rough shiplap walls. His phone pinged at him, and he dug it out of his pocket and looked at the screen. It was a text from Mindy Rogers, an old friend:

Thursday 10:47 AM
Want to do some dancing this weekend?

Nick thought about it, his thumbs hovering over his phone. He liked Mindy's company. A few years ago, they'd dated for about six months. Mindy was the sort of woman who didn't stay in a relationship long and always parted on friendly terms. Or maybe he was that sort? He didn't really know. But Mindy liked having a lot of ex-boyfriends she could call up when she didn't have a date. Nick liked her, and he liked to dance country western–style.

The only problem was that he hadn't been feeling very social lately. More like decidedly antisocial. Which, he concluded, was another reason he ought to go. He couldn't live like this forever, and he really hadn't been out of his house much in the last several weeks.

Three dots popped up on his screen:

Thursday 10:58 AM
Chuck, David, and Sarah are going.

Nick texted back.

Thursday 10:59 AM
Sure. Sounds like a good time.

Mindy texted where to meet up, and Nick shoved the phone back in his pocket. He looked up—and his gaze landed on the visitor area. Someone had put floral seat cushions on the couch, and had added a fluffy white rug to the stained concrete floor. There was a floor lamp painted turquoise, with a floral shade from which beads hung, in between two yellow chairs. The visitor lounge didn't look very barnish. Or ranchy. It looked girlie. Nick half expected a book club to show up and make themselves at home.

His gaze traveled to the reception area and the half moon desk made of old rail ties and sporting a tin countertop. He could just see the top of Charlotte Bailey's curly blond head behind a computer screen. Charlotte had been the office manager here for eleven years. His dad had hired her fresh out of college.

Nick strode forward, coming around to the side of the desk on the march toward his office.

Charlotte swiveled around in her office chair, propped a foot against the wall, and studied him up and down as she sucked on a lollipop. Pepper had curled up at her feet.

"How long have you been sitting here?" he asked.

She removed the lollipop from her mouth. It was grape. She knew he liked the grape ones best. "Since January," she reminded him. "Since you fired Imelda."

"I didn't *fire* Imelda," he said impatiently. The first person to go from the offices was Raymond Davis, their accountant. Nick's sister-in-law—Luca's wife, Ella—was doing the books for him part-time and for an embarrassingly small fee. It was all he could afford, and Ella had said she didn't mind, she just wanted to help out.

Imelda Ramon was the next to go. She'd been their receptionist for many years and made the best muffins of anyone Nick had ever known. "I let her go, and with a nice severance, I might add. That's a big difference from firing."

"Not really," Charlotte said. "What's got you

fee fi fo fumming in here?" Her eyes drifted over him.

Nick looked down, too. "What are you talking about? I came in like anyone comes in here."

"Mm-hmm. I thought you were meeting the new banker."

"I am."

"Looking like that?" She popped the lollipop in her mouth again and eyed him suspiciously. "You look like you've been digging ditches. Have you been digging ditches? Or did someone finally truss you up and pull you behind a mule?"

"What do you mean, *finally?*"

She shrugged. "It's bound to happen sooner or later."

So his T-shirt was sweat stained, and his jeans were beyond dirty. And it looked like he still had some mud caked on his boots. "Rafe and I have been branding cattle this morning, Charlotte. It's a dirty job. Besides, this dude is a cattleman's banker. He's probably been tagging his own cattle."

Charlotte dumped the lollipop in the trash and stood up. Her eyes were the color of swimming pools and framed with dark brown lashes. She had the lightest dusting of freckles across her nose and cheeks, like she'd dashed outside for a moment and had dashed back in before the freckles could darken. She glanced at his cowboy hat and reached up, removing it from his head, and held it away from her body between finger and thumb. "Eew."

He took the hat from her. He dragged his fingers through his hair, still damp with sweat. Okay, so she had a point. "I beg your pardon, but I'm dressed like a ranch hand today. That's what I do. I work the ranch and then I come in here and try and run it. It is what it is. Do you have the—"

She picked up the mail and slapped it against his chest. He glared at her. "What about—"

She held up two pink phone messages between her fingers.

He stared at her some more. Why did it always feel like her efficiency was somehow duplicitous? Why could he find nothing to complain about when it came to Charlotte, besides her stupid filing system?

He took the mail and his messages. "Come on, Pepper," he commanded.

Pepper looked at Charlotte. Charlotte's eyes never left Nick's as she extended one long, manicured finger and pulled open the top drawer of her desk. Pepper's tail began to thump hard against the floor. Charlotte picked up a small biscuit and tossed it. Pepper caught it deftly.

"You don't play fair," Nick said.

"No one ever said anything about fair."

"True," he conceded. That's not the way they did things around here. Nick knew when he was defeated, and strode the fifteen feet to his office like a messenger who had ridden all day with news for the king.

He reached the door of his office and tried to slide it open. All the offices in this building had faux antique barn doors that were suspended from metal rods. The doors slid back and forth to open and close. Nick's always stuck. Charlotte knew how to unstick it, but it was a little emasculating for Charlotte to have to unstick his door every other time he was in the office.

So he cursed under his breath and manhandled the thing into submission with one hand.

"Want me to call Buck and get him out here to fix your door?" she called over her shoulder.

"No," he said curtly, and walked into his office.

"I'll call him," she said, and he heard her pick up the phone.

He went to his desk, tossed down his mail and messages, and sat for a moment, his head in his hands, as he listened to Charlotte sweet-talk Buck into coming out tomorrow. He sighed, and looked around for the financial reports.

Now Charlotte was cooing to Pepper. "You're such a *good* dog, Pepper, such a *good* dog. Do you want a belly rub? Let me give you a good *belly rub.*"

"Charlotte!" Nick shouted. "Did you get—"

"On your desk! Red folder, remember?" she shouted back. She followed that up with some muttering that he couldn't quite make out, but judging by her tone, he was about ninety-five percent certain it was about him and not what a good dog Pepper was.

He had to be the only man in all of Three Rivers who didn't get along with Charlotte Bailey. Everyone loved her. His dad had said that if it weren't for Charlotte, Saddlebush Land and Cattle would have sunk a long time ago. She was very pretty, and she had a sparkling personality, a dazzling smile, and a bubbly defiance that most people found charming. She was quick to help out where she could, was able to laugh at herself, and fortunately for him, didn't get her feelings hurt too very often.

There was a lot to like about Charlotte Bailey.

It wasn't that he didn't get along with her, exactly, but there was always something big and large between them. A big ball of tension. The Jabba the Hutt of all balls of tension. It didn't make sense, really, because when Nick thought of Charlotte, he thought of someone who was super capable and better at this job than he was.

But he also thought of breasts that were the perfect size and thighs so firm and so soft that he could still remember how they felt when he sank between them the night of that Christmas party after one too many Mistletoe Margaritas.

So there was that.

He didn't have time to think about that right

now, however, because the new banker was going to walk in at any moment, and Nick needed to borrow forty thousand dollars.

He looked at his desk again, and there was the red folder with the financial reports. Had she ever been late with them? Had they ever not been on his desk? How come he couldn't see them half the time? Why was this color system so damn hard?

He opened the folder and glanced through and noticed that a copy of the monthly ledger was not in the folder. He wondered what color folder the monthly ledger occupied. He didn't want to ask—Charlotte really didn't like it when he didn't use or understand her system.

He heard some flowery music drifting up from her computer. He couldn't find the monthly ledger and was running out of time. So he walked out of his office to ask. He stood behind her a moment, waiting for her to notice him. The music was loud, and he could see words floating up from the bottom of the screen. *Is this method of fertility preservation right for you?*

"What does that mean?"

Charlotte jumped, then scrambled to close the browser windows. "Don't sneak up on me like that!"

"I didn't sneak up on you. I walked out of my office and right to your desk."

She shook her head. She stood up. But Nick

was inadvertently blocking the exit from the half-moon desk. She was standing close. So close that her eyes looked even more summery, if that was possible. If she drew one deep breath, her breasts would touch his chest, and damn it if he didn't feel a little flutter of anticipation at the mere thought.

She didn't take a big breath. She put her hands on her hips. "You're in the way."

He folded his arms. "I have a question. Where are you running off to?"

"To fill the water bowl for your dog, something you routinely forget to do."

He looked at her lips. Plump and brightly pink with some very glossy gloss. "Pepper prefers the toilet."

Charlotte made a gagging sound. "That's *gross*."

"There's no accounting for a dog's taste," he said, with an accusing look at his dog. "What's fertility preservation, anyway?"

Charlotte folded her arms. "None of your beeswax."

"Which means it's something."

"Which means it's none of your business, Nick."

"I guess it is my business since you're doing it at work."

She laughed. "As if you would know what the office manual says about personal use of computers. It's my lunch hour." She pointed to a Tupperware container on her desk. "And it's not porn, so no, it's none of your business."

"Huh," he said.

"What does *huh* mean?"

He could feel a corner of his mouth quirk up in a sort of half smile. "Well, generally, it means, you don't say. But in this context, it means *huh,* that's interesting, because last I heard, you were on the hunt for a sperm donor. I thought you were going to be pregnant before the end of the year or something like that."

"You don't have to make it sound so weird," Charlotte said.

"Just repeating what you said."

"So what if I was looking into sperm dona- tion? I've changed my mind. Will you please move?"

Nick took one giant step back. He gestured dramatically for her to go ahead. Charlotte brushed past him, her shoulder making contact with his chest in a move he was certain was purposeful. She walked to the filing cabinet and pulled out a drawer.

Nick took the opportunity to look at his traitorous dog, who, fresh off her belly rub, had settled in under the desk as if she wasn't going anywhere. He shifted his attention to the computer screen. Charlotte had closed one tab, but not another.

Google: *how to freeze my eggs*

People also ask:

Is freezing your **eggs** painful?
What is the best age to freeze your **eggs**?
How much does it cost to freeze my **eggs**?
Is **egg** freezing covered by insurance?

He was startled by a slap to his arm and turned around. "What's this?"

"The ledger. You'll need it to meet with the banker. It's our accounts. All of them, clearly labeled and color coded. You might notice that everything to do with the oil wells is purple. Yellow for cattle. Blue for minerals. Red for monthly finance reports. And if you forget, there is the *chart* that I *taped* to your wall so you *wouldn't forget.* We've talked about this."

The chart was right next to a calendar and a poster of Angus steers. It was a lot of wall noise, which he'd pointed out during their staff meeting. At the time, he'd somehow been convinced to give the color system another two weeks. He glanced at her computer, then at her, and went back to his office.

He hadn't even opened the folder—how could he, when the words *how to freeze your eggs* were dancing around in his vision—when he heard the door of the office open.

"Hello!" Charlotte said cheerfully. "You must be Mr. Rivers."

"Oh, please call me Colton," a deep male voice said.

He didn't have a Texas accent, Nick noted.

"I'm Charlotte, the office manager of this little barn."

Interesting. Charlotte's voice was different. About an octave higher than it normally was. He opened the ledger and flipped to the red tab to quickly review what was in the accounts.

Out in the reception area, Mr. Rivers said, "Very nice to meet you, Charlotte."

"Oh! This is Pepper. She's a great cattle dog, but horrible with her social skills. I'm not going to lie, her training was terrible. But I'm working with her."

Nick rolled his eyes. Charlotte happened to share a house with the laziest Labrador retriever in the history of man, and under no scenario could she claim that Rufus was well trained.

"I'm so sorry! It looks like she got mud on your pants. Let me get a wet cloth."

"No, it's okay," Mr. Rivers said. He was laughing. "It's nothing."

Nick heard the treat drawer slide open.

"Are you new to town?" Charlotte asked.

"Fairly new. I moved here about two months ago. Are you from around here? Looks like it's growing pretty fast."

"I was born and bred in Three Rivers," she said cheerfully.

Why didn't she just bring the guy back to his office? Nick stood up, rubbed his hands on his jeans, and then walked out into the reception area.

The first thing he noticed was that Colton Rivers had not been branding or tagging cattle this morning. He hadn't been anywhere near a ranch, that much was obvious. He was wearing a suit. And not an ill-fitting kind of suit that men sometimes pulled on for Sunday church services, either. This was a tailored suit with cigarette trousers and a figure-hugging coat and a stylish tie. His gold-brown hair was brushed back behind his ears. His goatee was perfectly trimmed. His tortoiseshell glasses framed his eyes and made them look fairly large. He was tall and trim and had the physique of a quarterback. If Nick were a woman, he'd be attracted. Hell, he was a little attracted as it was. And clearly, so was Miss Egg Freezer over there.

"Good morning," he said.

Mr. Rivers glanced up and cast a brilliant smile that knocked Nick back a mental step or two. "You must be Nick Prince. I'm Colton Rivers."

"Good to meet you," Nick said, and walked forward, hand extended, to greet him.

Colton Rivers tried to meet him, but Pepper was not ready to let him go, and put herself in his path. Rivers laughed and went down on one knee to greet Pepper properly. Points for liking dogs.

Mr. Rivers stood up and took Nick's extended hand, and Nick wished he'd listened to Charlotte and cleaned up a little. "Come on back," he said. "Sorry about my appearance—we're branding cattle today."

"Tough work," Mr. Rivers said.

"Pretty awful," Nick agreed, and gestured to the door of his office. "Charlotte, will you get us some coffee please? How do you take yours, Colton?"

"Black, thanks," Colton said.

Nick looked at Charlotte. "Two blacks."

"Sure," Charlotte said, and resumed her seat and swiveled around to her computer.

In his office, Nick asked Colton Rivers to take a seat. The young gentleman settled in. "What can I do for you, Mr. Prince?"

"Nick, please," Nick said.

"Great. And I'm Colton. I always feel like someone is looking for my dad when they call me Mr. Rivers."

"Yeah, me too," Nick agreed. "Speaking of my dad . . . I've got some wells I need to pay for." He looked around the desk. Where were the invoices for the wells? He'd just had them here yesterday. He lifted up some papers and quickly looked through them. "Sorry," he said sheepishly. "I've got it right here somewhere."

"Take your time," Colton said. He reminded Nick of James Bond, all cool and collected while Nick searched his desk.

"Hey, is that a Learjet?"

Nick looked up. Colton had stood to look at a picture of the jet Nick had owned but had to sell after his father died. He had one plane now. "It is."

"Nice," Colton said. "Is it yours?"

"It *was* mine. That is, it belonged to Saddlebush Land and Cattle, but I had to sell it when some of our financial woes became apparent."

"What's the range on that one? About two thousand nautical miles?"

That was not the standard question people asked him about planes, and Nick was impressed. "Do you fly?"

"Me? No," Colton said, and smiled. "I wish. I've always had a fascination with planes, to be honest."

"I still have a Cessna," Nick said. "A single-engine turboprop. Good utility plane."

Colton turned from the picture and sat again, crossing one leg over the other. "That's awesome. I'd love to have a look at it sometime."

Nick was liking this guy. Most people he knew didn't care much about planes, only that they got them from one place to another. "It's at our airstrip on the ranch. You need a plane to have a look at a ranch this big."

"I bet that's right," Colton said. "You shouldn't have told me you have it close by. I don't want to blow up your phone, but . . ." He grinned and shrugged.

They both laughed. "I get it," Nick said.

"So what can I do for you?" Colton asked.

"Yeah, about that. My dad drilled some water wells. Charlotte?" Nick called.

Charlotte appeared at the door. "Inbox," she said.

Nick looked at his inbox. He could have sworn he just looked at it, but there it was, the plain manila folder in his inbox. "Great, thanks. And the contract with the drilling company?"

He did not miss the look she gave him as she walked to the filing cabinet and opened it. She pulled out a folder and handed it to Nick. "Current contracts are green," she said, and pointed to the chart on the wall.

Damn color chart. "Thanks, Charlotte, you're a lifesaver. And the coffee?"

"Oh sorry," she said with a slight wince, on her way to the door. "The machine is broken."

This was news to Nick. Hadn't he spotted a cup of coffee on her desk? "It is?"

"Yep. Won't work."

"Probably just as well," Colton said. "I had plenty this morning." He patted his very trim belly and smiled at Charlotte.

Charlotte smiled back with a thousand watts,

then glanced at Nick and dimmed that smile to about seventy-five watts before walking out of the office.

With all the papers he needed, Nick began to explain his dilemma to Colton. In the middle of his explanation, he saw Charlotte stroll by carrying a coffee cup. A moment later, she strolled by again with the coffee cup, on the way back to her desk. She paused briefly and flashed him a smile.

Okay, all right, he'd deal with her later. Right now, he had to convince his new friend that he should loan him some money.

When Nick had finished going over everything, Colton nodded. "I think we can work something out. I should probably have a look at the wells."

"Want to fly out?"

"That would be awesome." Colton smiled boyishly.

Together, Nick and Colton walked out of his office. "I'll give you a call in a day or so," Nick said. "We'll have a good look at the ranch and the wells."

"Sounds great," Colton said as he shook Nick's hand. "You really ought to consider the idea of putting a development out there. There is a lot business going up on the road to Victoria. It could be that's what your dad had in mind."

"I'll run some numbers," Nick lied. There was no way his mother and his grandmother would ever agree to develop prime ranch land.

Colton paused at Charlotte's desk and smiled. "*Very* nice to meet you, Charlotte."

"Likewise," she said.

Colton started for the door, and Nick went with him. So did Charlotte. So did Pepper, for that matter.

"You should check out the Magnolia Bar and Grill if you haven't already," Charlotte said to Colton. "They have some fantastic craft cocktails. I know the bartender there and he's always experimenting."

"I wouldn't know where to start," Colton said. "I'd need a guide into the craft cocktail section."

"Well, lucky you!" Charlotte chirped. "My friends and I hang out there at least once a week. Maybe I'll see you there and introduce you to a few drinks and my friends."

Colton smiled, all snowy white teeth and dimples. "That could definitely be arranged. Thanks. You two have a good day." He walked out of the office with a wave.

Nick and Charlotte stood silently at the door and watched Colton jog to a sporty BMW.

"He's hot," Charlotte said. "He's got a swimmer's body."

"I'd say it's more of a quarterback's body," Nick said as Colton got in his car and drove away.

"Swimmer," she insisted.

"Quarterback," he countered, not because he was really invested in Colton Rivers's level of hot, but he wished Charlotte wouldn't drool like that. "Laying it on a little thick, weren't you, with the craft cocktails? Why didn't you ask for his number if you're so interested?"

She tilted her head back and smiled up at him. "What's the matter? Afraid I'll intrude on your budding bromance? You sounded a little breathless in there." She arched a brow that dared him to deny it. "Why didn't *you* ask for his number?"

"Because I already have it," Nick said.

She gave him a knowing little smirk, then walked back to her desk and picked up her coffee cup and drank.

"I thought you said the coffee machine was broken."

"That's right, I did," she said, as if mystified by that. "But I guess it wasn't."

Nick put his hands on his hips. "Charlotte, I swear—"

"I know, Nick, because you swear about something most days. But I'm not your maid, remember? We agreed on the ground rules. *Your* ground rules. *You* said we had to have ground rules. *You* said this has to be a professional working relationship and whatever happened in the past has to stay in the past, and *I* said, I am the office manager here and not the maid, and you agreed. I should have been in that meeting."

Nick clamped his jaw tightly shut. He couldn't argue with her. He had indeed set ground rules when he told her that there could never be anything between them, that he was leaving as soon as he could get out of here, and that they ought to keep it professional. And then, just like the putz he could definitely be at times, he'd laid out all the ways they could keep it professional.

"I know more about those wells than you do," she added irritably.

He wanted to say something like *You're right, you should have been in the meeting,* or *I don't know why I don't think of things like that,* or *I was too wound up about having to borrow money,* or *I own this pop stand, don't tell me what to do,* or *Why didn't you say something if you thought so,* or *Why are you freezing your eggs? What happened to the sperm donor?* But instead, he said, "Fine. I stand corrected." He stomped to the coffee bar, poured himself a cup of coffee, and stomped back to his office. At the door, he glanced over his shoulder. "Pepper, come!"

Pepper leaned against Charlotte. Charlotte put her hand down and scratched Pepper's ears as if assuring her they were united against Nick.

Sometimes it felt like the whole damn world was against Nick.

"By the way, I'm leaving early today," Charlotte announced.

Nick paused and glanced back at her. "You are?"

"Yep. I'm leaving at four."

"Doctor appointment?"

"No."

"Something to do with your family?" There were a lot of Baileys in town. Like on every corner.

"No."

"So . . ."

"So, if you must know, I have a date. In San Antonio."

"You have a *date?*" he asked, perhaps more incredulously than he should have. Charlotte had seemed so hell-bent on the sperm-donor thing, he thought she'd given up on dating.

"Yes, Nick, a *date*. Will you please stop looking at me like that?"

He blinked. "I'm not even looking at you. I mean, I'm *looking* at you, but not like . . . that."

"Yes, you are. You're looking at me like you can't believe someone would ask me out on a date. Either that, or you don't remember what a date is, and you're trying to remember."

He snorted. "I know what a date is, Charlotte. But I didn't know you were dating."

She folded her arms. "News flash—not all of us are fine with sleeping alone night after night."

There it was, that Jabba the Hutt tension rearing its big ugly head. He couldn't even say why, but it had something to do with *sleeping* and *alone* and *night* that reminded him of the night he hadn't slept alone. Hadn't slept at all, really.

Charlotte was thinking of it, too. He could tell by the way her cheeks turned pink. "Anyway, just so you know." She sat heavily and swiveled back around to her computer screen. "And Buck will be here to fix your door at nine tomorrow morning."

Nick stood there. He wanted to say he thought about that night, too. But he didn't see what good that would do. So he slowly turned around and went into his office and looked for the drilling reports. *Lord.* What color would that be? He squinted at that damn chart on the wall and tried very hard not to think of someone else between Charlotte's thighs.

Chapter Two

His name was Mark Tremayne, and he was a lawyer. On the dating app, he said he was six feet two, and he had hair almost as blond as Charlotte's. He said he was into water sports and had included a picture of his torso. Charlotte couldn't remember why she'd been drawn to him, but sitting in the lobby of Hotel Emma, where they'd agreed to meet for a drink, she was questioning her judgment.

She wondered idly what Nick would say if he knew whom she was meeting for a drink. If he had an opinion, he probably wouldn't say it out loud. He was the type who liked to smolder with his thoughts. He'd probably think Mark Tremayne wasn't *that* handsome or *that* ripped, just because she did. But his opinion would be one delivered with a shrug, because Nick didn't have strong opinions about anything, with the exception of a color-coded filing system, about which his opinion was ridiculously strong.

Colton Rivers, now *there* was a handsome guy. Almost as handsome as Ni—

Nope. She wasn't going there. And anyway, Nick wasn't classically handsome like Colton.

Nick was handsome like actors who played Wyatt Earp in movies were always handsome—in a rugged, badass way. Handsome like someone who played hard and drank hard and made love hard. Whereas Colton could have walked off the pages of a magazine. He had a beautiful smile and kind eyes.

She knew Mark Tremayne the moment he walked into the lobby. He strode in as if he'd just come from winning an important murder trial, loosening his tie as he checked out the women. Charlotte stood and gave him a little wave. She was wearing a blue dress she'd picked up at Mariah Frame's boutique and hair salon on Main Street in Three Rivers. "You should always wear blue, Charlotte," Mariah had said. "It makes your eyes pop." Charlotte didn't really care about her eyes popping most of the time, but she did want to make a good impression on the thin chance that Mark was The One.

He didn't look like he was six feet, two inches. And she didn't know what had happened to that sculpted torso on his profile, but he hadn't brought it tonight. She waved again, and when he spotted her, his eyes did the flick up and down, checking her out. Then he smiled. So did Charlotte.

"You must be Charlotte," he said, his arm outstretched.

"I am!" She extended her hand to shake his.

"Very nice to—" Mark went right by her hand and threw his arm around her shoulders, hugging her. "Oh. Okay," Charlotte said, a little startled.

"Been here long?" he asked, and sat on the couch.

Charlotte carefully sat, too. "Just a few minutes."

"What are you drinking?" he asked, looking around for a server.

"I'm having ro—"

"Nah, come on, we have to have a real drink," he said, and waved down a server. "Y'all still making the Three Emmas cocktail? We'll have two," he said, holding up two fingers.

"Wait, I—"

"You'll love it," Mark said, and squeezed her knee.

Oh-kay. He was gregarious! There was nothing wrong with gregarious. "So, Mark. You're a lawyer, right?" she asked as he scanned the crowded lobby.

"Litigator." He looked at her. "Do you know what I mean by that?"

Charlotte was momentarily stunned again. Was he kidding? "Yes, I know what you mean by that."

"I've handled some big cases you've probably heard of. *Tobin v. Texas*."

Charlotte shook her head. Why would she have heard about that?

"No? What about *Exxon v. Terlingua Limited*?"

She shook her head again. He rattled off a few more, watching Charlotte closely. She didn't know what he expected—she didn't exactly keep up with the civil court dockets. Did anyone?

"Well, that's okay," he said magnanimously. "I'll fill you in as we go along."

Great! There was nothing she liked more than being filled in on court cases involving companies she didn't know.

The server returned with the cocktails and set them on the little table before the couch.

"Thanks, sweetheart," Mark said to the woman.

Charlotte swallowed down a strong desire to punch this guy. She and the server exchanged a look before the server walked away.

Mark made her pick up the cocktail and clink glasses. "To the beginning of a beautiful arrangement," he said, and winked.

What the hell was an arrangement?

"So," he said, and his gaze drifted to her chest. "Tell me about you."

"Well, I live in Three Rivers and work for a land and cattle company."

"Okay. Forget about that—tell me your wildest fantasy," he said, and gave her a smile that made her want to pour her cocktail on the top of his head.

At the moment, her wildest fantasy was to end

this date. Mark Tremayne was not her guy. "Let me think," she said.

"Do us both a favor and think of something naked," he said, and chuckled as if that was supposed to be funny.

Yeah, no, this was definitely not going to work. Moreover, Charlotte didn't have time for this nonsense. She was thirty-two years old and she wanted kids. Correction—what she *really* wanted was a family, which in her mind included children, the requisite husband who loved her above all others, a two-car garage, and a big Christmas tree during the holiday season. She wanted to host backyard birthday parties and dress her kids up for Easter. She wanted another dog and maybe a cat and to pose for family pictures in the bluebonnets each spring and go to baseball games. The whole nine yards. The entire kit and caboodle. The real deal.

But time was beginning to run out.

Or at least it felt that way to her.

Mark gave her a knowing smile. "My guess is, you've got some kinky fantasies." He waggled his brows over the rim of his glass as he sipped.

"Not too kinky," she said. After a few years of dating guys on and off, Charlotte had reached a point last year where she'd had enough of men who turned out to have full-blown commitment phobias, and had made the decision that she was going to have her family without a husband.

She'd started researching sperm donation. Eight months into that quest she'd been ready to try it. She was ready to get impregnated with donated sperm. But one night she'd woken up in a sweat, panicked by a dream that she'd been impregnated with the sperm of a man who turned out to be a lunatic. The dream startled her so badly that she'd gotten on the floor with her dog, Rufus, and curled up against him, using him as a pillow while her doubts crept in to destroy any sleep she might have had left that night.

When the sun came up the next morning, Charlotte had a complete about-face—sperm donation was too clinical. And maybe a little too desperate for where she was at that point in her life.

She still wanted kids in the worst way. But she also wanted the family part of her fantasy. Maybe she hadn't hunted long enough for Mr. Right. Maybe Three Rivers was too small of a dating pool, and she needed to expand her net. Her sister Cassie was constantly dating someone new. Who was to say that the same couldn't happen for Charlotte if she allowed herself to explore the universe of available men?

Charlotte truly believed there was someone out there for her. She just had to find him, that was all. So she'd changed course.

Her plan was simple. She would date until she was thirty-four in the hopes that something with someone would click and she would find Mr. Right. If she hadn't found him by the time she was thirty-four, she was going to freeze her eggs. And if she hadn't found him by the time she was thirty-five, she was going to go the route of using her eggs and anonymously donated sperm.

One thing was certain: Mark Tremayne was not Mr. Right. She didn't want his sleazy sperm anywhere near her vagina or her eggs.

"So?" he said, and licked the rim of his glass. "Are you going to tell me?"

"I sure am," Charlotte said, and leaned toward him. "My kinkiest fantasy is to find a guy and make some babies."

Mark chuckled. He was smiling, but his face looked a little frozen. He wasn't certain it was a joke.

"As soon as possible," she whispered, and coyly licked her lips.

"Whoa, honey, slow down there," Mark said. "We haven't even finished our drink. And I was thinking of something a little sexier than babies."

"Really?" she asked, pouting a little. "But when you say *fantasy,* I think of adorable little baby outfits."

Mark's smile faded. "Yeah, okay," he said, and downed his drink. "I get it. You're not down with a little wordplay. You could have just said so." He looked away.

"You're right, I could have. But this was more

fun and will make for a better story. So I'm going to go now," Charlotte said. She picked up her purse and pulled out her wallet.

"I've got this," Mark said, waving his hand at her. He was already searching the room for a replacement.

"Great," Charlotte said. She stood up.

"Nice to meet you," Mark said.

Charlotte laughed and walked out of the Hotel Emma.

On the way home she decided that she really had no idea what she was doing. It had been too long since she'd dated around, and she'd never used a dating app. She was as rusty as Cassie accused her of being. As much as Charlotte hated to admit it, she was going to have to give in and take Cassie up on her advice. Cassie was desperate to help her. She was an experienced online dater—she had profiles on three different dating apps.

For some reason, that did not inspire a lot of confidence in Charlotte.

Miles south of San Antonio, on the western edge of Three Rivers Ranch, Nick was sitting on his back porch. His house was a ranch-style, built of river stone, and about as far from the family compound as a person could reasonably be. It had been built some time in the 1950s for ranch hands. It sat on a bluff and overlooked some undeveloped prime grazing land and a river. It was removed from town and any neighbors, and it suited him.

He and his dad had renovated the house. They'd pulled up the linoleum and restored the original pine hardwoods. They'd painted the rooms, restained the crossbeams on the ceiling, and completely revamped the kitchen and bathroom. Nick wasn't much of a cook, but if he ever decided to be one, he had the setup. He had high-end appliances. He had quartz countertops, milled just down the road. Pale gray cabinets made by the old man on Avenue E in town. A farmhouse sink, and the standalone center island that Nick and his dad had made together in the workshop at Three Rivers Ranch.

That was one of the last projects they'd done together. They'd spent hours in the ranch workshop, talking sports and planes. His dad had been one of the few who liked to listen to Nick talk about planes.

The house didn't have cable TV, and the internet was pretty spotty, but that was okay with Nick. He liked the solitude.

He heard his horse, Frank, knocking against the paddock gate. He liked to rub his flank against it for a scratch. Frank was a hundred and ten years old if he was a day. He once lived at a house that Nick used to pass on the way to town. He was never out of the small fenced yard and never with any other animal or person that Nick could see. After a few months, Nick couldn't take it. He stopped by one day and offered an outrageous amount of money. The man who answered the door—shirtless, with three or four kids hanging off his legs—had asked no questions. Frank had lost some muscle mass, and he couldn't see too well. But that old horse held on.

There were cows down in the valley, far enough away that they looked like someone had spilled their blackberries. There weren't many of them. Two longhorns retired from stud service that he'd bought at auction, saving them from slaughter. There were two heifers, too. One of them had made a mad escape from being corralled into a feedlot to be fattened up for slaughter, and her friend ran after her. It had taken the sheriff and his deputies up in Medina County two days to catch them. When they did, Nick was there with a trailer and made a deal with the owner on the spot. He didn't get a fair price, but that was okay.

He had one more cow, a bull that had been displaced by a storm. It had an ear tag, which, Nick would admit, he'd removed. He'd found him wandering around by a two-track road that went down to the creek, and he figured if that bull could survive the storms spawned from a hurricane, he ought to live out the rest of his days in peace. So Nick's little rescue herd had grown by a couple of calves.

In the morning, the cows were all up near the fence at the house. He'd go out and talk to them. Tell them about what was going on in the world. He didn't have that much to say, but the cows came every morning to hear him, and when he was done, they'd sort of wander on out, seeking better grass. Maybe they showed up just to assure themselves that he was still a vegetarian. He was. He'd made a pledge to them a long time ago. "I can't stop the world from wanting a good steak, but I won't betray you."

That was the one thing about him that his dad had not understood. "I've never heard of anything so dumb as a vegan cattle rancher," he'd proclaimed. "They're just cows."

"Not vegan. Vegetarian. They're still beings, Dad," Nick had said.

"There's that broken heart for you," his mother said. "Always crying about something."

Nick didn't think he was always crying about anything, and he thought it probably shouldn't matter to them what he ate or didn't eat. But in his heart, he couldn't look at those bovine faces every morning, faces that had fought hard to survive, and feel good about sending them off to be a burger. So yeah, he was a vegetarian cattle rancher.

He had a pig, too. She'd been Ella's—or rather, she'd been abandoned at Ella's old place, where his sister, Hallie, and her husband, Rafe, were living now. Hallie was six months pregnant and couldn't deal with that hungry pig every day, so Nick had hauled her out here. Priscilla liked it here. Nick suspected she'd gotten it in her head that she was a horse like Frank, because she followed him around half the day. Frank didn't mind and Priscilla seemed happy being a horse.

Nick had a couple of barn cats that kept busy. He'd had some abandoned chickens at one point, but they never made it long this far out. Coyotes or cats or something got them. And he had Pepper, of course, the best damn dog that ever lived.

So he wasn't entirely alone out here. Just didn't have anyone to talk to besides the cows.

Sometimes he thought about that. It wasn't that he didn't want someone to talk to. He did. But he had it in his head that he was leaving Three Rivers behind. He was getting on a jet plane for real, and he was going to see the world. It didn't make any sense to find someone to talk to.

His brother, Luca, reminded him that being in a relationship was not the same as having friends, and he didn't have those, either. "I know," Nick had said. "I know I need to get out more and meet more people. But then I am reminded that I don't happen to like getting out or meeting people."

Luca had sighed wearily. "Dude," he said.

"How can you go without sex for so long?"

"Who says I'm going without sex?" He was, save an occasional fling here or there, but Luca didn't need to know that.

It had always been hard for Nick to make friends. Even as a kid, he'd hung out with Rafe Fontana, who was the son of the family's majordomo, Martin Fontana. Now Rafe was his brother-in-law, married to Hallie. Nick and Rafe had gotten along because they'd grown up working together. But Nick had always been the quiet one in school. He'd wanted friends, and he supposed he'd had one or two. But he wasn't outgoing. He'd never had a knack for knowing what to say. He was too taciturn.

He wouldn't mind a friend or two now. He was, he would grudgingly admit, a little lonely. He could well imagine what Charlotte would say to that. He could just hear her, quoting some tea bag. *The creation of a thousand forests begins with one acorn, Nick. Hello!"*

Oddly enough, Charlotte was probably the closest thing to a friend that he had. And she couldn't stand him. But he liked Charlotte. A lot. He'd never be crazy enough to let her know, though. Whew boy, she'd take something like that and run with it.

Nick was pondering this with his beer when his phone pinged with a text message. He felt relieved by it—it was proof that he wasn't as pathetic as he was beginning to believe. But then he saw the text.

Thursday 7:15 PM
You can save a lot of money with Geico! Call today!

Nick groaned. "It's worse than I thought," he said to Pepper.

Pepper didn't even lift her head from between her paws. She knew.

From: Nick nickprince@saddlebushco.com
To: Charlotte charlotte@saddlebushco.com
Subject: You're Late

Good thing I was in the office this morning. Big Barb came by with the mail. And stayed to chat. So there's an hour I'm never getting back. Guess your date went pretty well.

From: Charlotte charlotte@saddlebushco.com
To: Nick nickprince@saddlebushco.com
Subject: Re: You're Late

I'm late because I'm the kind of person who sometimes shuts off her alarm and comes in late to work. I'm sure Big Barb was thrilled to have a chance to grill you about the goings-on at Three Rivers. I hope you gave her something because I can't keep making up things about you Princes. At least I had a date last night. What did you do?

From: Nick nickprince@saddlebushco.com
To: Charlotte charlotte@saddlebushco.com
Subject: Re: You're Late

It doesn't matter what I did because I wasn't late. Do you have Colton Rivers's number?

From: Charlotte charlotte@saddlebushco.com
To: Nick nickprince@saddlebushco.com
Subject: Re: You're Late

I knew it. You *do* have a crush on him. Maybe you could meet him at Magnolia for a cocktail.

From: Nick nickprince@saddlebushco.com
To: Charlotte charlotte@saddlebushco.com
Subject: Re: You're Late

Are you still mad about the thing with Colton? I said I was sorry. It wasn't intentional to leave you out of the meeting, Charlotte. I got a little wrapped up in my own head, worried about how I was going to present my dad's boneheaded decision to drill three water wells in a pasture. I. Am. Sorry.

From: Charlotte charlotte@saddlebushco.com
To: Nick nickprince@saddlebushco.com
Subject: Re: You're Late

Apology accepted. But stop asking me to get coffee for people. I'm not the help.

From: Nick nickprince@saddlebushco.com
To: Charlotte charlotte@saddlebushco.com
Subject: Re: You're Late

Should I draw blood? Will that help?

From: Charlotte charlotte@saddlebushco.com
To: Nick nickprince@saddlebushco.com
Subject: Re: You're Late

Only if I get to do the drawing.

From: Nick nickprince@saddlebushco.com
To: Charlotte charlotte@saddlebushco.com
Subject: Re: You're Late

Can I just have the number please? And by the way, you know I'm only 15–20 feet away from you. I can hear you muttering. I am not "another helpless male," I just misplaced his number. Thank you.

From: Charlotte charlotte@saddlebushco.com
To: Nick nickprince@saddlebushco.com
Subject: Re: You're Late

I was muttering about Rufus. I had to feed him again this morning because he can't figure out how to feed himself. It's 210-555-5555. ☺

Chapter Three

Charlotte Bailey had a very big family, all of whom liked to be involved in the business of all the rest of them. Constantly. It was easy for them, too, because they all lived in the Three Rivers and San Antonio area.

Having a big family within a fifty-mile radius of one's house had its pros and cons. For example, housing—there was no way Charlotte could have afforded to purchase her charming craftsman home right in the middle of Three Rivers. She rented it from her great-uncle Ken for dirt cheap. Uncle Ken had moved into independent senior living in San Antonio about four years ago. He said he preferred independent living to his home and garden in Three Rivers.

"But you loved that garden," Charlotte reminded him one Sunday when she'd gone to have brunch with him.

"I did. But there's lots of gals here," he'd said, and had winked at her. "This is the life, kid—they're *everywhere*." He wasn't joking—four old women stopped by to fawn over him while Charlotte sat with him.

Charlotte also drove an older-model Lexus

that her father had given her when he purchased a new car. "They weren't going to give me what that car should get on a trade, so you can have it," he'd said, as if it were no big deal to hand off a car.

"But you could sell it, Dad!"

"Well, I could. But I'd rather you have it. That car has been meticulously maintained, and I am not going to let just anyone have it."

So yes, there were definitely benefits to being from a large family.

But on the flip side of the coin, being one of the few unencumbered adults (translation: presently, Charlotte was without children or a significant other) meant that the family tended to rely on her. That was great—Charlotte didn't mind helping where she could. But it could be annoying, because her family had a problem with boundaries. Her phone was ringing or pinging all day, every day.

Yesterday, for example, Charlotte had received several texts. The first had come from her brother, Chase.

> Hey, will you watch kids tonight? Lori and I want to see new Marvel movie with cuz.

Cuz would be their cousin Grant and, presumably, his wife, Kit.

Another one, from her younger sister, Cassie:

> I don't know what to do about Ryan. Thought about it all night. Should I break up? Tell me if I should break up.

Charlotte texted Cassie that she couldn't really discuss whether or not she should break up with Ryan *while she was at work* and while *Cassie was also at work.*

Cassie had responded, Whatever. I'll talk to Caitlin, then.

Big-sister Caitlin had promptly texted Charlotte:

> Don't try and put me in the middle of Cassie and Ryan! No one has time for that much drama. Also, Mom is driving me insane. Also, need you to come and help me decide on paint colors for living room. Jonah wants white and I can't take it.

And of course, Charlotte's parents:

> Honey, Dad wanted me to ask if you'll come over and watch that Astros game with him next Wednesday night. I didn't have the heart to tell him that you're a

young woman who probably has better things to do than watch baseball.

After Charlotte said she'd come, her dad had texted:

Astros cut Gonzalez, that pitcher we like. Had an ERA of 3.05. What's the matter with them?

Charlotte didn't have the heart to tell her dad that she didn't really know or care about pitcher ERAs, and that she liked Gonzalez because he was gorgeous.

That litany of text messages was a typical day for Charlotte, in spite of explaining to them all more than once that she really couldn't tackle their problems while she was working, and if it was really so crucial that they had to talk to her, to *please* contact her after work and on weekends. They'd all agreed that of *course* she was busy, of *course* she had to work, they *totally understood.*

And yet, every single one of them continued to text at all hours.

Another great thing about big families is that there was always a reason for a party. Today, the Baileys in all their various configurations were trooping down to the riverbanks at the Magnolia Bar and Grill, where, under a canopy of live oaks, Stars, Boots, and Music happened every Saturday night during the summer months, weather permitting. It was an evening of hanging out with friends and family, listening and dancing to music, and eating and drinking. Residents brought their picnics and blankets and lawn chairs and, in August, when the heat was really brutal, portable fans. Or they backed their trucks up as close as they could get to the cordoned-off area and put the tail down for a tailgate party. The Magnolia had an outdoor stage and portable dance floor, and for those who didn't want to dine in the restaurant, food trucks arrived to complement Magnolia's outdoor bar.

The music was almost always country western, because people around Three Rivers generally liked a good two-step.

Charlotte's family would descend on her house to avoid the hassle of parking at the Magnolia, and they would carry their things the five blocks down to the river's edge and set up. Last year, in fact, her dad had purchased a rolling cooler expressly for Stars, Boots, and Music nights.

Charlotte's sister Cassie, the baby of their family, was the first to arrive. Cassie was the most audacious of them all in Charlotte's view, although some of the family might argue she was just as audacious. Okay, so she'd given the mayor a piece of her mind at a fundraiser, but a campaign promise was a promise. Charlotte could hear Cassie on the street, yelling at her father as he apparently tried to parallel park. "To the *right,* Dad! Not my right! *Your* right!"

Charlotte's parents had popped a kid out every two years until they had four altogether. Cassie was two years younger than Charlotte, and where Charlotte's hair was blond and curly, Cassie's highlighted blond hair was made sleek with an expensive blowout.

Charlotte was two years younger than Chase, who was the only one of the four to have dark hair. He had three kids and swore that was it. "They're too damn loud," he'd said of his children.

Chase was two years younger than Caitlin, who was also blond, but more honey than ash blond, like Charlotte and Cassie. Caitlin was currently seven months pregnant with her fourth child. "I've entered the waddling stage," she'd announced dramatically the last time she'd been at Charlotte's house, and then had collapsed onto Charlotte's couch so hard it squeaked.

In addition to her immediate family, Charlotte had lots of cousins, most of them married, most of them with kids. It seemed as if her entire family had what Charlotte wanted. Except Cassie, who did *not* want to be married or have kids. "I prefer the life of a single woman," Cassie would insist loudly to anyone who listened. She traveled the globe with her tech job, dated men with names like Ryan and Trace and Josh, and inevitably broke up with them in spectacular fashion. She was rarely alone.

Charlotte did not want to be a single girl who was rarely alone. She wanted a life more like Caitlin's. Which was why Cassie had anointed herself Charlotte's dating coach. "I'm not sure I need a dating coach," Charlotte had said over drinks one afternoon. "I just needed some help getting set up on the apps. Which you've graciously done. Your services are no longer required."

"You *totally* need a dating coach," Cassie had insisted.

"But should it be you?" Charlotte had asked, looking curiously at her sister. "You've been dating Ryan for two weeks, and you're already thinking of breaking up with him. That doesn't exactly recommend you."

"I'm teaching you how to *get* dates. The relationship is up to you," Cassie countered.

"She's right," Caitlin added. "You seem to be really bad at getting good dates."

"I've had exactly one date," Charlotte reminded them. Her first foray into online dating had been a rancher from Fredericksburg. He had looked so hot in his profile, and Charlotte had been excited. And as it turned out, he was very handsome in person. A very nice man. A true gentleman. Unfortunately, she'd discovered very early into the date that he dipped tobacco.

When she told her sisters later, Caitlin had gasped, then grimaced like she was going to be sick. "You mean like a pinch between cheek and gum?"

"That's chew, I think. This is just below the lip." Charlotte pulled out her bottom lip to demonstrate.

"Groosss!" her sisters cried in unison.

"Don't say another word," Caitlin had said, tossing up a hand. "I swear to God I'll vomit."

They'd all agreed—dipping tobacco was a total deal breaker, no matter how handsome and nice a man was.

After the conversation with her sisters, in which they'd adamantly insisted that Charlotte didn't know how to properly choose a guy from a dating app, she'd been so determined to prove them wrong that she had tried again on her own and had come up with boob-staring Mark.

Charlotte heard the unmistakable sound of the family's infamous rolling cooler being pushed around the porch. Cassie opened the screen door and shouted, "We're here! *Whoa!* What did you do to the house?"

Charlotte stepped out of the bathroom, where she was trying to do something with her unruly hair, and looked around at her cluttered little house. "What do you mean? I'm painting, obviously." A soothing color of pale green, too, thank you. Charlotte loved it. But she hadn't had time to put the room back together.

"Who is painting what?" Charlotte's dad asked, crowding in behind Cassie. He had a mad scientist look, with a thin build, wire-rimmed glasses, and hair that never seemed actually combed. He bumped into Cassie and forced her to hop over a pile of books that Charlotte had removed from the built-in bookcases and stacked on the floor during her painting project.

"Me," Charlotte said.

"Why didn't you call me? You know how I like a good project," her dad said, looking around. He was holding a big paper bag from H-E-B grocery.

Charlotte hadn't called her dad because while he liked a good project, he would have puttered around for three days, and she couldn't have her dad in her space for three full days. "What is that?" she asked, pointing at his bag.

"Juice drinks for the kids. Your mother and I made a trip to the new H-E-B in town. You should check it out. Go on a Saturday, though— that's when they have the best samples. They have really good pizza, too. You like pizza, Lot?" He stepped around Cassie and walked through the clutter to the kitchen. "I'm just going to put these in your fridge."

"Whew!"

Charlotte's mother was next, her silvery blond hair in a neat little ponytail at her nape. She was in her late fifties and kept her figure by running three miles every morning. She was the exact opposite of Charlotte's father—when her mother decided to tackle something, she did it with efficiency and a minimal amount of fuss.

"Goodness, what is all this?" her mother asked, and gestured to the strips of painted silk Charlotte had hung from a ceiling fan to dry.

"An art project," Charlotte said. "Plus, did I tell you? I'm going to teach myself to sew." She pointed to the sewing machine she'd bought at a thrift shop in San Antonio. "And I have an idea for a dress."

"You really need to date," Cassie said.

"Rufus wants a biscuit!" her father called from the kitchen. "Can I give him a biscuit?"

"No!" Of course Rufus wanted a biscuit. He was a big black Labrador retriever with a block head that weighed nearly as much as Charlotte. He had a thick tail that acted like a battering ram against the walls and tables. He was a little gray around the muzzle, too, given that he was nine years old now.

"He's had his supper, Dad," Charlotte called out. "What's he doing in the kitchen, anyway? He was on the back porch."

Her father appeared in the arched door that led from the front room to the large farmhouse kitchen. Rufus lumbered up to stand behind him, still licking his lips from the biscuit her dad had clearly given him. "He pushed the door open and came in," her father said with a shrug. "That door doesn't latch all the way."

"Uh-huh." Charlotte's old house had some quirks, but she loved it all the same. A lot of things didn't latch all the way, but the back door definitely did.

That door led to the sleeping porch Uncle Ken had added at some point, along with a little half bath on the other side of the laundry room. It was great in the summer, but freezing in the winter. "Uncle Ken was born before they had insulation," Charlotte's father had once explained.

Down the steps from the porch was her backyard, a deep green oasis shaded by bur oaks and loquat trees. She had kept up Uncle Ken's little kitchen garden, and every summer she tried to grow cantaloupe and tomatoes and vegetables with varying degrees of success.

In front of the kitchen was the large family room, and from there, a narrow hall that led to two bedrooms, separated by a large family bath with a black-and-white-tiled floor, a tub that was starting to rust, and a showerhead that couldn't be bothered to put out much of a stream. But it worked.

"Hello!"

Caitlin and her kids were coming in now. Rufus's tail began to work overtime, beating hard against the door frame at the sound of children's voices. Charlotte's two nephews and niece, all of them under the age of six, rushed inside and straight for Rufus. They loved him, and the feeling was mutual. The little darlings didn't bother to greet their aunt, but dropped down on their knees and threw their arms around Rufus's massive neck while Rufus happily panted along.

Caitlin barely made it inside before collapsing in a chair. "I need this baby *out* of me," she said. "Any takers? Just reach up there and get it *out*."

They were all used to Caitlin's pregnancy complaints and generally ignored her. "Where's Jonah?" Cassie asked, peering out the screen door.

"He and Chase and Lori and their kids went down to the river to stake out a spot," Caitlin said. She flipped open a fan and began to wave it at her face. "He said we always take too long and we always lose the best spots."

"Oh! We don't want to lose the best spots," Charlotte's mother said. "Come on, kids, let's go down to the river."

"What about these drinks?" Charlotte's father called from the kitchen. He appeared at the arch again, this time with a handful of chips.

"They need to go in the cooler, Paul!" her mother called impatiently over her shoulder as she walked outside. "Come on, kids!"

"What about me?" Caitlin asked irritably. "Does anyone have a wheelbarrow to wheel me down?"

"Aunt Lottie, can Rufus come?" little Noah asked.

Charlotte looked at her dog. Drool was forming in the corner of his mouth. "You bet. I'll get his leash."

When the dog was leashed, and the drinks had been put in the cooler, and Caitlin had been persuaded to walk, Charlotte and her family started for the river. The kids ran ahead, monitored by Grandma. Grandpa pulled the cooler, reminding anyone who would listen what a great investment it had been. When his daughters refused to listen, he caught up to some neighbors heading down to the river to fill them in on his genius purchase.

Charlotte and her sisters lagged behind at a pace that was comfortable to Caitlin.

"You're, like, *really huge,*" Cassie remarked as she studied Caitlin's belly.

"Gee, thanks, Cass. I wasn't sure." Caitlin shot her sister a dark look. "Can we talk about something other than this baby? He kicked me all night long. Let's talk about Charlotte."

"Yes! Let's talk about Charlotte!" Cassie said eagerly. "How was your second date? I was expecting a report on the boyfriend project."

Charlotte paused so Rufus could examine a mailbox post. "Is that what we're calling it now?"

"That's what it is," Caitlin said. "I'm invested. I have to live vicariously through you two, and since Cassie is breaking up with Ryan, that puts it all on you, Lot."

"I never said I was breaking up," Cassie complained, which earned her a look of disbelief from her older sisters.

"So?" Caitlin said with a slight shove at Charlotte's shoulder. "How was it? Was he cute?"

Charlotte tugged on Rufus's leash to hurry him along, or they'd be at that mailbox all night. "He was cute enough, I guess."

"What does that mean?" Cassie demanded.

"He did not have a winning personality."

"Ooh, give us the details," Caitlin said, and actually rubbed her hands together.

"Lemme see, where should I start? He said he was a lawyer, then asked me if I knew what a litigator was."

Her sisters gasped at the same moment. "You're joking!" Cassie said.

"He determined that my rosé was not good enough and ordered some high-octane cocktail without asking me."

"Ugh, what a jerk," Caitlin muttered.

"After he bragged to my breasts about some cases he'd worked on, he said, 'Let's talk about you, what is your wildest fantasy, and I hope it's a naked one,' or something close to that."

"Get *out*," Cassie shouted.

"So I told him my wildest fantasy was meeting

a guy and having babies right away, and then I got up and left."

"Good call," Caitlin confirmed.

"Okay, all right, you've had two strikes, but remember, we're just getting started here," Cassie said, sounding like a coach giving her team a pep talk. "You're learning. You're getting a feel for men and how they present themselves on the apps."

"Come on, Cass, it's not like I've never dated," Charlotte reminded her.

"Well, no, but you know," Cassie said with a shrug.

Charlotte didn't know, but she suspected that Cassie was referring to Adam, the man she'd dated for about three years in her late twenties. Their breakup had been mutual, driven by Charlotte's desire to settle down and his desire to never settle down. She hadn't had a truly *steady* boyfriend since. A few dates here and there. And, of course, the big cake-topper—that night with Nick.

"So we've established that you're not good at picking guys and you need to let me help you," Cassie said as they all paused again for Rufus to pee.

"I will concede that I haven't done so great on my own."

"Right, so I'm going to do some picking for you," Cassie said confidently.

"Before you let Miss One-Night Stand pick for you, it so happens I think I have someone for you," Caitlin said with a pert look at Cassie. "I may be hugely pregnant, but I've still got game."

"You have no *game,* Caitlin. Who is it?" Cassie demanded, as if it were beyond comprehension that Caitlin could know someone.

"A friend of Jonah's," Caitlin said with a coy smile.

"Who?" Cassie asked.

Caitlin smiled. "Tanner Sutton." She arched a perfectly done brow at Charlotte. "He's apparently available at the moment."

Charlotte knew Tanner Sutton, all right. Didn't *know* him, precisely, but knew *of* him like everyone in town knew of him. She stared at Caitlin. "You know who that is, right?"

"Of course I do," Caitlin said. "Who doesn't?"

"I don't," Cassie said. "Who the hell is Tanner Sutton?"

"He is Charlie Prince's illegitimate son," Caitlin said. "But apparently, no one knew that until Charlie Prince died and it was in his will."

That was sort of true. Tanner Sutton, the tall drink of water with the dark golden hair and gorgeous smile, was the love child of the affair Charlie had had with Margaret Sutton Rhodes. Tanner was a year younger than Luca and Hallie Prince, who were a year behind Charlotte. Charlotte remembered Tanner from school, mainly because he was in sports and was always winning awards for track or basketball or football. None of Charlie Prince's other children had known Tanner was their half brother until Charlie's funeral and the reading of the will. No one in town had known it, either.

Nick had once confessed to her in a moment of candor that the discovery of it had made him feel a little ill. "Not because of Tanner. He seems like a good guy from what I know. But because all those years we had a brother and didn't know it."

"Wow," Cassie said.

"Wow is right," Charlotte muttered. "I think dating Tanner Sutton would be a big showstopper around the office, Caitlin."

"Please. Who cares what Nick Prince thinks?" Caitlin asked with a wave of her hand. "It's not like he cares who you date."

Charlotte inwardly winced. Caitlin was probably right. And she didn't care what Nick thought. Not really . . .

Okay, maybe fifty percent.

Fine, she cared.

Nick drove her nuts, but she still liked him. More than liked him. She had a thing for Nick. She wouldn't say it was romantic, precisely, although the sex had been off the charts. It was something more than that. She got him. And she owed a lot to the Prince family for her job, and to Charlie especially. She'd come out of college with a business operations degree and no experience, and Charlie hadn't hesitated to give her a job. He'd taught her the ropes and then had let her run with it. And she'd run that place for eleven years. Did anyone really think *Charlie* was paying the bills and getting the contracts signed? Nope. All her. He'd even joked about renaming the business Charlie and Charlie, because she ran it so well.

So good, in fact, that outside of George Lowe, the Prince family attorney, and Raymond Davis, the family's accountant, Charlotte was the only other person to know that the company was hemorrhaging money before Charlie died.

She was also the only one to notice how big of a chip Nick lugged around on his shoulder, owing to his resentment at having been burdened with the worry of the Saddlebush Land and Cattle Company instead of pursuing his dream to be a pilot.

Charlotte was not without empathy for him. She knew Nick was angry with his dad for dying in that weird way people have of being angry at the concept of death. And he was terribly disappointed by the way his life had turned out— she'd never seen anyone as low as Nick Prince when he had to sell his jet. She certainly knew what it was like to have dreams derailed—a few of hers had been derailed along the way, too.

But she also knew that running the office

wasn't nearly the chore Nick made it out to be. She just wished he'd accept that she knew as much as him, if not more. She wanted her due.

Charlotte was still miffed that he hadn't invited her into the meeting with Colton Rivers. She could have said something, but it annoyed her that she had to keep saying something. It was like he didn't *want* to know how the office ran. As if the less he knew, the less it was real. He preferred to wear his grudge like a new leather coat—all day, every day.

But what annoyed her even more, what had made her blood pressure ratchet to near catastrophe, was how quickly and easily Nick slipped into Superior Male mode and asked her to bring coffee. He was lucky she hadn't punched him right in the kisser. She might have, too, if Colton Rivers hadn't been in the office.

"What do you think, Lot? I can arrange it so that you and me and Jonah could meet him for drinks at the Magnolia."

"You can't even drink," Charlotte said.

"I can't, but Jonah drinks like a fish, and I need a break from the kids. It will be fun!"

Nick's very handsome face and piercing blue eyes popped into Charlotte's mind. His eyes were so blue, especially when he was riled up, that they looked almost navy. Charlotte could still remember those eyes the night of the Christmas party when they'd made love like wild animals.

They had shone down at her like she was the only woman in the whole entire world.

Damn Nick. He never could get over the fact that they'd slept together. Couldn't let it go. Of course Nick would deny that was true up one side and down the other if Charlotte pointed it out, but she didn't have to point it out. It was glaringly obvious.

"Why aren't you saying anything?" Caitlin asked.

"I'm thinking," Charlotte said. "Hey, do either of you know Colton Rivers?"

"Who?" Cassie asked. "Sounds like the name of a subdivision. The Colton Rivers, homes starting in the four fifties."

Caitlin laughed.

Charlotte thought Colton was seriously cute. Was he single? Married? Gay? And why had his parents named him Colton Rivers?

"Charlotte, you're killing me. Can I set something up with Tanner?" Caitlin pressed.

Charlotte sighed. Nick was not going to like it. He wouldn't actually say it, but he would let it be known. "Okay."

"Hey! *Hey!*"

The three of them looked up—they had reached the river. Chase and Jonah were standing on the coolers, arms waving, trying to get their attention.

"Could they be any more annoying?" Cassie asked.

"Yes," Charlotte said. "I've seen them do it time and again." She pulled Rufus's leash closer to her and began to pick her way through the crowd.

Chapter Four

Nick was beginning to wonder why Mindy had invited him on this little outing—she was very obviously interested in dancing with Chuck Leffowitz, an attorney in town who was known for wearing a cowboy hat and boots to court. Ranch attire for people who weren't ranchers had always baffled Nick. To him, it was utilitarian wear—not a fashion statement.

Mindy and Chuck still hadn't come off the dance floor after forty-five minutes. Nick had danced once with Sarah, but he didn't know her as well as he knew Mindy, and it was hard for him to make small talk, a character flaw that had been pointed out to him through the years by more than one woman he'd dated. They'd said things like, *You don't say much, do you,* and *Cat got your tongue?* And his perennial favorite: *Is that all you have to say?* Yes. It was all he had to say. Was there something wrong with that? He didn't need a surfeit of words to express himself, and no cat had his tongue. He just found it difficult to think of things to say about topics that didn't mean much.

He'd always enjoyed the Stars, Boots, and

Music Saturdays, although he didn't get out to them very often. But tonight was perfect—it wasn't too hot, and it looked like the whole town had come out to enjoy the music. There were so many people that the dancing had spilled off the portable dance floor as more couples crowded around the band.

Sarah and David got up to dance and left Nick alone with his beer. He nursed it, waiting for someone to come back to the table. But when it became apparent that the two couples would not, he shook his head. He'd left Pepper, Frank, and Priscilla, not to mention the cows, to sit here alone as the fifth wheel.

Nick stood up to stretch his legs and downed the rest of the beer. He thought about heading home, but the music was good and it was such a nice evening that he decided to have another one. He thought he better get one before the band took a break and all those dancers swarmed the bar.

He was weaving through the crowd when he heard an all-too-familiar voice. "Nicky!"

No way. Nick paused and turned toward the familiar voice. *"Grandma?"*

It was his grandmother, all right, all one hundred pounds and eighty-six years of her, seated in a lawn chair in a group of fellow octogenarians. She had straight gray hair that hung to her shoulders and, in the midst of all that gray, a streak of bright pink next to a streak of bright orange. All his life, his grandmother had kept her hair short, neatly trimmed, and colored a silvery blond. But when his dad died, something had changed. She'd stopped coloring her hair. Psychedelic colors began to appear. Her fashion choices had changed, too, from trousers and button-down shirts to clothes like she was wearing this evening—button-up jeans and a T-shirt that read *Cooley Cougars,* the local high school sports teams. Over the T-shirt, she wore a leather vest with fringe. And of course she was wearing cowboy boots.

She gave herself a couple of rocking starts and hauled herself out of the lawn chair.

"What are you doing here, Grandma?" Nick asked as he bent down to hug her.

"Same as you, enjoying this fine summer evening. You know my bridge club, don't you?" she asked, and swept her hand at three old men sitting hunched over in their seats. Two of them wore Marine Corps ball caps. One of them had on the signature red *Make America Great Again* hat. All of them were wearing black shoes with Velcro straps. There was a woman with them, too, sitting slightly behind the line of men, her hair jet-black and her lips so brightly red that Nick guessed that later, those lips could light the way to the parking lot.

"How are y'all tonight?" Nick asked politely.

"This is my *grandson!*" his grandmother

announced proudly before any of them could answer. "He's a *pilot*. He flies airplanes!"

"That's okay, Grandma—"

"I was in the air force," said the man in the MAGA hat. He didn't seem to want a response because he looked away.

"I want to dance, Nick," Grandma said. "None of these old guys can dance."

"Well, that ain't true, Dolly," said one of the men in the Marine Corps hats. "I can dance. I just can't get out of this goshdern chair."

"Don't even bother, Lloyd," Grandma said, and slipped her hand into Nick's. "I'm dancing with my grandson." And she tugged Nick toward the dance floor with a surprising amount of strength.

Grandma couldn't dance, either, which Nick knew going in, but he would be the last to tell her so. She considered swaying side to side in a very slow and tight circle to be dancing.

"Who'd you come with?" she asked Nick as they rotated around like they were a pair of sausages on a spit. "Got yourself a sweetheart?" Her brows popped up into question marks above the red frames of her glasses.

"First of all, no one calls their girlfriends *sweetheart* anymore, Grandma. And no, I don't have one."

"Why don't you have a girl, Nick? You're a good-looking man. Maybe not as handsome as Luca, but still handsome in your own right."

"Well, thanks, Grandma. I feel really special," he said with a wry smile. He was not offended. Even he could see that Luca was astoundingly handsome, and even if he'd never seen it, it had been pointed out to him many times in his life.

"I'm just saying there is no reason you shouldn't have yourself a girl."

"Do you have a boyfriend, Grandma? Because I thought you said life was too short to shackle yourself to a man."

"I did say that," she said, as if just remembering it. "I thought maybe Lloyd and I had a little thing going, but I think he's just interested in finding himself a live-in cook. And besides, I like playing the field."

Nick smiled. When his grandfather had died many years ago, his grandmother suffered a serious bout of depression. After a couple of years, she somehow pulled herself out of a funk and had dated around a little. But she'd given that up pretty quickly. She was a sixty-nine-year-old woman and declared to the family one afternoon that no one would ever replace Rick Prince.

When their dance ended, Grandma rose up on her toes and hugged him. "Come to supper Sunday. Everyone will be there."

"Who is everyone?"

"Your family, son! We miss having you around. I told your mother you were avoiding us."

Nick snorted. "I'm not avoiding anyone,

Grandma. I've been busy, that's all." Of course he hadn't been avoiding his family . . . except that he'd been avoiding his family.

He loved them, it wasn't that. But there was a nebulous feeling of resentment in him that sat like a lump in his chest. It seemed like everyone in his family had moved on since Dad had died. Luca was getting to do what he'd always wanted to do, thanks to Dad. He'd left Luca some land he could conserve and turn into a biosustainable showcase. Hallie was six or seven months pregnant, and she and Rafe had opened up a pair of studios in empty warehouses that Dad had left her—one to teach ballet and dance to kids with disabilities, which Hallie would run. And one for training wounded soldiers in martial arts, which was Rafe's specialty.

Even his mom was doing better. She was getting out more, seeing friends again, and carrying on in the new normal without Dad.

The worlds of his entire family continued to turn on their axes. But not Nick's. His world was stuck and he was not moving at all. It was as if his feet were encased in concrete, and he stood in the very same place he'd stood all his life. He was cemented to this damn ranch.

"I can see you trying to think of an excuse," his grandmother said, wagging a finger at him. "Do it for your grandmother—it's not like I'm getting any younger, you know."

Nick snorted. "You'll outlive us all," he said, and hooked his hand in the crook of her elbow. "Okay, Grandma. I'll come for you. Regular time?"

"Regular time."

He escorted her back to her group of friends, helped Lloyd out of his seat so he could go to the bathroom, and then carried on to Magnolia's outdoor bar.

He had not avoided the crush of dancers—there was already quite a crowd, and Nick had to inch his way forward. When he was about three deep back from the actual bar, he noticed a very familiar head of blond curls. He reached forward and tapped Charlotte on the shoulder.

"Seriously, what takes you so—" Charlotte clamped her mouth shut when she saw he was the one who had tapped her on the shoulder. "Oh. It's you."

"A cheery hello to you, too, Charlotte. I'm not actually the grim reaper, you know." Nick slipped in between her and a broad man who was leaning with both elbows on the bar. It was so crowded that Nick had to turn sideways, and Charlotte's shoulder was pressed against his chest. He could smell her hair. It smelled like honeysuckle.

He noticed five drinks in red Solo cups in front of her. "Thirsty?"

"Hilarious! I'm waiting on Cassie to come and help me carry these." She tried to turn her head and look over her shoulder, but their bodies were pressed so tightly together that she couldn't turn far enough, and instead peered up at him. "What are you doing here, anyway?" she asked. "Shouldn't you be at your house staring at a rescue cow or something?"

"The cows are down in the valley. I wouldn't be able to get a good look." Nick caught the bartender's eye. "I'll have an Alamo lager, please." He propped his elbow on the bar as he reached into his pocket for his wallet. To reach his back pocket and not the guy's beside him, he had to lean forward and press a little more into Charlotte. He smiled apologetically into her pretty blue eyes. "Excuse me. It's crowded." He kept looking into her eyes, which were narrowed at him now. He couldn't help himself—those eyes were forever catching him by surprise, as if he kept forgetting just how blue they were.

"You're smothering me," Charlotte complained. "You never said why you're here."

"Same reason as you—I'm enjoying a nice summer evening." Jesus, he sounded like his grandma.

She snorted. "Who said anything about enjoying the evening? Apparently, I've been dragged here by my family to be the drink runner. Who dragged you?"

He pulled a five from his wallet and tossed it down on the bar. "Mindy."

Charlotte looked startled. She twisted around so that she was facing him. They were chest to chest—one could not have slid a penny between them. So close he was acutely aware of how soft she was.

"Mindy Rogers? I didn't know you were dating her again. Why do you never tell me anything? You know I'm dying for *something* to happen in your life."

He smiled lopsidedly. "I'm not dating her, I'm dancing with her. Or, I was supposed to be dancing with her, as that was the proposal she put forward when she invited me. But I guess she's got a thing for Chuck Leffowitz."

"What, *again?*" Charlotte wrinkled her nose.

"What's that?" Nick asked, gesturing at her face.

"I think it's my face."

"No, I mean that look. And what do you mean, *again?*"

"Oh, Nick." Charlotte said his name like he was addled. She put her hand on his arm. "Try and keep up with the town they named after your family's ranch. I feel like you have a responsibility to know what's going on." She smiled pertly and dropped her hand.

"The only real responsibility I have is to sign your paycheck and mine."

"Well, brace yourself, Nicholas Nickleby—there is a lot happening in this town that you never know about because you are off brooding somewhere."

Nick took exception. "I'm not off *brooding.* I'm just not a people person. What's happening in town?"

Charlotte's eyes sparked. She was enjoying this. "For starters, Mindy Rogers wants a husband. She tried to get Chuck Leffowitz to marry her just like she tried to get *you* to marry her—"

"She didn't try to get me to marry her," he scoffed.

"Okay, cowboy, yes she did, and it's okay to admit it. Chuck wouldn't bite, either, so she broke it off. I guess she's trying to rekindle that long-dead fire."

This was news. Nick didn't know Mindy had dated Chuck before. "Really?" The bartender handed him the beer as he contemplated it. He shook his head. "There's a flaw in your theory."

"I don't think so, but go ahead. What's the flaw?" Her smile had gotten deeper. She had one very cute dimple that appeared when she smiled like that.

"Why would she invite me if she wanted to get back with Chuck?" Nick smiled, too, pleased with himself for having bested Charlotte at something. It rarely happened.

Charlotte actually laughed. "You are so *dear,*" she said playfully, and laughed again when Nick grunted at her. "She obviously invited you to give Chuck some competition. Don't you know anything about how dating works?"

Apparently not enough, which sort of chapped him. "Don't need to," he said, and took a swig of his beer. "What else is going on in town that I should know about?"

Charlotte's smile was sparkling now, and it zapped right through him, like a zing from a light socket. "You seriously want a rundown?"

"Yeah, maybe not. Just file the information for me. What color would that be? Purple?"

She laughed. At least they were past the filing system debacle.

"Where are we going?" he asked, nodding to the cups.

"Don't worry about those—Cassie will make it over here eventually."

"She hasn't made it yet and people are trying to get a drink. Let me help you. Where is the Bailey clan tonight?"

"Straight through the crowd to the river. You can't miss them—they will be the loud ones. You know how my family loves to party."

Nick had been to a couple of Bailey events through the years. "Indeed I do." He put his beer in the crook of his elbow and picked up three of the cups between his fingers. He put his free hand to the small of Charlotte's back to guide her out of the crush around the bar.

It took some serious navigation, but they

managed to wend through the throng of people on the lawn. Charlotte was right—the Baileys were loud. He could hear them laughing before he could actually see them. They'd constructed a Baileyville island with lawn chairs and coolers.

Jonah, Charlotte's brother-in-law, noticed them first, and stepped over a fallen chair to rescue the cups from Nick's hand. Rufus noticed them a moment later, and the enormous dog hopped up and trotted over a blanket and the bags of chips, which earned him a collective cry of "Rufus!" That cry quickly turned to another one: "Nick!"

"Hello," Nick said as Rufus stuck his snout in his crotch. "You, too, Rufus," Nick said, and gave the dog a good head scratch.

"Nick! It's so great to see you!" Cassie sang out from their midst. Nick knew Charlotte's sisters fairly well, as they stopped by the office to see Charlotte. Chase had been a year ahead of him in school. He was there with his wife, Lori, and their kids. So were Caitlin and Jonah, and their kids.

"You were supposed to come help me, Cassie," Charlotte said as she helped Jonah hand out the drinks.

"I forgot," Cassie said, and swayed toward Nick with a big grin. "You just get better looking every time I see you, Nick!"

"Thanks," he said, and caught her before she

swayed into the ground. "How many have you had tonight?"

"Plenty!" Cassie cried with a triumphant fist in the air.

"Hey, bro," Chase said. He'd taken a cup from Charlotte and tried to hand it to his parents. But Mr. and Mrs. Bailey were holding each other tight, waltzing around Baileyville. "Dad, come on," Chase said.

Mr. Bailey ignored him and kissed his wife.

"*Dad!* Either get a room or take this drink. What is the *matter* with you two?"

Mr. Bailey grinned at his son and took the drink. "How are you, Nick?" he asked, extending his hand.

"Doing good, Mr. Bailey."

"It's so good to see you, Nick!" Mrs. Bailey trilled. Her cheeks were as flushed as Cassie's. "How is your mother?"

"She's doing well, thank you."

"Is she here with you tonight?"

Charlotte snorted into her cup. She was well acquainted with his mother and knew that Cordelia Prince would not rub shoulders with the masses if she could help it.

"She's not," Nick said. "I'm here with a couple of friends."

"Ooh, *friends,*" Cassie said, and she and Caitlin looked directly at Charlotte and laughed. "We didn't know you had *friends,* Nick."

At Nick's curious look, Charlotte sighed. "Okay," she said, holding up a hand. "I may have complained about you and said some things once or twice. So sue me."

"I was thinking more along the lines of firing you."

Cassie laughed loudly. "You'd be so lost without Lot you'd end up in Omaha, and everyone knows it."

"I wouldn't—"

"Hey, who *did* you come with?" Cassie asked with a drunken waggle of her brows. "Who are these *friends?*"

"Leave him alone, Cass," Chase said. "The man is out prowling and doesn't need to explain himself. Right, Nick? Charlotte says—"

"Charlotte doesn't say anything!" Charlotte shouted. She grabbed Nick's hand. "Come on, let's dance." She yanked him hard enough that he almost stumbled. He managed to put his beer down as she dragged him away.

"But you hate to dance," he reminded her as she pushed toward the dance floor.

"I don't *hate* it hate it."

"I have no idea what that means. Are there degrees of hate for dancing?"

She glanced back at him with exasperation. "Of *course* there are degrees of hate. I actually kind of like dancing when I've had a couple of drinks, as you may recall." She arched a brow at him, waiting to see if he remembered the Christmas party.

Oh, he remembered, all right.

"And besides, I have to do it. I'm sacrificing myself to save you from a full interrogation. You should thank me." She pushed onto the crowded dance floor, pulling him along. When she reached a spot she was satisfied with, she turned around to face him.

He slid his hand onto the small of her back, and Charlotte put her hand into his. Nick drew her a little closer. It was crowded, he told himself, and he drew her a little closer still. They were touching again. He couldn't think about that. He would think about what she'd been saying about him. "So what have you said about me to your family that has us running like a couple of scared cats?"

"Oh, you know. The usual stuff when two people work together." She smiled.

He couldn't begin to guess what "the usual" was when two people worked together, but Nick wasn't too upset about it.

He led her into the two-step and tried not to think about how good she felt in his arms. He definitely tried not to think of the way she looked the night of the Christmas party when she'd worn that green satin dress that fit her body tight from the waist up, but flared out in clouds of fabric from the waist to her knees.

He tried not to think about how damn pretty she was right now under the globe lights the Magnolia had strung up over the dance floor.

He tried not to think about Charlotte at all, but most of the time, he failed. Because in spite of all his trying, he couldn't help but think about how this little dance they were doing was exactly the way things had started at the infamous Christmas party. That night, she'd said she didn't like to dance. He'd told her she hadn't had the right kind of partner. She'd told him to cowboy up and show her, if he thought he knew so much. He'd said, "Then get over here." She'd fit his arms perfectly. He didn't have to lean over to hold her, and the way she'd tilted her face up to him, with that smile that ended in the dimple, and her eyes shining like two ornaments . . .

Yeah, he remembered.

He looked away from her, twirled her around to the right to avoid a collision with another couple. There was no point in trying to dance, really—it was too crowded. He pulled her closer and now her body was pressed against his. "So are you going to tell me what's up with the egg freezing?" he asked.

She blinked with surprise. "Well *that's* a personal question."

"It is? I figured it was one of those things going on in Three Rivers that everyone knows but me."

"It's not. And come on, Nick, you don't really care."

"You think I don't care?"

"I would say, given the trajectory of our acquaintance, that you've made it pretty clear that you don't." She stared at him, silently challenging him to deny the conversation they'd had after that long-ago party. The very morning after.

"That is *not* what I made clear, Charlotte," he reminded her, and she rolled her eyes. "Of course I care. I thought you were looking for a . . . a donor. Of sperm." For some reason, he didn't like thinking of sperm being donated to Charlotte.

"Why do you have to say it like it's some kind of personal science experiment?"

He opened his mouth to deny that he had said it in any way, but she was right. He had. "Sorry. It's just . . ." He tried to think of the right word. It seemed all wrong. It seemed like Charlotte ought to have the family she longed to have without resorting to the sperm donated by some guy who was getting a hundred dollars a pop.

"It's just you don't get it," she filled in for him.

"No, I don't get it," he admitted.

"I'd try and explain it to you, and probably get super frustrated with your inability to get it, but great news! I don't have to, because I've decided that I don't want to go that route. Not yet, anyway. I am saving that as a last resort."

"Really?" he asked hopefully.

"Yes, really." She looked at him like he was saying something strange. "Seriously, why do you care what I do?" Her expression was all suspicious and annoyed. He stared back. There were words he wanted to say, he could feel them rattling around in his head. But he couldn't seem to grab them. Like his brain wasn't working. The air felt thick and still around him, and even though people were moving, it felt a little to Nick like they were bobbing along on a current with no effort on his part. Just the two of them.

But then someone bumped into them, knocking Charlotte into his chest and waking him from that dream. Nick slipped his arm a little more firmly around her back. "I don't know why. But I do," he muttered.

She looked at him again, but her expression had softened. "I guess because I realized I would rather find someone to love and who would share the experience of kids with me," she said, sparing him the need to express himself, because she knew how hard it was for him to do. "But I'm thirty-two. I don't have all the time in the world to start a meaningful relationship and walk down the aisle and set up a house and then start a family, you know? So, I want to freeze my eggs just in case. If I haven't found the right guy in the next year or so, I'm going to go the sperm-and-egg route."

It still sounded clinical and undeserving of a

woman like Charlotte, but Nick nodded. "I get it. That makes sense."

"I'm so glad you agree, weirdo." She smiled a little. "I think I can safely say that outside of me, there is no one more interested in my sperm donor than you. Even my sisters." She laughed.

He was looking at her mouth, remembering the feel and taste of her lips. "It's not your sperm donor I'm interested in," he said quietly, then remembered himself. "Just how are you going to find the love of your life, anyway?"

"Mail order."

Nick's brows rose.

Charlotte laughed at his expression. "You're so gullible! I'm going to do it the old-fashioned way. I'm going to *date*. I know, horror of horrors, right? But I've decided to embark on some serious dating. I've got my must-have checklist and I'm going for it."

"You have a must-have checklist?" He grinned. "Let me guess. Six-pack abs? Money in the bank? Super sperm?"

"I will concede that none of those things would ever hurt a man's prospects, but I am much more practical than that."

"Let's hear the must-haves," he said as they moved slowly in the crush.

"Well, my first must is no caveman tendencies because I am not a housemaid. Must be able

99

to spell fairly well and have a general grasp of the proper use of an adverb. And he can't say *nu-ku-lar* for *nuclear,* because I will lose my mind. Must have a decent credit score and cannot, under any circumstance, be a hoarder. Oh, and he cannot dip tobacco." She shuddered. "You know, practical things."

"That rules out half the guys in America."

"And it would be really nice if he felt like I was the most important thing in the world. But, you know, *really* felt it."

"If he felt it, wouldn't he *really* feel it?"

"You know what I mean. I think it's easy to say that your spouse is the most important thing in the world. But to really feel it? That's a special guy."

"Still sounds the same."

"Okay, Nick, let me put it in cowboy terms. I want someone who would ride so hard to get to me. Someone who would ride all out until the horse was lathered and about to drop, and then he'd jump onto the back of another horse and ride just as hard. *That* kind of important." She smiled. "Get it?"

"I get it."

"So what do you think? Do I have a chance?"

Of course she had a chance for that. He had been surprised for years that there weren't guys lined up outside her door. But Nick didn't speak, because he felt a little shimmery inside. Like the night of the Christmas party, he felt shimmery and warm and—

"The music has stopped."

"It has?" Nick looked up. People were moving off the dance floor, others coming on.

"So you can let go now."

Nick looked at his arm on her waist, her hand in his, and frowned. "When did it end? Who can hear anything? This place is too crowded and everyone's too loud."

"Hey, everybody, Nick wants you to get off his lawn!" Charlotte shouted up to the globe lights overhead, then laughed and tried to pull away.

Nick wouldn't let her. "Let's dance another one. It's thinned out a little and a person can move."

As if on cue, the band struck up a jaunty two-step. Nick suddenly let go of her waist and twirled her under his arm, around his body, and back into his chest.

She was caught off guard by it, and actually slammed into him. *"Hey!"* she said, her voice full of delight. "You really *do* know how to dance."

"Of course I do. Did you think the only thing I knew how to do was cowboy?" He started two-stepping her around the edge of the dance floor.

"I definitely didn't think that!" she said with a snort. "I thought the only thing you knew how to do was grump it up."

"Well, look at that, Charlotte, you don't know

everything about me." He winked, then twirled her again so fast that her floral skirt swung out around her knees. He brought her around to one side with his arm draped over her shoulder so that they were two-stepping side by side for a few beats, then twirled her under his arm again and brought her back in front of him.

"Show-off," she said breathlessly.

"Yep," he agreed, and twirled her out again.

He could have danced the rest of the night with Charlotte. She was light on her feet, she was wearing red cowboy boots, and she was a hell of a lot of fun. She was the type of woman who could make a man forget his woes for an evening.

But when that dance was over, she breathlessly informed him that she needed a drink, and Mindy came wandering up from somewhere without Chuck, and the moment was over.

Still, Nick had enjoyed himself immensely for those two dances. He hadn't enjoyed much of anything in a while. He was too much in his own head these days.

He would have gladly taken that spot of fun back home with him and had a good night's sleep if he hadn't seen Charlotte a little later smiling up at Tanner Sutton like she had stars in her eyes.

Chapter Five

Early Sunday afternoon, Cordelia Prince was directing her majordomo, Martin, on where to put the solar lights around the cemetery. As the days had gotten warmer, she liked coming up the hill to the small family cemetery at night. Everyone in town now knew that Cordelia Prince, once the matriarch of a powerful Texas family, spent a lot of time at the grave of her husband. A man from whom she'd been separated at the time of his death. One might think her grief knew no bounds. Her grief knew bounds. It wasn't grief that compelled her.

Her family liked to point out how odd her behavior was. At first, when the earth on top of his little cremation grave was still soft, they worried about her. But as time went by, they began to roll their eyes and shake their heads about it.

Cordelia didn't know why she came up here. Sure, she missed Charlie. But it had been eighteen months, and as with all grief, the pain of the loss had dulled, and she could think about him again without tearing up or getting angry.

She felt peace being near him.

Frankly, it had taken a hell of a lot longer to get over her anger than it had the grief. She and Charlie had been separated for more than a year when he'd been cut down with a heart attack. It wasn't the first separation in their long marriage, either. She'd been so mad when she got the news, so *mad* at him for living like a frat boy most of his adult life. She was so mad about the cigars and the greasy food and the *gambling*—dear God, the gambling. He'd single-handedly taken a family dynasty and turned it to rubble. It was what George Lowe, the longtime family attorney, had said: "You're land rich and cash poor, Delia, and land doesn't pay the bills by itself."

Cordelia had had to let go of most of her staff and discovered it was pretty hard to keep up with a twenty-thousand-square-foot ranch house on seventy-five thousand acres of ranch land. They ran this massive property with a staff of two—Cordelia and Martin. They used to have ranch hands. Now, they had Nick, Martin's son Rafe, and occasionally, a couple of vaqueros.

There had been some talk of selling land to put some cash in the coffers. *Selling land.* To a rancher, that was the worst possible offense, the worst possible solution, and that they were even talking about it was all Charlie's fault.

So yes, Cordelia had been mad for a very long time. But she was less mad now. She was mostly numb.

Martin was almost done putting the lights up. He'd promised her that the lights would not detract from the stars. Cordelia was adamant about that. The stars seemed so much brighter up on this little hill. They were a huge blanket overhead, covering the earth and everyone below. It was her mother-in-law, Dolly, who wanted to string lights in the old live oaks that stretched their limbs and branches out over the two dozen or so Prince graves.

Cordelia had, at first, refused. "I will not have anything detract from that big sky, Dolly, do you hear me?" She'd felt completely entitled to this opinion. Dolly had inserted herself in Cordelia's sanctuary by dragging her own lawn chair up here and then instructing Martin to carry up the outdoor side table so they'd have a place to put their snacks. Dolly was the one who'd insisted on Christmas decorations around Charlie's grave, and she was entirely incapable of letting Cordelia have her space to breathe. If she saw Cordelia at Charlie's grave, here she came with a hearty *yoo-hoo* and a mouth that wouldn't stop working.

But it was Cordelia who had installed the sun umbrella and the cooler, and it was George's idea to add the fire pit and the lanai on the southern edge of the cemetery. George was at Three Rivers Ranch more than he was home. He liked to come up here, too. He said it was a break from the calls and texts he was constantly receiving.

"That's the last one," Martin said, and paused to drag a bandanna across his forehead. "Says you need to give them twenty-four hours to charge before they glow." He glanced at his watch. "Still got time to put in the pinwheels."

"The what?"

"Pinwheels," Martin said, and looked up. "Miss Dolly bought some pinwheels at Walmart and wants to put them up here."

"What is this, some old codger's garden? Are we going to be growing cantaloupe and cucumbers next? We're not putting any pinwheels up here, Martin. For heaven's sake."

Martin shrugged. "I'll let you break the news to Miss Dolly."

Cordelia snorted and took a seat in her lawn chair, waving him away. "Chicken. I'm not afraid of an old woman with an orange stripe in her hair."

"I guess that works out for both of us, then, because here she comes." Martin picked up his shovel. "Mañana," he said, and started down the hill. Cordelia heard him pause to speak to Dolly on the way down. She took the opportunity to sigh loudly with impatience and glared at Charlie's grave. "What did I ever do to deserve this?" she asked him. "Was I not good to you and your mother? Did you really have to leave her with me?"

"What are you going on about, Delia?" Dolly

106

asked as she paused at the gate in the iron fence that some ancient Prince had erected around the cemetery.

"I'm going on about pinwheels, Dolly. We are not putting pinwheels up here like we're some sort of Grey Gardens Texas franchise, do you hear me?"

"They're pretty!" she protested, and came huffing across a few old graves to take her seat next to Cordelia.

"No."

"Then will you let me put in one of those wind sculptures? Charlie loved those things. He bought that monster one in Taos and had it hauled all the way down here to put up at the offices in town."

Cordelia cast a look of exasperation at her mother-in-law. "That thing cost three thousand dollars, and the delivery nearly as much again. Your son was such a fool with his money."

"Oh, stop," Dolly said with a wave of her hand. "It's not like you never ran off and bought something outrageous."

"Like what?"

"How about that blue Maserati that appeared in our drive? Your own brother the car dealer told me it was the dumbest thing you'd ever done."

Cordelia looked away. So she'd bought an expensive car. She'd deserved it after all Charlie had put her through that year. "It was my fiftieth birthday," she said, as if that explained it. "And at least we got something for it when I sold it. We'll never get anything for that wind sculpture or the money Charlie lost in Vegas."

Neither of them said anything for a long moment. In the terrible wake of Charlie's death, they'd both learned a lot about the man to disappoint them. "What's in the cooler?" Dolly asked.

Cordelia leaned over and opened it, chose a grapefruit wine cooler, and handed it to Dolly.

"Saw something interesting last night," Dolly said as she opened the drink. "Do you want to hear?"

"Do I have a choice?"

"I went to Stars, Boots, and Music with my friends. Quite an interesting evening."

"Lay it on me," Cordelia said. In spite of her protestations, she was interested.

"For starters, your oldest boy was there."

Cordelia glanced at her mother-in-law to gauge if she was teasing her. She looked quite serious. "*Nick?* The hermit crab? My oldest son?"

"Unless you have another oldest son I don't know about."

Cordelia was shocked. Nick never did anything. He rarely left that ranch house of his. Since his father had died, her son could not seem to get out of his funk. Her beautiful firstborn, the baby her grandmother said was born with a broken heart. That used to infuriate Cordelia. Now she wondered if her grandmother had sensed something in Nick that Cordelia couldn't see because she was blinded by adoration for her baby. But it was true—if any of her children were prone to despair or depression, it was Nick. "Was he there with anyone?"

"Don't know. Maybe. I didn't see him with anyone but Charlotte. They danced."

"They *danced?*" Cordelia thought those two were at odds most of the time.

"Charlotte was there with her whole family. Let me tell you something, those Baileys can keep a bartender as busy as a beaver building a dam. But here's the *most* interesting thing," Dolly continued, and shifted around in her chair so she was almost facing Cordelia. "I saw Charlotte talking to Tanner Sutton."

Cordelia flinched when she heard that name. Tanner was Charlie's love child, the son he'd had in secret with Margaret Sutton Rhodes. Margaret had once been Cordelia's best friend a lifetime ago. Charlie had had this affair when Nick was one. Cordelia had found out, Charlie had begged her, said it would never happen again.

It happened again. When she was pregnant with the twins, he'd had another affair with Margaret. It had ended when Margaret got pregnant.

Those were definitely some of Cordelia's darkest days—she'd had three small children, a philandering husband, and had been too young and stupid to figure out what to do about it.

Charlie didn't have much of a relationship with Tanner, at least not that Cordelia knew. But he left the boy some land, like he was a Prince or something. Cordelia turned her head and glared at Charlie's grave. "Well, good for Charlotte," she said, with a lightness she certainly did not feel.

"You know I ran into Margaret in town not too long ago," Dolly said between swigs of wine cooler. "Saw her at the new place, Molly Maguire's cake shop. I still can't get over her opening that up right across the street from Jo's Java. Don't you know Jo Carol was hopping mad about that."

"What about Margaret?" Cordelia asked.

"Oh. I went in to see what Molly had in her shop. Curiosity, you know. Had a red velvet cup-cake that was so good—"

"Dolly. What about Margaret?"

"Oh, Margaret. She was buying a cake. She said she was having a dinner party because she'd just redone her kitchen and dining room. She asked me how I was getting on after Charlie, you know, and how things were up at the ranch."

Cordelia snorted. "Wouldn't she like to know."

"She said she was going to make her special King Ranch chicken casserole."

With a bitter bark of a laugh, Cordelia rolled her eyes. "She always did think her King Ranch chicken was the best. Like no one makes it any better than her, not even down at King Ranch."

"Well, it is pretty good," Dolly said.

"Excuse me?" Cordelia shot a dark look at Dolly.

"I had it at church," Dolly said with a shrug. "Hate the woman, not the casserole."

Cordelia figured she could hate both if she wanted. "So what is your point in telling me this? I don't care about Margaret Sutton Rhodes."

"I just thought you'd be interested to know that she looked a little rough around the edges, that's all."

Cordelia reached into the cooler and pulled out a raspberry wine cooler. "Don't we all," she muttered, twisted the top off, and drank.

Chapter Six

Charlotte often met her good friend Keesha at yoga class. Keesha was George Lowe's one and only paralegal. Which meant she knew almost as much as Charlotte did about the fabled Prince family. She also knew about the challenges of a two-person office, when one person was a Male Boss and the other person was the Woman Who Did Everything. At least George was outgoing and would talk about his weekend.

Keesha definitely knew about the scandal with Margaret Sutton Rhodes and her son, Tanner, and how their appearance at Charlie's funeral had started a family brawl, so her eyes rounded and her mouth dropped open when Charlotte told her she was having coffee with Tanner later that afternoon.

Charlotte had met him last night. When she'd come off the dance floor all flushed and made happy after dancing with Nick, Cassie intercepted her and shoved a red Solo cup at her chest. "Why in the hell are you wasting time dancing with Nick when you could be meeting your future husband?" she'd demanded.

"Tanner Sutton is here!" Caitlin had added

excitedly. "I made Jonah go and get him over here."

So, that happened. After introductions were made, Charlotte sat on a rock next to Tanner, each of them nursing a drink and chatting easily with her family. Rufus took to Tanner right away, but then again, Rufus took to any human being who showed him the slightest bit of attention. He leaned against Tanner's leg and kept his head on Tanner's knee. Tanner was a good sport and didn't hold it against Rufus or Charlotte, and just kept stroking Rufus's head.

Charlotte liked Tanner. He seemed like a nice guy. She'd ended up giving him her number.

"It's weird," she said to Keesha over frozen yogurts post-yoga. "He looks like Nick. And yet he doesn't."

"Genetics," Keesha said.

"Right." Tanner looked like Nick, but there was something about Nick that was more . . . virile. At least in her eyes. No one would think Tanner Sutton wasn't a handsome guy. "I should go, right?" she asked. "I should have coffee with him."

"Girl, yes, you should," Keesha said emphatically. "He *is* a nice guy, and he's easy on the eyes. Plus, he's rich." She winked. "He doesn't have to worry about Three Rivers Ranch going under."

"Three Rivers Ranch is not going under,"

Charlotte scoffed. She knew Charlie had left his illegitimate son some prime land. Charlotte didn't know all the details, but she knew from chatter around town that the land was a big bone of contention with the Prince family, and especially Mrs. Prince.

"He's fine, Charlotte. And you could use some fine in your life," Keesha said. "I think you should totally embrace the whole dating thing. Lean into it! Go out with as many men as you possibly can. Get laid. You know, work the kinks out. It's been a while since you've been in a relationship, and let's face it, you'll never be this young and pretty again."

"Wow. I'm not sure how to take that," Charlotte said.

"Text me immediately after your date," Keesha instructed.

Charlotte could not disagree with Keesha's logic. Since she and Adam had broken up more than two years ago, she hadn't had much luck in the dating department. She was a grown woman and she wanted sex just as much as anyone. Not that she was going to have sex with Tanner . . . not immediately, of course. But last night, the thought had definitely crossed her mind.

Charlotte left Keesha and returned home to prepare for this date-that-was-not-a-date. She searched through her closet for something to wear, settling on a light blue summer dress. She held it up to herself in the mirror. It was cute. She would have to tackle her unruly hair, but still. As she dressed, she began to fantasize about dating Tanner Sutton. Because what if he was The One?

She had a terrible habit of doing this before a date, imagining that the man she was about to meet was perfect for her, and that today was the day she was going to meet the man who would father her children and walk her dog and take the trash out and make love to her until she couldn't walk. And then she proceeded to be terribly disappointed.

But Tanner, well . . . it was easy to imagine a happy ever after.

By the time Charlotte got to Jo's Java, she'd worked herself up into a lather with her fantasies. She was early, a sign of overeagerness, which Cassie had said was a strike against her. She should not be the early one, and yet, here she was, assuring Jo Carol and her towering pile of hair that she would wait until her friend arrived before she ordered anything.

"Well, who's your friend?" Jo Carol asked, because she was, if nothing else, one Nosy Parker. "I'll keep an eye out for her," she added shrewdly.

"So will I," Charlotte said. "Shouldn't be a problem since no one else is here except Mr. and Mrs. Fenway." She took a seat in the window. She happened to glance down Main Street and saw that Nick's muddied truck was parked in front of the Saddlebush Land and Cattle offices. What was *he* doing there on a Sunday?

But Charlotte forgot all about Nick's truck when she spotted Tanner striding down the street. He was wearing joggers and cool tennis shoes. They had a name, but Charlotte didn't know what it was. He had on shades and a T-shirt that fit him like a glove. Even from a distance she could make out the words *Ramos Boxing Gym*.

He strode into the coffee shop, bypassing Jo Carol altogether, and with a warm smile walked straight to where she was sitting. Charlotte stood up. "Hi!" she said.

"Hi." He leaned in to kiss her cheek, which struck her as a very cosmopolitan thing to do. She tried to imagine Nick doing that and couldn't. But she liked it and grinned with delight.

"Sorry I'm late. Can I get you something?" he asked. "A latte?"

"Oh, ah . . ." She looked toward the counter. "It's a little warm for hot coffee."

"Good point. How about a frozen coffee drink? A caramel macchiato?"

"That would be great."

"Be right back."

Charlotte sat down. She watched him saunter across the room, easily moving through the scattering of tables. Oh, look—she was still smiling. Yep. She liked him.

He returned a few minutes later after some banter with Jo Carol and with frozen coffee drinks. He smiled sheepishly, like he was a bit shy. "Jo Carol said you love this drink."

Jo Carol and her matchmaking. She'd once tried to connect Charlotte with Cash Proctor, who was a notorious womanizer. "Thank you. Wow, you really do look like your dad, has anyone ever told you?"

Tanner froze. "What?"

Should she not have said that? "I ah . . . I'm sorry. I just . . . you *do* resemble him. I worked for him for years, you know."

"No, I didn't know that," he said. "I mean, you said you work for Saddlebush last night, but I didn't realize . . ." His voice trailed off and he looked away a moment.

"I've been there eleven years. Oh, this drink is delicious!" she said, trying to turn the subject. Tanner's eyes were blue, she noticed. Like Nick's, which were so darkly blue that they looked almost navy. And Tanner's hair, although sandy in color, was thick like Nick's, too. "So, Tanner, I didn't ask you last night. What do you do?"

"Ranch," he said. "Like everyone else, I guess." He smiled. "But my spread is pretty small."

A million questions were rumbling through her mind, but instead of asking what he did for fun, she asked, "Did you know Charlie?"

He looked at her for a long moment. "Yes, I knew him. But I hadn't seen him in a while. I was away at college, then lived in Dallas. I've only been back in Three Rivers for a couple of years."

Interesting. Charlie had never mentioned Tanner to her, but she'd once overheard him and George Lowe talking about him. She wished she could remember that conversation. Charlie had been a talker and ran his mouth all day, and like so many of his long conversations, she'd forgotten more than she'd ever heard. "Well, I'm glad you're here now."

"Thanks. I'm not sure I'm going to be here for the long haul, though."

Well, that was disappointing. There went the first picket out of her little fantasy fence—poof, just disappeared. "Why not?"

He shrugged. "I'm not sure there is anything here for me. Except my mother, obviously."

"But you have some prime land here," she blurted.

Tanner glanced up from his drink.

Oh, for heaven's sake. Why did she do that? Why was she always opening her mouth and inserting her foot? She held up a hand. "That did not come out right. I don't know, really. I mean, I *do* know about it." She sighed. "What I *mean* is I know what was in Charlie's will, because, you know, I worked for him." As if Tanner needed a reminder. "But I don't know the *details,* obviously."

He gave her a strange smile that sent a funny little shiver down her spine. "I guess by the time it was all said and done, everyone in town knew the details, didn't they?"

She couldn't argue that. Charlotte sipped her drink. She thought it was probably better if she didn't say anything more because she'd already said way too much. Unfortunately, that had never been Charlotte's way. It was a major character flaw, and yet, that that didn't stop her from asking, "If you don't stay, what will you do with the land and your ranch?"

Tanner settled back, leaving his drink on the table. He crossed one leg over the other and said, "Good question. I've been thinking about that land. I think I might sell it to developers."

Charlotte actually choked on the big sip of frozen coffee drink. "*Develop* it?" Her response was merely reflective—she knew how the Princes would feel about him developing that land. Mrs. Prince would lose her mind.

Tanner shrugged. "Why not? It's prime real estate, as you pointed out. I could put down town houses, maybe a city center like those that are being built all over the state. You know, live there–work there developments."

The coffee drink had gone down the wrong pipe. Charlotte coughed. She was both fascinated and alarmed. She felt responsible somehow, as if bringing up the topic had spurred him to decide to develop it.

"Are you all right?'

"Yes," she said hoarsely. "I thought that was prime grazing land for cattle."

"I know that's what the Princes think," Tanner said calmly. "I think its good for development. I could make a whole lot more money selling it off than I could trying to eke out a living with cattle."

Charlotte nodded because she was too afraid to speak. Too afraid she would squeeze another foot into a mouth already stuffed full of feet. But she realized he was watching her closely and she looked down at her drink. "So how long have you known Jonah?" she asked, determined to change the conversation. Before he could answer, she was startled by the buzz of her phone. She smiled sheepishly. "Excuse me." She pulled it out of her pocket and glanced at the screen.

At the office. Where is the tax stuff?

Nick! Was he serious right now? It was Sunday afternoon! "Ah . . . sorry about that," Charlotte said, and turned her phone upside down. "So, Jonah. Where did you say you met?"

"I didn't," he said, and smiled thinly. "But I met

him a couple of years ago at the Ramos Boxing gym." He gestured to his shirt. "You know Juan Ramos, right? He has the huge spread north of here."

"Quarter horses," she said. Her phone began to buzz again. "He's known for them." She ignored her phone.

"That and boxing," Tanner agreed. "It's a good gym."

Her phone was relentless. Tanner looked at it, then at her. "Do you want to get that?"

"I swear I'll make it quick." She picked up her phone.

> I forgot—I also need to know what you did with the plat surveys that show where Dad had the water wells drilled. I can't find them on your desk.

Charlotte glanced up and flashed a very sheepish smile. "One sec."

> If you are going to text me about work on a Sunday afternoon, in the middle of my date, there better be champagne and roses on my porch when I get home. I am OFF THE CLOCK. The taxes are in the chartreuse folders. The plat maps are stored with all the plat maps in the conference room.

She hit send and put the phone down.

Tanner smiled at her. "What do you like to do for exercise?"

"Exercise?" she repeated as if she didn't know what that word meant. She hardly did. Her phone buzzed again. She tried to ignore it, but Tanner gestured to it.

Charlotte grabbed up the phone.

> I double down on my apology. But I really need to get at the tax stuff. What is charter.
>
> *chartreuse

She smiled at Tanner. "Last one, I promise."

> GREEN. LIKE LIME GREEN. How can you not know what color chartreuse is? Are you color blind? I've been meaning to ask you because you have some serious color issues. Please don't text me again today, Nick. I am trying to have a good time.

She hit send, then shoved her phone in her pocket. "So! Exercise! I don't know, but I've created all the necessary playlists so I'll have them ready to go when I do get around to exercising." She laughed.

Tanner smiled.

They chatted a little more—where she liked to hang out, the kinds of music on her hypothetical playlists. He didn't get the appeal of the Magnolia Bar and Grill for hanging out when they were so close to San Antonio. He preferred rock and roll to pop music. And when she was halfway through her drink, and he had finished his, he looked at his watch. "I should probably go," he said. "I'm meeting some people later." He glanced up at her and said, "Maybe we can do this again sometime."

That did not sound like a commitment to Charlotte. "Sure," she said. She was fairly confident they both knew they wouldn't do this again sometime.

"Can I drop you off somewhere?" he asked as he gained his feet.

"Oh, no thanks. I'm going to finish this. I live just a couple of blocks away." She smiled and stood up, too. "Thanks for inviting me."

Tanner squeezed her shoulder. He turned to go, but before he did, he looked back at her.

Charlotte smiled uncertainly, then looked around the table. "Forget something?"

"Can I ask you something, Charlotte?"

"Sure!"

"Did anyone put you up to this?"

"Put me up to what?"

"To us getting together."

"Is it so obvious?" She sighed, and prepared to explain her sisters' over-involvement in her dating life, when he said, "Someone like, maybe . . . Cordelia Prince?"

Charlotte's mouth dropped open. "You think Cordelia Prince wanted me to meet you?" she asked, gesturing between the two of them.

He shrugged. "You asked a lot of questions."

"Well, yeah. I thought that's what you did when you were getting to know someone."

Tanner studied her, as if he expected her to confess that this date had been part of a vast conspiracy of Princes. "Jesus, Tanner, of course not. And I resent the implication."

"Sorry," he said, although he didn't sound sorry.

"My sister Caitlin really likes you and really wanted me to meet you. That's all the scheming that went into this."

Tanner nodded. But he didn't look the least bit chastised. He looked dubious. "Well . . . nice meeting you, Charlotte." He smiled again and then went on, pausing at the counter to exchange a few words with Jo Carol.

Charlotte sat in her chair, stunned by how south this coffee date had gone. It was her own damn fault—she should never have mentioned Charlie or his land. It was none of her business. "Man," she muttered, and pushed her drink away as she watched him jog down the street to a truck.

125

Her fantasy picket fence was completely gone now, and the little fantasy cottage was burning to the ground. Oh well. The quest continued.

She left her drink, and as she walked out of the coffee shop, Jo Carol braced her hands against the display case and said, "Well, *he* was a cute one. Can't do much better than Tanner Sutton."

"Don't make a big deal of it, Jo Carol," Charlotte said as she walked by.

"I'm just saying, sweetie." Jo Carol gave Charlotte a big smile as she chomped on her gum.

Lord. Charlotte had just played the part of Jo Carol, sticking her nose where it didn't belong into Tanner's business.

Out on the sidewalk, it felt hotter than usual. Charlotte thought about going home and having a long soaking bath with a book. The only problem was Rufus. He would sit by the tub and pant onto her tile floor. She glanced down the street, to the Saddlebush offices. Nick's truck was still out front.

She looked in the direction of her house, then at the office. She turned in the direction of the office.

Charlotte didn't know why she was doing it, exactly. She didn't know why she did anything as far as Nick was concerned. He was like an ant bite—something you should definitely leave alone but couldn't because it itched so bad.

Chapter Seven

Nick heard the front door open with a *whoosh* of air. "Who's there?" he called, and came to his feet, striding to the door of his office.

"Your color coordinator!" Charlotte shouted back. She stood in the foyer, staring at the visitor seating area. "What happened to my pillows?"

"What?"

"My yellow and turquoise pillows!" she said accusingly, and pointed at the couch.

"Ah . . . my office," he said, and rubbed his nape. He'd meant to put them back. "I wanted to see if it would look less . . . frilly . . . without them."

"Well, it does and I want them back."

Nick sighed. He pivoted and went into his office and picked them up from an extra chair. When he turned around, she was standing there, her eyes sparkling with ire. She snatched the pillows from his hand and marched out of his office. "I can't believe you don't love them!" she yelled over her shoulder.

A moment later, she returned to his office and stood just at the threshold, her legs braced apart, and looked him up and down.

He couldn't help it—his gaze lingered on her bare legs. "What are you doing here? I thought you were on a hot date."

"It wasn't a hot date. It was coffee. That's a lukewarm date at best. Actually, I'm not sure you can even count it as a date. It was really a meet and greet."

He looked at his watch. "It's already over? Because you clearly said *date* in your scorching text message."

"Are you timing my meet and greet?"

"It wasn't even a half hour ago that you told me to get lost, so yeah, I'm a little surprised your meet and greet is over." He looked at her again. "You look . . ." He tried to think of an office-appropriate word.

One of her dark blond brows rose in question.

"Pretty," he said.

Clearly surprised by the compliment, she looked down at her dress. "You think so? Thank you!"

Nick waved his hand as if it was nothing, and took a seat. Charlotte came over to his father's enormous desk, perched on the end of it, and crossed her legs. He really wished she wouldn't do that. They were right there, slender and long and smooth, six inches from his hand.

"What are you doing here, anyway? You're not normally the guy in the office on weekends," Charlotte said.

"Had some tax work to do." He had the lime green file in front of him—he still didn't believe chartreuse was a legitimate word—but he followed her gaze to his computer screen. He had the diagram of a plane engine on his screen. The internet reception was much better here than at his house. All right, so it wasn't just taxes that brought him into the office today.

"It couldn't wait until tomorrow?"

"I've got plans tomorrow. I'm taking Colton Rivers up to have a look at the ranch."

"Now *that* sounds like a date," Charlotte said, and laughed at his withering gaze.

"Who was your date with?" he asked. "For his sake, I hope it was someone who used adverbs correctly."

"So far so good," she said. "I met him just last night."

At Stars, Boots, and Music? That was a bit of a sucker punch for Nick after the fun he'd had dancing with her. It had been a while since he had such a good time, and he wished that last night had been just about them. But that was dumb and Nick felt the flush of dumb in his neck. He didn't look up from his desk.

"Don't you want to know who?"

"Probably don't know him."

"Oh, you know him. It was Tanner Sutton."

Nick jerked his gaze to her. "You were on a date with Tanner Sutton?"

"Meet and greet," she said, her expression entirely neutral.

He felt . . . befuddled. Yep, that's exactly how he felt because no part of that declaration made sense to him. So he asked, just to clarify in his own head, "You went on a date with my half brother?"

"No, I had coffee with him. Technically, a frozen drink. But I don't think that actually counts as a date, per se," she clarified, putting air quotes around the word *date*. "But I'm not going to lie. He's hot and I was hoping it would maybe turn into more. You look alarmed, Nick. Don't be alarmed."

"I am not alarmed," he said calmly, but it was a lie, because he was completely alarmed by this development. He didn't know how he would cope with Charlotte dating a half brother he'd known about for exactly a year and a half. "I'm just clarifying for my own purposes because half the time I don't understand what you are saying."

"So it bothers you."

"I didn't say that."

"But it does."

"No," he said.

She smiled. "Yes, it does."

"I guess I'm a little surprised," he blurted. "I'm still getting used to the idea of him myself."

"Well, he's a very nice guy. I think you'd like him."

He'd heard that. He'd heard Tanner Sutton was a decent guy, and maybe one day he could accept the fact that his father had deprived them all of the opportunity to know a brother and had dumped it on them when he died, which now made it weird for everyone involved. But he was certain of one thing—he didn't want to get to know Tanner as Charlotte's boyfriend. That seemed all kinds of wrong to him. "Yeah, maybe." He stood abruptly and went to the filing cabinet. "I've been trying to find last year's tax return in the chartreuse section and I can't."

Charlotte hopped off the desk and walked to the filing cabinet. She squeezed in next to him, pulled the drawer out a little farther, and found the prior year's folder. She pulled it out and pressed it against his chest. "If it was a snake, it would have bit you."

Nick covered her hand with his and held it and the file against his chest. "Are you going to see him again?" he blurted helplessly.

Charlotte's eyes seemed to turn bluer as they stood there. "Probably not, no thanks to you," she said, and slipped her hand free.

"Me?"

"You." She wandered over to his computer and leaned over to have a look at the plane.

"Why me? I stopped texting when you said you were busy."

She straightened up from looking at his computer screen. "I mean you as a Prince. Your family. He asked me if your mother had put me up to the date."

"What?"

She shrugged. "I guess he thinks your mom is trying to get information about him through me."

That was so ridiculous that Nick felt irrationally murderous. Who the hell did this guy think he was? First of all, anyone who knew Cordelia Prince knew that if she had something to say, she'd say it directly to your face. Second of all, how dare he think that of Charlotte? She was the most honest, straight-shooting woman he'd ever known. "Did he say that? Because if he did, I'll set him straight, Charlotte. I'll—"

"I already set him straight," she said with a flick of her wrist. "I guess I asked a couple of questions he didn't like. Also, I may have been reading more into his reaction than was really there."

"Why? What did you ask him?"

"What he was going to do with the land Charlie left him."

Nick blinked. "You didn't."

She laughed. "I did! You know me, Nick. I tend to speak first and think about it a day later."

True, he did know that about her. It happened to be something else he admired about Charlotte. You never had to guess where she stood on any issue. "What did he say?"

"He said he might develop it. Put town houses and a town center on it. I don't know if that's really true. Honestly, I had the feeling he was saying it because he didn't like me asking."

"I don't know why you'd want to date him anyway," Nick said, and resumed his seat. "Doesn't seem your type."

Charlotte gave him a funny look. "My type?"

"He's not it."

Charlotte folded her arms across her middle and leaned against the desk beside him. "This is news. I didn't even know I had a type. What is it?"

"Come on, Charlotte," Nick scoffed. "You know you do."

"I do not!"

"Sure you do. Look at Adam."

"Adam!" She gave his shoulder a healthy shove. "What does *that* mean? What type is Adam?"

Nick wondered why he'd said anything at all.

"Seriously, what type is Adam supposed to be?"

Did she really not know? "Like a party guy," Nick said vaguely.

"Not following."

"If I had to describe him, I'd say he was the type of guy who'd show up in Cancun every spring break cheering on the wet T-shirt contests."

Charlotte's gaze narrowed. "Are you trying to tell me my type is a *bro?*"

"Yes, like that," Nick said. But she looked perplexed. "Am I wrong?"

"I am so insulted right now," she said, and pressed her lips together for a moment, then sighed. "But you're probably right. I haven't thought about it, but now that you say it . . ." She glanced off a moment. "Do you think Tanner is a bro?"

"I don't know Tanner well enough to say what kind of guy he is. He could be a serial killer for all I know. But I bet Adam isn't the first bro you've dated, if that's what we're calling them."

She suddenly smiled at him. "You sound almost jealous, Nick."

He gaped at her. Then laughed. "Trust me, I am not *jealous*."

"For your information, it's not like the dating pool in Three Rivers is great. And I haven't had much luck in my new online dating regimen."

"It's a regimen? And why haven't you had any luck? I thought those apps were filled with people wanting to hook up."

"Maybe because I'm not interested in hooking up? And besides, dating is just hard any way you look at it. I mean, not that you'd know, living under your rock out there in the hinterland. Maybe I'm not a good picker. Maybe I'm picking too many *bros*," she said dramatically.

"I thought the app route was supposed to

help you pick. To weed through the chaff, so to speak."

She stared at him as if he'd just landed on planet Earth. "Don't you know how any of this works?"

"Judging by your expression, I guess not. You should show me."

Charlotte laughed loud and long. "No! You can't just go on and troll. That is so rude! Anyway, you have to have an account."

"*You* have an account."

Her cheeks flushed a little. "I am not showing you my account, Nick."

"Why not?"

"Because it is my dating profile!"

He didn't see what the big deal was. "Okay."

"*Not* okay. It's for guys who might be interested in me, and *you* are not, remember?"

She was never going to forgive him for the morning after the Christmas party. "If you're worried about attracting the right guy," he said, ignoring her jab, "maybe I can give you some pointers from a male perspective."

Charlotte gasped. "Are you insane? *You* cannot give *me* pointers."

"Why are you looking at me like I'm some sort of animal? I didn't mean to offend you, but I'm a man, and I'm attracted to women, and you might be surprised how helpful that makes me."

"I would be, like, struck dead with surprise if

you could help me. Even so, it's a no. It's my *dating* profile. It's things about me, and things I like."

He swiveled in his chair and looked her directly in the eye. "Who are you talking to right now? I know what you like, Charlotte. I probably know you as well as anyone." You didn't work beside someone day in and day out and not learn a thing or two about them. You didn't sleep with a beautiful woman at a Christmas party and not remember what she liked in bed, either. Yeah, he knew Charlotte all right. And Charlotte knew it, judging by how her slight flush morphed into a full-metal-jacket blush.

"Whatever," she said. "I don't know why I care. It's not like you'll have a clue what you're looking at. Fine. I'll show you." She walked around the desk and picked up a chair, and brought it back, setting it down in front of the computer. "Is it okay if I click out of this scintillating picture of airplane guts?"

"That happens to be one of the fastest airplane engines made, but go ahead, remain ignorant about the wonders of flight."

"*Thank* you." She closed the window with the engine and pulled up a dating site.

Nick rolled closer.

The site opened to a page where Charlotte's face was front and center. It looked like she was on the river, the sun dappling the water behind her. Her face was illuminated by her smile, her eyes sparkling. She looked happy. She looked pretty and vibrant and sexy. He would definitely swipe up or down or whatever it was you did on these things.

Under her picture was the name she'd given herself: TacoLover32. Below that was a quote from a Journey song: "Just a small-town girl living in a lonely world . . ."

Below that, she'd written, *But I keep missing the midnight train going anywhere. I'm a drugstore cowgirl by birth and a princess in a previous life. I'm easily distracted by dogs, books, and fancy craft cocktails. I'm looking for someone to share adventures, Sunday brunch, hikes, trips to the coast, and art galleries. I'm up for anything! In my head I'm a gourmet cook, a graceful ice skater, and a skilled orator. In real life, I've never been on a pair of ice skates, but I'm willing to try if you are! Must love dogs, wildflowers, and at least tolerate* The Bachelor.

Below that were links to her Instagram page (Nick didn't even know Charlotte had an Instagram page) and her Spotify playlist.

"Interesting," he said.

"Okay," she said. "Go ahead and lay it on me. What's wrong with it?"

He read her profile again. "Nothing. There is not a thing wrong with it." He looked up at her. "You look great."

She smiled with delight. "Thanks! So from here, you scroll down to see your matches." She scrolled down.

Nick was stunned.

There were dozens upon dozens. He was completely gobsmacked by the sheer number of men who had swiped on Charlotte's profile. Not because of Charlotte—that, he understood all too well. But because he really was a hermit crab and didn't know so many people were on these sites.

Hi TacoLover32. I know the best place to see the wildflowers in the spring. I'll tell you where if you DM me.

Hey pretty lady. I love dogs too.

Hi TacoLover32. I like your profile. What was your last Netflix binge?

"This guy is cute," Charlotte said.

Nick looked at the picture of the guy who liked Netflix and then at her. "You absolutely hate fishing, Charlotte. He's standing on a boat holding a giant catfish. That's a clue."

She looked at his profile picture again and wrinkled her nose. "I *do* hate fishing."

They looked at the next one from the man proclaiming to have a bead on the best place to see wildflowers. Nick suspected it was somewhere deep in the country where no one would hear her if she screamed. "No," he said, and pointed to the semiautomatic rifle in the background.

"He's a hunter," Charlotte said.

"That's not a hunting gun. I'm going to have to insist you pass on this one. You're not into guns, remember?"

"I remember."

They scrolled to the next one. "What about this guy?" Nick asked. This was the man who said he loved dogs, too. He looked safe, like the kind of guy who would help you with some algebra. "He's cute, right?"

"You think so?" Charlotte asked. "His dog is cute."

"Agree."

They both stared at the profile picture. Charlotte cocked her head to one side. "Is he a bro?"

"I don't think you can be a bro if you own a corgi."

"Okay, he's a possibility," Charlotte agreed.

They scrolled to another one.

"He's really cute!" Charlotte said excitedly. Nick had to admit the next one was a good-looking man. He clicked on the profile. The first thing they noticed was a picture of a robot made of Hot Pocket sleeves with the caption *I build things out of Hot Pocket sleeves. Don't @ me.*

"Good Lord!" Charlotte said, horrified. "How many Hot Pockets did he eat to make that?" She looked at Nick and they both burst into laughter.

They scrolled through several more in search of another one they both considered acceptable— meaning, Charlotte thought the man was cute, and Nick thought he was safe enough. They landed on another potential candidate who wore glasses and said his last good read was a Harlan Coben novel. "He has definite possibilities," Charlotte said. "Does he look like a bro?"

"Not to me," Nick agreed. "And he loves to read. So do you. Have you ever heard of Harlan Coben?"

Charlotte gave him that *what planet are you from* look again. "Seriously, Nick? I mean, do you *really* live under a rock out there on the ranch? We all think it's a house, but tell me the truth—do you go out there every night and crawl under a rock and lick your crab-claw hands?"

"I take it you have heard of Harlan Coben," Nick said drily.

Charlotte shook her head and looked at the pro- file. "Okay, which do you think I should choose? The man with the corgi? Or the man with the book?"

"The book," Nick said. That guy looked the opposite of a bro. He looked smart and harmless with that book in his hand. It was possible he was wrong about that, but from his standpoint, any dude holding a book seemed like the safer option.

"Should I?" Charlotte asked.

Nick couldn't bring himself to say yes. He couldn't make himself agree that Charlotte should meet a total stranger via some dating site. But she wasn't waiting for him to agree. She swiped on the profile picture of the man with the book, and they watched that swipe disappear into a cloud that dissolved into hearts.

"Now what?" Nick asked.

"Now we wait for Book Boy to respond."

"How long does that take?"

"Depends," she said with a shrug. "On a Saturday night, you can get a very quick response." She smiled pertly. "So I've heard."

"And on a Sunday?"

"I have no idea. It's not like I do this all the time."

That was, at least, somewhat comforting. He was feeling entirely too protective of her, and that wasn't good. He glanced at his watch. "It's later than I thought. I need to go."

"Rushing back to your rock?"

"You know that no one thinks you're as hilarious as you think you are, right?"

"Oh yeah, I know," she laughingly agreed.

"I'm on my way to the ranch. I promised Grandma I'd come for Sunday dinner." He looked at Charlotte as he picked up the chartreuse files. "Want to come?"

"Ha! Good one, Nick. Your mother would not appreciate me showing up unannounced."

Nick stood up. "You'd be doing me a favor, to be honest."

"How so?"

"Because if you come, questions about me will be kept to a minimum. All the questions will be directed at you." He smiled.

Charlotte did, too. "Thanks, but I have Rufus to worry about."

"We'll swing by and get him. You know that dog would love a trip to the ranch."

"I am one hundred percent positive Rufus would love a trip to the ranch. But I'm only about fifty percent positive that your mother would be excited to see me *and* Rufus. So that's like a fifty-fifty chance that me and my dog showing up out of the blue will be a disaster."

Nick stared at her. "That is not even remotely close to how percentages work. Or any kind of math for that matter. Are you coming or not?"

She hopped up. "I think I will! I *like* those odds."

"They aren't odds," he said with a smile, and realized, as he gathered up some papers, how happy he was to have Charlotte come with him. And not for the reasons he'd stated.

Whatever the reason, he'd think about it later. All he knew was that he was looking forward to Sunday dinner for the first time in a very long time.

Chapter Eight

When Charlotte was about ten years old, the Prince family held a Fourth of July fireworks display on the ranch for everyone in Three Rivers. A big Hollywood studio had just finished filming a movie about the Alamo on the property, and the sets had not been struck. Practically everyone in town had come for the event, cars and trucks loaded with picnic gear driving through the wrought iron gates marking the entrance to Three Rivers Ranch. From there, they went down a long drive that meandered along the river until the river turned south, and then turned toward a vista of hills. The ranch was set at the base of gentle hills and at the mouth of the river, amid ancient live oaks, acacias, and cedars, as well as the occasional patch of prickly pear.

The family house was an old Spanish-style mansion that had been the seat of the fabled Prince family for more than one hundred years. The mansion had graced magazines and postcards that could be found in Market Square on the Riverwalk in San Antonio. It was twenty thousand square feet if it was one, with a red-tiled roof and a mix of stucco and limestone fascia.

One could imagine a Spanish princess walking out the enormous iron doors.

Behind the house was a terra-cotta patio that gave way to a modern, zero-edge pool. Below that were tennis courts and a multicar garage, and just below that, a paddock and stables. Horses grazed alongside cows at the fence line, their tails swishing in unison.

When she was ten, Charlotte was awed by the house. She had thought it a fancy hotel.

On that Fourth of July, the traffic from town was diverted around the house and down a dirt road to a pasture near a stock tank so large it was the size of a small lake. There her family had spread their blankets and dragged their coolers. Kids were allowed to play in the town and Alamo that had been erected for the movie that had finished filming. What Charlotte remembered most about that night was the fireworks. She couldn't imagine they were any better in a big city or even in Washington, DC. It was a brilliant display of pyrotechnics that burst against an endless canvas of dark sky and thousands of glittering stars.

All these years later, Charlotte was still awed by Three Rivers Ranch. She never drove through those ornate iron gates without feeling a tiny swell of excitement, and the house and grounds never failed to impress her.

Tonight, she noticed that a string of clear light

bulbs had been strung in the trees up on the hill behind the house where Charlie's ashes were buried. She'd heard about Mrs. Prince spending time up there since her husband had died—everyone in town talked about it, said she was going crazy. Charlotte had also seen the sun umbrella that went up in the afternoons. She thought it looked downright festive up there.

Nick pulled up to the garage. He hopped out and went around back to lower the tail of the truck. Rufus, in an uncharacteristic burst of energy and mobility, leapt from the tail and raced off to have a smell of the fence line.

Charlotte got out with the bottle of wine she'd insisted on bringing.

"The last thing anyone needs to do at Three Rivers is drink," Nick said.

"Don't be a spoilsport. And besides, I can't show up empty-handed."

They walked up through the gardens and through the rosebushes Mrs. Prince had planted the spring after Charlie died. Charlotte could smell burgers on the grill, and her belly rumbled. "Smells fantastic."

"Rafe must be making burgers," Nick said. "Never knew a man who liked to grill as much as he does."

The Prince family voices drifted down from the patio as Charlotte and Nick walked toward the wrought iron gate. Charlotte reached it first and stepped into the pool area. The Saltillo-tile patio wrapped around the back of the entire house, beneath a lanai, and bled into a vine-covered pergola over more patio. Ceiling fans turned lazily on a gentle breeze. Someone had planted giant pots of chrysanthemums that added a lot of color.

"No way!"

Hallie was the first to spot them. Charlotte grinned and waved. Hallie was Nick's sister and Charlotte's very good friend. Hallie was six months pregnant, just a few weeks behind Caitlin, but looked like she would pop at any minute. As it was, she had to leverage herself out of the lounge chair near the pool. "Charlotte! This is *great!*" she said happily.

"Charlotte is here?" Ella, Luca's wife, suddenly appeared at one of the open French doors that led into the house. She was laden with a platter of buns and burger fixings. "That's great!"

"Who is here?" Luca asked, crowding in behind his wife at the door. "Hey, Charlotte! Long time no see. Get over here, girl," he commanded, and threw his arm over her shoulders when she came around the edge of the pool, and squeezed her tight. "So good to see you, Lot."

"See who?"

"Charlotte!" Hallie announced happily as she pressed both hands to the small of her back. Charlie's mom, known as Miss Dolly around town, used the door frame to steady herself as she stepped outside. She had on a Mexican patio dress and some very colorful beads. She was trailed by an old man wearing a Marine Corps hat. "Well, Charlotte Bailey! Now isn't this a pleasant surprise!"

"What surprise?" Rafe asked. "Move, everyone. Coming through." He was carrying a platter of meat, presumably to add to whatever was already on the grill. But when he saw Charlotte, he paused and grinned. "Well, look here, it's Charlotte, the prettiest girl in Three Rivers."

"Hey!" Hallie said.

"After Hallie, of course," Rafe cheerfully amended. "What brings you out here?"

"Literally? Nick," Charlotte said, and jerked her thumb over her shoulder.

All of the Princes turned to look at Nick at the same moment. He was standing at the pool's edge, his arms crossed over his chest, gazing back at his family. "Don't everyone start greeting me at once," he drawled.

"Well, now there's a sight for sore eyes." George Lowe had entered the gathering, stepping carefully around Miss Dolly, his gaze on Charlotte. He was carrying a tray of what looked like martinis. "How are you, Charlotte? Can I offer you a martini?"

"I'm great!" she said. "Thanks, but I'll pass on the martini, George. I've had yours. I hope no one minds if I'm here. Nick said it was okay. I brought some—"

Her general hello was abruptly interrupted by a great splash in the pool.

"Rufus, no!" everyone shouted at once.

"Oh my God," Charlotte said. "Rufus, get out of there!"

Rufus did not get out of the pool, but swam in circles, his giant block head skimming the surface.

"Rufus, *out!*"

"Save your breath, Charlotte. He's not going to suddenly start obeying now," Nick said.

Nick was right. Rufus paddled around the pool a few times before finding the steps. He hauled himself out of the water and trotted into their midst. Before Hallie could shriek no, he shook off his coat, spraying Hallie with pool water tinged with old Labrador coat.

"Hallie, I am so sorry!" Charlotte cried. She shoved the bottle of wine at Nick and tried to grab Rufus's collar, but the old dog was too quick for that, and darted around Hallie to have a run at Miss Dolly's friend.

"It's all right," Hallie said, wiping away the drops from her legs. "It's not like Sulley doesn't do the same thing every day. Where is Sulley, anyway?" she asked, looking around for her dog.

Rufus had reached the old man and stuck his snout in his crotch. The old man smiled.

"Rufus! Come here!" Charlotte demanded.

"What's going on out here?" That was the unmistakable voice of Mrs. Prince. She'd appeared in the doorway, looking so put together, as always. She wore slim-fit jeans and a sleeveless red blouse that matched her red sandals. She'd brushed her silvery blond hair into a short tail at her nape. When she saw Charlotte, her face lit up. "Charlotte! What a delight!" She came forward with her arms open to hug Charlotte.

"I'm a little wet," Charlotte said apologetically. "I'm really sorry about my dog." Mrs. Prince hugged her with a surprisingly tight grip. "Nick said it would be okay to bring him," Charlotte said over Mrs. Prince's shoulder.

"Well, of course it is! We are always happy to see you and old Rufus. Is my son actually *here?*" Mrs. Prince asked, and released Charlotte.

"Hi, Mom." Nick stepped forward and leaned in to kiss her cheek.

"I guess my heart will live to beat another day after all," she said, and rose up on her toes to hug Nick's neck. "The prodigal son has returned."

"Yeah, okay, Mom," Nick said with a wry smile. "Don't get dramatic."

"Well, I'm just surprised to see you. You never come home anymore. I was beginning to think you'd run away and joined pilot school."

"Flight school," Nick said quietly.

Rufus, fresh from his inspection of the old man,

trotted over and tried to push his gargantuan head in between Mrs. Prince and Nick.

"What the devil! That dog is *wet*," Mrs. Prince said, and brushed impatiently at her leg where Rufus had pressed against her.

Charlotte caught his collar and hauled him back to sit beside her. "Again, so sorry. He used to mind me."

"That's the problem with old dogs and old men," Miss Dolly said. "They get to where they're going to do as they please."

"We're used to unruly dogs here at the ranch, aren't we, Hallie?" Mrs. Prince asked, and slanted an accusatory look at her daughter.

Hallie rolled her eyes. "I *told* you, Sulley was trying to be helpful when he dug up the bush."

Sulley, a blue heeler, must have heard his name, because he appeared at the pool gate, trotting in with muddied paws and nose. He, too, decided to greet Mrs. Prince, and left a mark on her jeans.

"All right, that's enough. Can someone usher these beasts out the gate and latch it shut?" Mrs. Prince asked. "This isn't a barn." The largesse she'd extended to the dogs had come to an end, and she turned about, walking toward the house, brushing her pant leg where Sulley had left a bit of mud.

"I told you," Charlotte muttered to Nick.

"Everything is fine," Nick muttered back. "Rufus! Sulley!" he called, and whistled sharply. The dogs obediently trotted after him, crowding in beside each other, trying to be first. He opened the gate and ushered them through, then closed the gate and latched it. Both dogs promptly turned around and sat, facing the gate, watching the people on the patio and wearing pitiful expressions.

Hallie eased herself back onto the chaise with Luca's help and rested her hands on top of her belly. Miss Dolly sat beside her on another chaise. Her friend was sitting in a chair, his legs spread in old-man fashion, his arms resting across his belly, much like Hallie.

"Charlotte, have you met my friend Lloyd?" Miss Dolly asked. "Lloyd, this is Charlotte Bailey. She runs our company."

"Well," Charlotte said, "I mean, I do, but with help from Nick." She smiled at Nick. He steadily returned her gaze.

"And you met Nick at the Stars, Boots, and Music, Lloyd, do you remember?" Miss Dolly asked.

"Of course I remember," he said gruffly, and raised a hand.

"Lloyd," Nick said with a nod.

Miss Dolly turned a smile to her grandson. "We're having burgers, Nicky! Rafe makes the *best* burgers. He says he has a secret ingredient."

"Family recipe," Rafe confirmed.

"They smell delicious," Charlotte confirmed.

"Oh goodness, Nicky, I just remembered, you don't eat meat," Miss Dolly said. "What are you going to eat?"

Nick accepted a beer that Luca put in his hand. "I'll be all right, Grandma."

"Have you ever heard of a cattle rancher who doesn't eat meat?" Miss Dolly asked Lloyd. "Isn't that about as crazy as a dancing cat?"

If Lloyd had on opinion, he didn't offer it. But he did give Nick a good study.

"Nick?" Mrs. Prince appeared at the door again. "I don't know what to do about your dinner. Should I make some rice for you?" She held up a box of instant rice and shook the contents. "Or I could make you a cheese sandwich."

"Cheese is an animal product, Mom," Hallie said in a tone that suggested they'd had this conversation before.

"I'm okay with cheese, Hallie," Nick said, and held up a hand. "But don't go to any trouble on my account, Mom. I'll make a salad."

"I didn't say it was any trouble. I just don't understand all the rules. I'd be happy to whip something up for you, but you're going to have to tell me what. It's not my fault you're a vegan, you know. I swear, these diet fads are getting out of control."

"It's not a fad," Nick said quietly. "And I'm not a vegan. But I don't eat meat. I'll make a salad."

"Well, whatever, be my guest. But I agree with

Dolly—a cattleman who doesn't eat meat is about the most ridiculous thing I ever heard."

"I know. You've mentioned it," Nick said.

Charlotte could almost feel the tension building in him. She smiled and took the beer that Luca offered her. No wonder Nick didn't come to the ranch as much as his mother would like. She wouldn't, either, if this was the reception she could expect.

"I guess I'll just make a salad, then," Mrs. Prince sighed, as if preparing a salad were as taxing as whipping up a lasagna at a moment's notice.

"Delia," George said softly.

"What?"

"Nick said he'd do it."

"Seriously, Mom—I don't want you to go to any trouble," Nick reiterated.

"Oh, she won't go to any trouble, you can rest assured," Miss Dolly snorted. "She's still mad we had to let Frederica go."

Mrs. Prince glared at her mother-in-law. "Fine. Do what you like, Nick. But I'm telling you, a man needs real protein." She turned and went back inside. "People are supposed to eat *meat,*" she complained as George followed her inside.

"Not all people, Delia," George said calmly.

Charlotte glanced at Nick. She'd never wanted to make a salad for someone so bad in all her life.

"Well!" Hallie said cheerfully. "Now that we

have Mom's total disdain for vegetarians out of the way, how is Caitlin doing, Charlotte?"

"She's miserable," Charlotte said with a laugh. "We were talking about you the other day, wondering if you have any names picked out?"

Hallie and Rafe had decided not to know the sex of their baby until it was born. Recently, Hallie had been complaining about the names Rafe liked. "They're so . . . I don't know, *boring,*" she'd said.

"Well, if it's a girl, we're going to name her after one of my more illustrious ancestors," she said proudly.

"Eldagirt Wirt?" her grandmother asked.

"What? *No,* Grandma, definitely not *Eldagirt Wirt.*"

"I don't see why not. She was mayor of Silo when Silo was a town," Grandma said. "It's just a crossroads now. They shut down the silo there and that was the end of Silo. How about naming her after your great-aunt Hannah Prince?"

"*Yes,* Hallie!" Luca said suddenly and vociferously. "Hannah Fontana! Think about it."

"I have thought about it, and I will not have a baby named Hannah Fontana," Hallie said. "We have a couple of names in mind. Alberta, like our great-grandmother, and we'd call her Albie or Bertie. Or Amelia, after our great-great-great-grandmother. She was the one who fought off that band of thieves, remember?"

"Such a pretty name," Ella agreed. "And if it's a boy?"

Hallie sighed and looked at Rafe. "He wants to name him Lauriano, after his grandfather."

"What's wrong with that?" Luca asked.

"Everyone would call him Laurie," Hallie complained.

"Maybe they would call him Lauriano," Rafe said.

"You know how I feel, Rafe," Hallie said.

Ella must have sensed an argument brewing, and asked Charlotte, "Does Caitlin have names picked out?"

"Liam," Charlotte said. Caitlin was having a boy.

Ella said she'd seen Caitlin at the grocery store with all her kids and she'd looked exhausted. Hallie complained about the summer heat, and said she moved from fan to fan all day long. They laughed about some of the ridiculous games at baby showers, and about first-baby jitters. Hallie had a strange and unnatural fear of smothering her baby with a bad swaddle.

Luca and Ella squeezed onto a chaise together, and Ella said, "Okay, Charlotte. I'm dying to know. How is the dating project going?"

Charlotte had not been shy about telling all her friends she was embarking on a yearlong dating experiment to find Mr. Right. In fact, one day last week, she'd had drinks with Ella and Mariah and told them how Cassie had set her up on a couple of dating apps.

"I'm not sure. So far, I've been on three first dates."

"That's great!" Ella said.

"Wow," Luca said, nodding appreciatively.

"But not a single second date. I am learning that I am not very good at picking out the best Texas has to offer."

"Well, that's the thing with dating apps," Hallie said. "You have to kiss a lot of frogs."

"And how do you know that, Hal?" Rafe asked from his place behind the grill. "Is there some part of your dating history I don't know?"

Hallie laughed. "Okay, so I have no personal experience. But I've had friends use them and I know how they work. First, you have to get through all the players who flood your inbox. You know, the guys with feet fetishes and that sort of thing."

"*Feet* fetish?" Rafe asked, looking up.

"She doesn't know what she is talking about," Ella said with a wave of her hand.

"Actually, Nick very graciously helped me pick out two guys today," Charlotte announced.

That declaration was met with stunned silence. For a moment. Luca's loud laugh interrupted it. "I thought you said *Nick* helped you pick out two guys." He laughed again and looked around at the others.

"I did," Charlotte said.

"Wait," Rafe said. "Are you saying that *Nick* is on a *dating* site?"

"Now, that's the funniest thing I've heard in a long time," Charlotte said. "No, he helped me on *my* dating site. We went through some of my matches and he picked out two."

"Oh my God," Hallie said. "Charlotte, I wouldn't go there if I were you. Nick doesn't know anything about this kind of dating, trust me."

"Okay, everyone, I'm sitting right here," Nick said. "Why not help out? I don't actually live under a rock as I am often accused." This he said with a meaningful look at Charlotte.

"Don't be silly, Nick. You're not that kind of guy," Hallie snorted.

Nick looked wounded. "*What* kind of guy? I've dated. I've dated a lot."

"Not since, like, 2012."

"That is a gross exaggeration," Nick complained, pointing at his little sister.

"Fine. But you have to admit that since Dad died, you've been living the life of a lonely recluse out there with your bubble baths and herbal tea and staring at the sky wishing you were someone else."

"Bubble baths," Luca said with a snort.

"It's true!" Hallie insisted. "You don't know that Nick loves bubble baths?"

Nick sat up in his chair. "Well, I guess I didn't get the memo, Hallie. Is there supposed to be something *wrong* with liking a good bath now and again? When was the last time you wrangled a calf?"

Charlotte couldn't help herself—she burst into laughter at the image of Nick lounging in a bubble bath.

"May I ask what is so damn funny?" Nick demanded.

"Oh my God, Charlotte, have you not seen his bathroom?" Hallie continued excitedly. "He had a big picture window installed and set this *giant* claw-foot tub in front of it. It's a *great* tub. I took a bath in it once."

"When?" Nick exclaimed.

"That does sound relaxing," Miss Dolly said. "I like a bath, too, Nicky. I just don't like having to get in and out of bathtubs. Hard to do at my age."

"Not me," Luca said. "Shower guy all the way. Get in, get the job done, get out."

"So do you, like, soak?" Ella asked curiously.

"I don't know!" Nick said with great exasperation. "I take a bath!"

"And exposes the entire world to his luscious self since he put that picture window in," Hallie said.

For some reason, that made Charlotte feel a little warm around the hairline. She had a sudden, and not completely unwelcome, image of Nick in the buff.

"I'm not exposed to anyone but a few cows, a blind old horse, and maybe a coyote or two," Nick complained. "There isn't anyone for miles around."

"So, like, how often do you soak in a bubble bath?" Luca asked curiously, as if this were a concept so foreign to him that he couldn't quite grasp how it worked.

Nick looked around at them all. "I never said I soaked! So I like a hot bath! You're all looking at me like I'm a freak."

"Just own it, Nick," Hallie said cheerfully. "Otherwise, we'll sit here all night debating how weird my brothers are."

"What'd *I* do?" Luca asked with some offense. "*I* didn't take a bubble bath."

"Anyway, we were talking about Charlotte," Hallie said. "Charlotte, you were saying?"

Charlotte was having trouble getting that image of naked Nick out of her mind. "Hmmm?"

"Nick's picks for your dates," Ella reminded her.

"Oh! Well, one of them has a corgi. He's adorable."

"Which one?" Ella asked. "The dog or the man?"

"I'm not going to lie," Charlotte said. "I'm more excited about meeting the corgi."

"Smart," Ella said. "Dogs are awesome."

"You can tell a lot about a man from the dog he picks," Rafe said as he flipped burgers.

"Rafe, I hope those burgers aren't too well done," Miss Dolly said loudly. "I don't like mine well done."

"I know, Miss Dolly. Believe me, I know," Rafe said with a fond grin.

"And the other guy?" Hallie asked Charlotte.

"The other guy loves books. We swiped right on him."

"You mean you swiped," Luca said.

"Actually, Nick did the swiping on that guy. He likes the way it dissolves into little hearts."

Luca looked at his brother. "Who *are* you right now?"

"The book guy looked nice and said he'd just read the latest Harlan Coben novel," Charlotte added.

"Oh!" Hallie cried. "So did I! It was *so* good."

"Wasn't it?" Charlotte eagerly agreed. She'd devoured it over a weekend. "Guess who's never heard of Harlan Coben?"

"Who?" Ella and Hallie asked in unison.

"Nick!"

Ella and Hallie looked at Nick. *"Seriously?"* Ella's brows dipped, and she looked him up and down as if she couldn't quite comprehend it.

"Come on, I can't be the only one," Nick said, looking around at them all, and rather pointedly at Luca, who, Charlotte knew, had been working to overcome dyslexia and had only recently learned to truly read. "I know *you* haven't," Nick said to his brother.

"Haven't read him," Luca agreed, and Nick smiled smugly at Hallie and Ella.

"But I listen to his books on audio."

Nick turned to Rafe for support.

But Rafe shook his head. "Sorry, bro. I read his latest after Hallie finished."

Nick looked helplessly at his grandmother.

"Well, I can't say I've read any of his books," Miss Dolly said. "I like a good World War II book, you know. But of course I've *heard* of him."

"I haven't," Lloyd grunted.

Charlotte guessed no one was surprised by that.

Nick seemed discombobulated by the popularity of Harlan Coben among his family. "Okay," he said, nodding. "All right, I get it. It's pile-on-Nick day. He takes baths, he hasn't heard of Herman Corbin—"

"Harlan Coben!" they all shouted at him.

"Now see, Nicky, if you dated Charlotte, you might learn a thing or two," his grandmother said with a waggle of her brows.

The mere suggestion made Charlotte choke on her beer and then laugh with something that sounded close to hysteria to her own ears.

"Please, Miss Dolly. I already have to work with him," Charlotte pleaded.

"Hey," Nick said.

"Charlotte, have you met Colton Rivers?" Ella asked. "Now *there* is a great guy. He came out to look at our project. I really like him. And he's single."

"You actually asked him that?" Charlotte exclaimed. Ella wasn't exactly front and center when it came to meeting new people.

"No, silly! Luca did. You know he can talk to a fence post."

"How else are you going to know what's up if you don't ask questions now and then?" Luca asked.

"Nick is taking him flying tomorrow," Charlotte said.

"Oh yeah?" Luca asked, shifting his attention to Nick. "Where?"

"I'm showing him the ranch. Looks like Saddlebush is going to need a loan until we sell some cattle."

"A loan!" Miss Dolly said.

"Trust me, Grandma," Nick muttered.

The issue of a loan seemed to create some tension between grandson and grandmother, so in an effort to change the subject, Charlotte said, "I think Nick has a thing for Colton." And she arched a brow at Hallie and Ella.

Nick sighed wearily. "I happen to like the guy.

Is *that* okay? Or is that another unpardonable sin, ranking up there right next to baths and not knowing who Herman Corbin is."

"Harlan Coben!" Hallie shouted at him.

"Of course it's okay!" Ella said. "Who wouldn't like him? He's kind and fun, and he's hot in a sort of bankery way. You should totally date him, Charlotte. You're kind and fun and pretty in all the best ways. It's a perfect match."

"Oh, I don't know," Charlotte said, blushing a little. Not because of the flattery—Ella was good at that. Because the thought had certainly crossed her mind, almost the moment Colton Rivers walked into the Saddlebush offices. He was definitely hot in a bankery way.

"Maybe he's got a dog," Rafe said. "Then it would be really perfect."

"A Lab, like Rufus," Ella suggested.

"I like a good cow dog, personally," Nick said. "Pepper is a great dog. They don't get any smarter than a cow dog." He took a swig of beer. "I mean, if we're going off the kind of dog that recommends a man, I'd say cow dog. Not a Lab."

"We're talking about how amazing Colton would be for Charlotte, Nick," Hallie said.

"She's already picked a guy. Two, in fact."

"But I should have a backup plan, shouldn't I?" Charlotte asked this question directly of Nick, for no other reason than to goad him. Honestly, she didn't know why she stirred up trouble with

Nick when there was no trouble to be stirred. She was smart enough to know that it had something to do with the aftermath of that damn Christmas party, but she didn't pretend to understand the psychology of it, other than a juvenile desire to zing him because he'd zinged her. She was very adult like that.

And Nick always took the bait. His gaze settled on hers. "Maybe you should have a backup plan that is not our banker."

"You mean *your* banker. Not mine. Are you worried he won't have time for you?"

"Not at all, Charlotte. Because I'm the one with all the problems that enable the bank to make money, so I'm sure I'll see plenty of him. I just think we should let the man breathe before we marry him off. He's new to town."

"I think Charlotte is right," Hallie said, grinning. "I think you do have a thing for him."

Nick stood up from his chair. "What I have a thing for is food. Are those burgers ready, Rafe?"

"Just about."

"I hope they aren't too well done," Miss Dolly said.

"If you are all through torturing me, I'm going to make a salad," Nick said, and walked toward the French doors. "Anyone need anything?" he called over his shoulder as he disappeared inside. But he didn't wait for anyone to answer.

"Burgers are ready," Rafe announced.

"Luca, help me. I can't get up," Hallie moaned.

They all stood up, Charlotte and Miss Dolly helping Lloyd from his chair. They trundled inside, gathering their drinks and empty beer bottles as they went. George directed them to the informal dining room, not to be confused with the formal dining room, which, Charlotte understood, could seat twenty-four people if necessary. She and Charlie had spread the plat maps with the oil wells on that expensive, hand-polished table once, and Mrs. Prince almost had a coronary.

The interior of the house, like the exterior, was something to behold. From the hand-scraped hickory floors, to the marble foyer, to the ceilings that soared overhead into box beam construction, it felt as if one was walking through a museum. Priceless paintings were artfully arranged on the walls, and crystal and glass chandeliers hung in the massive family room as well as the foyer. The furnishings were made of the finest leather, the rugs handwoven from wool and silk. Charlotte knew this because *House and Garden* magazine had once done a feature article on the house, and she'd devoured every word of it, had studied every photo of every room.

They passed through the enormous kitchen with its marble countertops and gleaming high-end appliances, with its cozy hearth and seating area. Nick was at the counter, creating a salad.

The informal family dining room was tucked into a rounded corner of the house with windows overlooking the gardens. Sulley and Rufus had already made their way to sit outside the windows and stare in with boundless hope. Just below the gardens, a pair of horses stood at the fence and seemed to be looking in, too.

Charlotte smiled at the sight of the animals. That was the way of things around this town—everyone, even the animals, wanted a peek inside the lives of the Princes.

Charlotte often wondered why Nick would want to leave this spot of paradise as badly as he seemed to want to do. The house was clearly built for generations of Princes to reside here. He could probably have his own wing. But for reasons Charlotte didn't understand, he preferred to live in that old ranch house miles away from anyone, with a big picture window in his bathroom.

That was just another of what seemed like many little mysteries swirling around this man, another piece of a puzzle that she couldn't seem to wrap her head around. What really annoyed her about it was that she wanted to wrap her head around it at all.

Especially after that Christmas party.

Or maybe the Christmas party was the reason she did.

Chapter Nine

Nick's mother had whipped up a batch of instant rice and frozen peas for him, which she presented to him at the table like a wise man presenting a gift to the baby Jesus. Nick suspected she'd done it so she could make her comments, like, "It's probably bland. I didn't use butter because God forbid any cow be put out by having to produce a little milk to make a little butterfat."

Nick had learned a long time ago to ignore his mother and bite his tongue. But he'd once asked her why it bothered her so that he preferred not to eat cows. That he didn't feel right about it.

"It doesn't *bother* me," she'd lied. "It's just not the way Princes do things."

His mother was all about the way Princes did things. She was a slave to appearances, an annoying trait that had seemed only to worsen since Dad died. It was as if she was determined that no one see the cracks in their collective facade. She didn't care that it was beyond her ability to control, that the whole town knew about the cracks and could see them widening. She was determined they would not get even a hint of scandal from any member of the Prince family.

But it was obvious Three Rivers Ranch was not what it once was. The crew of groundskeepers who had kept the estate looking immaculate were gone, replaced by a yard crew. The bunkhouse was empty except on those occasions a couple of vaqueros would appear to help with some of the cattle operations. Their household staff had been let go, and a cleaning service now came in twice a month.

Everything was different now, and sometimes, Nick thought he was the only one who could see it. It was like he was living in a parallel universe sticking Band-Aids on all the places they were hemorrhaging, while the rest of them carried on in another universe with only a few new inconveniences. His mother acted as if nothing had really happened, as if they were still a powerful ranching family that could throw money at any problem without breaking a sweat.

They were not that family. The economy of ranching was changing, and they were struggling to change with it.

Rafe and Hallie had set up a burger bar on the hutch in the family dining room. With burgers and chips, everyone sat around the table and chatted about old times. Somehow, an old family tale surfaced, and Nick's grandmother tried to explain to Charlotte the Disaster of the Year 2000, as it was known in their family.

"Not Y2K," Luca said, laughing, referring to

the panic that automated systems weren't pro-grammed to handle the date at the turn of the century. "But we were ready for that one, too. You've never seen so many batteries. Dad had them stacked in one of the garage bays, floor to ceiling."

"Well? You can never be too careful," Nick's grandmother said. "But I'm talking about the afternoon Delia lost her fool mind in the middle of that high tea for the San Antonio Arts Asso-ciation and almost sold you three to slave labor."

George chuckled.

"It's not funny, George," Nick's mother warned. She was seated at the head of the table and had predictably filled her plate with a burger patty, some lettuce and tomato, and nothing more. "That happened to be one of the premier events of the spring. I negotiated it right out from under the nose of Marybeth McIntyre, and she was fit to be tied."

"That woman has some strong opinions," George said.

"I think she has a slight drinking problem," Grandma added.

"You both speak as if there is something wrong with a woman having strong opinions and a slight drinking problem," Nick's mother said grandly with her martini glass in hand. "My com-plaint with Marybeth has always been that she does not own the annual spring arts fundraiser."

"So what happened?" Ella asked.

"My kids happened, that's what. I have never been so embarrassed in my *life*." She pressed a hand to her chest as if the mere memory of it gave her heart palpitations. "Nick was what, twelve or thirteen?"

"Twelve," Nick said. He glanced at Charlotte and rolled his eyes. Her eyes sparkled back at him with anticipation.

"The twins were ten," his mother continued. "Why the three of them thought that afternoon was a good time to be complete idiots, I'll never understand."

"You told us to disappear, Mom," Luca said.

"I meant for you to go to your room, Luca. It was Charlie's fault, anyway," she said with a dismissive flick of her wrist. "He gave you all way too much leeway. 'Oh, they're just kids, Delia,' he'd say. 'Let them be.' Well, that was exactly the sort of thing that would happen when I let you kids be."

"For heaven's sake, Delia, are you going to tell the story or not?" Nick's grandmother demanded.

"I'm getting there. While I was presiding over the loveliest of spring flings, far better than Marybeth McIntyre could *ever* put together, my children determined it was a good time to teach each other how to drive."

"Luca and Hallie," Nick pointed out, although

170

the detail would be lost in his mother's dramatic presentation of events.

"You were there," she countered. "Guilty by association. And you can't deny it was with your help that they backed one of the work trucks out of the garage. Luca was driving, and hit the gas so hard that he rammed into a light pole and toppled it."

"Which is why I made him get out of the driver's seat," Nick pointed out.

"*That* must have made a noise," Charlotte said. "They were lucky no one was killed," she said, looking at Nick.

"It did indeed make a dreadful noise. I thought we were being attacked! But it was nothing compared to the sound of that truck careening around the house and then crashing into the water fountain in the drive."

Nick noticed that Charlotte was biting her lip to keep from laughing. That water fountain was an ostentatious display in the middle of a circular drive. It had been built in the style of a Roman fountain, but instead of Neptune lazing about, it was three horses.

"That was Hallie's doing. She was behind the wheel and could hardly see over it. And here came Nick, running after them, shouting at Hallie to put the thing in park. It was too late for that—the fountain was spewing, and the top of the sculpture had fallen onto the drive."

"Oh my God," Ella said. "How come I've never heard this story before?" she asked, casting a suspicious look at Luca.

"You'd think that would be the worst of it," his mother continued. "You'd think that having to face the shame of what my foolish children had done would be punishment enough. But oh no—my guests couldn't leave because the wrecked truck and the wrecked fountain blocked the drive."

Charlotte's laughter burst out of her, and even as she clamped two hands over her mouth, it didn't stop her from shaking with it. To be fair, Ella, George, and Rafe were laughing, too. Lloyd sat stoically—probably hadn't heard a word of it—and Grandma was predictably amused by her daughter-in-law's ire.

Nick and his siblings exchanged weary glances.

"I'm happy you all find it so amusing," his mother said regally. "It required two wreckers from town to remove the obstacles. Charlie came home from the golf course and laughed until he cried. Didn't care at all about the damage that had been done. And then he proceeded to help my guests drink us bone dry while we waited for the drive to be cleared." She lifted her martini glass to her lips and sipped. "I am sure it goes without saying that I was never invited to host the San Antonio Arts Association spring tea again." She set her glass down

172

with a thud. "And Marybeth crowed about it for *years*."

"I never understood why Luca and I were grounded for two weeks and Nick only one," Hallie said. "That didn't seem fair."

"*You* should have been grounded for the rest of your life, Hallie. It was your doing."

"Actually, it was Nick's doing." Hallie pointed at Nick. "He said, 'I bet you can't drive that truck.'"

"Give it up, Hal," Luca said. "Nick is Mom's favorite."

"Not true," their mother said. "I love all my children equally."

"It is, too, true, Delia," Grandma said. "Admit it."

"Well." Nick's mother shrugged. "I guess he is my favorite in a way."

Luca gasped. "Mom!"

"You just said it yourself!"

"I know, but I didn't expect *you* to say it," Luca said.

"What? You and Hallie have always had each other. It was like the two of you didn't even need me. But Nick, he needed me."

All eyes turned to Nick, but he remained stubbornly silent. He didn't remember it quite like that, but he wasn't going to set off another round of arguments.

"Nick *needed* his father," Grandma said.

"Okay, Dolly, go ahead, dig the knife in," Nick's mother said.

"Remember when Nick played baseball? Charlie was out there every day. Every practice, every game."

"I was out there, too!"

"Not like Charlie," his grandmother insisted.

"All right, Dolly, okay—I am a horrible mother."

"I wouldn't go *that* far," Dolly said.

"Mom? Grandma? Can you not do this right now?" Nick asked. "It's water under the bridge. I haven't played baseball in fifteen years."

"And we have company," Hallie added, waving a hand at Charlotte.

"Charlotte is not company," Grandma said. "She's practically a Prince."

"Practically," Charlotte cheerfully agreed.

That was another thing about Charlotte, Nick decided. She'd heard all the Prince family dysfunction through the years and hadn't gone running yet. Why hadn't she? He'd tried to run but couldn't get very far, no matter how hard he tried. She could work for anyone in town or San Antonio. Why did she stay?

"My mom has favorites," Charlotte continued. "Right now, it's any one of us who can give her the next grandchild." She laughed. "Caitlin is winning."

"Maybe that's my ticket to my mother's love,

174

huh, Mom?" Hallie asked, and ran her hand over her enormous belly. "When are you going to get on the baby bandwagon, Ella?"

"That's a personal question, Hallie," Luca said, and Ella smiled so gloriously at him and Luca returned one so smitten that it tugged on Nick's heartstrings a little. He had a brief moment of curiosity about what it would be like for someone to look at him like that. He sort of had seen it once, but the memory of a dark night in bed with a particular woman jolted him back to the present. He shifted, turning his gaze to the window and the evening sky.

"We'll have them when the time seems right for us," Luca said.

"You're so New Age," Hallie complained.

"I can't wait to have kids," Charlotte announced.

"We know," Rafe said with a gentle laugh.

"Yes, I'm kind of a nut about it," Charlotte admitted. "But time is slipping away from me."

"You have all the time in the world, Charlotte," Nick's mother said.

"What about you, Nicky?" his grandmother asked. "When are you going to settle down and give us some grandkids?"

"What?" Nick squirmed slightly. He hated this question, posed periodically to him by a mother or grandmother. *When will you marry? When will you have kids? Aren't you lonely living out there all by your lonesome?* "I haven't thought about it."

"You better think about it, son," his grandmother added. "You're not getting any younger."

"All he wants to do is jet off here and there," his mother said, in a tone that suggested she thought that was a dumb wish to have. "He thinks he can just flitter around the globe like some sort of nomad. Unfortunately, that's not how life works."

Nick pinned her with a look. "I haven't flittered anywhere. I've been right here, taking care of the ranch for you."

His mother guiltily averted her gaze from him. "Well, it's obvious that's what you want to do."

"Yep. It's been obvious since I was eight years old."

"Life doesn't always turn out the way we want," his grandmother said. "You just haven't met the right girl yet. When you meet the right girl, you'll want to settle down. Mark my words," she said with a smug smile.

"Is dinner over yet?" Nick could feel the tension rising in him, the aggravation he felt every time his family tried to push his square body into the round Prince hole. He didn't want the right things; he hadn't found the right things. "So anyone following baseball?" he asked, and looked up. "Rangers look good this season."

"Not as good as the Astros," Luca countered.

Nick successfully turned the conversation to sports, but beneath the table, his leg was bouncing with impatience. When the sound of a large splash in the pool reached him, Nick had never been so grateful to a dog in his life.

"What was that?" his grandmother asked.

"I think I know," Charlotte said. "Will you excuse me?" She was already out of her seat and headed for the dining room door.

Nick stood up, too. "I'll give her a hand." He strode from the dining room, following Charlotte out the mudroom door and around to the patio.

"Rufus! Get out of there! What is *wrong* with you?" Charlotte shouted as Rufus happily paddled around the pool again. "Get out!"

Rufus ignored her.

Nick whistled. "Rufus, truck!" Nick started for the gate.

Rufus immediately clambered out of the pool and shook his coat, spraying Charlotte and Sulley. Rufus then paused to lift a leg on a rosebush before trotting after Nick.

"How do you do that?" Charlotte demanded.

"A dog won't ever turn down a ride." And indeed, Rufus was wagging his tail like it was Christmas morning. So was Sulley, ready to get in the truck, too.

George wandered out of the house to see about the commotion as Charlotte held on to Sulley's collar while Nick helped Rufus into the truck. "Anything I can do to help?"

"Not unless you can take the dog out of a dog," Nick said. He closed the tailgate.

George studied Rufus in the bed of the truck. Rufus tried to crane his neck to lick George, even though George was standing several feet away. "I don't think that dog's got a lot going on upstairs."

"I think that's pretty clear," Nick said with a chuckle. He rubbed Rufus's wet head, much to the dog's utter delight.

"Rafe!" Charlotte cried, maneuvering Sulley back into the gate. "Come and get your dog!" She disappeared into the garden.

"You know, Nick," George said quietly, "your mom means well, but sometimes she can't see the forest for the trees. You know what I mean?"

Nick wasn't sure he did know, but the less time he spent talking about his mother, the better.

"I guess what I'm trying to say is, if you want to fly, you ought to fly."

Well, that was interesting. George Lowe was not in the habit of offering unsolicited advice, and Nick was not in the habit of asking for it. He glanced curiously at George.

George kept his gaze on the dog. "Delia wouldn't like it, but she'd get over it. She always does. It just takes her a little time. But Rafe and Martin are perfectly capable of running this ranch. Martin's been at the ranch for thirty years."

"I don't know if Rafe would even be interested," Nick said. "He's put a lot of time and effort into the martial arts studio. He has a degree in social work. Not animal husbandry."

"He could do both," George offered. "And I think Rafe is interested in being wherever Hallie is, period." He turned to look at Nick. "You could at least talk to him about it. He'll keep it confidential if you ask him to."

Nick thought about the next flight-training course in Dallas. It started in October. "Yeah, maybe," he said vaguely.

George turned his attention back to Rufus. "You're a lucky man, Nick. I know it doesn't feel that way at times, but you are. You have the means to do what you want, and not everyone can say that. If it were me? I'd stick to what I'd always wanted."

"It's asking a lot of Rafe. It's a thankless job, a busy job. And then there is Mom on top of that."

George chuckled. "Rafe has me to help him. I know the Saddlebush business as well as you do. And with a good sale of cattle this fall, we should have a little breathing room. Moreover—you didn't hear it from me—but I think I've got Dolly and Delia convinced we ought to sell some of the land along the highway to the city. We could hire a couple of hands then." He turned to face Nick.

"Charlie never expected you to sacrifice your dream for this ranch."

A sharp stab of resentment landed in Nick's gut. "Maybe. But then he died."

"That doesn't change the way he felt." George gave Nick's chest a fatherly pat. "Just think about what I've said."

Charlotte suddenly banged through the gate. "I should take this dunce home. He'll sleep for two days after all this excitement." Rufus was so happy to see Charlotte that he wagged his tail hard enough for Nick to worry he could break something on his truck.

"Are you leaving?" Hallie and her mother appeared at the mudroom door.

"I think we should," Charlotte said. "Rufus's behavior doesn't get better with time."

"Come back anytime, Charlotte!" Hallie said. "Come back next week. And the week after. You don't have to come with Nick. You're a lot more fun than he is."

"Thanks a lot, Hallie," Nick said. He put his arm around his sister's shoulder and hugged her into his side.

"Thank you so much for letting me crash your Sunday evening," Charlotte was saying to his mother.

"We were so glad to have you," his mother said graciously, but she shot a look at Rufus.

"Bye, Charlotte!" Nick looked up to see his

grandmother near the pool, waving her hand overhead.

"Bye, Miss Dolly! Bye, Lloyd!"

"Don't run off without saying good-bye." Rafe, Luca, and Ella came out the mudroom door, too. Rafe hugged Charlotte. "Always good to see you, kid. You too, Nick."

When the good-byes were said, Nick's family stood on the drive watching them pull away, waving like he was going off to war. Charlotte waved back. When they turned out of the gate, Charlotte sank in her seat and put both hands on her belly. "I'm *miserable,*" she announced. "It's true—Rafe makes the *best* burgers. I think I ate twice my body weight."

She looked pretty. If that's what Rafe's burgers did for her, Nick could put aside his queasiness about it.

Charlotte suddenly looked at him. "Can I say something?"

"It depends. Usually when you say that, it's not something I want to discuss."

"It's a little controversial," she agreed.

Nick expected some tips on how to eat. He'd discovered the world was full of people who wanted to tell a man how to eat. "Is it about my eating habits?"

"No. I know you're a vegan or vegetarian or whatever."

"Vegetarian," he said. "It's just a personal

thing—I don't want to eat animals. It's like eating a dog. Very unappetizing."

"Nooo!" She grimaced, squeezing her eyes shut. "Why'd you have to say *that?* You don't have to explain it to me. I know you don't eat meat because you're a big fat cow lover."

"They have personalities and feelings too, you know," he said defensively.

"Anyway, that's not what I was going to say."

He glanced at her as he turned onto the main road through town. "So what were you going to say?"

"That your family borders on bat-shit crazy." She smiled pertly. "I mean, I've always known that, but when you have them all together, whew boy, that's a trip to crazy town. And what is with Lloyd? Is he deaf? Is he *real?*"

Nick laughed. "I wondered the same thing. You think I don't know how crazy my family is?"

"Don't get me wrong," she said, tapping her fist to his leg. "Mine is, too. You should come to dinner with my family for the sake of comparison."

"I have a feeling the Baileys would give the Princes a run for their money in the crazy department." He smiled at her. "I've met your little sister."

Charlotte laughed. Her smile was soft, and maybe almost adoring, and it sank into him fast and hard like an anchor into a sea of volatile emotions.

He didn't look at her again until he pulled up in front of her house. In the bed behind them, Rufus began to pace. Nick got out and opened the tailgate, and Rufus launched his body off the back. He raced up the steps and stood facing the door, his tail wagging, as if he expected the door to magically open.

Charlotte walked up the porch steps, and leaned around Rufus to open the door. The dog bolted inside, and a moment later, from his place on the porch steps, Nick could hear him lapping up water somewhere.

Charlotte returned to the top step. She was eye level with him, a step or two above him. He hadn't come onto the porch because he didn't want to give the impression that he wanted to come inside. Part of him did want to come inside. *Really* wanted to come inside. Come in and wash away all his disappointments and resentments and general lethargy with something that felt good.

But he thought too much of Charlotte to take her down that path again.

Her eyes moved over his face, and she adjusted her handbag on her shoulder, keeping her hand on the strap. Her gaze slipped to his mouth. She might as well have thrown a flame at him.

"You know what?"

"What?" He was looking at her mouth, too. He was remembering the kiss that had started it all. He was remembering it in Technicolor DreamWorks cinema style, which, frankly, was not a good idea at the moment. That sort of memory had a tendency to cloud his better judgment.

"You can be a really good guy sometimes. This evening was not unpleasant." Her voice was full of wonder, as if she was surprised by this revelation.

Nick felt his mouth quirk up into something of a wry smile. "You really know how to flatter a guy."

"It's a gift."

He moved up one step. They were no longer eye level—he was looking down at her. He was so damn close to her, and a million thoughts raced through his head—how she'd felt that night, how intensely he wanted to kiss her right now, how he would miss her most of all if he actually took George's advice and went to flight school. "You know what, Charlotte?"

She gave him a lopsided smile. "Probably. But what?"

Nick didn't know what he was going to say, exactly, but he felt some words forming on the tip of his tongue. Words that wanted to desperately put themselves in order so he could convey what she meant to him. Words that were growing and expanding and moving around. But they were too slow—before he could deliver them, her phone pinged.

She instantly dropped her gaze from his and reached into her handbag. She retrieved her phone and looked at the screen. She gasped. She grinned. "Oh my God, it's that guy."

That guy. Should he know that guy? "What guy?" he asked, confused.

"The book guy!" She held up the phone, the screen illuminating the soft darkness around them. The book guy's face and profile were on her screen. "Should I respond? I shouldn't respond right away, should I? Like, maybe in the morning. If I respond now, it looks too eager, doesn't it? What do you think?"

What he thought was not something he could say aloud. What he thought was that he would like to kick the book guy's ass up one side of the street and down the other. He'd been so close to those words coming out, so close to *kissing* her. "You should respond," he said, and stepped back, down a step.

"You think?" She was looking at her phone.

He went down the last two steps to the ground. "But make it sound like you're doing him a favor when you do. Like you've got lots of other options. He'll want to win that imaginary contest."

"Really?" She sounded skeptical.

"Or don't. I'll leave you to decide. Have a good night, Charlotte." Nick turned about and started for his truck.

"Nick!"

He was a foolish man, because he turned back with some vague and desperate hope that she would put away her phone and invite him in. "Take your own advice. Don't come on too strong with Colton tomorrow. You don't want to chase him away." She laughed.

"You're hilarious, Charlotte," he deadpanned, and walked on to his truck.

He drove home in something of a fog, his thoughts warring in his head. Part of him was annoyed with himself. He'd come dangerously close to starting something with Charlotte. To saying things he ought never say, and maybe even ending the night with sex. Part of him was relieved—if he'd done that, it might have ended them forever. And he didn't want that, whatever it was between them.

Maybe he should send a thank-you to the book guy for saving his ass from making the same mistake he'd already made with her.

At his house, Nick was greeted by Pepper and Priscilla the pig. He fed those two, then filled Frank's bucket with feed. When he'd finished puttering around, he went into his kitchen and opened his laptop. He typed in the words *Herman Coben.* Google informed him it was including results for **_harlan_** coben, and then pulled up several references to the author.

Nick ordered the author's latest book. And then he went and started a bath. He made sure the water was scalding hot.

Chapter Ten

From: Nick nickprince@saddlebushco.com
To: Charlotte charlotte@saddlebushco.com
Subject: Need Password

I need the password to our contracts database.

From: Charlotte charlotte@saddlebushco.com
To: Nick nickprince@saddlebushco.com
Subject: Re: Need Password

You're not supposed to say things like "password" in an email because we could be hacked and that's like a big neon sign pointing to valuable information.

From: Nick nickprince@saddlebushco.com
To: Charlotte charlotte@saddlebushco.com
Subject: Re: Need Password

You're not supposed to say things like "password" in an email because we could be hacked and that's like a big neon sign pointing to valuable information.

That makes no sense. How am I supposed to ask for a password?

From: Charlotte charlotte@saddlebushco.com
To: Nick nickprince@saddlebushco.com
Subject: Re: Need Password

P a s s w o r d

From: Nick nickprince@saddlebushco.com
To: Charlotte charlotte@saddlebushco.com
Subject: Re: Need Password

I am going to pretend that I didn't just lose the last five minutes of my life. What is the damn password, please?

From: Charlotte charlotte@saddlebushco.com
To: Nick nickprince@saddlebushco.com
Subject: Re: Need Password

Adam418.

From: Nick nickprince@saddlebushco.com
To: Charlotte charlotte@saddlebushco.com
Subject: Re: Need Password

Adam? As in jilted boyfriend Adam from two years ago? How come when I used Pepper as a password, you said I was a technology Neanderthal, but when you make a password from the name of an old boyfriend, it's okay?

From: Charlotte charlotte@saddlebushco.com
To: Nick nickprince@saddlebushco.com
Subject: Re: Need Password

The answer to those questions is so far above your ability to understand that I can't even. Let's just agree that, generally speaking, when you do something, it's ignorant. When I do something, it's adorable. And FYI, I set that account up a long time ago. If I change it now, I'll never remember the new one. I'm going to the store to restock the break room fridge. Do you need anything?

From: Nick nickprince@saddlebushco.com
To: Charlotte charlotte@saddlebushco.com
Subject: Re: Need Password

The last time you went to the store to "restock the break room fridge" you came back with a new printer and a giant cake meant for ten people. So if you have the urge to pick up a jackfruit and a riding lawn mower, I'm asking you nicely to keep purchases to the break room. BTW, we're out of stamps. Get the smallest book they have. They're like 55 cents or something now. Outrageous.

From: Charlotte charlotte@saddlebushco.com
To: Nick nickprince@saddlebushco.com
Subject: Re: Need Password

Okay, Grandpa.

It was Thursday, and Thursday meant happy hour with the girls. Charlotte met up with Keesha and their mutual friend Mariah Frame. Mariah owned a dress boutique and hair salon on Main, and outside of Jo Carol of Jo's Java House, Mariah knew more than anyone else in town. She did not disappoint today—she had news that Jo Carol had exchanged fighting words with Molly Maguire for opening a new bakery just across the street. "Randy had to break them up before it came to blows," Mariah reported as she stirred her frozen margarita into the perfect slush consistency. Randy was her husband.

"That's crazy," Keesha said. "Cakes and donuts can coexist peacefully on the same street. Get it together, people!"

"Apparently, Jo Carol has been catering the Baptist Ladies Auxiliary monthly meeting for a while now, but this month, they ordered cake from Molly, and Jo Carol lost her mind."

"I heard about that cake," Charlotte said, pausing to lick the straw from her frozen margarita. She glanced around the crowded bar area of the Magnolia and then whispered, "I heard the cake was dry."

Mariah gasped. Keesha laughed. "Kidding," Charlotte said, and Mariah rolled her eyes.

"Okay, baby doll, enough about Jo Freaking Carol," Mariah said. "How's the dating going? Ella said you're really into the apps. That's what they call it now, you know. The apps," Mariah said.

"I didn't know that," Charlotte said.

"Cassie told me. She was in, too, and she said you were really picking some duds."

"I will have to thank my sister for making sure everyone knows my business," Charlotte said drily. "In my defense, they don't look like duds on 'the apps,' " she said, making air quotes around the term.

"What about Tanner Sutton?" Keesha asked.

"Tanner Sutton!" Mariah gasped. "Get out. *Really?*"

"I met him for coffee. I'm surprised Cassie didn't tell you that," Charlotte said. "It went great until he accused me of being in cahoots with Mrs. Prince."

"Wait, what?" Keesha asked.

Charlotte sipped from her margarita. "I got a little too nosy, so I guess it looked like I was asking questions for a friend."

Mariah and Keesha groaned at the same moment.

"I can't help it!" Charlotte insisted. "It's in my DNA. I have an insane need to be up in people's business."

"Charlotte, you have to up your game," Keesha said. "I'm living vicariously through you, you know. I've been married for so long it's hard to remember what actual butterflies feel like."

"Truth," Mariah said.

"I had another date last night that Cassie doesn't know about yet," Charlotte said coyly. Last night, she'd met Book Guy at the Twig bookstore in San Antonio. They'd talked online for a couple of days, and he seemed great. Charlotte was excited. And the date had started off well.

"Don't sit there!" Mariah said. "Give us details!"

"His name is Tracy, and in his profile, he said he was a booklover, and he'd just finished Harlan Coben's latest."

"Great book," Keesha said.

"I thought so, too," Charlotte said.

"Okay, so match made in heaven," Mariah added.

"On paper, yes. I can't believe I'm going to say this, but . . ."

Mariah and Keesha both leaned forward, as if they were afraid they would miss something terribly salacious.

Charlotte winced. "I think he reads too much."

Her friends stared at her, unblinking, waiting for her to explain herself.

"I know, right?" Charlotte said. "It makes absolutely no sense, because I *love* to read. So we met at the Twig—"

"Love that bookstore," Keesha said.

"Great choice, right? It was his idea. I thought he chose it because there are some great spots for a drink around the Twig, but when I got there, he said he thought we could sit there and read a little. I thought, yeah, okay, not exactly what I had in mind, but they close at six, and I guessed we'd probably get a drink then. So we sat. He had a book."

"Okay," Mariah said carefully.

"I hadn't brought anything to read, obviously, and I was looking for something, and I picked up the new Liane Moriarty book. And he took one look at it, and he said, 'There are some great books over here,' and pointed to the new release table that had new literary fiction. And I said, 'Oh, that's okay, I love Liane Moriarty.' " Charlotte paused to take a sip of her drink.

"And?" Keesha prodded her.

"Well, he kind of chuckled, and he said, 'That's chick lit.' And I said that all *lit* is chick lit because chicks read a lot, and widely, and he said, 'But I'm talking about serious literature.' "

Mariah and Keesha gasped in unison.

"So I pointed out that was a sexist thing to say, and that I liked books about relationships, and if they are funny books, even better.' "

"That's so true," Keesha agreed. "I love a good romantic comedy, you know?"

"Me, too!" Charlotte said.

"So what did the book guy say?" Mariah asked.

"Well, he gave me the old *Jane, you ignorant slut* look, and handed me a book with a gloomy cover about a dysfunctional family in New Orleans. And I think someone died."

"Jesus," Keesha said.

"He said it was a tour de force that addressed issues of race and class and made a person think. I said I preferred more upbeat fiction. And then he proceeded to explain to me that I like fiction that entertains, but the beauty of well-crafted fiction is in its art form, and that if I read only entertaining fiction, I am missing out, and I should really stretch my horizons."

"Yeah, okay, we're done with him," Keesha announced.

"*So* done with him. I told him I also liked my men to be entertaining, and maybe I had stretched my horizons too far on this date because it wasn't very fun. And I bought the Liane Moriarty book and left."

Mariah laughed.

"Why do men always have to be mansplaining everything?" Keesha asked. "I had this pro-fessor—"

"*Whoa,*" Mariah said suddenly. "Who owns *that* smoking-hot body?"

Charlotte turned to look. Interestingly, Nick and Colton Rivers had walked into the bar. It was so odd—Nick was not a bar guy. "That's Nick," Charlotte said. "You know Nick."

"Not *Nick,*" Mariah said. "The hot guy!"

Surely Charlotte didn't have to point out to Mariah that Nick was seriously hot. "You said *body,* and I thought—"

"That's Colton Rivers," Keesha said. "He's the new banker."

Mariah's mouth gaped. "Seriously? Wow. I think I need a new loan or something."

"Roll your tongue up, Mariah. You're married," Keesha reminded her.

"A girl can pretend. Is he married?"

"Single. Hasn't been in a serious relationship in a year." When Charlotte looked at her with surprise, Keesha said, "What? He came to see George one day and we had a chat."

"Why aren't you dating *him,* Lot?" Mariah demanded, playfully slapping Charlotte's arm. "Why are you wasting your time on Book Guy while that single man is walking around town?"

Charlotte turned her attention back to the two men . . . but her gaze kept sliding to Nick. He *was* smoking hot. She'd always thought so, still did, even when she wanted to kick him most days. He had what she would call rugged good looks. Like the kind of guy who could sweep you off your feet with one arm. The sort of guy who rode in from a hard day's work with the shadow of a beard and a little sweat on his shirt, and you wanted to jump his bones. The kind of guy who ended up on the cover of romance novels, could lift this building and toss it across the river if it meant saving the woman he loved.

Wait—had she really actually just thought that? She definitely needed to reel her imagination back in.

But damn it, it was hard to reel it in. She'd been thinking a lot about Nick the last few days, and not in the usual *I'm going to kill him* way. Now it was more of an ongoing internal debate as to whether he'd been about to kiss her on Sunday night. It had sure felt like it in the moment.

She'd been sort of shocked by the sensation and anticipation, by the way his eyes darkened while he looked at her. It had felt like he was only moments away from launching himself at her, and she stood there, not moving, because she had to see what he'd do. She couldn't believe that after their disastrous pseudo breakup after the Christmas party he would even *dream* of kissing her. And yet, the way he'd looked at her on her front porch was the very same way he'd looked at her the night he took her on a ride to the stars and back.

Honestly, she'd caught him looking at her like that before Sunday night.

It was an expression that was hard to describe, but it was indelibly seared into her brain. Like he missed her, even though she'd been right there all along. Like he longed for her, even though he generally kept her at arm's length. Like he was a little sad but dangerously hungry, and wanted to consume her. Just eat her up. It was a look that no other man had ever given her, and frankly, it was a bigger turn-on than any other she'd experienced. It sank deep into her core—because it was so raw and so unguarded that it felt quite intense and tended to set off all kinds of warning fires in her.

It was a very stark contrast to the usual brusque manner of the man who emailed her from twenty feet away.

And then there had been her ongoing internal debate as to whether she had *wanted* him to kiss her. Correction—she had *definitely* wanted him to kiss her when she was standing on her porch steps, because the moon was shining on them, and she was still experiencing the glow of good company and good food and maybe too much beer. She'd definitely wanted to feel his lips on hers again, the iron grip of his arms around her. She'd wanted to taste him, to touch her tongue to his, to feel the hardness of his body pressed to hers.

Lord. Charlotte squirmed in her seat. She really needed a boyfriend.

But when the sun came up Monday morning, Charlotte was glad Nick hadn't kissed her. She didn't want the inevitable aftermath of all the second-guessing she knew he would do. Jesus, she could hear it even now. *That shouldn't have happened. We can't go there. This isn't about you, it's about me.* Blah. Blah. Blah.

But that didn't keep her from thinking Nick Prince was about as hot and virile and attractive as a man could be.

Colton was a very handsome man, too. But in contrast to Nick, he seemed like the kind of guy who looked sexy while he fixed the glitch in your email. A very different kind of sexy.

"Go say hi," Mariah commanded Charlotte.

"I can't."

"Why not?"

"Nick wouldn't like it. That's his new best friend. They've been hanging out."

"Who cares if Nick likes it or not?" Keesha said. "Colton is a prime baby-making specimen, Charlotte, and you can't pass up the chance. Just say hi. Invite them over for a drink. Mariah and I will do the rest."

The sip Charlotte took went down wrong, and she sputtered. She could just imagine how Keesha and Mariah would "do the rest." "Thanks, but I think I can handle it."

Keesha seemed dubious. Mariah seemed like she was on the verge of drooling.

But Keesha had a point—Charlotte couldn't pass up what might possibly be her perfect match because of Nick. "Okay," she said. She slid out of the booth and smoothed her dress. It was the white one with the little bumblebees that Nick said made him feel anaphylactic just looking at them. "How do I look?"

"Fabulous," Mariah said. "Of course you do— that's a dress from my shop."

"My hair?"

"Wild and woolly, but there's nothing you can do about that today," Keesha said. She grinned. "You're as charming as always, Charlotte. *Go.*"

"Okay. Don't drink my cocktail while I'm gone."

"Would we do that?" Mariah asked, but she was already reaching for it.

Charlotte threaded her way through the crowded tables to the bar, self-consciously tucking ringlets behind one ear before they promptly fell forward again. Nick and Colton were standing at the bar. They were in the middle of a conversation, and Charlotte hesitated, not sure how to interrupt.

Colton turned his head slightly and saw her, and Charlotte was treated to a small thrill when his face lit up at the sight of her.

"Hey!" he said, turning from Nick. "Fancy meeting you here!"

Nick turned, too, and the look that came over his face sent a much stronger shot down her spine—it was the most curious mix of surprised delight and annoyance.

Charlotte smiled brightly at Colton as she walked up to the two men. "*Hey!* What are you two doing here?" She clapped Nick much harder on the shoulder than was necessary, but kept her gaze on Colton.

"Hello, Charlotte," Nick said.

"This is a lucky coincidence," Colton said. "We've been flying around the ranch and decided we'd worked up a thirst."

"Flying again?" Charlotte asked, and shot a look at Nick. Hadn't he been complaining just last week about how much it cost to put his plane in the air?

"Can I buy you a drink, Charlotte?" Colton asked. "I was just about to order."

"Oh, she's probably got one going already, knowing Charlotte," Nick said. He gently pulled her arm so that she had to drop her hand from his shoulder, and gave her elbow a squeeze. "She's a big fan of happy hour. Oh, I see Mariah and Keesha—tell them hello for us. But don't feel like you need to interrupt your happy hour."

"I don't feel that way at all, Nick!" Charlotte said with an overly enthusiastic bark of laughter. "And I'd *love* a drink, thank you! But let me get Mateo over here," she said, gesturing to the bartender. "I promised you I'd introduce you to some craft cocktails." She squeezed in between Colton and Nick, and leaned across the bar. "Hey, Mateo!"

Mateo lifted his chin in acknowledgment, and headed down the bar to them. "What's up, Lot?" he asked, then smiled at Nick. "Buenos días, Señor Nick."

"Hi, Mateo," Nick said.

"This is Colton Rivers," Charlotte said, and put her hand on Colton's arm. "He's new to town and I told him you would hook him up with some great craft cocktails. What have you got?"

"So glad you asked," Mateo said. "I've had some really good reviews on the Poisoned Prickly Pear. It's so good you won't know you're going down till you're gone."

"Yikes," Charlotte said. "That sounds deadly."

"Oh, it is," Mateo said proudly.

"Sold," Colton said. "Nick?"

"I've had Mateo's cocktails. I think I'll stick with beer, thanks."

"For you, madam, I have the Maybe Mañana," Mateo said. "Maybe you'll see tomorrow, maybe you won't." He laughed.

"Wow, okay, I'll give it a go. Shake 'em up, Mateo! And don't forget Grandpa's beer." She smiled at Nick.

He smiled, too, but it was one of those he gave her at the office when he wanted to strangle her.

Charlotte turned her back to him and faced Colton. "So what did you think of the ranch?"

"Awesome," he said. "I've heard of the big Texas ranches, but a man's imagination can't stretch that far—you have to see how big it is to believe it. This weekend we're going to go deep into the ranch and a do a little target shooting."

"Oh," Charlotte said. "So you're pulling out the big guns, huh?" She glanced at Nick.

"I think Mariah is trying to get your attention," Nick said.

Charlotte didn't bother to turn around and look. "Why don't you join us?" she asked Colton.

"Nah," Nick said. "You don't want us to bust up your girls' happy hour. We're not into shoes or Real Housewives."

Colton laughed. "Depends on the shoe."

204

"Hey, didn't you have a hot date with a book nerd?" Nick asked.

"Book *guy,* thank you, because breaking news, Nick, people who like books are cool and not nerds. Anyway, I already had it, thanks." She turned back to Colton. "Want to say hi to my friends?"

"I'd love to meet your friends," Colton said with enthusiasm as Mateo set the drinks in front of them. "I had an ex that was into shoes. I think I can hold my own."

Charlotte couldn't help it. She smiled triumphantly at Nick.

"I'll just grab these," Colton said. He looked at Mateo and said, "Thanks, buddy."

"Let me know what you think," Mateo said.

"The corner booth, right?" Colton asked.

"Right. Just head for the dark-haired white woman who is waving you down. I'm right behind you." But she wasn't right behind him. She shot a dark look at Nick. "What is your problem?"

"You," he said as he dug in his back pocket for his wallet. "You're one hundred percent my problem right now. You're going to dominate the conversation and I'm not through with him yet."

"No, I won't. Mariah will, hello—you know how she is. Anyway, what if I did? Are you afraid he'll like me better?"

"Yes!" he said, as if that were obvious. He

tossed some bills down on the bar, then put his hand to the small of her back to give her a nudge forward. "I like hanging out with him. If you date him, where does that leave me?"

"Well, I like him, too, Nick. So what are you going to do?"

"Fine," he said, and with the neck of his beer bottle he pointed at Colton, who had turned to see what kept them. "Game on, then."

She gaped at him. "Game *on*," she said, and started after Colton.

By the time Nick and Charlotte reached the table, Keesha had introduced Colton to Mariah, and predictably, Mariah was doing all the talking. Charlotte shot an *I told you so* look at Nick.

"Sit, sit," Mariah said eagerly, gesturing for Colton to slide in. Charlotte went next, but the booth was not really made for five people, especially when one of them was as big as Nick. Charlotte didn't want to sit in Colton's lap, so she kept a bit of space between them. But that didn't leave much room for Nick, and when he sat, he tried to shove her over, but she refused to budge. That left the two of them squished together. Nick had to stretch his arm across the back of the booth to keep from falling out of it.

Charlotte smiled at Colton, but she was painfully aware of the length of her leg pressed against Nick's hard, muscular leg. She was aware of the heat of his body against her bare arm and hip. She tried to shift about, but it was impossible, and she ended up pressed even more closely against him. The hot shiver of a memory flashed through her of another time she was pressed against him.

She tried to ignore Nick's very firm body by focusing on Colton, who was talking about meeting Lyle Timmons at Timmons Tire and Body Shop, who thought Colton needed a shotgun rack on his SUV. Charlotte was laughing too loudly, leaning forward too far. When Colton looked at her and smiled, clearly pleased with her laughing, Charlotte felt Nick tense beside her, and her laugh got louder.

She desperately needed to take it down a notch, especially when Mariah gave her a worried look across the table that suggested she thought Charlotte was having some sort of attack, but she couldn't. She didn't know if it was Colton's smile that had turned a little alarmed, or if it was the fact that she could feel Nick's vexation turning her skin hot.

Keesha stepped in to stop Charlotte from making a complete ass of herself by talking about some things around town Colton should check out. Naturally, Mariah felt like her boutique should be high on his list and launched into an unnecessarily lengthy explanation. Colton was polite enough to feign interest, but when Mariah began to go into the history of her shop, Keesha intervened again. "Hey," she said, when Mariah paused to take a breath, "I know how you can meet people in town."

"I'm all ears," Colton said.

"The city softball league. Most of the businesses field a team. You could put a bank team together and meet half the town."

"As it happens," Colton said, "the bank already has a team. I think our first game is scheduled against the Tool and Diehards."

"That's my team!" Keesha said with delight. "I mean my husband's team. He works at Prince Tool and Die."

"I don't think we have a team name yet. But I'm looking forward to it," Colton said.

"That's such a great idea!" Charlotte said enthusiastically. "I love softball."

"Saddlebush Land and Cattle should have a team," Mariah said with a snort. "A team of two."

"Wait a minute," Charlotte said, perking up. She'd never really thought of it before. "That's a great idea, Mariah!"

"Charlotte." Nick put his hand on her shoulder.

"No, wait, Nick," she said, anticipating his rejection of the idea. Nick was not a joiner. "This is *great*. We can get Rafe and Luca, and my brother Chase. He played baseball."

"Has to be coed," Keesha pointed out.

"No problem—I'll make Cassie play. And my friends. Like Mariah—"

"Nope, leave me out of it," Mariah said. "I am not a sporty person."

"I'm sure I can come up with some women—"

"Charlotte," Nick tried again.

"Don't be a stick-in-the-mud, Nick. We can call ourselves the Saddlebush Sweethearts!"

He blinked. *"No,"* he said emphatically.

"That sounds like powder puff," Keesha said. "You're clearly the Saddlebush Sluggers."

"Great name," Colton agreed.

"That's perfect!" Charlotte exclaimed. She was winding up to discuss uniforms, because before anyone could properly play a sport, they needed a proper uniform, and she twisted around to face Nick, which was nearly impossible because they were wedged together, but Nick burst her bubble before she could even *suggest* the blue and green combo by saying loudly, "I'm trying to tell you that I'm playing for the bank."

Charlotte gaped at him. "You're doing *what?*"

"Playing for the bank," he said, and nodded across the table at Colton. "With Colton."

"Sorry, Charlotte," Colton said cheerfully. "I got to him first."

"What the hell?" Charlotte said to Nick.

He looked only slightly chastised. "Third base," he said, and for the benefit of the group, he added, "I was a varsity player in high school."

"It's been a while since I played ball," Colton said as Charlotte stared at Nick in disbelief. Nick tried to avoid her gaze. "Nick, we ought to throw a ball around sometime," Colton added.

"Great idea," Nick said.

Mariah had some ideas for what Colton's team name should be, which they batted around. But while they did, Nick gave Charlotte a perplexed look. "What?

"I can't believe you are playing for the *bank*," she whispered loudly.

Nick arched a brow. "Did you honestly think the two of us could field a team? And since when were you so interested in softball anyway?"

"I would have been if you'd asked. You know I would have had a team together by the end of the day. You don't want to play with me."

He chuckled. "I am pretty sure that until today, you wouldn't have wanted to play softball with me even if I were the last guy on earth. Look, if you want to play softball, I'm sure we can find you a team."

"Okay," she said, smarting at the truth in his accusation. "I'll play for your team."

"Nope." He shook his head. "It's a business league." He leaned closer and whispered in her ear, "You can't just hook up with a bank team because you have the hots for the banker."

She whispered in his, "*You* are."

A slow smile appeared on Nick's face. He brushed one of her curls that had stuck to the stubble on his chin. "I warned you not to invite us to sit down," he muttered. "Now look how mad you are."

"Well, you should have kept your big fat softball at home," she whispered hotly. She had no idea what that actually meant.

He dipped his head to look her directly in the eye and said, "Don't be such a sore loser."

"Loser? Who said I've lost?"

His bit of a smirk said otherwise. "Where's the book guy, anyway? Do you really have time for softball with your race to find the perfect man?"

"He's somewhere reading highbrow fiction. And for your information, it's entirely possible to date and play softball at the same time."

"Maybe," Nick said with a shrug. "But you better ask Book Guy how he feels about soft-ball."

"I'm going to see how he feels about playing, and if there is anything he can bring to my team, because guess what, cowboy? I don't need you to start a team."

"Yeah, if you are going to form a Saddlebush team, I think you need me." He finished that with a small snort of indignation.

"I *don't* need you," she insisted. "You think I do, but I don't."

Nick's eyes narrowed. He looked like there was something he wanted to say. But he bit out a single, *"Fine."*

"Fine," she shot back.

"Geez, do you two need a room or something?" Mariah said.

Charlotte started—she hadn't realized everyone was listening to the two of them argue about an imaginary softball team that hadn't existed fifteen minutes ago. "Ugh, *Mariah,* don't make me vomit," she said dramatically.

"For God's sake, Mariah," Nick said with just as much disgust.

"Are you really going to form a team?" Mariah asked Charlotte.

"Ha!" Charlotte said defiantly at the exact same moment Nick said, "Ha!" with a tone of disbelief.

She glared at him. He smiled at her.

She was going to make a team all right, and they were going to beat the pants off Nick and his bankers.

And with that, she twisted around, making sure her back was to Nick, and smiled at Colton. "How about the Bank Batters?" she suggested cheerfully.

She completely ignored Nick's groan.

Chapter Eleven

Nick couldn't figure it out.

A few days after cocktails at the Magnolia, he was still trying to understand what the vibe was between him and Charlotte. He'd gotten the turbocharged part of it, loud and clear. But charged toward what? He had this strange feeling that she wanted to throw him down on the desk and take him and then hang him when she was done.

He'd been brooding about this seismic shift in their joint atmosphere. This morning, he and Rafe—and a vaquero, who was an excellent roper, borrowed from a neighboring ranch—had chased down a cow and her calf who had managed somehow to get themselves separated from the herd. The calf was easy, but the damn heifer was stubborn—it had taken all three of them to get her into a hauler, and then Nick had walked off without closing the tailgate.

"Nick!" Rafe had shouted. "Where's your head at, man?"

An excellent question—point to Rafe. Nick leapt back to close the tailgate before the heifer could decide she and her calf needed more alone time. He drove the two of them back to the rest of the herd to release them, his cheeks red with shame beneath the three-day growth of beard he had going on. He didn't make rookie mistakes like that. He was methodical and careful in what he did. But this thing between him and Charlotte felt like it was amping up, and it was messing with his brain, nudging in beside his growing desire to follow George's advice and fly.

He'd talked to Colton about what George had said when they'd gone target shooting. He'd explained his desire to fly commercial jets, to see the world. But that the ranch was holding him back.

"Really?" Colton had asked. "How?"

"Someone has to run it," Nick said.

Colton had considered that before taking aim and firing wildly off target. "The thing is, if you want it bad enough, you'll figure it out. From what you've said, Charlotte could probably run the office."

"She could and she does, practically speaking."

"So you'd be shorthanded around here, is that it?" Colton asked.

It was so much more than that. It was his mother, and the directions he wanted to take the ranch if he were to stay. Directions she didn't want to go. It was the need to sell some land that no one wanted to talk about. It was so much family history and feelings about his dad's death and his need to leave, to see the world, and this thing he felt for Charlotte. Good God, he was all over the place. But he said simply, "Yeah."

"Dude. That can be worked out," Colton said, and smiled confidently.

Nick was hot and hungry from chasing cows when he pulled into the lot of the Saddlebush Land and Cattle Company. The lot was empty, but Charlotte's blue bike was on the porch, tucked in behind the rocking chairs, as usual. He would never admit it to another living soul, and certainly not to her, but he always felt a little swell of happiness at the sight of her bike. Even if she pretended she couldn't tolerate him half the time. Maybe she couldn't. Nevertheless, every day, he looked forward to sharing an office with sassy Charlotte.

He let Pepper out of his truck and walked into the offices. Charlotte was tidying up the visitors' seating area, her colorful pillows returned to their places. He debated mentioning that it looked like someone's sunroom, but decided against it. She did seem awfully proud of that seating area.

Pepper was so excited to see Charlotte that she started turning in circles.

"Pepper!" Charlotte cried with delight. And then, "Well, hello, Nicholas Nickleby."

Before he could respond, there arose such a ruckus that for a moment he thought a pipe had

215

burst. The enormous half-moon reception desk actually moved before Rufus came trotting out from behind it to greet him and Pepper.

Nick looked at the big black dog with the slobbery grin. "Please tell me you didn't ride over here with him in your basket."

Charlotte laughed. "I couldn't fit him in that basket. He trotted alongside. Well, it was more of an easy amble, because he is a very lazy dog and determined to smell every rock and tree stump. I'm taking him home at lunch. You'll be here, right?"

He hadn't planned on it. He'd planned to stop by and then go and get something to eat. "Sure," he said, and started for his office. He could probably find something to graze on in the kitchen. Charlotte liked to have her snacks around. As he passed her desk, he noticed a yellow legal pad on top of it. He glanced down and noticed a list of names that made him halt. *Rafe, Luca, Ella.* "What's this?" he asked, pausing to look at the names of his family.

"That? That is a list of my team."

"Your what?"

"My softball team."

She walked across the room to stand beside him and study the list, too. "I have to register by Friday."

"A team?" he asked, still not quite following. "A Saddlebush team?"

She glanced up at him with her aquamarine eyes. "Yes, Nick, I am going to register a softball team for the Saddlebush Land and Cattle Company. Hey, can I donate some money from Saddlebush to sponsor the team's T-shirts?"

"What? No."

Charlotte turned so she was facing him. Her eyes were dancing now. "Okay. I'll get it somewhere. Because I'm the team captain. Which, for the record, is a way better position than third base."

His eyes narrowed. "Are you serious right now?"

Her eyes narrowed, too. "Deadly."

He looked again at the list. Rafe, Luca, and Ella. Big Barb the mail lady, who was one of the biggest gossips in town, and her husband, Ed. Charlotte's brother, Chase, who Nick remembered was a great ballplayer. "Who is Kyle?" he asked. "Who are Nora and Olivia?"

"Kyle Rudd is a friend of Chase's who, like you, played baseball in high school. So he must be *really* good, right?" She laughed.

Nick suddenly remembered Kyle Rudd. If Nick wasn't mistaken, Kyle had gone on to play college ball.

"Nora and Olivia are my cousins. And don't forget Jo Carol's son, Benny," she said, pointing at the pad of paper.

"Benny?" Nick said with disbelief. Benny was

several inches over six feet and just as broad. "He's a mountain. He can't run bases."

"Maybe not. But I bet he can hit that softball into kingdom come while the rest of us run the bases."

Nick's hands found his waist. "So you're really going to field a team called the Saddlebush Land and—"

"The Saddlebush Sluggers," she said, nodding along as he spoke, as if she knew what he was going to say before he said it.

"While I, the proprietor of this business, will be playing on another team?"

"Looks like," she said cheerily. "But let us not forget that it was your choice to play with your new BFF instead of the company team. You know what? I can't *wait* to meet you on the softball field."

He tried to be annoyed, but it was impossible to look at her pretty face and stay annoyed. That light in her smile of triumph wouldn't allow it. "The feeling is entirely mutual," he said. "Just so I know the landscape here—are you doing this because you are jealous of my friendship with Colton? Or to torment me?"

"Torment!" She laughed gaily. "That's just a happy side effect, Nick! I'm doing it because, like I said, I *love* softball." Her smile faded a little, and she tilted her chin up, her gaze locked on his. "And just so we're clear, if I ever

218

set out to torment you, you're going to know it."

Little fires flared in Nick. "Is that right?" he asked her mouth.

"It's so right, you should think of surrendering now."

He could feel the little fires stirring in him and sparking dangerous thoughts. This was a perfect example of his confusion. His body believed her torment would be pleasurable. But his mind wasn't so sure. His mind told him to step away. Run, even. But his body shifted closer.

"Is everything a contest with you?" he asked the purse of her lips.

"Pretty much," she said, and the purse turned into a smile that ended with the dimple he wanted to touch.

For the thousandth time, Nick thought about kissing her. How easy it would be to slip his arm around her waist and pull her into his embrace. How good it would feel to sink his fingers into those springy blond curls and kiss her.

He wasn't going to kiss her. But he did something probably just as wrong—he lifted his hand and placed his palm against her neck, sliding in under all those curls. Her skin was warm and downy soft. The fires were flaring. "Okay, slugger," he said, and stroked his thumb along the base of her jaw. "I guess I'll see you on the field, then." He reluctantly stepped back, dropped his hand, and stepped around her as he started toward the office.

He'd only made it a few steps when she said, "What is the name of your team?"

He glanced back over his shoulder. Charlotte was still facing the windows, her back to him, leaning up against the desk. Like she was frozen there.

"Frontier Bank. Why?"

"That's it? That's the name of your team?"

"That's the name."

"Lame!" She turned around, her back to the desk, one leg crossed over the other. Her eyes were dark now, and the glisten in them was something other than laughter. She reminded him of a cat who was about to pounce on its prey. She took him in, head to toe, mapping him. "*So* lame," she said again, her voice much deeper, and Nick didn't know if she meant the team name, or the fact that he hadn't kissed her. He couldn't disagree on either count.

So he smiled—probably lamely—and went into his office, the dogs on his heels. He sat at his desk, where Rufus joined him, his tail sweeping a copy of the *Cattleman* magazine off the low end table before he crammed himself under the desk to lie on Nick's boots.

Pepper wisely chose the better option of the two humans and trotted out of his office to be with Charlotte.

"My foot is already going numb," Nick informed Rufus, but the dog was not inclined to move his giant body.

Nick was halfway through his email when he heard the office doors open and someone come in. Rufus didn't stir.

"Oh. Hi, Mr. Mitchell," he heard Charlotte say. "Did you have any luck finding the invoice?"

Nick wondered idly who Mr. Mitchell was and what invoice. He hoped it wasn't a big one. He felt like they were running on fumes as it was.

"Nope. That's because I sent it to you. *You* should have it."

"Right," Charlotte said, and Nick heard the subtle change in her voice. "I left you a message—"

"Yeah, I got your bullshit message."

Nick's head came up.

"I'm sorry you feel that way. But I've really looked everywhere, and I haven't been able to find—"

"Now look here, woman," the man said, "I don't know what kind of game you're playing, but I want my money."

Nick's heart leapt with fury. He didn't know who this man was, but he had no right to speak to Charlotte like that. He shoved out of his chair and strode across his office.

"I understand you're frustrated, but I don't have any record or knowledge of the work. I have to have *something* in order to see that you're paid."

The man must have brought his hand down on the reception desk, because Nick heard a thud and the clink of glass, and a yelp from either Charlotte or Pepper just as he strode through the door. "What the hell is going on here?"

Charlotte whirled around toward him. She looked terrified.

Nick walked around to the front of the desk, putting himself between Charlotte and a man he'd never seen before.

"Who are you?" the man snapped.

"I'm Nick Prince. Who the hell are *you?*"

"Tim Mitchell, and this place owes me some goddamn money."

"For what?"

"Serviced one of your oil wells, that's what."

That made no sense. Their oil wells had been capped several years ago. "They're dormant."

"Not Karankawa," the man said, referring to one of the wells. "Charlie Prince hired me to get that one ready to pump again. That's sixteen thousand dollars he owes me."

His father had asked this man to ready a capped well? Nick didn't believe it—it was ridiculous. Opening up a capped well was a massive under-taking, and in this case, there was no point. Those wells had been capped because there wasn't enough oil to make it worth the cost of operating.

"Charlie Prince was my dad. And he's been dead over a year."

The man's eyes narrowed. "I didn't know that until recently. I work out of Corpus. But that don't change a damn thing. He hired me, and I told him I'd get to it when I could. I got to it about eight months ago and I sent that invoice, but this *woman*," he said, gesturing angrily at Charlotte, "is trying to rip me off—"

Nick stepped closer. "You better think twice about speaking against Miss Bailey. If she says she doesn't have it, *she doesn't have it*. If you did the work and you invoiced us, you ought to have a record of it. So if you don't mind, I'll drive out to Karankawa and have a look at the well and see what was done."

Tim Mitchell's face mottled. His lip curled into a sneer. "Let me tell you something, big shot," he said, and poked Nick hard in the chest. "If I don't get my money, I'll sue."

Nick laughed low. "If you don't have a record of your work, we can't help you. And neither will a lawyer. But you go ahead and do what you think you need to do."

The man pressed his lips together and glared at Nick. For a moment, Nick thought he might have to fight him. "Fucking cheat," the man snapped. "You'll hear from my lawyer." He pivoted on his heel and strode out.

Nick and Pepper followed him to the door and

watched him stride across the lot to his truck, cursing the whole way. He got in, slammed the door shut, and peeled out of the lot.

Nick turned around and looked at a wide-eyed Charlotte. "Are you all right?"

"Yes. But . . . not really." She dragged her fingers through her curls. "I mean, *yes,* I'm fine, but . . . but what if he comes back?"

Nick knew what she meant—she was often alone in the office. Moreover, there wasn't much that rattled Charlotte, but she was definitely rattled. He started back to the reception desk.

"I mean, if he does, I'll just lock the door, right? But I don't have a gun, Nick. I don't *want* a gun—"

"We're not talking guns," he assured her. He knew her distaste for them, even the sort they needed around the ranch. He knew, because they had been in the same school the year Bill Bromley found his dad's gun and accidentally shot himself. Charlotte still talked about it years later.

"But the thing is, he might come back even madder, and Rufus is a great companion, but he's a horrible protector. I mean, look, he hasn't even come out of your office. It could have been *bad,* Nick. It could have been so bad—"

Nick reached for her elbow and pulled her forward before she spun off into a full panic.

"Take a breath," he advised. "He's not coming back."

"I'm not freaking out, I'm just thinking. You know what? Now is a good time to mention a few things I've been thinking about."

"Do you want to sit down?"

"You should sell this office, Nick," she said, and seemed not to notice that he was pulling her into his body, his arm around her back. "It's ridiculous that this huge office only holds the two of us, isn't it?"

"It's pretty ridiculous," he agreed, and hugged her.

Charlotte gripped his arms. "You should *sell* it," she said again.

Her eyes were wide and unblinking, and Nick wrapped his other arm around her and held her tight. She kept talking, her voice muffled against his shoulder. "Charlie used to work out at the ranch, remember? You could go there to work. Me, too! It would save you some money and then the office would be behind a gate."

"Charlotte? I won't let anything happen to you. Do you understand what I'm saying? That guy is not going to bother you again. He won't be back."

She lifted her head and looked up at him. "Are you sure, Nick? Because you're not here a lot and he was *scary.*"

"I'm sure," he said. He didn't think the man

would be back, but he'd do something to make her feel safer. Install a lock on the door that she could activate from her desk, maybe. An extra expense he didn't need, but he wouldn't have Charlotte afraid to come to work.

She was staring at him. He couldn't read her expression. Her grip on his arms had relaxed, and he couldn't decide if she was looking at him like that because she didn't believe him, or if it was something else. All he knew was that they were staring into each other's eyes, and the air seemed to have left the room, and there was nothing but electricity crackling around them.

Nick's gaze drifted to her full pale pink lips. Her chin tilted up. Those lips were so close to his.

It was funny how things happened, how a man could think he was in full control, that he knew what he was doing, and in the very next breath, find himself kissing a woman without knowing exactly how he'd gotten there. But he was kissing her all right, and it was slow and careful and so deliberate that he was one giant erection of want. She felt so good in his arms, just like he remembered. So perfect, so soft, all curves and mounds and pliable flesh.

She slid her hands up his chest, around his neck. She pressed into him, like this was what she'd had in mind all along. She kissed him with her butter-soft lips and sent tiny shivers waving through him as her fingers grazed lightly over the stubble on his face. Nick was suddenly tumbling hard and fast down a chute into desire that had simmered and boiled for too long, and alarmed by it, he lifted his head and locked eyes with Charlotte.

She was so unbelievably alluring to him. He felt like he was floating in a waking dream, somewhere between reality and fantasy. "That . . . that was not what I intended," he heard himself say.

"I *knew* it," she said in a breathless whisper. "I *knew* you wanted to kiss me." She grabbed his head and bent it down and kissed him again. She kissed him so hard that he lost his balance and they knocked into the reception desk. Nick caught her by the waist and twisted her around when Pepper and Rufus came to investigate. He anchored himself to her, feeling every inch of her against him, and though he knew he had to stop this, and stop it now, he couldn't make himself give up on this kiss.

Because Charlotte damn well knew how to *kiss*.

But Nick was raging with arousal, and the sexual beast in him, hammered into hibernation over the last year, was up and moving around. *What the hell am I doing?* He'd done this before and he hadn't stopped, and it had caused a rift between them that he didn't want to repeat. Not to mention they were standing in the middle of the Saddlebush offices where God and everyone could see them, and there had to be one million reasons why this was all wrong, a horrible, terrible idea.

Nick suddenly shifted back from her. "Charlotte, I . . ." He what? He regretted it? Not the kiss. But he regretted . . . he regretted . . .

He didn't know what he regretted. He dragged his fingers over his crown and noticed that Charlotte was staring at him wide-eyed.

A smile slowly appeared on her face. "I was *right,*" she said. She grabbed onto the desk and bent backward as if she were exhilarated. "I was right! I am *right* all the time, have you ever noticed that? It's like, how can one person be so right all the time? But I knew you wanted to kiss me earlier, and then you did! This is crazy! I know you so *well,* Nick. Ha!" she said, and slapped her hand on the desk before walking away from him and turning a very tight little circle in the middle of the room.

Nick sighed. "Did you pretend to be scared so I'd—?"

"No! That guy scared the living daylights out of me! But then you were standing next to me, and I thought, he really wants to kiss me—"

"I should apologize—"

"Don't you dare!" she exclaimed, and smiled brightly. "Do *not* make this weird, Nick. I hate when you make things weird."

Her mouth, plump and moist, was still enticing

him. "I make things weird?" he asked, but immediately shook his head. "Never mind. I have to apologize—that was way out of line. If we had an HR department, I'd report me."

"We do have HR and it's me and I already reported you." Her smile broadened. "Don't look so worried!"

"I'm not *worried*—"

"I'm not going to ask you to marry me or anything."

"What? God, Charlotte, I didn't—I'm not thinking *that*."

"Well, you don't have to look so relieved."

"I'm not!" Nick suppressed a groan. He didn't know what he was doing. She was toying with him, making him suffer for that kiss. "I'm . . . I'm mad at myself."

Her smile started to fade. "*Mad?* Oh, geez. Well, *you* wanted to kiss me and I just helped you like I always help you. You don't have to act like it's the end of the world as you know it, because it's not. See? You're already making it weird."

Wasn't she the one who was making this entire episode weird? "No, I'm—you're misunderstanding me. It's inappropriate."

"Oh, that," she said with a dismissive flick of her wrist. "We're still coworkers. Everything is the same. You're still incapable of following a simple color-coded filing scheme, and I'm still running things while you're out roping cows or whatever. The only difference is that today, you kissed me, and yes, I kissed you back because it was fantastic, because we both know we've got the chemistry thing down," she said, gesturing between the two of them. "Oh! I almost forgot that on top of that, some guy came in who looked like he might blow the place up, which everyone knows pushes people together, but other than that? It's just another day in paradise."

She was moving too fast, glossing over that burning kiss. He tried to get his head back in the game. He didn't believe she thought it was nothing, no big deal, business as usual. Because that had been a kiss that lingered. It was still sizzling in him, and he wanted more, but he didn't know how to have more without making a big mess of both their lives. So he mentally shook it off. He turned so he wasn't looking at her. "Can we just get back to work and the business of oil?"

"Of course," she said curtly.

"Do you know anything about Tim Mitchell?"

"Not a thing. The first time he came in, he told me about it and I said I'd look for an invoice. I went through everything and couldn't find any record of this. Charlie never told me he was having those wells looked at. I called Raymond, too," she said, referring to their former accountant. "And he'd never heard of Tim Mitchell. So I left him a message and told him that I couldn't find any record, and could he please send a copy of the original invoice."

"Did you ask George about it?"

Charlotte shook her head.

"We'll start there." Nick rubbed his forehead. He suddenly had a very bad headache. His body was desperately wanting something it wasn't going to get.

"Nick." She spoke softly, and Nick looked up expectantly. "Don't sweat it, okay?"

"I'm not," he insisted. "That's not—"

"You are. I know how you are. You're a by-the-book guy, and that was not in the book."

He wanted to argue, but Charlotte did know him pretty well. And when she smiled with empathy and patted his cheek, he wanted to grab her up and bury his face in her curls.

"We're not the first coworkers to have insane sexual tension and just keep going. It's sort of like that show. You know, the one with the two detectives, and they are totally into each other, and they kiss once or twice but then duty calls and they go back to work and pretend it never happened?"

"What?" he asked, confused.

"Don't you have a TV?"

"I don't watch it."

"Are you kidding?" she asked. "I seriously do not get people who don't watch TV. Okay, it's like . . ." She paused, thinking. "It's like a bull

231

and a heifer. They're going to mate, but once they have, they go back to eating grass and doing whatever it is cows do. They don't make a thing out of it."

This woman was amazing. "I don't think you can compare cows to this."

"Fair enough," she said, and folded her arms. "But until you can tell me what *this* is, I am going to pretend it's nothing more than a detective show. Are you going to be around today?"

He nodded.

"Great. I'm going to take Rufus home, then swing by Mariah's and see if she has a Xanax I can have. Would you like me to see if I can get you about ten of them?" She giggled.

Nick was grateful that she was making light of it, but confused by it, too. What had just happened here? "Take all the time you need."

"Thanks!" She stepped away from him, walked back to her desk, and began to gather her things before she called Rufus.

Nick and Pepper stood at the door and watched Charlotte ride off on her bike, Rufus trotting alongside her. Pepper melted onto the concrete floor like a mop, her legs splayed, her head between her paws. Like she was as bummed as Nick was to see them go.

Charlotte thought she knew everything, but what had just happened between them was not like two cows or some detective show. Nick didn't know how to tell her the million things on his mind. He didn't know how to say that he had talked to Colton and George about flight school. He didn't know how to tell her that the plan to sell this office building was already in the works. He didn't know how to explain that if it weren't for this burning need to be out of here, to fly, he would be all in on her. One hundred percent in, no need for dates or playing kissing games or anything else.

But he wasn't going to be around because he had to be true to himself. And he wasn't going to provide her with babies, and it wasn't fair to take her off the market, given what she wanted from life.

None of it was fair, but life seldom was. So he had to stop acting like a schoolboy. And yet, he couldn't stop thinking about her.

Chapter Twelve

What Charlotte really wanted was to ride away from that office like death was chasing her. Not because of Tim Mitchell, although he had given her the creeps in a major way. But because of Nick's knee-melting kiss.

Unfortunately, she ended up walking her bike because Rufus was such a slowpoke. Nevertheless, her body was still thrumming by the time she and Rufus reached her porch. She parked her bike, took Rufus inside, and waited until he'd had his fill of water and slung it everywhere and collapsed on the threshold between the living room and the hall, apparently exhausted by the day's events.

She, too, was exhausted by the day's events, and felt like she needed a nap. Or a good, stiff drink. She sat on her couch. And then she slid off, lying on her back on the floor beneath the ceiling fan and the silk panels that fell gently from the blades. She needed to take those down. She needed to clean up her house. And she definitely needed to stop goading Nick into doing things, like kissing her.

Yessir, that kiss had been all her doing, whether

he knew it or not. She'd *made* him kiss her. She should have kept her distance, but she could see by the way he looked at her, like there was fire coming out of his eyes, that he'd wanted to kiss her but wouldn't, because he was a gentleman and a freak. So she'd made it happen. Everything had felt so crazy after Tim Mitchell had pounded the desk and threatened to sue them, and Nick was holding her, and she'd felt this urge to bury herself in his chest.

If there was one thing that hadn't changed in the last two or three years, it was the attraction between them. If anything, it had intensified.

Why did it have to be so hot and tense between them when he was the one guy who would never be the man she wanted? Why had she made him kiss her? What sort of perversion *was* that? Did she do it to prove that she could? Did she do it to prove to herself that he still wanted her, no matter what he said? Did she do it to show him she still wanted *him?* Did she do it because she'd been scared and wanted to climb him like a tree?

What really shamed her was that she was not a game player. She was the straightest shooter she knew, a what-you-see-is-what-you-get person. She liked to know where everyone stood on every subject, and to make it known where she stood. So why was she doing this with Nick? Why was she teasing him and standing too close and ratcheting up the tension between them at the most inappropriate moments?

Hell, she knew why. Because the night of that Christmas party, Nick had looked at her with such adoration that she'd been moved by it, and she'd been seeking that look on the face of any other man since.

That kiss, that night, had happened the Christmas before Charlie died, and if there was one thing Charlie Prince knew how to do, it was throw a party. The booze had flowed, the lights had twinkled, and by midnight, everyone was drunk.

Charlotte didn't usually drink to excess, but she'd had quite a nice little buzz that night, and she ran into Nick in the kitchen, standing to one side by himself, nursing a beer. He'd smiled at her. She'd smiled back. Up until that point, every time Nick had come into the office, Charlotte would try to engage him. She would talk about things, chatting away, and he would just look at her, smiling or nodding, occasionally saying yes or no or a few words here and there. Every once in a while, she'd hit on something that would make him talk. Like his rescue cows. She'd said she knew he'd saved the cows that had escaped the slaughterhouse. She would never forget the way he'd looked at her. Suspicious at first, then relieved. Then grateful, she suspected, because she admired him for it and didn't make fun of a cattle rancher rescuing cows from slaughter.

In spite of his general lack of communication, there was always something there—a spark or a current that seemed to flow between them.

But on the night of the party, they'd really talked. She'd wondered why he was by himself in the kitchen. He said Veronica Littman, a real estate agent, was getting too handsy. Charlotte had said she was surprised by that, because Veronica generally liked them a little younger than Nick. He'd laughed. But it was true.

Charlotte couldn't remember now what all they'd talked about. She recalled telling him she'd seen him flying around Three Rivers in his smaller plane. He'd said he liked the bird's-eye view, and that once, he'd seen her in her back-yard with her dog. At least he thought it was her. He had conceded it could have been any one of the Baileys, and they'd laughed about how many of them there were in town.

She'd said he was lucky she wasn't sunbathing in the nude. He'd said he might have crashed the plane. And somewhere in there, he'd shifted closer. She'd said she'd never heard him say as much as he had that night, and he'd surprised her and said he was often a little tongue-tied around her in the office. She hadn't asked him what he meant. She hadn't had to—his expression had said it all. His gaze had moved languidly down her body, and his breathing had deepened. When someone ran into the kitchen with mistletoe, that had been that. He'd kissed her. "In the spirit of Christmas," he had said, and then . . . well, then, at some point, they'd found their way here, to her house.

She would never in her life forget the way the rain had pattered against her windows as he'd moved in her with such deliberation, so in tune to every one of her sighs and moans. His hands, callused by his work around the ranch, had felt strangely tender on her skin as he caressed her. He had filled her up, emotionally and physically, and her climax had been a great thunderclap of pleasure and awakening and hope.

Nick Prince was the best lover she'd ever had. He knew what he was doing. He moved over her body like they'd been sharing a bed for years instead of one night.

What had been the difference between them that night? Was it the Mistletoe Margaritas? Was it the heat that swirled around them every day? What had brought the walls down between them?

Whatever it was, Charlotte had believed that a night like that could only be the start of something really spectacular. The next morning, she'd gotten up to make breakfast. She had been puttering around her kitchen in a T-shirt, feeling so gloriously sore and alive and happy that she had been convinced she had to be super adorable. And then he'd come in like someone had died.

She had known just by looking at him what he was going to say. It wasn't the start of anything but a long period of regrets. "Last night was amazing," he said. He'd kept talking while she just stared at him, shocked that he was suddenly able to speak. *Sorry I got carried away. Should never have happened. Of course we have to put this behind us . . .* And on and on.

That morning, he had not once asked her what she thought. So Charlotte had spent the last couple of years making sure he knew what she thought. She'd cut him a little slack after Charlie died and he'd had to take over the business. But he was so grumpy and so afraid of her, like he feared she was going to jump his bones in the office. So she'd begun to push back in ways big and small, subtle and not so subtle. But even so, that thing between them had not gone away. If anything, it had been amplified.

But today? She closed her eyes. She really had to grow up. She had to get over Nick and the disappointment he'd caused her and move on. Which, truthfully, she thought she had. She was only needling him half the time. But then today . . . what was that? What was it about that grumpy, generally unhappy man that kept her clinging to the idea of him?

Charlotte couldn't figure out her feelings. She was a mess of internal conflict. She really did want kids and a family. She really did want to settle down. Nick was not settling down. He'd made it clear he didn't want to be bound by family or tradition or legacy. So why did she keep toying with a man who was only going to disappoint her in the end? It made no sense.

She heard something outside and her heart leapt—her first thought was Tim Mitchell. She rolled onto her hands and knees, and crawled forward to look out the window. When she saw who was on her porch, she sighed, stood up, and opened the door. "Mom, what are you doing here?"

Her mother shrieked. "Charlotte! You scared the dickens out of me! What are *you* doing here? Shouldn't you be at work? I was leaving you some tomatoes—it's the end of the season and Dad wanted you to have the last ones."

Charlotte looked down at the paper bag her mother had placed near her door. "They definitely look like the last ones. They look like they were forgotten. And something has been eating them."

Her mother looked down into the bag, too. "Just trim that part off," she said with a flick of her hand. "What are you doing home in the middle of the day?"

"I brought Rufus back from the office."

She must have sighed, because her mother looked at her closely. "Are you all right, Lottie?"

"I'm fine."

"You look a little pale." She put her hand on Charlotte's forehead like she was a little girl.

"What are you doing?" Charlotte asked, batting away her mother's hand.

"You don't look good. You look like you've lost your best friend."

She probably had, in a manner of speaking. "My best friend is Cassie and she's definitely not going anywhere."

Her mother smiled sympathetically. "Is it the dating thing?"

"The dating thing?"

"Cassie can move through men like they're candy bars, but not you, Lottie."

"*No,* Mom," Charlotte said, and opened the screen door so that her mother could come in. Rufus managed to get to his feet to come over for a pat, then moved to the kitchen to lie on the cool tiles.

"Then how is the dating going?" her mother asked as she plopped herself down on the couch.

"Well, you're right. I'm not Cassie and it hasn't been great. I have to force myself to do it, and I'm always excited by the profile, but then disappointed with the reality, and then I find myself wondering if I am just pushing myself down a path that my life isn't going to go, you know?"

Her mother tilted her head to one side. "You mean having a family?"

Wasn't that what she always meant? "I really do want one."

"Oh, Charlotte, honey. There is plenty of time for you to have a family. You're only thirty-two! I think you're overly anxious about it."

"I may be only thirty-two but I've got nothing on the horizon. No prospects, Mom. Caitlin had her first kid by the age of thirty-two. And I haven't had a serious boyfriend since Adam."

"You're not Cassie, and you're not Caitlin. Even if you don't meet someone in the immediate future, or next year, or the year after that, and your timeline gets pushed back, there is a lot of fertility science that can help you if you need it."

Charlotte knew all about that. But she didn't want to leave it to science if she could avoid it. She really wanted to go about this the natural way. "It's just that sometimes I wonder if I should accept that my life is going to be different than the one I always thought I would have. Maybe I need to accept that I'm trying to fit a life into mine that isn't really possible for me. What do you do when life doesn't turn out the way you planned?"

"You make a new plan," her mother said.

"See?"

"But I don't think you've reached critical mass yet. I think you are unnecessarily giving yourself anxiety about it."

Charlotte couldn't disagree. "I don't know why I want kids so bad, but I always have. Caitlin and Chase's kids drive me nuts half the time. But it's this thing in me, this pressing need."

"Some women are bent that way," her mother said.

"Were you?"

She shrugged. "Not particularly. Not until I had Caitlin. And then I wondered what I had been doing before her, why I'd wasted so much time getting to her." She smiled. She stood up and leaned over to kiss the top of Charlotte's head. "Stop worrying about things you don't need to worry about just yet. Enjoy your life, Lottie. Date the boys and pet the dogs and let life come to you."

Yeah, tell that to her womb.

"I have to run to the store. Avocados are on sale this week. Want me to pick some up for you?"

"No thanks." She saw her mother out and took the tomatoes into the kitchen. All of them had been nibbled on by insects. Charlotte tossed them in the trash and looked out her kitchen window.

She had kissed Nick on principle, really, because she knew he still had a thing for her. And she still had a thing for him. But why was that so important for her to prove? All it did was make her want the one guy who was the worst choice for her future.

"Okay, enough," she said aloud, and Rufus

thumped his tail on the floor. She had to go back to work, she had to face him, to pretend none of this had ever happened.

Just like the last time.

But in order to do that, Charlotte was going to need some help. She was going to need something to think about other than Nick. So she went into her living room, found her phone, and clicked on the dating app. She swiped right on the dog guy.

Chapter Thirteen

From: Nick nickprince@saddlebushco.com
To: Charlotte charlotte@saddlebushco.com
Subject: Karankawa well

Have you had any luck tracking down any information about the well?

From: Charlotte charlotte@saddlebushco.com
To: Nick nickprince@saddlebushco.com
Subject: Re: Karankawa well

Nope. Spoke to Keesha and she said George had no recollection of it. Have you looked at the ranch?

From: Nick nickprince@saddlebushco.com
To: Charlotte charlotte@saddlebushco.com
Subject: Re: Karankawa well

Not yet. I'll get out there tomorrow or the day after. The lock guy will be here at three today to install the buzz-in lock on our front door. BTW,

Colton and I had lunch. He said you came by the bank a few days ago.

From: Charlotte charlotte@saddlebushco.com
To: Nick nickprince@saddlebushco.com
Subject: Re: Karankawa well

That is correct. I needed to make a deposit and that is where you do it. At the bank. Is there a reason he is reporting my appearance to you?

From: Nick nickprince@saddlebushco.com
To: Charlotte charlotte@saddlebushco.com
Subject: Re: Karankawa well

No reason. He just thought it was interesting that you volunteered to take his softball registration paperwork to the city.

From: Charlotte charlotte@saddlebushco.com
To: Nick nickprince@saddlebushco.com
Subject: Re: Karankawa well

I was going there myself and thought I'd save him a trip. I'm very helpful that way. I would hate for him to leave the bank and someone come in and he not know it and then fail to report it to whoever.

From: Nick nickprince@saddlebushco.com
To: Charlotte charlotte@saddlebushco.com
Subject: Re: Karankawa well

We were just wondering if it was you who registered our team as the Fred Savages. Or perhaps that was a gross clerical error on the part of the city?

From: Charlotte charlotte@saddlebushco.com
To: Nick nickprince@saddlebushco.com
Subject: Re: Karankawa well

Nope, that was all me. You're welcome.

From: Nick nickprince@saddlebushco.com
To: Charlotte charlotte@saddlebushco.com
Subject: Re: Karankawa well

Charlotte. Why did you do that? The city says we can't change it, they've printed up the schedules.

From: Charlotte charlotte@saddlebushco.com
To: Nick nickprince@saddlebushco.com
Subject: Re: Karankawa well

Why did I do it? Because A, It is hilarious, and everyone laughs when they hear it, and B, *Frontier Bank Softball Team* is so lame that I can't even.

From: Nick nickprince@saddlebushco.com
To: Charlotte charlotte@saddlebushco.com
Subject: Re: Karankawa well

It wasn't even your team to name. That was really uncalled for. You owe Colton an apology. You owe everyone on our team an apology. Actually, you owe us at least a round of beers. There are acceptable forms of pranking in a softball league, but changing a team name is not one of them.

From: Charlotte charlotte@saddlebushco.com
To: Nick nickprince@saddlebushco.com
Subject: Re: Karankawa well

You're right. I feel so bad about what I did. I will bring beer to the first practice.

From: Nick nickprince@saddlebushco.com
To: Charlotte charlotte@saddlebushco.com
Subject: Re: Karankawa well

Thank you.

From: Charlotte charlotte@saddlebushco.com
To: Nick nickprince@saddlebushco.com
Subject: Re: Karankawa well

You're welcome.

Wow, did you see that thing shoot past the window? LOLOL—for a minute there, I thought it was you! I thought you'd leapt on your high horse and galloped away!

PS Practice fields open Saturday afternoon. See you and the Freds there.

Nick closed the email tab on his computer. He should have been annoyed, but when Colton had told him what she'd done, he had had to work hard not to laugh outright.

He and Charlotte had gone back to pretending that nothing had happened between them. That the spark wasn't glowing red hot between them. They were very good at pretending. Maybe because they'd been doing it for a long time now.

This time, it was Charlotte who had turned the tide for them. She'd come back to the office the day it happened, humming cheerfully, and with a bag of cookies from Molly Maguire's cake shop and a story about how Jo Carol and Molly had argued in the middle of the street and Randy Frame had had to break them up. She'd been very entertaining in her telling of it, because Charlotte knew how to spin a good tale.

They'd pretended every day after that.

It felt to Nick like he had to work a little harder than Charlotte to pretend there wasn't a palpable tension between them. He'd spent the next few days going home from work, feeding his animals, and reading his new Harlan Coben book to take his mind off of her.

Saturday morning, it rained. He wandered around his house in pajama bottoms, carrying a pink coffee mug that read *Born to be a girl boss*. Of course Charlotte had given it to him on Boss's Day last year. He sat on the covered porch for a while and watched Priscilla roll around in the mud pit she'd created. He finished the Harlan Coben book. It was good. He was looking forward to the next family gathering when he could report that he, too, had read it.

When he finished his coffee and the book, he and Pepper went back inside, and he sat at the kitchen bar with his laptop and opened it up to a saved tab.

Flight school.

There were still slots available in the fall. Nick was dithering about it, wondering if he ought to risk making the initial payment. He'd done that once before, had paid the not-insignificant fee. But then a couple of months later, his dad had died, and Nick canceled. If he got in this fall, he calculated how long it would take him to achieve his goals. A year in aviation school, more time to reach the number of flight hours required by a major airline, and with a little luck on his side, it was conceivable that he could make captain at a commercial airline by the time he was forty. At least forty-five.

It wasn't too late for him. Not yet. But the more years that ticked by, the longer he put it off, the later it became.

The idea of flying around the United States and seeing every dusty corner of it—and perhaps even the world—was exhilarating to him. He'd always been filled to the neck with wanderlust, an intense desire to see different places where there was something more to look at than cows and cactus. As a kid, traveling was the best part of family life, even when his parents fought through an entire trip. They spent winter holidays in the Swiss Alps or the Colorado Rockies. They used to have a beach house at a Cabo San Lucas resort—that was the first thing to go when Dad died. They'd gone to New York and

Los Angeles and London for various reasons through the years, too, but they'd never really ventured beyond the exotic locations for skiing or boating, or the big cities that were comfortable to them. His parents were not adventurous. They never wanted to be away from the ranch long.

Nick had wanted to be away from the ranch since he could remember.

He thought about what the ranch would be like if he left. Would it run as bare bones as it did now? Would Rafe and George manage okay? And what about Charlotte? He tried to imagine her with someone else in the office. Would she spout tea bag wisdom at Rafe? Would she color code him into crazy town? Would she tease him, smile at him, and love his dog?

Would she miss *him?* Would she think about him and remember the Christmas party? Or would that fade with time? Would she think about the kiss in the office?

That kiss. It had stirred up a hornet's nest all right, and it still hadn't settled. Every time he walked into that office it felt like he was walking through a frying pan and the tiny little burns of a thousand slices of sizzling bacon.

He wondered if he was the only one feeling it. Maybe Charlotte really could turn it on and off like a spigot. He thought she was feeling the same sort of tension, but she wasn't obsessed with it like he was. He'd overheard her on the phone with her sister. Apparently, she'd had another date last night. He'd distinctly heard her say she was meeting the dog guy at a dog park. It had occurred to him that his attempt to reduce the sizzle between them by helping her find a guy to date might have been the dumbest thing he'd ever done.

His feelings about that were extraordinarily complicated. He wanted Charlotte to find the right guy for her, someone who would ride hard for her, like she'd said. More than anything, he wanted Charlotte to be happy. He just didn't want her to find the right guy while he was around to see it.

He looked again at the flight school website. He hit the button to apply and filled out the form. There was no harm in applying, was there? He could cancel again if he had to. If he were accepted, he would have a couple of months before the first payment was due.

When he finished the application, he hit send. And then he picked up his phone and texted Rafe, asked if they could meet up next week to talk about a few things.

Rafe, assuming it was ranch business, texted back right away:

Saturday 11:42 AM
Sure. Name the time and place.

They agreed to meet at George's offices on Wednesday of next week. Now, all Nick had to do was talk to his mother. He would prefer to put that conversation off as long as he could. His mother had a way of slicing right through you if she didn't like what you were doing. Unfortunately, he couldn't avoid seeing her today. He needed to go to the ranch and look in Dad's office for that invoice, if it even existed. He and George had driven out to Karankawa and had a look around. There were some tire tracks. But if any work had been done on that well, they couldn't determine it. That didn't mean much, to be honest. A well that wasn't running looked like a well that was running.

He glanced at his watch and noticed the time. The Fred Savages were meeting for the first time today, and he didn't want to be late. They'd signed up for a practice field adjacent to one scheduled by the Saddlebush Sluggers.

Nick showered and dressed, and then trimmed the beard that he'd decided to try on for size. He donned joggers, a T-shirt, and tennis shoes, and rummaged around in his closet for his glove and a hat.

The sun had appeared from behind the clouds by the time he walked outside. It was so bright that at first he didn't see the car bouncing down the road to his house. He paused, watching it. This was curious—no one ever came out this way unexpectedly. Occasionally he'd get a delivery, but this wasn't any sort of delivery vehicle. It looked like a small Honda.

Pepper started barking as the car rolled to stop. Even Priscilla, muddy from snout to tail, came running around the house, hoping it was something to eat. A guy got out of the car. He was wearing a knit cap in spite of it being summer, long pants, and leather sandals. "Hey, man, are you Nicholas Prince?"

"Yes," Nick said.

"Great. Got something for you." He reached in through the window of the back seat and pulled out a manila envelope, then jogged up to the porch with it. "Here you go."

Nick could see his name written on the envelope and took it from him. "What is it?"

"I don't know," the man said. "I just serve them up."

Nick looked at the man. Then at the envelope. He ripped it open as the guy dipped down to pet Pepper. "Cool dog," he said, and jogged to his car. Nick didn't notice him leave—he was staring at a lawsuit, filed on behalf of Tim Mitchell. *Damn it.*

He took the notice into his house and left it on the bar next to his laptop, then drove out to the ranch.

The ranch looked deserted. When he walked inside, he shouted, *"Hello!"* It was so odd to feel the emptiness in the mansion. Growing up, there were always people around. Plenty of staff. Visitors, too. His dad and Martin off in a corner solving the problems of the world.

Now, his footsteps echoed. It was like walking into a ghost town.

Nick made his way to the kitchen. This house had more rooms than a hotel, but the family always congregated in the kitchen. The kitchen light was on, and when Nick strolled in, he found his grandmother sitting in the kitchen nook. She was wearing her favorite jeans and a tee that read *This ain't my first rodeo*. A little girl in buckskins, boots, and a cowboy hat had lassoed the words. Grandma's pink-and-orange-striped hair had been updated to purple tips.

She sat with her feet, encased in red Keds, propped on an ottoman, and a magazine was draped across her lap. "Well, look here, it's my favorite grandson."

"That's gonna hurt Luca's feelings," Nick said as he crossed the room to kiss her cheek.

"I'm throwing caution to the wind. What are you doing here?"

"I need to look for something in Dad's office." He helped himself to some popcorn from a bowl on the table between the two armchairs. "How's that going to go over, do you think?"

"Good question," Grandma said. "You better speak to your mother first. She's left his office untouched, you know. It's like a dang mausoleum in there. I fear next she's going to drag out Charlie's sarcophagus."

"Yikes," Nick said. "Where is Mom, anyway?"

"Where is she ever at this time of the day on a Saturday? Up at the cemetery. Are you going up there to talk to her?"

"I guess so," Nick said.

"Well, do me a favor and carry that up there, will you?" Grandma asked, gesturing to a bag. "I told her, if we're going to spend all our time up there, we ought to install some sort of lift. It's not as easy to get up and down that hill like it once was. But your mother won't hear of it. *'I am not going to ruin the landscape because you're old,'*" his grandmother said, mimicking Nick's mother. "Can you believe she said that to me?"

"Yep," Nick said, and smiled at his grandmother. He looked inside the bag. It held a six-pack of hard seltzer and some pretzels. "Please tell me you're not drinking hard seltzer, Grandma."

"Don't you get snooty with me, mister," Grandma said. "I've earned the right to drink motor oil if I want. Just take them up," she said, waving a hand at him. She picked up her magazine to indicate the conversation was over.

"Yes, ma'am," Nick said. "And please don't drink motor oil." He picked up the bag and walked outside.

The family cemetery sat on top of a small

259

mesa. Someone long ago had planted live oaks, and they formed a canopy over most of the two dozen or so graves. A wrought iron fence surrounded the plot. It was a nice spot—when you were standing on the mesa, you could see for miles around. You could see down into the backyard of the house, too. He and Rafe used to come up here when they were kids and spy on their dads. But his mother's constant presence up here was a little concerning. He and Luca and Hallie had talked about it once. Did it require an intervention? They had decided that she seemed her normal self the rest of the time, and when she was up there, she wasn't bothering them. They decided to leave well enough alone.

Nick could see his mother in a chaise longue as he trudged up the hill. That was an upgrade from the woven lawn chairs that had been here several months ago. She had three chaises in a row, looking south, over the vast expanse of empty ranch land. Martin had built a lanai over the three chaises after his mother had complained that her sun umbrella kept blowing over. Nick had suggested she move her seats under the trees, but his mother had dismissed that idea. "Can't see as well. And besides, I don't think Charlie can hear me from there."

"But Great-Aunt Hannah can," Nick's grandmother said. "As I recall, you had a few choice words for her, too."

"Well that was a lifetime ago. But a person can't criticize someone's style and expect it to go unchallenged."

Nick didn't know what his great aunt Hannah had said about his mother's style. He could only vaguely remember his great aunt at all.

He opened the gate and it squeaked.

His mother had her feet propped on Dad's headstone and didn't turn around. "Dolly, if that is you, I am meditating. Consider yourself warned."

"It's me," Nick said.

His mother bolted upright and turned around. A smile lit her face. "What a surprise! Come over here, Nick. Come sit next to me in George's chair."

"George has a chair?"

"Oh yes. He's as bad as Dolly. I don't know why those two won't let a woman mourn her husband in peace."

Nick put down the bag on a table between them and eased himself down on the chaise. "Are you still mourning, Mom?"

"No, not really," she said thoughtfully. "I've gone past mourning to wishing. I wish he was still here, but I'm not sad about it anymore." She shifted her gaze to the landscape.

So did Nick. He could see cows off in the far distance. "You should put some goats in here," he said. "Keep the grass down."

"I hate goats," his mother said.

"How can you hate goats?"

"I just do. They seem judgmental to me."

Nick laughed. "Goats are fine."

"If you like them, put them out at your house."

"Maybe I will." He wouldn't.

She glanced at him from the corner of her eye. "Is Ella's pig still living with your band of misfit toys?"

"She's still there and her name is Priscilla. You'd like her, Mom. You ought to come out and say hello."

"I told Luca he should have sold her for the meat. We could have had us a nice Easter ham."

"Mom!" Nick said.

"Well? That's what pigs are for. Really, Nicholas, I certainly hope you don't turn into a Cathy Feldman."

Nick looked curiously at his mother. "Who is Cathy Feldman?"

"Oh, she used to be on the charity circuit with me," she said with a flick of her wrist. "But she was all into the animals and their rights, and went completely over the edge."

"I'm not an animal rights activist."

"Well, she was. She lost her damn mind. There she was, living up in Alamo Heights in San Antonio with three grown pigs *in her house.*"

"The potbellied kind?"

"No! The full-bodied bacon kind!"

Nick laughed loudly. "I don't believe that for a minute."

"It's true! She had three of them. They had to pig-proof that house by taking all the furniture out. And she had three kids to boot! I never did understand her or her husband."

"If it makes you feel better, Priscilla has never been in my house. She sleeps outside in an old shed."

"That makes me feel a little better." His mother eyed him suspiciously. "Why are you here, anyway? I'm not used to you dropping by just to say hi."

"Can't a man pay a call on a mother with strong opinions and a slight drinking problem without having to defend himself?" he asked with a grin.

His mother laughed. "Yes, of course you can."

"Speaking of drinking, Grandma sent these," he said, and pulled the hard seltzer from the bag. The package of pretzels tumbled to the ground.

"Oh!" she said, and her eyes flashed with delight. "That's the new flavor! Thank you." She pulled one free of the package and popped the top, then drank. "It's good."

Nick was old enough to remember when his mother had French champagne flown in from a dealer in California.

"You didn't answer my question. Did you come for one of my strong opinions?"

"I came to tell you that I was served with a lawsuit today."

"What?"

Nick nodded. "A man out of Corpus Christi says Dad hired him to service the Karankawa well."

His mother frowned with confusion. "The Karankawa well? Why would he do that?"

"I don't know. I was hoping you'd know the answer. The man implied Dad was going to open the well and start producing."

His mother snorted. "That's ridiculous. There wouldn't be anything there to pump. It would cost more money to get it up and running than you would ever make back."

Nick's thoughts exactly. "So this is news to you, too."

"Yes. Did you ask George?"

"News to him, too."

"It's a lie," his mother said flatly.

"Maybe," Nick agreed. "This guy wouldn't be the first to come sniffing around looking to cash in on the Princes. But . . ."

"But?"

"But Dad was in a desperate situation, Mom. It's possible he thought he could squeeze something out of that well to pay down some debts."

She clucked her tongue. "Then he was a bigger fool than I believed."

"I need to look in Dad's office," he said.

Her head snapped around. "For what? George and I went through all those files after he died. There is nothing in there."

"This man says he invoiced us and we owe him money. Charlotte and I can't find any record of it. If Dad was doing something a little off the grid, he might have tucked the evidence away somewhere in his office."

She looked off into the distance a moment, and then back at Nick. "You're not going to tear everything apart, are you?"

"No, Mom. What are you worried about? Are you going to leave that as a shrine to Dad or something?"

"No," she said, as if that were preposterous. "I don't know. It still smells like him."

"The last time I was in there, it smelled like stale cigars."

"Exactly."

"Dad's gone, Mom," he said softly.

"Well, I know that, Nick. Do you see where my feet are right now?"

"We need to move on," Nick said gently. "Dad left us in a world of hurt, and we've got to fix it now. Leaving his office untouched isn't helping either of us."

"Fine," she muttered, and took a long draw from her seltzer.

Nick stood up with the intention of leaving, but his mother said, "Just how do we fix it, anyway?"

"What?"

"You said we have to fix the world of hurt he left us. How?"

"We need cash to fix it. We could sell some land. We could sell more assets."

"I knew you were going to say that."

Nick knew this was not what she wanted, but it was the truth. They couldn't fix it any other way. "What did you want me to say?"

"Honestly? I wanted you to say that you will *fix* it. That you are committed to us, and you aren't selling things or whatever so you can go fly planes around the world." She suddenly sat up and twisted around to look at him. "Do you have any idea how many Princes, and Princes before them, worked hard to get and *keep* this land? Do you have any idea what sort of legacy a ranch like this in this day and age is for your children? You're not a kid anymore, Nick. You're an adult, and that means responsibilities. It means you have to look at the big picture and do what's best for everyone, and not just you."

Nick stared at her. He shouldn't have been surprised, but he was. "Thanks for that vote of confidence, Mother. I thought what I'd been doing was looking after the big picture. Here's a question for you—why am I the only one who is expected to sacrifice what I want for the sake of this ranch?"

"Don't be ridiculous. We've all sacrificed."

"Really?" Nick asked, folding his arms over his chest. "Hallie and Luca? *You?*"

"I lost my husband."

"You and Dad were separated when he died. You two talked about divorce more times than I ever talked about flying."

"Listen, mister," she said, jabbing a finger in his general direction. "I poured my whole adult life into this ranch and maintaining the Prince name. I did it with no help from *him.* And I will *not* be defeated because he died."

"Defeated!" Nick protested loudly. "Is this some sort of contest for you? I am not pursuing what I want in *my* life because Dad left me this goddamn mess. I never asked for it. I never wanted it."

"But you've been groomed for this since you were a boy! We made sure of it."

"You should have asked me," Nick said. "You and Dad should have asked me, Mom." He suddenly felt so tired. He thought he'd done everything that was asked of him. He'd put off flight school, for God's sake. He'd been here for his family and it still wasn't enough. "You have to be the only mother in Texas who would discourage one of her children from pursuing his dream," he said with some bitterness.

"I'm a practical mother and I am trying to make *you* see that sometimes what we want from life isn't *practical,* Nick."

"But you don't get to decide that for me. So thanks, Mom. Thanks for the pep talk. Always a pleasure." He turned to leave, walking through the family graves.

"Nick," she said pleadingly. "Nick!" He didn't respond. He didn't look back. He was afraid of what he might say if he did.

"For the love of Pete, get that chip off your shoulder! I didn't die, your father did! If you want to be mad at someone, be mad at him!"

There was enough anger and disappointment to go around. Nick strode down the hill, away from her.

He marched into the house and ignored his grandmother, too, when she called out, "Is that you, Nicky?" He kept walking until he reached his father's office.

He paused just inside and looked around at the richly paneled walls, the bookshelves that held more trophies and golf memorabilia than they did books. The room still smelled like stale tobacco. Nick didn't know where to start, exactly, but after an hour of going through the desk and a filing cabinet, he had a box of things he wanted to look through. He hoisted that onto his shoulder and left without saying good-bye to his mother or grandmother. He loved his mother. But sometimes, he didn't like her much.

He shoved the box into his truck and drove away from Three Rivers. As he moved away from the house, his mood lightened. He thought of the softball fields. He thought of his desire to do something physical, to hit a few balls with all the strength he had, just knock those suckers out of the park and work out the tension his mother had put in him.

And of course he thought of Charlotte, she with the bouncing blond curls, the turquoise eyes, the sparkling smile.

Chapter Fourteen

Charlotte arrived at the softball fields before anyone else to set up their "dugout," which was basically a metal bench on one side of the field. She had chips, water, beer—and a suitcase of beer for Colton's team, as directed by Nick—and best of all, T-shirts. They were red, and on the front, they had the Saddlebush Land and Cattle logo, and on the back, she'd had the team member's name stenciled. It had been a rush job, but Charlotte knew the lady at the print shop and had brought her donuts from Jo's Java to sweeten the rush. She'd paid a steep upcharge, but she thought it was important to make an impression, even in the practice rounds. The Saddlebush Sluggers were not messing around.

The league was set up for each team to have practice time, then a four-inning practice game if the teams so desired.

She had finished setting up a couple of extra lawn chairs when her brother, Chase, and his friend Kyle arrived. Chase had the bag with the bats. He was wearing his baseball pants from high school. Charlotte was secretly envious that he could still wear them.

Luca and Ella came next, and it looked as if they'd stopped in at Walmart on the way over and picked up gloves—they still had the tags hanging from them.

"You're going to need to soften those up," Chase said, and took the one Ella was holding and began to bend the leather. "Here's what you do—you rub it with baby oil, then put it in the oven for about fifteen minutes."

"The oven?" Ella repeated skeptically.

"And then, when the oil is baked in, you get a ball-peen hammer and start hammering the pocket," he said, mimicking the action of hammering the glove. "Because until you do, you're not going to catch anything with these gloves."

"The odds are stacked against me with or without a glove," Ella admitted.

"We're not in the majors, Chase," Charlotte reminded him.

"Well, no, but we still want to win, don't we, Lot? I mean, are you here to play or to look cute?"

Charlotte rolled her eyes. "Please. Obviously both," she said, and thrust a T-shirt at him.

Rafe arrived next, walking in with Charlotte's cousins Nora and Olivia, both of whom were wearing shorts so short that Charlotte cringed. Behind them were Big Barb and her husband, Ed, and Benny, whom they'd picked up on the way over. After everyone said hello, Rafe asked

Charlotte, "Who's that?" and nodded in the direction of the other field.

Charlotte turned around to glance at the field behind them. "That," she said, watching the other team wander aimlessly out onto the field, "is the Fred Savages."

"The who?" Rafe asked.

"The Fred Savages," Charlotte repeated. "Formerly known as the Frontier Bank Softball Team." She grinned. "I sort of renamed their team when they weren't looking."

Ella burst out laughing.

The Freds looked a little motley from where Charlotte was standing. Not that she was watching.

Okay, she was watching. She spotted Nick right away—he was taller than most of them, and much larger in frame. He was throwing the ball around to people who had been sent out to the bases, but no one could seem to catch. There were two middle-aged women with gray curls springing out from beneath their ball caps. Charlotte knew they were the sister bank tellers who worked at Frontier. Colton had arrived, too, looking trim and athletic. *A swimmer's body, not a quarterback's,* Nick, Charlotte thought, and he looked pretty good throwing the ball . . .

But not as good as Nick.

There were two other men, both of them wiry and thin. One of them was windmilling his arms like he was about to take off in flight. He stepped up onto the pitcher's mound and threw the first ball. It bounced on the ground and shot off to the right.

Luca appeared at Charlotte's side and adjusted his ball cap as he squinted across the field at the Fred Savages. "I don't know, but I think we might win this league before it even starts."

"Right?" Charlotte murmured.

Kyle joined them. "Hey, Luca, isn't that your brother, Nick?"

"Yep, that's him," Luca confirmed.

"He was a really good player in high school."

"High school was such a long time ago," Charlotte pointed out with a shrug. She didn't want him to be good. She wanted to beat him in the worst way.

"Are we going to practice?" Chase shouted at them. He was already walking out onto the field, and Charlotte hadn't finished handing out the T-shirts. Her brother completely ignored her when she explained to him that *she* was the captain.

They took turns at bat and practiced their fielding, then threw the ball around to the bases. After some discussion, it was decided who would play where. Charlotte got second base. "For now," Chase had said, his voice full of warning, as though if she missed a ball, she'd be sent straight to the metal bench on the side of the field.

They'd practiced for about an hour when they decided they wanted to engage the Fred Savages in a few friendly innings. Luca jogged over to see if the Freds were even interested. From where the Sluggers stood, it looked like the Freds were debating it. There was a lot of lively discussion before Luca jogged back. "They'll play," he said. "But Nancy has to leave by two to pick up her kids, and she's the catcher."

"Then let's go," Chase said, and immediately jogged to the other field.

"I'm the captain!" Charlotte called after him.

Colton walked out to greet each of them individually as they filed over. He was wearing sweats and an old T-shirt with the LA Dodgers logo across the chest, and a red ball cap. He shook Charlotte's hand with a tight grip and a grin. His smile was blazing. "I like your shirts! You guys are on the ball, aren't you?"

"Thanks! I had them made up."

"From one captain to another, you've put me to shame," he said with a wink. "I guess I should get the team shirts, huh?"

"Of course! You really *are* new to the world of municipal softball, aren't you?"

"I need someone to help me figure out how to be a team captain. Maybe you could help me?" he asked as they began to walk toward home plate.

"Are you sure?" Charlotte asked. "I'm the one

who made you the Fred Savages, you may recall. No telling what I'd do with a T-shirt."

Colton laughed loudly. "I thought the name was fun."

"See?" Charlotte said to Nick, who had walked into their path. "I told you I am hilarious."

Colton laughed again. "I didn't say *that*."

"You will," Charlotte said confidently. "And sure, I'd be happy to help you with shirts."

"What shirts?" Nick asked, eying her suspiciously.

"Our team shirts," Colton said. "That's great, Charlotte. I'll call you?"

Nick jerked his gaze to Colton. "That sounds great," Charlotte said. She loved it. It was as if before her very eyes Nick was discovering that Colton was not the same man he'd fallen in love with flying around in his plane. And Colton was openly flirting with her—seriously, who needed help making team shirts? *And* she had a second date with a corgi tonight . . .

Well, technically speaking, she had a date with Jake, Gus's owner.

But still, when had she become *this* girl? She glanced at Nick with a ridiculously big smile on her face. Since her breakup more than two years ago, she'd had no luck meeting a man who could possibly give her a life and a baby. Now it felt like they were lining up. It was impossible and heady, and no matter how it had happened, she didn't hate it. "I should *bottle* this," she murmured to herself.

"What did you say?" Nick asked, his eyes narrowed.

"I said, let's play ball!" She jogged to her team and listened to Chase give instructions.

The Sluggers were the first to take the field, and as they walked out to their positions, Ella gave Charlotte a friendly shove. "That banker is totally into you, girl."

"I mean, *right?*" Charlotte said excitedly, and glanced over her shoulder at Colton.

"Just don't get *too* excited," Ella warned her. "You have a tendency to sound like a hyena when you're too excited."

It was too late. Charlotte laughed with delight and she did, indeed, sound like a hyena.

The Freds were as awful as they'd appeared from across the field. The first three batters all struck out. The Sluggers came in and took their turns at bat, almost every one of them getting a hit off the man with the whirling arms. But just before Charlotte was to step up to the plate, the man suddenly grabbed his shoulder. "Damn it!" he shouted. "I think I threw my shoulder out!"

There was quite a hullabaloo as the Freds gathered around him. After a few minutes, the man walked off the pitching mound and Nick took his place.

"Oh *great,*" Charlotte said, but Nick smiled a Maleficent sort of smile.

"You can do this, Lot," Chase said. He put his hands on her shoulders and roughly moved her around. "Just keep your eye on the ball. He's no pitcher. Okay? Loosen up. Easy swing."

Charlotte shrugged him off. "I told you, *I'm* the captain."

"Come on, Charlotte!" Rafe called to her. "Hit it out of the park!"

As Charlotte walked up to the plate, Nick called out, "Bring it in, guys. She won't hit it past home plate."

"Yeah, okay, we all know who's winning," she said back to him, and assumed the position. His first pitch hit the plate. The second pitch was pretty good, and Charlotte almost put her back out swinging wildly at it. She did not make contact. She swung into air at the next pitch, too. That was followed by two wildly errant pitches by Nick, but then one right across the plate that she swung so hard to hit that she almost corkscrewed herself into the ground.

"You're *out!*" some Fred shouted.

Charlotte glared at Nick as he jogged off the pitcher's mound. He grinned at her. "I think you might be the worst batter in the league, kid."

"What are the odds the worst batter would be on the field the same day as the worst pitcher in the league?"

Nick tapped her arm with his glove. "Hope you didn't hurt yourself with that last swing."

"You're so funny, Nick! Too bad that your team really sucks."

"Tell me about it," he said out of the side of his mouth, and cuffed her on the shoulder before jogging off to join his team.

After another inning, people from both teams began to complain about needing to go, and Charlotte was one of them. "Come on," she shouted at Ella, who was pitching. "I need to go home and get gussied up!"

Rafe, on first, looked at her. "*Gussied up?* Who talks like that? Did you go behind our backs and get a role on an HBO western or something?"

"If you must know, I have a hot date."

"Okay, I quit," Ella said. "My arm hurts anyway."

"Quit! You can't quit!" Nick shouted. "I'm on third, and you're pitching. It's a guaranteed run!"

"Hey!" Ella protested.

After a bit of negotiation, it was agreed they would finish the inning with the next at bat. Nick was right—Ella was awful and it was a guaranteed run.

As everyone gathered up their things, Charlotte walked over to present the suitcase of beer to their opponents. "In the spirit of good sportsmanship, I present this suitcase of beer to the Freds," she said grandly. "But really, consider it my mea culpa for messing with your name."

"I mean, could you maybe call us the Savages?" one of the women asked as she helped herself to a beer.

"I *could*," Charlotte said. "But I probably won't. You're definitely a team of Freds. Anyway, enjoy! Bye, Freds!" She turned to jog away, but not before Colton said, "I'll call you about the shirts, Charlotte!"

She did a little pirouette to give him a thumbs-up, then turned back to her team. Chase and Rafe had her things, and as they walked together to the parking lot, Charlotte was aware of a pair of eyes boring a hole through her with every step she took.

And they were not Colton's. They were dark blue.

Charlotte met Jake for drinks at the Down on Grayson watering hole near the Pearl Brewery. Their first meet-up had been at a dog park. His dog Gus was adorable, and Jake hadn't done anything weird like spit tobacco or make a pass. It was like she'd told Cassie—she'd spent more time talking to Gus than to Jake, but still, she thought Jake had potential, so she'd agreed to see him again.

"That's great! Now your water's boiling on the

front burner! Maybe this guy is the one," Cassie had chortled.

Charlotte didn't think Jake was The One. But he was a nice guy.

He was already there when she arrived. He stood up, waving at her so she could spot him on the crowded lawn. He grinned as she took her seat on the picnic table across from him. "I hope you don't mind, but I took the liberty of ordering us two Ranch Waters. It's a specialty drink here."

Charlotte would never object to a specialty drink, but it turned out the drink was neither water nor from any ranch she'd ever visited— it was simply a lot of tequila, a splash of Topo Chico, and a twist of lime.

They sipped the drinks while Jake talked about his job. He was in finance, and was very excited about a stock he thought was going to be a game changer. As Charlotte didn't make the kind of money that required her to ever think about stocks, she listened politely and without yawning. But Jake was interested in her, too, and when he'd finished his explanation about his five- and ten-year plans for his finances, he asked about her work.

"Oh, I manage a ranch office."

"Where?" he asked. "Like on a ranch?"

She smiled. "In the town of Three Rivers, just a few miles south of here. It's a land and cattle company."

He shook his head. "Don't know what that is."

"Typically, a land and cattle company buys, sells, and leases land for the grazing of cattle. But in this case, it's a little more. We manage all the Prince ranch business."

"Ah," he said. Charlotte wasn't sure, but she thought his eyes might have glazed over. "I don't know much about ranch life."

"You're not into cattle futures?" She laughed.

Jake looked at her blankly.

Charlotte waved her hand. "It was a joke. I'm not into cattle futures, either. I really don't even know what they are." She wasn't into cattle futures, but she was, she realized, into ranch life. She hadn't really thought about it before, but she knew more about ranch life than anything else. Funny how things worked out. When she finished college, she'd had this fantasy she'd get a job in New York or Los Angeles. Someplace urban and cool and away from Texas. She'd imagined herself something of a Bohemian, wandering around the planet. At least the United States. But the need to pay rent had driven her to get a job, and Charlie Prince was hiring.

And then there was her family. Someone was always calling, needing her to help out, to check in on parents, to pick up something or babysit. Just this morning, Caitlin had called and asked her to sit with the kids for a little while—she was feeling super pregnant and super tired. Charlotte hadn't hesitated. She'd packed up a book and Rufus, and had gone over, giving Caitlin and Jonah a Saturday morning to themselves. It's what family members did for one another. And it's what her family relied on her to do for them.

"I always think of ranches as a bunch of cows and cowboys," Jake said. "Like in the movies."

Charlotte looked at Jake appraisingly. "Don't you ever go out to the country?"

"Like where?"

"I mean like out of the city."

He thought about it as he sipped his drink. "I've been to Eisenhower Park. Does that count?"

Eisenhower Park, although rugged and untouched by sprinklers or concrete, was a San Antonio city park. But it was smack-dab in the middle of development. That was not what she meant at all. She was thinking about the *country,* where there were miles and miles of open land and trees. Like where her parents used to send them to cowboy camp every summer—way down in the Hill Country, with nothing for miles around them. "Eisenhower Park is not what I'd call the country."

"No? What would you call the country?"

Charlotte thought about the drive out to Nick's house. The road went through empty acres, following a river, then veering off into mesquites and pin oaks. She thought of how carpets of wildflowers would push up in spring. First came the bluebonnets, blue stretching as far as the eye could see, sometimes dotted with pink evening primrose. Then came the Indian paintbrushes and the fire wheels that grew so thick a person could hardly walk through the flashy red and yellow flowers. Then came the black-eyed Susans, the daisies, and the poppies. There were wine-cups and spider lilies, all of them blanketing the ground through March and April. And when the heavy spring rains came, the rain lilies would pop out, the fragile white flowers tall and stately for their brief two days on earth. *That* was the country.

There was no place that she knew of where one could see the brilliance of spring except in the country, and especially when driving across a portion of the seventy-five-thousand-acre Three Rivers Ranch. It felt as if you were in another world.

"I would call country at least ten miles past the last billboard," she said.

Jake smiled and shrugged. "Yeah, I don't know. Rural is not my thing."

She'd never really thought it was her thing, either, but Charlotte wondered if maybe it was. It wasn't only the land, really, but the people, too. Some of her best friends were cowboys. Like Nick and Rafe. Some of her friends that had come from the country looked at life differently than people from San Antonio. She didn't know how to explain it really, other than there were certain conveniences city living afforded a person. And that perspective had to be changed in a rural setting. Some of those conveniences existed on a different scale in the country. Sometimes smaller. Sometimes bigger. Sometimes not at all.

"I'm sorry, did I offend you?" Jake asked.

"Not at all! I was just thinking it's a different mind-set in a way." She thought about Nick for some reason, and the way he had quietly gone about his life when the conveniences didn't stack up. He'd taken it all on, the ranching and company management, while trying to hold his family and his own desires together. Yes, he was a grump, but look at what he'd had to contend with. She looked at Jake and wondered how he would cope if his world fell apart and he had to do all the jobs—except the one he really wanted to do. Jake was a nice guy, but she couldn't picture it.

"You mean conservative," he offered.

That wasn't at all what she meant. She meant hardy. Forbearing. "Down to earth," she countered. She couldn't explain the mind-set to anyone—she just knew it was something you had to experience in your blood. "Hey, how is Gus?" she asked brightly, changing the subject.

"Gus is great," Jake said, and began to tell her about a showdown between Gus and a neighbor's cat.

They talked about their dogs for the rest of the date. And as the date came to an end, and Jake kissed her cheek before she left—he was, after all, a self-proclaimed gentleman—Charlotte smiled and thanked him for the evening.

But as she was thanking him, she was thinking of Nick's kiss. That boiling, heart-aching kiss that she wondered if only a boy from the country knew how to make happen.

Chapter Fifteen

A muggy haze had had settled onto the tops of the trees and the fields behind Nick's house on Sunday morning. In the distance, the cows looked as if they were undulating in the heat. Nick sat under a fan on his covered porch, his bare feet propped on an overturned bucket. Pepper was sitting alertly on the top porch step, her ears pricked to any sound. There was no sound out here except the occasional breeze that rustled the leaves of the cottonwood trees. There was no vehicle traffic, no planes overhead. Nothing. He lived that far away from civilization.

When he'd first moved out here at the age of twenty-six, he'd chafed at the vast emptiness around him and the lack of sound. But at the time, the alternative was his parents' house, an enormous home built for generations. And yet it wasn't big enough to separate him from his parents. Living with them was worse than living in San Antonio, which would have required a substantial commute each day. He had access to family properties in San Antonio and Houston, and when he was younger, he would decamp to those cities on weekends. But he'd never been a partier like Luca, or social like Hallie. And besides, his work on the ranch sometimes took him deep into the massive acreage. He'd needed something closer. So he'd taken this old house, originally built for vaqueros.

He and his dad had been enthusiastic about renovating it in the beginning when they put on the new roof and installed new flooring. But after they'd added the second bathroom, the work went from a father-son project to hobby work for Nick. He'd tinkered along for a few years, replacing all the trim and painting the rooms. And then, about four years ago, he and his dad had tackled a kitchen renovation.

Now, he liked it here. He'd learned to appreciate the silence and the fact that he had so much raw land around him. This space had a way of settling into a man's bones and putting him in touch with his thoughts. He'd started to actually hear the birds chattering at each other in the mornings and missed them when they weren't. He listened for the coyotes calling to each other. He could probably hear a snake slither across his small bit of green lawn if he listened hard enough. His nose was filled with the scent of wild honeysuckle and Ligustrum every day and, if he was lucky, the scent of rain.

Nick might be alone out here, but he was truly in tune with the world. He understood his brother's desire to turn part of the ranch back to its natural state, to replant the native flora and repopulate the native fauna. He understood how easy it was to want to be part of the earth when you actually saw it and felt it beneath your feet. Nick still wanted to see the world—that desire burned as bright in him as it had in his twelve-year-old brain. But it was nice to have this place with its peace and quiet to retreat to.

The only downside to it was that sometimes, he was lonely. There was only so much Pepper, Priscilla, and Frank could do for him in the way of companionship. Hallie would argue that he brought the loneliness on himself, which she'd reminded him of just a couple of days ago when she had come out to visit, walking around his house with her hands on her incredibly large pregnant belly.

"What's up?" he'd asked when she arrived.

"Nothing. I needed a break from . . . people. Let's just leave it at that."

He knew what she had meant. She had needed a break from Mom.

"Your house is so clean!" Hallie had said, walking around. "Who cleaned it? I mean, did *you* clean it?"

Nick had looked at her curiously. "Who else is going to clean it?"

"You could eat off this floor!" she had insisted, bending over at the waist to see past her belly. "I am a terrible housekeeper. I keep thinking

Mayrose will come around and pick up after me."

"Mayrose hasn't worked at the ranch for six months. And she never worked at your house."

"See? That's my problem." She'd moved to the big sliding glass doors he'd installed along the back of the house. At certain times of the year, Nick opened them up. "It's, like, so solitary here," she had said. "No wonder it's so clean." And then she'd looked over her shoulder at him in a way that seemed almost accusatory.

"I like it that way."

"No one likes *that* much alone time, even someone as super grumpy as you."

"I'm not . . ." He'd sighed. This was the picture his family had of him. Super grumpy instead of laconic.

"Why don't you date, Nick? You're a pretty good-looking guy."

He'd snorted. "Thanks a lot. Why are you always so nosy?"

"You used to date, but since Dad died, you're so . . . *weird*." She'd said this with a strange flutter of her fingers.

"I don't think I can take all the compliments you are throwing my way, sis. I'm not weird. It's just that I don't expect to be around long."

Hallie had sighed, and wow, did she look and sound like his mother when she did. "Are you still playing that game? You're thirty-three, Nick.

You've been doing this since you got out of college. You're not going anywhere."

Nick had silently bristled. He feared she might be right. "I might surprise you," he'd said tightly.

Hallie's smile had been full of pity, and Nick had bristled more. She had walked over to him, and even though he'd told her not to touch him, she had, hugging him tightly. He'd stood awkwardly while she did. "For real—don't you get lonely?" she'd asked him.

Nick had looked out the window, at raw land as far as the eye could see. Nothing but trees and rescued animals out here. "Sure."

"Well, you did that to yourself." And then she had smacked his arm.

"*Ouch,* Hallie," he'd said, rubbing his arm.

"I just don't get it. You're really an amazing guy if you'd ever crack a smile and let someone see it. But no, you have to stomp around like Shrek."

"If this is supposed to be a pep talk, you're doing a terrible job," Nick had pointed out.

She hadn't been listening. At that point, she'd wandered into his master bath. "Hey! Is it okay if I take a bath?"

"Knock yourself out."

"Do not walk around in front of these giant windows!" she had shouted, and shut the bathroom door.

Nick hadn't walked around the house to the big bathroom window. But Rafe had when he'd come out to find her. "My wife's car is out front, but I don't see her, and she's pretty hard to miss these days."

Nick had laughed. "She's taking a bath."

"Taking a *bath?* In the middle of the day? At your house?"

Nick had shrugged. "Who knows with that one?"

Rafe had walked around the side of the house, and Nick had heard Hallie's scream, followed by cursing. He had laughed roundly—she got what she deserved, that little strawberry blond sassy pants.

But upon reflection, Nick conceded that Hallie had a point. He hadn't dated in a long time because he did think he was getting out of here. Now, he really believed it. He was meeting with Rafe this week, and he was eyeing the October start for flight school.

But Hallie was right—he did feel alone a lot of the time. He felt alone in his emotions at having lost his dad, of inheriting the Saddlebush company when his father knew that was the last thing he wanted. He felt alone in what he'd had to learn about his father, what he'd had to pick up and fix after his death. He felt alone in what he wanted, what he hoped to achieve with his life. He felt alone with his hopes. With everything.

And the only person who seemed to really get him was Charlotte.

On that muggy morning, Nick was thinking about her. Obsessing over her date with the damn dog guy. Nick remembered him from the app. He'd seemed clean-cut and safe, which was why he'd suggested him. He'd like to kick his own ass about now.

He looked at his phone. He'd typed out a message earlier that he hadn't sent because he was questioning his motives. Did he *really* need what he said he needed? Or was another motive driving him? He didn't know how Charlotte would take this request. Maybe she was just waking up to Dog Guy and a corgi. Maybe she had plans for the day.

He looked at his watch. He'd been sitting here with this unsent message for a half hour, questioning himself and everything he thought he knew about the two of them. It was ten fifteen. "For Chrissakes," he muttered irritably, and in a sudden burst of decisiveness, he hit send.

Sunday 10:15 AM
Hey Charlotte, it's Nick. I know you don't like to hear from me on weekends, but I could use your help today. Assuming you're home. Assuming you can spare me a few hours. I was served with a lawsuit by the Corpus guy yesterday. I

have a box of files from the ranch that might have something useful but need help going through it. Let me know, thanks.

He studied the text he'd sent, and then quickly amended it.

Sunday 10:16 AM
I forgot to say I will pay you overtime.

Charlotte did not respond right away. Maybe she wasn't home. But wherever she was, he knew she had her phone. So maybe she was torturing him by not answering, because the Lord knew she liked to do that, too. In fact, she let a good half hour pass before she answered him.

Sunday 10:49 AM
OMG do you not know that I am a salaried employee and you can't pay me "overtime" without approval from the HR department and the CEO?

The corner of his mouth ticked up in a smile. He texted:

Sunday 10:50 AM
I see you ate your Wheaties this morning. What do you say? Maybe come out this

afternoon? You don't have to gussy up and you can bring Rufus if you like.

Three dots appeared at the bottom of his screen.

Sunday 10:51 AM
This just in from HR: Permission granted. Submit invoice first thing Monday in orange HR folder. Not to be confused with red finance report folder. Try not to be a goob about it. JK! I know you can't help being a goob.

Nick's smile broadened.

Sunday 10:51 AM
Shall I take from this that you will come and help me?

She responded with:

Sunday 10:53 AM
Hey, what do you call two people who work on Sunday afternoons?

Sunday 10:54 AM
?

Sunday 10:55 AM
Pathetic losers! Hahaaa. Yes, I'll come.

But you better have snacks, Nick. Treat this like a staff meeting and do not screw it up. I'll see you around 2.

Nick laughed softly. That girl was crazy.
He liked crazy. He might even love crazy.

At ten till two, he heard her car and walked out onto his front porch to watch her drive down the road at a snail's pace. He understood why—Rufus was halfway out the window, his big head pointed toward the ground as if he intended to jump. But when she parked, Rufus pulled his head back in. Charlotte got out and opened the door to the back seat, and Nick could hear her telling Rufus to get out. A moment later, Rufus launched himself from her car and bounded straight for Priscilla, who didn't know what to make of a giant black dog galumphing toward her and went squealing into the shed. Rufus looked like he might career into the shed, but veered off at the last moment and trotted over to the feed Priscilla had been eating.

"Rufus! Get out of there!" Charlotte shouted.

Rufus obediently raced away as fast as he could—which wasn't particularly fast, given his girth—heading into the pasture to see Frank, with Pepper gleefully racing alongside him. Frank ignored both dogs.

Charlotte sighed and shook her head. "I'm serious—Rufus is not a smart dog."

Nick laughed. "I've noticed."

She turned toward him and smiled. She looked, in a word, delectable. She'd used a rolled-up bandanna to tame the curls off her face, and the tied ends of it stuck up like a bow on the top of her head. She was wearing cutoff jean shorts and a sleeveless snowy white linen top that billowed around her. Her long, tanned legs seemed even longer and tanner out here than they did in the office beneath the knee-length dresses she wore. Either way, Nick really liked seeing them.

And of course there were her summer blue eyes that he could never seem to get out of his head.

Charlotte put her hands on her waist, and tilted her head to one side, assessing him. "I've been meaning to ask, did you lose your razor?"

He put his hand to his chin. "Nope. I'm giving a beard a try."

She lifted one hand and lightly touched his cheek. "Got a little gray right here."

"Thanks for pointing that out."

"That's what I'm here for!" She suddenly whirled around. "I have to say hi to Frank! Oh my gosh, is that wild honeysuckle I smell? It's so *sweet*. Hey, look at your *roses*. Those are gorgeous! I didn't know you had a green thumb, Nick. You are constantly surprising me."

She kept talking as she walked out to the pasture fence, remarking on this and that. Nick looked at the honeysuckle that grew wild along the fence, then at the shrub roses the vaqueros had planted years and years ago. They showed up every spring and summer, red and dark pink, no matter what he did or didn't do.

She was talking to Frank now, and her voice rose up like the chatter of the mockingbirds that he listened to in the early morning. His place wasn't silent anymore—it was very much alive.

Nick stood beside her as she leaned over the fence to stroke Frank's nose. The old horse's eyes were cloudy—he was almost blind. Nick wondered fleetingly what he'd do with Frank when he left for flight school.

"Frank's got a little gray on his muzzle, too, don't you, Frank, don't you, big boy," she cooed to him.

Nick was about to speak for Frank when both of them started at the sound of a big splash of water. They looked up in the direction of the creek. Pepper was standing on the bank, her legs wide apart, her tail wagging furiously as she looked down at the creek.

"You have got to be kidding me," Charlotte muttered. She came down off the fence. "Okay, cowboy, let's go have a look at this box of stuff. You have no idea how much money you're paying me to stand here and pet your horse." She winked at him. "Bye, Frank!" she said, and started for the house.

"The HR department is scaring me," Nick said,

and the sound of her laughter rose up over her head and drifted off with the breeze that rustled the cottonwoods. The sound of that laugh made him feel happy. It made him look forward to this Sunday afternoon. When was the last time he'd looked forward to an afternoon?

On his porch, he opened one of the big sliding glass doors into the house. Charlotte walked in and looked around. "You know, I've seen your house before, but I forget how nice it is. When you're driving down the road to the middle of nowhere, you don't expect to find this. Frankly, I'm always a little shocked and a lot annoyed that your house is cuter than mine."

Nick looked around. "I wouldn't call it *cute*."

"Oh, it's cute." She smiled at him. "If the cowboy thing doesn't work out, maybe you could try interior design."

He arched a brow. "Interior design? I think I'll stick with cattle. Do you want coffee?"

"Yes!" She shook her hands to the ceiling as if she'd been begging him for coffee and he had only just heard her. "I drank tequila last night and it really slows you down. Why is there tequila, anyway? Do we really need that in the world?"

"You were drinking tequila?" he asked curiously.

"In San Antonio."

With his back to her, Nick winced. He made himself ask the question suddenly burning in his brain. "So, you had a good time with Dog Guy, I guess."

"I did indeed, sir. He's a really nice guy." Nick heard her slide onto a barstool as he took down coffee from the cabinet. "You chose well for me. Who knew?" She laughed.

Nick forced himself to turn and smile in her direction. He wished he'd never spotted Dog Guy. He wished he'd never even played that game.

"Gus is *really* cute," she said as he put coffee in the machine. There was that word again, *cute*. Cute house, cute guy, all for a cute girl.

"And he's so smart!"

Nick flipped the switch on the machine and turned around to lean up against the counter. "I'm really glad you found him."

"Yeah," she said, and propped her head onto her fist and sighed wistfully. "I wish I could have him."

Nick supposed she could. That's why the guy was on the dating app after all, and any man would be a damn fool to not want Charlotte.

"I'd love to bring him home."

What, to meet her parents? Was she already thinking like that? Seemed sudden. Nick looked down at his feet and tried to hide his . . . what? Disappointment? Regret? Idiocy?

"He is *so* well behaved. More like Pepper and completely unlike Rufus," she added.

Nick blinked. He had to think about that a moment and slowly lifted his head. "What are you talking about?"

"Gus. The dog guy's corgi."

A shaft of sunlight suddenly spilled through a skylight, illuminating Charlotte.

She laughed at his expression. "Did you think I was talking about the guy?"

Nick frowned. He shrugged. And then he laughed. Jesus, but his emotions about this woman were all over the damn map. He wanted her to be happy, he wanted that more than anything. And yet . . . he didn't want her to date. What nonsense was that? *He* certainly wasn't going to make her happy. He had no claim to her. He was nobody, a bystander. And yet, he felt possessive. "Are you dating a man or a dog?"

"Both! Between you and me, I'm more interested in the dog." She giggled, then abruptly brought both hands down on the top of the kitchen bar. "Okay, pal, we're wasting daylight talking about dogs. Where is this mysterious box, anyway?"

He pointed to the dining room table. "I'll just get the coffee. Cream, right?"

"Yes, please."

He made them coffee, and they sat at his dining table and started to go through the file folders. There was no rhyme or reason to the way Nick's dad had stuffed things in the files. All of them were filled with random bits of paper. In one, Nick found a scorecard from a game of golf, an old drilling report, and the receipt for a diamond pendant his father had bought for his mother . . . at least he hoped it was for his mother.

"This is why I had to take over the files," Charlotte said, holding up a clothing tag from a shirt. "Your father, may God rest his soul, was a horrible record keeper."

"He was a horrible gambler, too," Nick said.

"*My* father, on the other hand, is so organized it's ridiculous. He keeps every single receipt, sorted by month and year and type of expenditure. He's even got a filing system for his tools, and if you borrow a hammer, you have to sign the checkout log in his workshop. Like a library." She looked up from the file she'd just gone through. "Once, he came over to fix a loose faucet handle on my bathroom sink, and lined up all his tools by size," she said, her eyes shimmering with amusement. "It actually took him longer to lay out those tools than it did to fix the loose handle. I kid you *not*."

"That must be where you get your love of oddball filing systems," Nick observed.

Charlotte giggled. She picked up another file, and several photos slid out of it, tumbling onto the dining table. "Oh, hey, look at this!" She picked up one of the photos and held it up.

It was a picture of Nick. He was about twenty-six and was standing in front of the small Learjet he'd had to sell after his dad died. He remembered the picture, although he hadn't seen it in years. They'd just finished extending the runway up by the main house to accommodate his jet, and he'd flown back from dropping his mother in Denver and landed on that strip.

That plane had way too much range for the kind of flying he did. It was overkill. But Nick hadn't cared then—what had mattered to him was having the plane.

He took the picture from Charlotte and studied it.

It had cost them a fortune to extend that runway, probably more than actual GDPs in some developing countries. Given the state of the family coffers today, it was astounding to him how easily they used to throw around money. Like they had a bottomless bucket of it. "I miss this plane," he said longingly.

"Your dad was really proud of you and your flying, you know," Charlotte said.

"Was he?" Nick asked absently.

"He used to say things like, *'Nick's going to be flying one of them big planes before long,'*" she said, mimicking his dad's voice.

Nick couldn't remember now what his dad thought about his flying—it was his mother who was always quick with an opinion. He wished he knew what his dad thought. He wished his dad were here so he could tell him that he gave it his best shot, but he couldn't fit his square-peg body into the round hole of running the ranch, and he was going to flight school.

He glanced at the younger version of himself. He was thinner then, he noted. And something else he found curious about the photo—he was smiling. That was what you'd call a shit-eating grin. He didn't smile like that anymore.

"You still want to, don't you?" Charlotte asked.

"Huh?" Nick handed her the picture to return to the file.

"You really want to fly. I mean big planes."

"I really do," he admitted. "Probably sounds dumb, a grown man who wants to fly airplanes."

"It sounds like a grown man with a passion. Not dumb."

"For me, that yearning is never going to leave me. It just gets stronger. From the first time I flew in a little crop duster with my uncle when I was six or seven, I have felt different in the air. Weightless. Like I was omnipotent some-how, able to see the world." He realized he was revealing his innermost thoughts, and felt himself flush. "I know it doesn't make a lot of sense."

"It makes perfect sense," Charlotte said. "On the other end of the spectrum, I feel like a sardine when I fly, crammed into a seat that's hardly big enough for a child. Half the time, I can't even see out the window."

Nick shook his head. "I should take you up sometime so you can experience it from my viewpoint."

"I would love that! But you said the cost of fuel was eating into the budget you'd allotted for flying. And you've flown twice with your boyfriend this month."

Nick chuckled. "You do keep your finger on the pulse of Saddlebush Land and Cattle, don't you?"

"That's why you're paying me, remember?"

That was one reason he was paying her. The other was less tangible. He was paying her to keep her right where she was. So he could suffer her insults and steal her lunch on occasion and mostly, just look at her.

Charlotte showed him the other pictures—one of his parents at some event, Luca and Hallie with a box of kittens, a few other old ones—then returned them to the file, and the file to the stack of files they'd examined. She took another one out of the box.

"I told you my passion," Nick said. "What's yours?"

She snorted without taking her eyes off the folder. "I think all of Three Rivers knows what my passion is. I want a family." She looked up at him. "That's it, that's all I've got. Nothing exciting or noteworthy."

"Why do you say it like that?" he asked,

confused by her apparent put-down of her desire.

"Because, Nicholas Nickleby, a modern woman is supposed to want it all. She's supposed to want a career and a family and some hobbies and passions on top of that, didn't you know? I have the hobbies down, but my passion, the thing I think about, is having a family. Trust me, having a passion to fly is a whole lot easier and probably a lot saner."

"So if you had the family, you wouldn't be working?"

"Not if I didn't have to. I like my job, don't get me wrong—but if I had it my way, I'd be at home with my kids, making dinner every night and helping with their schoolwork and being a supportive wife and entering my pies in pie contests."

"Wait—you bake *pies?* Why do I not know this?"

"I *don't* bake pies, and that is exactly the point! I've only made one pie in my life and it took forever and I overbaked it. The *point* is that my fantasy includes that. All of that. In my fantasy, I am Wonder Woman to people who love me." She picked up another file. "Now who has the dumb passion?"

"Not you," he said. "I think it's an outstanding passion or desire or whatever you want to call it. What sucks is that we both want what we can't have."

That brought her head up. "You think I can't have that?" She sounded alarmed.

"No, no, that is not what I meant. Of course you can have it. I meant right now, that's all." She didn't look convinced. "You *will* have it, Charlotte," he said, trying to reassure her.

Her eyes narrowed. "Do you *really* think so, Nick? My family says that all the time, but sometimes I have to wonder if it's not in the cards for me."

"I think you will, if for no other reason than you want it. I've never known anyone quite like you—when you put your mind to something, it happens. You're pretty amazing that way."

She smiled a little lopsidedly. "You don't really think that," she scoffed.

He snorted. "I really think it. You're amazing."

"Damn, Nick, if you keep up that kind of talk, I might not charge you as much for this overtime. Okay, but what about you? Are you going to make flying happen? Or are you going to grump around for the rest of your life?"

He couldn't suppress his smile. "I don't grump around. As a person once said, 'That's just the kind of person I am, *Nick.*' "

She laughed. "You didn't answer the question."

He didn't know how to answer her, exactly. "I want to fly, more than anything," he said. "But Dad specifically left the running of the ranch to me, and you know as well as I do that it would take some maneuvering to get out of it now." He averted his gaze and shrugged. "Life gets in the way of the best-laid plans, right?" He picked up another file and opened it.

She was silent for a moment. "I hope you find your happy. I really do."

"I'm not sure it's possible." A thought occurred to him, and he laughed wryly. "They say I was born with a broken heart, you know."

"What?"

He grinned at her look of shock. "I never told you? Apparently I cried a lot when I was a baby, and my maternal great-grandmother theorized it was because I was born with a broken heart."

"That's absurd!"

"I'm starting to believe there might be some truth to it. I know I'm a grump, as you say, but it's not because I want to be. Dad's death cut a new road through our family, and honestly? I haven't been able to find my stride on it."

Charlotte's gaze went soft, and she reached across the table and grabbed his hand, squeezing it. "You weren't born with a broken heart, Nick. If your heart was broken, would you accept a hand-me-down pig? Would you keep Frank hobbling around as long as you have? Would you take on runaway cows and love them?"

He laughed. "You make me sound like a moron."

"If you were born with a broken heart, how

could you care so much about your siblings, or even me for that matter?"

He turned his palm up and wrapped his fingers around hers. "That might be the nicest thing you've ever said to me. I do care about you, Charlotte."

"I *know* you do. I also know you don't like to show your feelings, and that you have a lot of rules when it comes to us. I mean a *lot*. Sometimes I think, maybe you should just write up a manual—"

"Okay," he said, squeezing her hand. "So I went overboard. I want to be careful because I do care about you."

She smiled and withdrew her hand from his. "That's what I'm saying. You *do* care. You care about a lot of things, and you *feel* them, and maybe your heart is a little bruised by tragedy and disappointment. But you weren't born with a broken heart. You were born with a big open one, and from what I know about you, it's working just fine." She smiled pertly. "It's your personality that needs work."

He laughed.

Charlotte looked away and opened another file. Nick didn't. He watched her brow furrowing as she read over the file, and how she tugged on her earlobe. A habit he'd noticed when she was concentrating on something.

He couldn't sit here staring at her like she was

some sort of work of art. But he couldn't seem to turn back to the files and the history of his family and his father, either. It was both comforting and arousing to look at her.

He had to get a grip of himself. Squishy, warm feelings that made him want to squeeze a puppy or kick a rock or kiss her were crazy. So he forced his gaze away. He had to stop feeling things when Charlotte was around. What good did it do?

"Ta-da!" Charlotte said suddenly, and held up a pink sheet of paper. "An invoice from Tim Mitchell of Corpus Christi. *Damn* it—I was hoping he was a fraud and a cheat, and we could have him arrested."

"Let me see?" Nick asked.

She handed him the invoice. "Wait a minute," she said as Nick began to read. He looked up.

Charlotte was lifting up yellow and pink papers. Invoices. Receipts. She handed them to Nick. He looked through them—they were all for work done in the old oil fields. One was from a survey company to examine the right-of-way and easements into the ranch from the southern end, as if his father had anticipated having a road built. Another was for a feasibility study to determine if oil tanks could be built for storage. When the wells had operated before, they'd trucked out the oil.

"What is all this?" Charlotte asked. "I don't remember any of these things."

Understanding began to dawn on Nick. "You wouldn't. Dad was looking to see if he could squeeze blood from a turnip."

"Huh?"

"I may be wrong about this, but these invoices are all fishing expeditions. I think he wanted to open those wells. They're dry for all intents and purposes, we know that. My grandmother will tell you they ran dry fifty years ago. But my dad wanted to see if he could get at least something out of them to pay off his debts. All he did was create more debt." He put the invoices down. He shoved the fingers of both hands through his hair. "He got himself into a vicious cycle. I wish he'd talked to me about it. Maybe I could have helped him somehow." He dropped his hands and pushed the invoices away from him.

"Are they all unpaid?" Charlotte asked, picking them up.

"I don't know. We'll need to investigate them." He stood up and walked into the kitchen, his mind reeling. And then, forgetting why he'd come into the kitchen, he braced his hands against the sink and privately cursed his dad. He had loved him, had thought he was a god among men, and in many ways he was. But he'd also created a mess that he'd left behind for them to fix, and Nick resented the hell out of him for it.

"What are we going to do?" Charlotte asked.

"I'll have to talk to George and figure out

what's been paid and what hasn't. If these companies are sending notices, I don't know where they're going."

Charlotte's head was bent over the paper. She was studying each one. "Were his gambling debts really that bad?"

"They were really that bad," Nick confirmed. It was an admission the Princes never made outside the family. "He deceived us all."

Charlotte quietly put the invoices into the file folder. "I loved Charlie. He was great to me. He was a great boss."

"A great dad, too," he added softly.

Charlotte slowly slid down into her seat until her head was propped against the back of the chair. She closed her eyes. "I don't know about you, but I'm so . . . *disappointed.*"

"Join the club."

"Okay, that's it," Charlotte said, and suddenly sat up. "It is what it is, Nick."

"Why do people always say that?" he asked. "Like I don't know what it is?"

"Because they don't know what else to say," she said, and stood up. "And sometimes, people are ready for a snack." She walked around the long bar that separated the kitchen from the rest of the living area, passed him, still braced against the sink, and opened the fridge door like she lived here and bought groceries. With a hand on one hip, and the fingers of her other hand drumming on the fridge door, she said, "This looks too healthy. How much lettuce does one man need?"

Nick straightened up, reached around her, and shut the fridge door, and then reached above her to open a cabinet. He pulled out a box of donuts. Not just any donuts—Jo's Java donuts. To say Charlotte's face lit with delight was an understatement. She beamed. "How did you *know?*" she squealed.

"Are you kidding? Do you not recall your most recent staff meeting demands?"

She opened the box and took one out. "You love them, too, cowboy, don't act like you're above donuts." She took a bite. "You ate three that day."

"What else was I going to do while you were ranting at me?"

She held the donut up to his mouth. He took a generous bite, and she laughed. The sparkle in her eye had a way of making even his worst moments feel sunny and conquerable. He looked at the flecks of glaze on her lips, and watched as she deliberately swept them away with the tip of her tongue. She raised the donut up, as if she intended to eat the rest of it, but they stood there, the two of them looking at each other, so close that a slip of paper could scarcely fit between them. The air felt as if it were cracking around them, like it was a thing, giving way—

And then something hit the glass door.

Chapter Sixteen

"Rufus!" Charlotte was going to have her dog committed to the Home for Useless Dogs. Not only had he literally just run headlong into a sliding glass door, he'd left a huge smear of mud and dirty dog water. She stuffed the rest of the donut in her mouth as she marched to the door to give him a piece of her mind.

"Don't open the door!" Nick said quickly.

Rufus sat down, his tongue hanging out the side of his mouth, his tail swishing on the porch and against Pepper so hard that she moved away from it.

"What am I supposed to do with him?" Charlotte demanded through a mouthful of donut.

"Ignore him. He'll settle down."

"I meant, like, in an existential sense." She glared at Rufus. But Rufus was incapable of reading a room and continued to grin up at her while his drool dripped to the porch. Charlotte turned away from his pleading eyes, and when she did, she noticed a Harlan Coben book on the small end table next to a chair. "Hey." She pointed at the book. The significance of that particular book drifted over her thoughts like snowfall. It wasn't coincidence. He'd read the Harlan Coben book because . . .

Well, because of her.

Something fluttery went through Charlotte. She picked the book up and then looked at Nick.

Nick seemed almost embarrassed. "Don't make a big deal out of it."

It was genetically impossible for Charlotte to not make a big deal out of it. She grinned.

"Just put it down," he said, gesturing to the end table. "So what, I read a book. Don't get that *I win* look on your face. There was a lot of discussion and I wanted to check it out, that's all."

Except that was not all. She put the book down. "Did you like it?"

He looked at his feet. "Yeah, it was good."

Oh, but she was terribly pleased with this development. Nick folded his arms self-consciously across his body. He looked around the room. He clearly did not care to be discovered in this. "I may order another one," he said, and glanced up.

"*Order?* Dude, you need to come with me to a bookstore."

"See? You're making a big deal out of it. I don't need anyone to escort me to the bookstore."

"Yes, you do. I'm so happy that you have something to do out here besides staring at your navel!" she exclaimed as she started back across the room to the bar where he was standing.

"Do you honestly think I don't have anything to do here?"

"Seriously? You don't even have Netflix. You are literally a caveman." She came to a halt right in front of him, beaming at him with this small victory.

"I have plenty to do. I happen to be reading a book about airplane engines at the moment. Would you like to hear about that?"

"Yes!" she said with feigned enthusiasm. "Promise to start at the beginning and do not leave out a *single* word."

"You are *such* a smart-ass, Charlotte Bailey," he said, smiling at her with affection she could actually feel in her breast.

"I know, Nick Prince. That's what you like about me." She lifted her chin and smiled up at him. "You like me a lot. More than you want me to know. More than you want to admit to yourself."

"Whatever gave you that idea?"

His gaze moved over her face, and Charlotte felt like she'd been stung by baby bees all over her body. Her skin was sizzling, everywhere he looked. "I just know. I know you." She was a reckless, stupid fool, because more words popped out of her mouth that shouldn't have. "And I know you want to kiss me right now. Just like I knew it the other day. I made you kiss me, you know."

He didn't move. One brow arched dubiously as his gaze moved lower, to the V in her shirt. "You *made* me?"

"Mm-hmm."

"No, you didn't."

"Yes, I did. I stood close, like now. I smiled. I may have batted my lashes at you a time or two."

"Are you saying you came on to me?" He touched her collarbone and traced his finger across her skin along the neckline of her shirt.

"I guess I did," she agreed. "But subtly, because I didn't want to freak you out. I'm not trying to freak you out now, either, but, dude, you want to kiss me again."

One corner of Nick's sexy mouth tipped up and he shook his head. "You think you know so much," he said, and casually swept a curl from her collarbone. "The thing is, if I wanted to kiss you, Charlotte, I'd damn well do it. I'd kiss that smug look right off your pretty face."

Her smile deepened. "You mean you'd be kissing this sexy look off my face," she said, pointing to herself. "And then what would you do?"

"I'd have to keep kissing you so you'd stop talking," he said to her mouth.

"That's not physically possible. But let's agree you gave it the old college try. Then what?"

"Then?" He slid his hand down her bare arm. "I don't think you want to know." He lifted his gaze to hers. "I don't want to freak you out," he said, borrowing a phrase from her. He laid his hand against her neck. "I don't think you could take it."

Charlotte was vibrating from inside out. Her legs felt unsteady. "Yes, I can. What would you do?"

He moved his other hand to her back and pulled her into his body, all muscle and bone. Charlotte was indescribably inflamed. She was beginning to realize that she didn't care what he did to her after he kissed her face off, as long as he did it.

"First, I'd take your clothes off. One piece at a time," he said, and sank his fingers into her curls as he pulled her head forward. He bent down, nibbled her earlobe, and sent little white-hot shivers through her. He whispered, "With my mouth."

Oh. *Oh.* Charlotte steadied herself with her hands to his waist and turned her head slightly so that her cheek was against his mouth. "And then what?"

"Then I would use my hand," he said, and ran one over her breast, "and touch you in all the places you're afraid I'll touch you." He gently squeezed her breast. *"Because you can't take it,"* he added in a whisper.

That sharp intake of air was hers. The sizzle in her skin was radiating through every limb. "I can take it. I'm not afraid. And then what?"

He pressed his lips to her neck, lingering there a moment, and then said softly, "*Then,* Charlotte, I would slide my cock into you so long and so slow that you would come before I could get all the way inside you."

Charlotte's breath hitched. Her heart was fluttering madly in her breast. "That is *intense,*" she said breathlessly.

Nick's hold of her went tighter. She could feel his erection against her belly. "What are *you* going to do?" he muttered.

She turned her face to his. His dark blue eyes looked like oceans, deep with desire. "I'm going to let you."

A light flickered in Nick's dark eyes. Someone drew a deep breath, but Charlotte didn't know which one of them had. All she knew was that his lips were on hers, teasing her with a feathery little kiss that was hardly a kiss at all, but one that struck her like a bolt of lightning, streaking through every vein, striking at every neuron.

She felt weightless. Wasn't that what he'd said about flying? She was flying and she was weightless, and the only thing tethering her right now was her grip on his trim waist. She kissed him back, her tongue sliding in between the seam of his lips.

After a moment, Nick lifted his head and caressed her face. "Charlotte?"

She waited, thinking he was going to say

something, but Nick smiled and shook his head. And then, without warning, he picked her up and twirled her around, setting her on the kitchen countertop.

All of Charlotte's feminine senses revved into overdrive and careened recklessly into her groin. She wrapped her legs around his waist, took his head in her hands, and kissed him. He pressed his hardness against her, caressed her body with one hand. The tension between them escalated quickly—something clattered to the planked floors, and one of the dogs barked somewhere in the distance, but all Charlotte cared about was Nick's mouth on hers, his body pressed against hers. She was out of control, on a sudden and ardent carnal bender, and amazingly, they hadn't really gotten started.

This thing between them, this fire that seemed to erupt out of nowhere, was just like the night of the Christmas party. She'd become hypersensitive just kissing him, because she was acutely aware of every place he kissed her or touched her. His hands roamed her body, sliding up under her shirt to her breasts and sliding into the waist of her shorts, his fingers digging into the flesh of her hips. Her nose was filled with his scent— musk and cardamom and wild honeysuckle. Or maybe she imagined it—all she knew was that he smelled like an aphrodisiac and she was inhaling it like oxygen.

Nick pressed against her, and Charlotte pressed back, wishing he'd unleash that bad boy and do what he'd threatened. She forgot any question of how this might not be the best thing for her in the long run. She forgot how pissed she'd been at him the day after the Christmas party. She forgot that he was her boss and a grouch on his best day. None of that seemed to matter when a very handsome, sexy, *virile* man was kissing you and his hands were on you, and he was groaning softly like it wasn't enough.

It had been a while since she'd had sex, and if she was going to share this moment, this entry back into the world of full-throated sex, she wanted to share it with Nick. Not Dog Guy, not Book Guy, no one but Nick.

His hands swept up to her breasts again, squeezing, and Charlotte wrapped her arms around his neck. It was always Nick, wasn't it? For the last few years, it had been Nick, because he was so damn hot and they were a raging bonfire of need and desire together, and as he unbuttoned her shorts and slipped his hand into the waistband of her panties, she couldn't think another coherent thought. She was going to explode all over his kitchen if he wasn't careful.

Nick suddenly faded away from her. Charlotte almost fell over, but she caught herself with both hands on the counter.

Nick took a step back and wiped the back of

his hand across his mouth. His eyes were so full of want they almost looked black. He kept them locked on her as he ripped off his shirt and tossed it aside. He stepped back in between her legs. "Put your legs around my waist," he commanded, and when she did, he hoisted her off the counter and began to move across the kitchen, carrying her down the hall.

Neither of them spoke. He'd actually achieved the impossible and had kissed her into silence. They merely looked at each other and allowed an entirely silent conversation to pass between them. *We're doing this. We're not going to think about the last time, or the next time. We are going to go in with all guns blazing and let the chips fall where they may.* "Got it," Charlotte whispered.

"What?" he asked breathlessly as he moved into his bedroom. He deposited her on his bed and stood over her, kicking off his shoes, undoing his jeans, and then shoving them down his legs, revealing his naked body to her.

This man was *cut,* his body trim and toned and hard. Is that what ranch work did to you? And then there was his erection, thick and hard, and she was ready. She moved to take off her shirt, but Nick grabbed her hand. "Nope. I'm going to do that." And then he smiled so provocatively that Charlotte's blood began to rush in anticipation.

He lifted her arms and slowly slid the shirt over her head. He threw it aside, his gaze on her breasts. He reached behind her and unhooked her bra, and with two fingers, slid that undergarment down her arms. He drew a shallow breath as he looked at her bare breasts, and with the palm of his hand, he pushed her back as he skimmed her abdomen, down to the waist of her shorts, and began the long torturous slide of the clothing from her body.

Charlotte was as bare as he was. They stared at each other for one highly charged moment, each of them taking in the other, and then at last their eyes met. It was one final unspoken check-in.

Charlotte answered his silent question by slowly leaning backward, until she was lying on his bed. Her curly hair pillowed her, and she couldn't help it—she smiled.

Nick came over her, holding himself above her and dipping down to kiss her. "I *knew* it," she whispered, and caressed his face. "I knew you wanted me."

"Funny, I was thinking the same thing about you," he said, and began a gentle descent over her body with his mouth and hands. Charlotte closed her eyes. She arched her back, sank her fingers into his hair. She allowed the sensations to wash over her, riding along on the wave as he moved between her legs, his mouth and tongue dipping and sliding, making her crazy with want. She found his shoulders, dug her fingers into them, trying not to buck against him but powerless to stop herself. When Nick rose up and put his body between her legs, he reached across her to a bedside table and pulled open a drawer so hard that it came out of the table. But he managed to snag a condom out of it before the drawer fell to the rug.

"Want me to help? I can help," she said, reaching for it, eager to be on to the next round.

He pushed her hand away and quickly rolled it on. In the next moment, the tip of him was pressing against her body.

"Okay," she said, breathing raggedly now. She rose up and kissed him, dotting his face with them. "Okay," she said again. "Let's do this."

Nick smiled. He slid his tip into her and stopped.

"No," Charlotte said, and cupped his face. "Don't tease me. Do you want to make me beg? Because I will," she said. "I have no problem doing that."

He chuckled low and slid in a little deeper. He leaned down and gently kissed her cheek. She could feel her body pulsing around his, trying to draw him in. "Before I go all in, I want you to remember one thing."

"Okay. Tell me," she said, closing her eyes. "Hurry up." She expected him to say something about how this was just scratching an itch, that they still had to work together. *Yes, yes, okay, let's go.*

He wiggled around a little, slipping out of her,

then sliding the tip in once more. "You know all those emails you send me? The color-coded filing system? Registering the Fred Savages?" he whispered in a very sexy voice as he shifted inside her.

Her eyes flew open. "What are you doing right now? *Yes,* I remember! But why are you *talking* about that?" She was panting. She caught his hips, tried to push him in.

Nick smiled wickedly. "Consider this payback."

"No!" she whimpered.

"Oh yeah," he said, and moved inside her again before descending to her breast and taking it into his mouth, nibbling lightly at the peak.

It was highly pleasurable torture, but it was torture. Nick was right—she was going to climax before he ever was fully inside her. He shifted again, a little deeper, and moved to the other breast.

Charlotte arched her back into his mouth, thrust her hands into his hair. She rubbed her leg against him, slid her fingers down his back, even reached between them, trying everything she could to spur him on.

But Nick was steady. He pushed in another inch. His breathing was ragged, too, and she squeezed him, making him groan. He caught her bottom lip between his teeth, then kissed her hard before pressing his forehead to hers.

"You're making me crazy," she said, and kissed

his cheek. "Mission accomplished. I have been tortured for all the things I ever said to you. I need you to move, now, Nick. I need you to *pump*."

He kissed her neck, feathered her chest with kisses.

"What is the *matter* with you?"

"You," he said, and smiled as he reached his hand between their bodies and began to stroke her. "You are always the matter with me." And with that, he thrust into her so deep that Charlotte gasped. Her knees came up; she wrapped one leg around his back. He began to move, and she was there for it, meeting each thrust, gasping with euphoria. Tiny little earthquakes reverberated inside her body. It had been a million years or more since she'd felt like this, since she'd wanted to feel another human being quite like this.

Nick began to move faster, and when she opened her eyes, she found him looking at her. There was something in his dark blue eyes that she wasn't sure she was supposed to see, something that she sensed had percolated up, and she realized in one stunning moment as her arousal reached its natural end that she had seen that look once before—one night after a Christmas party.

Only, this time, she wasn't imagining it.

Nick *did* care for her. And when she cried out, it was in part her release and in part the confirmation that the sparks between them were very real. She cared for him, too, and she had for a long time.

The light around them seemed to grow brighter and brighter as Nick moved, and in a moment, he followed her, growling his release with one final thrust.

He slowed his pace then, kissed her neck, her cheek, and then her mouth, lingering there until his body stopped moving. He kissed her tenderly, with regard. Charlotte wouldn't try to understand him just now. She only wanted to bask in it. There were emotions bubbling in her that she hadn't counted on. This is what happened when desires were left unattended for too long.

Nick slowly lowered himself onto her. She wrapped her arms around him. There was nothing left of her—she'd released it all. She'd let him see how she truly felt about him, had left it all on their private playing field. It was his to do with what he wanted now.

She couldn't think about what was next. She couldn't think about anything but being with Nick like this, and how safe and comfortable she felt with him, and how she wished he would see he felt that way, too, and let go like she had. Maybe he had. Maybe the sea of their lives had turned over on itself while they were in his bed, and everything was new.

They remained like that for a few moments until Charlotte's stomach began to growl. Nick lifted his head and looked at her. "What can I say?" she asked, grinning. "It was quite a workout."

He smiled, and he kissed her again, and he rolled off the bed. "Stay there. I'll bring you a donut."

He walked out of the room, completely bare. "That's about the sexiest thing anyone has ever said to me," she said softly.

Chapter Seventeen

When Nick left Charlotte in his bed, she was naked and munching on a donut, looking quite pleased with herself, and it was an image he suspected he'd hold on to for a very long time. She watched him dress to go out and feed the animals.

There was a bit of a spring in Nick's step as he went outside and fed the dogs, the horse, and the pig. He'd almost forgotten how great a man could feel after some wall-banging sex. Especially with an enthusiastic lover like Charlotte. He could tell she was one who liked to steer the boat, and next time, he thought he'd allow it.

Would there be a next time?

Nope, he wasn't going to do that today. He wasn't going to box this up and put it in some impossible place inside him. He was going to enjoy the moment.

But when he returned to the bedroom, Charlotte was wearing her shirt and her panties and sitting cross-legged on his bed. Her smile was not shy—she didn't have a smile at all. She was just watching him.

Nick leaned against the door frame and folded his arms across his chest. "What's up, Lot?"

"Nothing! I'm just waiting."

"For . . . ?"

"For . . . for any announcement you think you might want to make," she said, and slowly arched a brow.

"What sort of announcement?"

"Oh, I don't know. Something you think you might need to get off your chest?"

He had no idea what she was talking about.

"The thing is, if you have an announcement, I'd rather hear it now instead of, you know . . . at breakfast."

He suddenly understood. He was not going to make any announcement. He was feeling things for Charlotte he'd not felt at this magnitude for any other woman. He was feeling fantastic and unsteady, and so many emotions were swirling in him like some freakish carnival ride that it was a wonder he wasn't sick. But one emotion that was *not* stirring in him was a sudden desire to disentangle himself from her. Not only did he not want her to go, he didn't want to return to the world of work. He wanted this day to stretch on forever, or until one of them did something stupid.

He pushed away from the door frame. "Yes, Charlotte, there is something I think I should say," he said gravely.

She glanced down at her hands, and sighed wearily. "Okay, Nick. Get it off your chest."

"I don't want to hear about this later, if it's all the same to you."

She clucked her tongue and looked at the window. "Just say it."

"Okay, here goes. I installed some cow scratchers and I thought you might like to see them."

She was silent for one long moment. She turned her head to him again. "Don't mess with me, Nick."

"I'm not messing with you. I installed them, and I want to show you. But you better not make fun of me."

"*That's* your big announcement?"

"Yep."

"What about—"

"Nope," he said with a single shake of his head.

Charlotte's smile of happiness returned in full force and speared his heart. "You are such a *jerk*," she said, and threw a pillow at him.

Nick deftly caught it and, with it, launched himself onto the bed and caught her in his arms. He kissed her, tangled his fingers in her hair. "I hate to ask you to put on pants, but if you want to see my cow scratchers, you're probably going to want them. Do you want to see my cow scratchers?"

"Like . . . more than anything," she said.

"I'll get the ATV."

By the time Charlotte appeared on his back

porch, Nick had pulled his ATV around and had loaded the dogs into the wagon on the back. She had taken one of his gardening hats and shoved it down onto her curls. He watched her walk down the steps, and wondered why he'd never noticed how sexily she moved. Everything she did right now exuded some sort of sexual message to his brain.

Charlotte popped into the passenger seat. "So cow scratchers. Really?"

"You'd want to scratch something, too, if you never got to take a bath." He put his hand on her tanned knee and left it here. Like they'd been doing this for months or even years. Like this had been them all along.

He drove down a two-track dirt road that cut through some acreage and came up on the side of a pasture where the cows were grazing. Three Rivers had a lot more cattle than this, raised for beef, which Nick moved around so they wouldn't overgraze. But his personal cows, all seven of them, got to do as they pleased. He pulled up next to a corral. There was a pond in the pasture, full from some summer rains they'd had recently, and a pair of cows were standing in it.

"There it is," Nick said, and pointed to steel poles with a bar running horizontally between them that he and Rafe had erected. The two vertical bars were covered with what looked like giant blue spherical scrub brushes. From the horizontal pole were two smaller scrub brushes on rollers that hung down. It so happened that one of the cows was rubbing her side against one of the vertical brushes.

Charlotte laughed. "What are the smaller ones for?"

"Their heads," he said. He reached down to a sack between them and pulled out two cold beers. He opened one and handed it to Charlotte. He opened the other, then tapped the neck of his bottle to hers. "Cheers."

"To cow scratchers." She drank. "What about Frank?"

"What about him?"

"If these cows get one, Frank should have one, too."

"What next? Priscilla?"

"Absolutely. Fair play, Nick."

He returned his hand to her knee as the dogs decided to jump out of the back and have a look around. The sun was behind them, the shadows starting to lengthen. Charlotte propped one leg against the dash and asked him who he thought would have a good softball team. They chatted about that for a while, and then their conversation turned to the Harlan Coben book.

There was never was an awkward moment with Charlotte. There never seemed to be space to fill when they were together. Conversation flowed easily. Charlotte was one of those people who came along in one's life and filled the air with happiness and hope. It was hard to imagine a woman as buoyant as her having a bad day. She was funny, and she could laugh at almost anything, including herself. She almost fell out of the ATV when he described her batting stance, she was laughing so hard.

It felt invigorating to be out in nature with someone like her. It made him feel invincible to feel sexual again, to know how brightly desire could burn. At one point, he leaned over to kiss her, and before he knew it, she had straddled his lap. Yep, he was right—she wanted to steer the boat. "What about the cows?" he asked, brushing her hair back from her face.

"Will they be offended?"

He never answered—they were startled by a loud splash. Charlotte squeezed her eyes shut. "Are you kidding me?"

She slid out of his lap and they both looked at the pond. The two cows who'd been cooling off were suddenly scrambling to get out as Rufus swam in their direction. "What am I going to do with that dog?" she moaned.

Nick laughed. They started back to the house, the dogs loping alongside the ATV, Rufus pausing to shake off his coat every so often and then racing to catch back up. Nick pulled the ATV into a garage, and when they walked back out into the sun, they were standing directly in front of Charlotte's car. They both looked at it.

"Hmm," she said. "I guess I ought to—"

"Eat," he said.

She looked at him.

He smiled at her. "I've got some quinoa in the house," he said, pronouncing it *kwin-no-ah.* Some habits were hard to break.

"Oh my God, it's *quinoa!*" she said, bending backward a little. "Is that all?"

"Nope. I've got some tofu, too. I like to make this dish—"

"Say no more," she said, holding up a hand. "This, I have to see, the tofu-quinoa dish. My only regret is that I didn't bring anything to contribute."

He put his arm around her shoulders. "You can reciprocate by doing the dishes afterward."

"Be still my beating heart," she said, and wrapped her arm around his waist.

They walked back to his house, their arms around each other. The dogs had found the porch, and both of them were stretched out on their sides. Rufus was snoring.

In the kitchen, he started to pull things together to make his dish, but one thing led to another, and somehow, they ended up on his couch, their passion as intense as it had been earlier in the afternoon. When they were done, they got up to finish making the meal. Charlotte's hair looked like she'd been through a windstorm, and her cheeks were red from all the kissing he'd done of her face.

They talked, of all things, about interior decorating as they put the final touches on their meal. "I should have *you* decorate the office," she said, and held up her wineglass in a toast. "You have excellent taste."

He lifted his glass, too, and tapped hers. "I think we should leave it the way it is. The decor of bright expectations."

Charlotte laughed. "You mean ranch lite. I don't know why Charlie thought he ought to make those offices look like a barn."

"Another mystery that will go unanswered," Nick agreed.

Charlotte insisted on cleaning up. Night had fallen, and he wanted her to stay. When she came out of the kitchen, he put his arms around her waist. "I'm going to make you an offer you can't refuse."

Charlotte gasped. "A bath in the ginormous bathtub I've heard about?"

That was not what he had in mind, but Nick grinned. "That's just what I was about to say."

So they took a bath in his extra-long bathtub. Charlotte had a grand time making fun of the bath pillow he'd hung on one end. But as big as the tub was, the two of them hardly fit, and there were feet in places they should not have been.

Nick had never been so crammed and so

content. This, right here, was the reason people wrote love songs. Steam lifted off the sudsy water, and with nothing but a few candles to light the bathroom, they had a view of a star-studded Texas night sky so vast that it glittered down on them.

"I get it," Charlotte said. Her curls were slicked back on her head, her breasts riding the surface. "I get why you put these windows in and why you like a bath. I'm even starting to get why you live out here all by your lonesome."

"I needed some space," he said. "The ranch is huge, but sometimes, it feels pretty damn small."

"Still," she said, tracing a line across the water with her finger, "you must get lonely."

"Sometimes," he admitted.

She smiled sympathetically. "And sometimes you can be in a room full of people and still feel alone."

"True," he said. He didn't know how to explain his solitude, really. It was nothing anyone had done to him. It was more a need to be who he was, and not who everyone wanted him to be.

"Do you think you'll always live out here by yourself?" she asked curiously.

"I'm not by myself. I have three animals and some cows that come up to the fence every morning for a weather report."

"But I mean . . . will you live out here away

from people? Are you going to remain a mysterious recluse?"

He grabbed her big toe, which had found its way to his scrotum. "That remains to be seen," he said, and lifted her foot from the water and put her toe in his mouth.

Charlotte giggled.

When the water cooled, they were in his bed again, no questions asked, no *should I stay?* It felt like the most natural thing to do. They reached for each other at the same time, taking their time and moving slow and easy.

Nick couldn't say when they drifted off to sleep. It seemed like one minute he was inside her, and the next, she was leaning over him, her curls brushing his face. But he was asleep, because he awoke with a start. Charlotte was leaning over him again, her fingers on his cheek. "I have to go."

"What time is it?"

"Six."

"Wait," he said, reaching for her. "Don't run off."

"I have to. I have to get ready for work." She leaned down and pecked him on the mouth. "Promise me you won't make it weird today."

"Don't *you* make it weird," he countered, and yawned.

"As if," she said, and popped up. "Bye, Nick!"

He listened to her go out the door. He listened

to her tell Rufus to stop licking her, tell Pepper what a *good* dog she was. He listened to her go down the steps and say good-bye to Priscilla and Frank, and explain to Priscilla, presumably, that she was too huge to get into her car. And then he listened to her drive away.

When he couldn't hear her car anymore, he listened to the silence fill his house again, creeping in under the doors and through the windows, slowly pressing in until it had filled every corner, every closet.

Nick didn't make it to the office until half past nine. When he pulled into the parking lot, he saw her blue bike tucked in behind the rocking chairs.

He steeled himself. He didn't know how this was going to go in the office, now that the sun was up and blazing, now that Sunday had faded into a very pleasant memory. He didn't know if she would pretend that nothing had happened between them, or if she would want or expect him to be different. He opened the glass door to a rush of cold air and stepped inside. He could see her curly blond hair above the computer screen. He looked at the seating area with its tropical colors and thought, for one insane moment, about throw pillows.

Then he made himself walk. "Good morning, Charlotte," he said.

"Good morning, Nicholas Nickleby. You're late."

"Thanks for watching the clock on my behalf."

"I can't help it. It's enormous and it's right over your head."

Nick glanced up at the big Roman numeral clock. He continued to walk across the office.

"How was your weekend?" she asked as he reached the reception desk.

He paused and turned to look at her. She kept her gaze on her computer screen. "Fan-fucking-tastic. How was yours?"

A grin lit Charlotte's face. She swiveled around in her seat. "Same!" She stood up and handed him a green folder.

"Were there any—"

She shoved a pink message slip at him. "Yes. Colton called. Something about needing a lot of practice." One of her brows quirked up. "You will be happy to know that I restrained myself and did not offer an opinion."

"That's an interesting turn of office dynamics, you not offering an opinion. Good to know."

"I'll keep you posted if I have one to offer today, but surprisingly, I'm feeling a little mellow."

"Well," he said. "I'll have to do my best to keep it that way."

"Okay, then," she said.

"Okay, then." He carried on to his office, aware that he was sporting the goofiest grin a grown man could possibly sport. But he had no idea how to get it off his face.

Chapter Eighteen

Over the next few weeks, Charlotte worked very hard not to put a label on whatever it was that was happening between her and Nick, but everyone else in Three Rivers was determined to slap one on them. She supposed it couldn't be helped—she and Nick were openly spending time together.

Soon after that remarkable Sunday, Nick came to her house. She made a salad and salmon after he assured her he had no emotional attachment to fish.

"How can you discriminate?" she teased him.

"I don't know. It's easy to discriminate against fish."

They sat on her back porch and laughed about Mariah's ongoing battle with the UPS man, who refused to come out of his truck and tended to toss her packages to the door. They talked about Charlotte's garden, which was bursting with squash and cucumbers and cantaloupe—so much that she could stock a small grocery. They packed some of the overripe fruit and vegetables for Nick to take home to Priscilla.

When dinner was finished, the two of them had

cleaned the kitchen between kissing and fondling. "What happened to us?" Charlotte asked, amazed by this turn in their relationship. "It wasn't that long ago we were fighting over a filing system."

"Hey," Nick said, pointing his finger at her. "We're not done fighting about that." And then he nuzzled her neck.

She insisted that he stay that night so they could stream something from Netflix. "It's called Netflix and chill," she said.

"Who calls it that?"

"*Everyone* calls it that, Herman's Hermit," she informed him with a shake of her head.

Nick seemed transfixed by the movie she chose. "That was really good," he said. "You do this every day? Stream movies or whatever?"

"Every day!" She laughed as if that were ridiculous. "Not *every* day."

It was every day. What was she supposed to do? It wasn't like she lived in the middle of nowhere with a pig and a horse and cow scratchers to keep her busy.

Nick also admired the silk strips she'd hand painted in that burst of creative energy in a search for appropriate hobbies. They were still hanging from the ceiling fan. "What are you going to do with them?" he asked.

She studied the fluttering strips of silk. "I have no idea."

He took one off the fan and walked to her

window and held it up against one of her sheer drapes. Charlotte gasped—the early evening light coming through the window and the sheer drapes made the art she'd painted look almost ghostly. It was a beautiful contrast and looked expensive.

"You need two more, and you've got enough for these windows," he said.

"That's a great idea, Nick! You're an interior-decorating genius."

"No, I'm not," he said sheepishly.

Those strips had been hanging from her ceiling fan for weeks, and all kinds of eyes had seen them, and not one set of those eyes had any suggestions for them. Nick had a knack for it, whether he wanted to admit it or not.

He came again the next night, and this time, they picked squash from the garden and made a squash casserole. "Just like Frederica used to make," he said, then slanted a look at Charlotte. "She was our cook."

"You had a *cook?*" she asked, both amused and fascinated by it. What had that life been like? To come home from school and find your room cleaned and tidied, your meals cooked for you, and your horses ready to ride. Nick had never given off that air of wealth like Charlie had. Nick had always seemed like a regular guy to her.

Charlotte also made a pie. An *apple* pie, as she thought America's favorite would be the easiest to tackle. But the crust wasn't flaky like her mom's and the apples didn't soften as much as she would have liked. So she smothered the pie in ice cream, and if Nick had any complaints, he didn't voice them. She watched him eat the pie and imagined the two of them like this in five years. Ten years. As two old people. In a house, with a pie, and their dogs, and their children and their children's children.

She was startled out of that dream when Nick said, "May I ask you something personal?"

That didn't sound good. Did he want to know her religious beliefs? Her political leanings? "To stop making pies?"

"I would never ask you that." He looked down at his plate. "I've been wondering about Dog Guy," he said, and glanced up. "Are you still seeing him? Or . . . what?"

What? was the million-dollar question here, wasn't it? Charlotte didn't know quite what to say. She didn't want to admit that she was all in on Nick and maybe had been for a while. It was too soon for confessions. In spite of the great sex and compatibility, there were some outstanding questions she had. But damn if she could think of even one in that moment. She averted her gaze, concentrated on sawing through an undercooked piece of apple. "No."

Nick didn't ask anything more. He made no comment and she offered no explanation. She took that to mean they had an unspoken agreement that they were seeing each other. That they were both all in.

They spent time at Nick's house, too. He was in the process of renovating an old barn and made her hold things like levels and then made her hammer nails into boards. Since there was no Netflix and bad TV reception, they spent those evenings talking about life in general. There had been some cattle rustling in the area, and Nick worried about keeping the Three Rivers stock safe. He said it would be time to separate the calves from their mothers soon, and she could feel his anguish about it. It was a necessary evil if one was in the business of beef production.

They discussed his theories about a mysterious plane crash in Asia. She talked about a new series of fantasy books she was reading.

What they didn't talk about, she noticed, was anything beyond the next day or the day after that. It didn't seem pertinent, not in these early stages. They lived in the moments together, getting to know each other in new and different ways than they'd ever really known each other. She knew some things about the future, but they were all vague. She knew, for example, that he'd applied to flight school—he'd told her that first night at her house. But he'd said it like it wasn't certain he would be accepted, and even if he were, he remarked with a bit of a laugh, "It's not cheap."

He knew she was going to at least freeze her eggs if she reached the age of thirty-four without a partner. She'd decided that if she was unmarried at the age of thirty-five, she would get a sperm donor.

They talked seriously about selling the Saddlebush offices. "It's a waste of good space, just the two of us," she said. "We can work anywhere, you and me. We don't need an office like that."

Nick didn't disagree. "George and I have chatted about it a couple of times. Nothing concrete. Just talk." He sighed. "The office is one of many questions I have for a father I will never see again," he said thoughtfully. "Questions maybe I should have asked but didn't when he was alive. Like why build such an extravagant office for a land and cattle company? Why leave the running of the company to me, when he knew that I wanted out? And again, why did I never discuss it with him?"

She stroked his face and kissed his cheek. "I'm sorry he's gone, Nick."

"Thanks," he said, and smiled at her. "Come on, I know you have some other cost-saving ideas. Let's have 'em."

"Are you kidding? *Loads,*" she said. "Expect an email."

"Baby," Nick said with a grin, "I *always* expect an email."

Perhaps predictably, there had been a subtle

shift in the dynamic between them at work. Nick had always been easy to work for, no matter what she said to him. He'd let her run the place and had dragged himself in as if under duress, agreeing to almost anything she wanted. But it felt different now. Like they were truly partners in this business. Charlotte wasn't naive enough to think that they were *really* partners—she wasn't a Prince, and she was still on salary. But he made her feel like it, and that was important to her.

It was the members of the softball league who first noticed the difference between Charlotte and Nick. On the first official pairing of the Saddlebush Sluggers and the Fred Savages, Big Barb followed Charlotte onto the field after the Sluggers scored two runs and said, "I don't know if you noticed, sweetie, but Nick Prince dropped that ball to get you to third, and Colton Rivers overthrew the catcher to let you score. What's *that* about?"

"That's not what happened," Charlotte exclaimed, and then she laughed so gaily you'd think there was a maypole nearby for her to dance around. She was horrible at keeping secrets. "Come on, Big Barb, I told you guys I was good."

"Are you good? Or lucky?" Big Barb asked, and with an appraising look, she carried on to her position in right field.

On the night the Freds had a bye, Nick came to

watch the Sluggers take on the Tool and Diehards, the team Keesha and her husband played for. When Luca noticed Nick in the stands, he stared at him awhile, and then looked suspiciously at Charlotte. "Why is he here?" he asked, jerking his head in the direction of Nick.

Charlotte tried to keep the smile of pleasure from her face, but it was impossible—it made her happy to see him sitting in the stands. "Ah . . ." she said, and tried to think of a plausible reason. "He's not an *official* member of the Sluggers, obviously, but—"

"Obviously," Luca interjected. "But?"

"But he's got a vested interest. It's the company rep on the line."

"The company rep?" he scoffed. "*No one's* reputation is on any line. What else you got?"

She could feel herself coloring as Big Barb sidled over to hear her answer. "I guess he really likes softball?"

"*Mm-hmm,*" Luca and Big Barb said in unison.

Keesha was more direct with her inquiries. When Charlotte visited the Lowe Law offices to drop off some papers they needed to deal with the Tim Mitchell lawsuit, Keesha didn't even look at the papers. She was too busy eying Charlotte up and down.

Charlotte looked down. She was wearing a new dress, a pink one with little black dachshunds trotting around in various directions.

"New dress?" Keesha asked.

"Yep."

"You've been wearing a lot of new dresses lately."

"Mariah had a sale."

Keesha didn't seem satisfied.

"I bought some because I'm learning how to sew and I like to see how they are made."

"That is so . . . bogus," Keesha said, her eyes narrowing.

Charlotte tucked a bit of hair behind her ear. It was extremely difficult to get one past Keesha.

"I've got another question," Keesha said, and folded her arms. "If you're dating him, why not just say you're dating him?"

"What?" Again, Charlotte laughed and laughed, just like she had at Big Barb. "I'm not . . . we're not *dating,* Keesha."

"Then what would you call it?" Keesha demanded. "And before you answer, consider that I am one of your best friends, and if I see it, you know damn well those sisters of yours will see it. So you might as well practice your answer on me. What's the big deal, anyway?"

Charlotte swallowed down a swell of alarm. Keesha was right about every bit of that. "The big deal is that he's my boss," she whispered hotly, and glanced nervously at George's open door.

Keesha snorted. "George isn't here. And no one

is anyone's boss at Saddlebush. Please. We all know that."

"Okay, we're hanging out a little," Charlotte admitted. "I wouldn't call it *dating*."

Except that she would call it dating. It was as close to dating as she'd been in a very long time.

She didn't know why she was so reluctant to admit it. Keesha was right—no one was exactly a boss in their office. So why couldn't she say it? Why couldn't she admit that after all these months in close proximity, she and Nick had developed feelings?

Because she and Nick hadn't defined it. They were still in the mind-set of seeing where this thing went, even though it was going pretty fast and furiously down that path.

Or, perhaps, she didn't trust that it was real or could last.

Whatever her reluctance, Charlotte wanted to enjoy it a little while longer before the whole world weighed in. But something else Keesha said gave her pause—once her sisters got wind, there would be no pretending it wasn't happening.

That wind blew in soon after the conversation with Keesha, when Charlotte met up with her sisters at their parents' house one afternoon. Caitlin was nearing the end of her pregnancy and was very grouchy, especially around her kids. So her mother had asked them to come over to give Caitlin a break.

It was raining, and the kids seemed extra wild, running around Charlotte's parents' house and shrieking at one another.

Cassie arrived late. She rushed in, kissed each kid, and then plopped down on the couch. "You would not believe the week I've had," she said dramatically. "I mean seriously, it's beyond your ability to comprehend."

"Please don't," Caitlin moaned, and closed her eyes as she leaned her head back against the chair. "Please don't tell us how important you are at your job again."

"But I *am,*" Cassie said. "What's wrong with a woman being confident in her value to an organization? That's a problem in this society, you know—women are considered difficult if they stand up for themselves."

"Cassie?" Charlotte said, and cast a meaningful look in the direction of their pregnant sister. "Maybe save the rally speech for the next Women's March."

Cassie rolled her eyes. "Fine. Whatever. Hey, what happened to the dog guy? You haven't mentioned him in weeks."

Charlotte blinked. Caitlin opened her eyes. Eyes that had been dull with fatigue and now looked bright and shiny. "Yeah, what happened to Dog Guy?"

"Mom," Noah said, tugging on Caitlin's sleeve. "Mom. Mom. *Mom.*"

Caitlin ignored him.

"Umm," Charlotte said. She tried to think while Noah yanked on his mother's sleeve. She'd seen Jake only once after that Sunday at Nick's. On a day Nick and Rafe had a meeting in George's office, she'd arranged to meet Jake for lunch. He'd brought Gus like she'd asked, and she buried her face in Gus's fur as she scratched him behind his adorable upright ears. "I love your dog," she'd said wistfully.

"Thanks!" Jake said. He'd brought his lunch and had laid it out on the picnic table. Peanut butter and jelly. Doritos. An orange. Charlotte pictured him packing up the same lunch every morning.

"So listen, Jake."

His head had come up.

"I need to say something."

His expression had turned to steel almost immediately. *"Great,"* he said darkly. "So what is it, Charlotte? Am I too nice for you?"

"What? No!" She'd been startled by the sudden change in him, uncertain what to say. He had even *looked* different. Almost menacing. "You're a really nice man, Jake. That's not what I was going to say—"

"All I ever hear," he had said as he'd begun to repack his lunch, "is that girls want to meet a nice guy. Well, I'm a *nice guy,* Charlotte. What's *wrong* with that?"

"Nothing! I think you're great—"

"Sure you do," he had said bitterly, and grabbed the end of Gus's leash.

"Jake, it's not what you're thinking. There's someone else—"

"I don't care."

But Charlotte had cared. She had wanted him to understand. "He's someone I've liked for a really long time."

"How long?"

"How long?" she had repeated.

"You said you've liked him for a really long time, Charlotte. How long is that? Weeks? Days? Years? Are you just picking up guys off the app and stringing them along?"

"*No*. He's not on . . ." She had thought the better of saying too much. "It's been a couple of years?" She had unintentionally framed her response in a question because she really didn't know. Somewhere along the way, grumpy Nick had gotten under her skin and there he'd remained, like someone had inserted a homing chip just below the surface, and she kept going back around to him.

"Whatever," Jake had said bitterly, and had walked away with his Gus, who trotted obediently along but looked back twice for Charlotte.

"MOOOOOMMMMM!" Noah shouted.

"Are you going to get that?" Charlotte asked.

Caitlin looked at her son. "Go play, Noah.

Mommy is having an adult conversation. I'll come look in a minute."

Charlotte wondered how looking was involved. But Noah seemed satisfied with the answer and shouted, "Grandma!" And ran toward the kitchen as Caitlin leaned forward as much as she could.

Cassie put her hand on Charlotte's arm. "Are you sure you want in on this, Lot?" she asked, and gestured in the general direction of Caitlin's belly.

"Would you stop pointing at me like I'm a whale?" Caitlin insisted.

"But look at you!"

"Mom!" Caitlin shouted.

"All right, children," Charlotte's mother said, appearing with a glass of white wine. She sat down. "Cassie, stop antagonizing Caitlin. Charlotte, what happened to the dog guy? We'd all like to know."

"Well, the good news is, I really like his dog. It's a corgi named Gus."

"But what about the *guy?*" Cassie pressed.

"I like Gus better," she said flatly.

"You have to give it time!" Caitlin said, and exchanged a look with her mother that told Charlotte they'd discussed this before.

"I cannot believe you are so bad at this," Cassie said, her voice full of wonder. "You find something wrong with everyone you date."

"No, I don't!" Charlotte said, wondering if

there was any truth to that. "I'm not *bad* at it, it's just that I'm sort of seeing someone else."

Cassie gasped. "*Please* tell me it's Colton Rivers!"

"No," Charlotte said, and frowned at her sister.

"Then who?"

She had a moment of indecision, the same moment her father chose to walk through the room with his reading glasses and a manual of some sort. "Hello, girls. Oh, hey, Lottie, I saw Nick's truck outside your house last night. Are you still having trouble with that faucet? I'll bring my tools over if he didn't get it fixed."

"No, Dad, the faucet is fine," Charlotte said weakly, aware that every female in the room was staring at her. Even her little niece.

"Okeydoke," her dad said, and wandered out of the room.

"Are you . . . are you *kidding* me right now with this?" Cassie demanded.

Charlotte shook her head.

"But he's such a grump!"

"Does Hallie know?" Caitlin asked.

"No, and don't anyone here tell her," she said, and looked directly at Cassie.

"Why not?" her mother asked.

"Because." She had no good reason. "We're kind of trying it out. I mean, why not? We know each other really well. Rufus *loves* him—"

"Rufus loves everyone!" Caitlin shouted. "That doesn't count."

"Okay, look, I like Nick," Charlotte said flatly. "And he likes me. And he could really use a friend right now because he's being sued over some stuff his dad did and it's really awful."

"So are you *friends?*" her mother asked, sounding confused.

"We're figuring things out, Mom. Why does it have to be settled right this minute what we are?"

"It doesn't," her mother said soothingly.

"Yes it does!" Cassie exclaimed. "He wasn't exactly great to you before."

"What was before?" their mother asked.

Charlotte shot Cassie a dark look, willing her to shut up. "Nothing, Mom. We had a little . . . run-in way before his dad died, that's all. And that's all I'm saying about it, okay? It's only been a few weeks. I don't understand why everyone is so concerned about it, anyway."

"Interested," Caitlin said. "Not concerned. And we are interested because we live in a tiny little town where not a lot happens. So indulge us."

Charlotte would not.

But she discovered later that week that her own sisters' "interest" paled in comparison to Hallie's. Hallie was so incensed that she had not been informed that she made a rare appearance at the Saddlebush offices. Charlotte was compiling some monthly reports when Hallie banged into the offices, Mariah right behind her. "I saw your bike outside," Hallie said breathlessly.

"Are you okay?" Charlotte asked. She looked at Mariah, who shrugged, even though Hallie looked a little red-faced.

"I have been trying to get Nick on the phone and he won't answer. Why is that?"

Charlotte said, "Because he is flying today?" She came out from behind the reception desk. So did Rufus, who was overjoyed to see Hallie and Mariah. His whole body wriggled with delight.

"Hi, Rufus," Hallie said. She walked to the seating area and dropped heavily onto the couch. "So were you going to tell me?" she demanded without looking at Charlotte. "Was Nick? Did I have to find out from *Mariah?*"

"Hey!" Mariah said, offended.

Charlotte released a small sigh and eased herself down next to Hallie. "How did you know?" she asked Mariah.

"Jo Carol told me."

"I'm sure Jo Carol's told the entire town," Hallie snapped.

"Oh, and Ella suspected," Mariah added.

"How does everyone know?" Charlotte asked.

"I don't know! Does it matter, Charlotte?" Hallie demanded. "Everyone knew but me, and supposedly, you are one of my best friends! Even

Rafe knew and he never knows anything! Not even my own brother could be bothered to tell me."

"I'm sorry, Hallie. We haven't told anyone."

"Yes, you have! You obviously have because everyone knows but me!" Hallie suddenly lurched forward and buried her face in her hands and began to sob.

"Hallie!" Charlotte cried. She put her hand on Hallie's back. Hallie shrugged it off. "Please don't cry! Can I get you something? You want some water? I made some cookies, you want a cookie?"

"She loves cookies," Mariah said.

"Shut up, Mariah!" Hallie said tearfully.

"But do you want a cookie?" Charlotte asked carefully.

"Yes," Hallie howled.

Charlotte jumped up to fetch the cookies. By the time she came back, Hallie had composed herself.

"I'm sorry," Hallie said. "I seem to be unusually weepy. I'm driving to Austin to finish my degree, and I'm so tired, and this baby is just enormous, and then I find out that everyone knows that you and Nick are together except me, and it hurt my feelings."

"I'm so sorry," Charlotte said again. She set a plate of cookies in Hallie's lap, then sat next to her and rested her head on Hallie's shoulder.

362

Mariah sat on one of the chairs so that she could rub Rufus's ears.

Hallie bit into a cookie. "So where is this going, Charlotte? I mean, you're not . . . you guys aren't thinking . . ."

"I'm not thinking at all, Hal. I'm just living in the moment. Can't two people just figure things out without having to declare what they are?"

"Are you sleeping together?" Mariah asked.

"Jesus, Mariah!" Hallie said loudly.

"What?" Mariah demanded. "Don't you want to know?"

"You guys," Charlotte said. "We're just enjoying ourselves. That's it."

"Good attitude," Mariah said, and reached for a cookie. "If I were you, I wouldn't trot out the baby stuff right away. Tends to scare guys off."

Charlotte gave Mariah a withering look. "Thanks. But he's known me for a minute, Mariah. He knows all about that."

"Whatever happened to dating Colton Rivers?" Mariah blithely continued. "Now *there's* a good-looking guy. I could totally see you with him. Nick, not so much." She munched her cookie as Hallie and Charlotte stared at her.

Hallie put her hand on Charlotte's arm. "Lottie, listen," she said softly. "Just be careful, okay?"

Charlotte laughed. "Do you know something I should know? Is Nick a serial killer or some-thing?"

Hallie didn't smile. She shook her head. "I love my brother to pieces. I just know him, that's all." She looked away.

Charlotte didn't know what that warning was supposed to mean. She thought she should probably press a little more, but Mariah was staring at her, and frankly, Charlotte didn't want to hear the answer.

"Hey, if you and Nick get married, are you going to get married at the ranch?" Mariah asked.

"Mariah! Stop talking!" Hallie demanded. She sighed and closed her eyes. Mariah looked at Charlotte and mouthed the words *call me* and mimicked a telephone to her ear.

Charlotte got up. "I'm going to get you a cool cloth, Hallie." She walked to the bathroom, working hard to ignore Hallie's warning to her. Be careful of what? What did she know that Charlotte didn't?

Chapter Nineteen

Cordelia was up at the cemetery sitting under the lanai. The vines had grown like crazy this summer, and now they provided a nice bit of shade. There was a coolish breeze tonight, and the flowers Dolly had planted were blooming, their heads dancing in the wind. It was lovely. Peaceful.

George was sitting beside her. "Sure you don't want to drive to the Magnolia for dinner?" he asked.

Cordelia had thought about it. "I'm sure. I'd have to change clothes and do something with my hair, and then be nice when people said hello. And anyway, why go there when this is the most beautiful spot in Texas?"

"Because the Magnolia has food. You don't."

"I have food," Cordelia said. She sat forward and opened an outdoor storage box that also doubled as a table. She pulled out pretzels, Cheetos, and a jar of peanuts. Dolly had made a run to Walmart earlier in the week.

George looked at the pile. "I can't believe you two eat that crap. Hand me the Cheetos."

Cordelia handed him the bag and then stood

up and walked to the newly installed portable indoor-outdoor bar. This was a hard-fought compromise between her and Martin. It was made of plastic, and it was inexpensive, which was a big consideration these days. Martin was happy—he didn't have to get bricklayers up here, and in winter, he and Rafe could roll it down and store it in one of the outbuildings. Cordelia opened the top of it and pulled out a bottle of gin, and some tonic and limes. "Double?" she asked.

"Single."

She mixed two drinks and returned to her seat. George already had orange Cheeto coating on his mustache. Cordelia set his drink on top of Charlie's gravestone and smiled at her companion. He was handsome, this old man. Well, she was as old as he was, but Cordelia liked to think that she looked a lot younger.

They turned their attention to the landscape. It was like this between them recently—they could sit in companionable silence for what seemed like hours. This was Cordelia's favorite time of day. She loved how the late-afternoon sun turned the river's surface into a kaleidoscope of orange and yellow and white. And how turkey vultures would return to the trees in lazy swoops to roost for the night.

"Nick wants to sell the offices in town," George said. "There is a realty company interested in buying it."

This was not a surprise to Cordelia. She'd told Charlie it was over the top when he built it. "Where is he going to work?" she asked curiously.

"Don't know yet," George said. "He and Charlotte could use some space in my offices. Or he could work out here. Charlie's office is plenty big. There'd be space for Charlotte, too."

"He's not going to come anywhere near me, George, you know that. He hates me." She sipped her drink.

"He doesn't hate you." George shoved his hand into the Cheetos bag again.

"Well he doesn't like me, that's for sure. How did I manage that, do you reckon? How did I screw up the affection of my favorite child?"

"Woman, I told you to stop saying that," George said curtly.

"I can't help it. He *is* my favorite. You think I'm the only mother in the history of earth to have a favorite child?"

"I think you're the only mother in history to actually say it. Listen, Delia—Nick wants to go to aviation school."

Something sharp and painful ran down her side, like the stitch she used to get when she ran for exercise all those years ago. She cast a sharp look at George. "I thought he put that on hold."

"He did put it on hold. For almost two years he's put it on hold. But he recently submitted another application. And then he talked to Rafe about running things."

"How do you know that?"

George shrugged as he tried to knock the orange off his fingers. "I might have hosted the meeting in my office."

Cordelia stared at him in disbelief. *"Traitor,"* she whispered.

George sipped his drink and kept his gaze on the ranch land before them.

Cordelia took a gulp of her drink. "What did Rafe say?"

"He wanted to negotiate the compensation because he's a smart man, and he knows that running this place is a thankless job. And he said if the offices were sold, and there was some money for it, he'd want to hire on two new hands. We're running an awful lot of cattle over a big expanse right now. It's time to get some hands on board again."

Cordelia felt like she was shaking. It was a quake, coming from the inside. "I can't even look at you right now. Thanks to you, my son is going to leave me, too."

"He's not going to leave you, Delia," George said patiently. "But he wants to live his life. And after thirty-three years, I'd say he's entitled."

"Well that's just it, George. You don't get a say." She winced the moment she said it, and instantly regretted her sharp words. She reached for George's hand without even looking at him and gave it a squeeze. "I'm sorry, George. Charlie was right, my tongue is deadlier than a two-headed serpent. I wish I could hold it, but I've never been able to perfect that."

"I know."

"Of course you have a say," she said apologetically.

"It's okay, Delia." He pulled his hand free of hers.

Cordelia could feel unshed tears in her eyes and she hated them. She hated herself for it. Why couldn't she hold her tongue? Why couldn't she be more supportive of her children? "The thing is, after Charlie . . . I don't want to lose Nick, too." Her voice sounded wobbly.

"You won't lose him. You might see him more than you do now. He plans to fly home weekends."

Cordelia considered this. It wasn't as if Nick was coming around to see her now. He was smart enough to avoid her and her serpent's tongue. Poor George apparently wasn't. He kept coming back time and again.

Nick had always been such a good kid. And when he became a man, he was always there for her and Charlie. He'd especially been there for her since Charlie had died. Oh, but she knew how desperately Nick wanted to fly. From the time he could walk, he had wanted to be in a plane.

She remembered bringing him the Little People airplane play set when he was three or four. He had loved that thing, spent hours pretending the plane was flying. He had loved for his father to lift him overhead and make him fly like a plane. When he was twelve, he had begged her to subscribe to an aviation magazine.

Yes, she knew what Nick wanted and how badly he wanted it. And she did want him to reach his dreams. But she didn't want to ache with missing him while he was off doing it.

"If it's okay with you, Delia, I'm going to give you a piece of friendly advice."

"Great," she said, and took a big sip of her drink.

"If Nick comes to tell you he's made up his mind and he's going, wish him well and tell him that you're there for him. You can tell him that you need to hear from him from time to time. But he needs you to support him. Otherwise, he'll go. But he'll go with guilt, and I know you don't want that."

"I know," she said wearily. She didn't want that at all. She turned her head and smiled at George. "I love you, George." It was not a romantic declaration. She meant to convey the kind of love a sixty-year-old woman had in her—love that was appreciation and gratitude.

One of George's bushy gray brows rose above the other. "I love you, too, Delia."

"Well what's going on up here?"

Cordelia groaned at the sound of her mother-in-law's voice.

"Good evening, Dolly," George said, and winked at Cordelia as he came to his feet.

"Hope you saved some of those gin and tonics for me. You know, I've come to really enjoy our happy hours up here. I told Lloyd he ought to come up, but he said he didn't want to be in a cemetery before he absolutely had to be."

George laughed.

Cordelia got up to make Dolly a drink.

"I still think we need some palm trees up here, Delia," Dolly said. "They'd look so pretty around Charlie's grave."

"They would make it look like we were having a luau up here. What's next, a pig roast?"

"Well, at least think about it. You have to admit I've had some good ideas for this cemetery. And Walmart has those little fan palms on sale right now." Dolly took her seat on the other side of George. She was wearing capris, and hiked them up over her bony knees.

Cordelia handed her a drink. Dolly took a generous sip, then burped. "Excuse me," she said. "It's good, Delia. I always knew that eventually you'd learn how to make a decent gin and tonic."

"At least I'm making them," Cordelia said, and sat down. "What have you done for us lately?"

"Oh my, I may have spoken too soon," Dolly said. "This is a *little* heavy on the gin."

George looked between Cordelia and Dolly, and said, "Listening to you two makes me understand your children a little better."

"Me, too," Cordelia admitted.

"What was that?" Dolly asked, looking up from her drink.

Chapter Twenty

It was another Sunday, more than a month since the Sunday everything had turned for them, and Charlotte was once again at Nick's, this time with a dog and a pie that was missing a sliver.

"Look, your pie didn't fill the tin," Nick pointed out.

She gave him a pert smile. "I had to test it. I am happy to report that it is delicious."

Nick didn't fully understand why the ability to make pies figured so prominently in Charlotte's wish for the future, but he was liking the outcome.

Over a dinner of vegetable soup, which Charlotte had made especially for him, she asked him how a meeting with George about the Tim Mitchell lawsuit had gone. George had done some digging into the other receipts and invoices they'd found.

"Three invoices were not paid. We are settling with Tim Mitchell for a whole lot more than the sixteen thousand. The other two were with big companies, and that's going to take more work to come to an agreement. They've got a lot of lawyers and accountants."

"How are you going to pay for invoices and lawyers? Not to mention George and Keesha's time."

"And the forensic accountants we had to hire," Nick added. The more he'd discovered about his father's attempts to hide what he'd done, the more resentful he'd become. "George is working on it."

Charlotte looked up from opening a bottle of wine. "Do you want to talk about it?"

That was the thing with Charlotte. She knew him well enough to understand his myriad feelings about his dad. And she'd known his dad well enough to understand. But Nick shook his head. He was exhausted by talk of it, by having to revisit his emotions every time he and George had a conversation. He changed the subject. "Hallie came to see me."

"Where? Here?" Charlotte asked, surprised. "I thought she was supposed to be on bed rest."

"She is. She made Rafe bring her out because she is as stubborn as our mother. Don't tell her I said that—she'd kill me. She said she wanted to say hi to Frank and Priscilla."

Charlotte snorted.

"She is *really* pregnant," Nick said.

"She really is," Charlotte agreed. "But that's not why she came out here. She came out here to yell at you for not telling her about us."

"You know my sister well."

"I do. Plus, she yelled at me. What did you tell her?"

Nick grinned. "That it was none of her business."

Charlotte's eyes widened. "You didn't!"

"I damn sure did."

Charlotte laughed. "What did she say?"

"That she was going to tie my tongue in a knot and shove it down my throat if I wasn't going to use it."

Charlotte laughed as she fetched two wineglasses. "That's just the hormones talking."

"No, that is definitely my sister talking. So I told her that yes, we are dancing around this thing."

Charlotte paused just before she was to pour the wine and looked at him. "Is that what we're doing? We're dancing *around* it? Or are we dancing right in the middle of it?"

"We're dancing, baby," he said, and grabbed her up, moving her around the kitchen.

It was not an answer. Because Nick didn't know what the answer was. He loved Charlotte—loved her like a friend, a companion, certainly. But it was more. He was falling *in* love with her, too. He didn't know what to do with that. He didn't know if Charlotte and his plans for the future could exist in the same place and he didn't know how to reconcile the two. At the moment, it didn't seem like a pressing issue.

After dinner, they took a bath. That had become their favorite thing to do at his house. Frank stood at the fence facing the house, and although the old horse was nearly blind, it looked like he was staring at them.

"Can't he, like, turn his head?" Charlotte asked.

"He can't see you."

"I don't care, I feel entirely conspicuous. Completely exposed."

Nick had been feeling exposed since Hallie came to see him. It was clear the news about him and Charlotte was all over town. That didn't surprise him—he knew how Three Rivers functioned. But it made him uneasy. Almost as if he was living a lie. But he *wasn't* living a lie, because he did love Charlotte. So why did he feel like such an imposter?

Charlotte stayed over, but they were both tired from a busy day. Nick pulled her into his side and held her there, content to just be. They fell asleep in the middle of a conversation about the AC. Charlotte liked it Icelandic cold when she slept. Nick preferred not to shiver all night. As usual, Charlotte got her way.

In the middle of the night, the dogs began to bark. Charlotte pushed up from a mound of covers. "Who's here?" she mumbled.

"No one. Probably a rabbit or coyote. Go back to sleep," Nick said sleepily, and kissed her forehead. He looked at the clock next to his bed—it was half past three in the morning.

The dogs wouldn't stop barking. And then Nick heard something that sounded like a vehicle. But also like the clanking of a gate. He got up, thought about putting on some thermals, but grabbed some dirty jeans and shoes and stepped out of the bedroom, taking care to close the door quietly. He went to a small front room he used as a library and unlocked his gun cabinet.

The dogs had moved to the front of the house, and it sounded like they were just outside the front door, barking and snarling at something or someone. "What the hell," he muttered, and took down a shotgun, quickly loaded it, and went outside. When he stepped out onto the front porch, he couldn't see a vehicle, but he could hear it bumping down the road, moving away from the house. The dogs were still barking and he instantly saw why. There, in the drive, about twenty yards from the house, stood a sway-backed white horse. Even in the moonlight, Nick could see that the horse's ribs were sticking out.

"You've got to be kidding me," he muttered. Someone had just dumped on old, malnourished horse on him. From time to time, horses were dumped when they got too old to work and too expensive to feed—he knew that happened. But it had never happened to him. He'd never had anything bigger than a dog dumped out here.

He returned to the house and put the gun away,

then went back outside to deal with an abandoned horse.

It took some doing—the horse was scared—but Nick managed to get the horse roped and convinced her to follow him to a paddock with a bucket of oats. Frank was in a pasture beside the paddock and stood facing away from them, almost like he didn't want to see the white horse. Nick got her in the paddock and went to make sure the water trough was filled. When he came back, Frank had moved away from the horse, and the white horse stood with her head hung, as if she were ashamed of having been dumped.

Nick stroked her nose. "Don't worry, old girl. He won't bite. None of us will. You're safe here."

She was still standing with her head hung when he went back inside.

He crept back into the house and pulled off the dirty jeans and tossed them into the laundry basket. He walked back to his room and found the door open. Somehow, Rufus had come inside while he was out, and someone had let him into the bedroom and onto the bed. He had his whole body pressed against the mound that was Charlotte. Nick lured Rufus off the bed with a biscuit, sent him back outside, then returned to the bed and crawled under the covers.

Charlotte rolled into his side.

"It's freezing in here, Charlotte. It's, like, zero degrees. There are literally no Fahrenheit degrees in this room in the middle of summer. What sense does that make?"

For some reason, his irritation made her giggle. Before Nick could say that he did not find it the least bit amusing, that he was freezing, she kissed his nipple, her teeth grazing it and sparking a fire.

"Where were you?"

"We had a visitor."

She kissed his neck. "In the middle of the night? Who was it?"

"A horse."

"A horse. It's awfully late for a horse or anyone else. I don't like unexpected visitors. I once had a friend from college pop in and stay three days. Who does that? Whose horse is it?"

"I don't know. Someone dumped her."

Charlotte kissed his shoulder. "Someone dumped an entire *horse?*"

He smiled. "I think it would be pretty hard to dump half a horse."

"What are you going to do?" she asked, returning to his chest.

"I had in mind sleep," he said, and yawned.

Her head popped up. Her curls spilled onto his chest. "Right this very minute?" She looked so desirable in the weak light of the night. "You woke me up, Nick Prince. The least you can do is entertain me."

He shoved his fingers into her curls. Nick was exhausted, but he was aroused, too. Charlotte bent her head and kissed his ribs. Nick jerked violently. "That tickles," he said.

Charlotte moved lower, her hair trailing down his arm as her mouth moved across his abdomen and her hand slid down his body to his cock.

"I smell like horse," he complained.

"I love it when you smell like horse." She moved lower.

Nick wouldn't fight it—he was incapable of mounting any kind of defense, especially when this was so pleasurable. Her tongue teased the tip of him, and he sighed, giving in completely.

If there was one thing he was certain about, it was that sex with Charlotte was off the charts. They seemed to be in tune with each other in a way he had never been in tune with a woman. And Charlotte wasn't shy about anything, always enthusiastic to try new things. "I have to be up at five thirty." He sounded like a grandpa.

"I'll be just a minute," she said, and took him into her mouth.

Nick's eyes fluttered shut as her lips moved over him, her tongue circling the girth of him. All it took was a touch or a kiss in the right place, and he was at her mercy. He appreciated her lustiness, and the way she could stoke desire in him that made him want to lift houses off their slabs.

She was true to her word, quickly driving him to the point of oblivion, and Nick suddenly surged up, catching her between the arms and pulling her up at the same moment he twisted around with her and put her on her back. He grabbed a condom while she frantically removed her panties. He moved between her legs, pushing them aside with his knees, and pressed his massive erection against her, moving in tantalizingly slow motions against her warm, wet body.

Charlotte grabbed his hips and pulled him closer. He slid into her body, and Charlotte flung her arms wide with a sigh of pure pleasure. Nick closed his eyes and lost himself in that exquisite sensation of movement in her body. He was enslaved by the sensation, and the deeper her panting became, the more sounds she made, the more he burned to give her.

He clasped her tightly, lifted his hips, and thrust deep into her until Charlotte cried out and her body spasmed around his. His own release followed, the force of it racking his body.

He dropped his forehead to her shoulder, and it was several moments before he could find the strength to lift his head again. When he did, Charlotte smiled like a fat cat. "You should rescue horses more often."

He kissed her.

On some level, Charlotte terrified him. She had the ability to steal his breath with a look or a smile. He eased out of her body and rolled onto his back. Charlotte sighed happily and nestled against him with her head on his chest, her arm draped across him.

When Nick awoke the next morning, Charlotte and her dog were gone.

The white horse had moved to one side of the paddock, her head still down. Frank was casually grazing.

Nick made it to the office at a quarter to twelve. He expected to see Charlotte's bike there, but it was not. And the offices were locked.

He went inside and looked around. Her coffee cup was still on her desk. Maybe she'd gone out for lunch. But she usually left him a message, tacking it to his door so he wouldn't miss it. She liked to slide that door closed just to make him open it. Today, it was standing open. He went into his office and pulled up his mail.

From: Charlotte charlotte@saddlebushco.com
To: Nick nickprince@saddlebushco.com
Subject: Caitlin's baby!

CAITLIN HAD HER BABY!! It's a boy, his name is Liam, he weighed 7 lbs, 4 oz, 21 inches long. Mom and baby doing great! Look at this squiggly little face! Doesn't it make you smile?

She'd attached a picture of the newborn, swaddled in blue and wearing a little blue knit cap. He was red-faced, and had something that looked like Vaseline smeared on both eyes. The squiggly face did not make Nick smile. It actually made him recoil a little. He stared at it, wondering how a newborn could be so . . . *ugly.*

From: Nick nickprince@saddlebushco.com
To: Charlotte charlotte@saddlebushco.com
Subject: Re: Caitlin's baby!

Congratulations to the happy parents.

He didn't know what else to say. He didn't know Caitlin and Jonah very well, only in passing. He was happy for them, mildly interested, but right now, the more pressing issue for him was an abandoned horse.

Nick spent the afternoon trying to find someone who would take the mare, and without much luck. It was the same answer everywhere he looked—who was going to pay for the vet and food? He found an equine rescue up near Austin, but in his Google search of it, he ran across a news article that claimed complaints had been made to the sheriff and accusations of neglect of rescue horses had been levied against the organization.

At four, it started to pour, and Nick thought of the mare standing in the rain, her head down. He wanted to get her into the stable. Which was really a barn. He'd taken out the horse stalls when it became too hard to maneuver Frank into one.

At a quarter to five, the rain looked like it was being dumped from enormous buckets.

His phone pinged.

Monday 4:47 PM
Nicholas Nickleby! I need a huge favor. Can you come pick me up at the hospital? I was in such a hurry I rode my bike.

Nick replied that he would, and thirty minutes later, he drove across town and parked in the hospital lot. He texted Charlotte to let her know he was waiting for her in the parking lot and asked where she'd parked her bike.

Monday 5:25 PM
In the bike stand. But you have to come up and meet the newest member of our family!

Nick blinked. He wasn't planning on doing that. He didn't know Caitlin *that* well.

Monday 5:26 PM
I don't want to intrude.

Monday 5:26 PM
You're not intruding. Please come up.

You have to meet Liam! He is adorable and you will fall in love. Room 312.

This was a bad idea. First, Nick wasn't into babies. Every once in a while a friend would show up with one, and he would observe from a distance. Second, he hadn't even been formally introduced to her family as her boyfriend. The Baileys knew him, but they didn't know him in *this* capacity, and what, he was going to waltz in there and present himself to her family and meet a newborn all in one fell swoop?

His phone pinged again.

Monday 5:27 PM
No one but you thinks it is weird. Half the town has already been by to see the baby. Please come up.

Charlotte could read him like a Harlan Coben novel. She couldn't even *see* him and knew what he was thinking. "Damn it, Charlotte," he muttered. But he shoved his phone in his pocket, got out of his truck, and made a mad dash through the rain to meet this baby.

He was directed to Caitlin's room, and when he pushed the heavy door open, he was greeted by all of the Baileys, crammed inside like so many pickles in a jar. *"Nick!"* they all shouted.

"Ah . . . hi," Nick said.

"Hey, we're rained out tonight," Chase said.

"No one cares about softball right now," his wife, Lori, said.

"Speak for yourself," Chase said. "Nick might."

"Chase, move! Let him see the baby," Charlotte insisted. Cassie, Chase, and Lori moved aside to give him a path forward. Charlotte was standing by a plastic box on a wheeled stand. She was beaming, the sparkle in her eye visible from across the room.

"Come see, come see!" she said eagerly, waving him over.

"Ah . . . sorry for the intrusion," he said to Caitlin and Jonah.

"It's no intrusion," Jonah said. He was grinning. "We want everyone to see our new little guy. I'm going to go get the kids, Cait. They can't wait to meet their little brother." He popped out of the pickle pack.

Caitlin was lying in the bed, her hair a twisted mess on top of her head. She looked like she'd been to hell and back, but that was overshadowed by the sheer happiness on her face.

Nick went to the plastic box and looked down. The baby was swaddled. Up close, he looked like a little old man. "He's . . . he's great," Nick said.

Mr. Bailey laughed. "He looks like a Martian."

"Dad!" Cassie warned him.

Charlotte reached into the box and picked the baby up. She cradled him in her arms, cooing to him, swaying softly from side to side. "He's amazing. Isn't he amazing?" she asked, and before Nick realized what she was doing, she held the baby out to him.

He panicked. He backed up so quickly that he knocked into Mrs. Bailey. "I'm so sorry."

"It's fine, Nick. Charlotte, he doesn't want to hold a newborn."

"No," Nick said quickly. "I might break his neck—"

"No you wouldn't!" Charlotte said jovially.

"Let me hold him," Cassie said, pushing past Nick.

Charlotte handed Cassie the baby as Caitlin asked anxiously, "Cassie, did you wash your hands?"

"Of course I washed my hands," Cassie said. "This is like the hundredth baby in this family. I think I know to wash my hands."

Nick caught Charlotte's eyes and motioned with his head toward the door.

She nodded. "Okay, I have to go," Charlotte said. She bent over Caitlin and hugged her. "I'll be back tomorrow. And then, when you go home, of course, I'll be there to help."

"Thanks, Lot," Caitlin said, and yawned.

"Liam is beautiful," Charlotte said.

"Isn't he?" Caitlin asked dreamily.

Nick waved good-bye to everyone and ushered Charlotte out of the room.

On the way down to the parking lot, Charlotte filled him in on the details of Caitlin's labor, which, honestly, Nick wished he didn't have to hear. The rain pummeled them as they dashed to his truck. He drove around to the bike rack and, in the rain, struggled with the lock on her bike as Charlotte shouted out the combination to him through the window. When he had the bike in the bed of the truck, he got in the cab and wiped his face.

"You're soaked," she observed.

He gave her a withering look. Charlotte laughed.

She chattered about the baby all the way to her house. The words were bubbling out of her. She was a fountain of excitement, spewing words of happiness. She had plans for this baby, she said. It was Caitlin's fourth, and she was convinced Caitlin would want to share her baby with her sisters, pass off some of the care. Mothers never wanted to do that with their firstborn, she explained, but by the fourth, they would accept help wherever they could get it. She was absolutely glowing, her eyes shining like two pools in noonday sun.

"I told Caitlin we could babysit," she said as he pulled into her drive.

"What?"

Charlotte laughed at an expression he was certain was sheer panic. "Not *now,* obviously, but when he's a little older. Like a couple of months. My God, you look almost green! Don't worry, Nicholas Nickleby, I'll handle everything."

Nick was too stunned to say anything. The idea that they would *babysit* an actual *baby* had not crossed his mind. He didn't want it to cross his mind. He didn't want to think about how much he did not want to do that.

But surely he knew this would come up at some point. Surely, somewhere in his head, he'd understood that Charlotte's desires for her future would enter into the picture.

"I'll get your bike," he said.

He met Charlotte on the porch and deposited her bike. He leaned forward to kiss her.

"Aren't you coming in?" she asked as she searched her bag for a key.

"I need to go see about the horse."

"Oh, of course!" she said. "I completely forgot the horse in the excitement of the day. I hope he's okay."

"She," Nick muttered.

"I'll call you later, okay?" She smiled up at him. So happy. So full of joy.

Nick kissed her once more. Softly. Tenderly. Sadly. "Talk to you later." He ran back to his truck.

He was bothered on the drive home by something so vague he couldn't quite capture what it was. He only knew that for the first time since he and Charlotte had acted on the heat that had swirled around them for so long, for the first time since that Sunday afternoon, he felt unsteady with this relationship. Strangely uncomfortable. Like he didn't really know her.

That was absurd. Of course he knew her. Maybe it was that he knew her too well. It was kids, he realized. It was babies. He didn't like them. Not that he didn't *like* them—it wasn't as if he held a personal grudge against children. But he wasn't interested in them. He didn't care to be around them. He definitely did not want to babysit and hold newborns and talk about hours of childbirth.

But Charlotte did. She wanted children, lots of children. She wanted them around, she wanted to raise them. She'd said it so many times, and he hadn't thought much of it because she was nowhere near having children.

He had to think about it.

The rain was still coming down when he arrived home, and his animals had all sought shelter. But the white horse was standing under a tree, her head still hanging low with deep dejection. He had never seen a horse so depressed and wondered what horrible life the old girl had been living.

Nick pulled on his mud boots, raincoat, and a hat, and walked out into that field with a bridle in his hand. The horse hardly even looked up.

"I've been there," Nick said softly, running his

hand over her cheeks and muzzle, her withers and flank. "Right where you are. I thought I was all alone in my place in this world, too. But I wasn't, girl, and neither are you. You give me a few days, and life will be smelling like roses again. No more starving. No more loneliness. Just roses and sunshine for you."

The horse nickered. Her tail swished a little.

Nick smiled and stroked her cheek. "You like roses and sunshine, huh? Sunny. That's what I'm going to call you. Because that's what your life ought to be now. Sunny." He'd whisper that name into the universe and hope that it would come back to the mare.

She let him slip the bridle onto her head and, with a little coaxing, she began to plod along behind him to the stables.

Frank was standing at the back, near the hay, and when Nick came in with Sunny, Frank lifted his head and nickered in her direction.

"See? That's what I'm talking about," Nick said as Frank began his arthritic walk forward to greet Sunny properly, as if he'd just been made aware of her presence. "You have to cut Frank a little slack," Nick explained. "He's old and blind."

Nick made sure the horses bedded down, then walked back up to his porch and shed the mud boots and hat. Priscilla appeared at the door of her shed and oinked at him. "You have plenty of food, Pris," he called out to her, and went inside with Pepper. He changed into dry clothes, then wandered around his kitchen, looking for something to eat. Fortunately, with Charlotte in his life, there were plenty of leftovers. He heated up vegetable stew and sat in front of his laptop at the kitchen bar.

He lazily scrolled through his emails, barely reading the subjects . . . until one in particular caught his eye.

It was from the flight school. They would be happy, they said, to reinstate him in October.

Chapter Twenty-one

Caitlin and the baby went home the day after Liam was born. Charlotte was on hand to help with Caitlin's other children, Ethan, Noah, and Hannah. The kids were giddy with excitement and couldn't wait to hold their little brother. It was hard to keep them away from Liam while he was sleeping.

Charlotte spent the afternoon with them, then went home to see about Rufus. The next morning, she'd just arrived at work when her mother called her. "I need you to come to Caitlin's right away."

"Why?" Charlotte asked.

"Something is wrong. Caitlin has a fever and we are taking her back to the hospital."

"What?" Charlotte shouted into the phone. Her heart began to race with panic. "Is she all right?"

"I don't know, Lottie, that's why I need you to come and be with the kids and Liam."

Charlotte didn't hesitate. She fired off a quick email to Nick:

From: Charlotte charlotte@saddlebushco.com
To: Nick nickprince@saddlebushco.com

Subject: Problem with baby and Caitlin

Sorry for the late notice, but something is wrong with Caitlin. My parents are taking her to the hospital and I'm going to go sit with the kids. I'll let you know when I know something.

From: Nick nickprince@saddlebushco.com
To: Charlotte charlotte@saddlebushco.com
Subject: Re: Problem with baby and Caitlin

Take all the time you need. Keep me posted. Don't worry about the office—I'll see if Hallie can come and fill in this afternoon.

It turned out that Caitlin had a significant bladder infection whose symptoms had been masked by giving birth. She would be in the hospital overnight, and when she returned home, she would need to rest. "She's going to need our help for a few days," Charlotte's mother said.

"I've got this," Charlotte said confidently. "If you can cover the mornings, I'll take the afternoons off."

"Are you certain?" her mother asked. "What about Saddlebush?"

Charlotte never took time off. She was at the Saddlebush offices every day, as dependable as the sunrise. "Nick can spare me a few after-noons." As soon as he knew what was going on, he'd probably insist on it because that's the man he was. He might come across as gruff, but he was really very caring. She picked up her phone.

"Hey, gorgeous," Nick said when he answered her ring.

Charlotte smiled into her phone. "I was going to say that to you. How are you? How's the horse?"

"Rancher and horse are doing fine, thank you. I named her Sunny. She's feeling a little better today. The vet is coming out tomorrow to have a look at her. How is Caitlin?"

Charlotte explained the situation to him, and as she knew he would, Nick immediately told her to take what time she needed. "Hallie came in yesterday, and I don't think she minds stopping by, if for no other reason than to soak up that chilly office air and sleep on the visitor couch."

"Thanks, Nick. You know, the worst part about this is how much I'm going to miss your face," she admitted. They'd been almost inseparable since they'd crossed the line into lovers, or boyfriend and girlfriend, or whatever they were going to call it. And yet, she'd never really told him how she felt about him. It was implied.

There was only a beat or two on the other end of the line. "I'm going to miss you, too, Charlotte. More than you know."

Charlotte grinned into her phone. She tucked her hair behind her ear and thought about saying more. Something like, *I'm in love with you, you old grump,* but instead, she promised to update him. She had her laptop and would keep up with work emails when Caitlin's little natives weren't restless. "This is just a small bump in the road," she said, and she believed it. She believed everything would go back to normal as soon as Caitlin was on her feet.

From: Charlotte charlotte@saddlebushco.com
To: Nick nickprince@saddlebushco.com
Subject: I'm not dead yet

I am exhausted! Who knew this was so much work? Do you know that babies eat like every two hours? That's more than you! I have to say, the kid thing is not what I thought it would be like. They talk constantly and all of them at the same time. And Liam! As adorable as he is, he cries a lot. That could possibly be due to the fact that Rufus keeps licking his feet.

Caitlin is home but feels awful. She keeps trying to get out of bed just like her kids try and get out of bed.

Charlotte hit send, then slumped in her chair. She looked at the mess in Caitlin's kitchen, the mess of toys strewn across the floor of the living area. And what was that? A half-eaten piece of jelly toast on the couch? Why did she want this life, again? What part of this did she find appealing?

Oh, right. Because when she held Liam, she felt a swell of big love and saw a beautiful baby boy with a fabulous future stretching in front of him. And because at night, when she and Jonah managed to corral Ethan, Noah, and Hannah into bed, they looked so angelic. Also, that's when Jonah made his famous whiskey sours.

This life was hard, and she felt for Caitlin. But it felt so warm in this house. There was so much love.

From: Nick nickprince@saddlebushco.com
To: Charlotte charlotte@saddlebushco.com
Subject: Re: I'm not dead yet

Glad to hear Caitlin is home. Looked all afternoon for the hole puncher. Found it in the dog's toy box???

From: Charlotte charlotte@saddlebushco.com
To: Nick nickprince@saddlebushco.com

Subject: Re: I'm not dead yet

You have not been authorized to punch holes in anything. The answer to your ??? is Rufus. Need I say more? How is Sunny?

From: Nick nickprince@saddlebushco.com
To: Charlotte charlotte@saddlebushco.com
Subject: Re: I'm not dead yet

Sunny followed Pepper and Frank into the field this morning. We're making progress.

Charlotte loved her niece and nephews beyond compare, but they were driving her nuts. This afternoon, when she told Ethan to put on his shoes before they went to the park, he refused. He shouted no at her. When she told him again with a more authoritative voice, he shouted, *"No means no!"* and dashed out of the house and into the backyard. By the time she'd calmed him down and convinced him that shoes were necessary at the park, Hannah had pulled out all her dolls again, and Noah had found a box of dried fruit and eaten half of it.

"You have to be firm," Caitlin said wearily. "Throw them in time-out."

It wasn't that easy for Charlotte to simply

throw them in time-out. She wanted to put herself in time-out. She wanted to soak in Nick's tub and stare at the cows and horses in complete silence. But Caitlin had looked so wan when Charlotte left that she couldn't imagine how her sister would manage all those kids without her help until she was completely back on her feet.

She texted Nick.

Thursday 7:15 PM
Hey . . . was going to come over tonight, but I'm beat. Today I got in trouble for putting tap water in the kids' sippy cups instead of bottled water. Also, who knew you needed a blowtorch to open kid-proof packaging? Not me.

Thursday 7:18 PM
Sold some cattle today. BTW, we need a new ledger. Please point me in the direction of the appropriate ledger store. I would not want to get the wrong color.

Thursday 7:19 PM
The appropriate ledger store is called "Walmart" and the ledger is in the "office supply" section. I can't believe I'm going to say this, but I really miss your crazy questions. Plus, I have major anxiety

about what's happening to my carefully crafted filing system. I have to find something to eat that doesn't involve goldfish crackers. TTYS

Friday 3:20 PM
Your dog apparently ate the color chart because I can't find it anywhere. When are you coming back? Pepper and I need you.

Friday 3:31 PM
Did you check the bulletin board next to the filing cabinet? I moved it so you would see it and USE it. I am incensed on Rufus's behalf at your accusation. He doesn't eat EVERYTHING. Speaking of which, these kids will not eat anything I make. Even my pb and j has too much pb on it and the eggs I made them for breakfast were yucky. Oh, how I long for the days when Rufus would eat anything I put in front of him.

Friday 3:33 PM
Before you rush to Rufus's defense, please know that the other day when you asked if he could come out to my place for a little activity, he ate the top half of one of my boots. Didn't chew it.

ATE it. I would eat your eggs. I miss your eggs.

BTW, I'm selling the office.

He had decided to sell the office? Just like that? She thought that there would be meetings, or cost-benefit analyses. Something.

Maybe she was just tired. Honestly, she'd never been so tired in all her life. She was so happy that Caitlin was feeling much better. Her sister was up and around, and said she'd be fine to go it alone by Monday. Charlotte didn't remember it being this hard when Hannah was born, but then again, Caitlin's kids were younger then, and they had designated nap times. This time, they wouldn't take their naps and ran circles around Charlotte all day.

Friday 4:20 PM
I'm headed home to my dog. I know you have a game tonight. I'll be back at work on Monday. Probably won't see you this weekend. Jonah had a weekend fishing trip with his brothers planned, so I'm going back into the fire so he can get a break. In the meantime, please enjoy this new photo of Liam. I have an entire catalog of them now. Look how he holds the edge of his blanket. Adorbs!

Over the weekend, Caitlin got much stronger. Jonah came home midafternoon on Sunday, and Charlotte immediately retreated to her house and her dog. She thought about texting Nick, but she decided she needed the time to rejuvenate.

On Monday morning, she was back at work. The building was empty and the air frigid. As she shut and locked the door behind her, she happened to notice the seating area. Her bright tropical throw pillows were missing. Again? What did he have against her throw pillows?

She worked all morning to go through her inbox and tackle the filing that had built up in her absence. She was cleaning out the fridge when she heard Nick come in. "Charlotte?"

She walked out of the break room as he strode across the office.

"Hello, stranger."

"Hello yourself, beautiful. I'm sure happy to see you." He wrapped her in an embrace and kissed her thoroughly. Oh, but Charlotte had missed this.

"I'm so happy to see you, too," she said.

"Are you busy tonight? I'll take you to dinner."

That sounded like the most divine thing in the world. "Will you?" she asked with relief. "I need someone to feed me real food and not complain about how yucky it is."

"I promise not to complain. How about the

Magnolia Bar and Grill?" he asked, and kissed the top of her head.

"Perfect. Hey, how's the horse?" She tried to remember what it looked like. The horse's appearance now seemed a lifetime ago.

"Sunny is doing great. She and Frank are inseparable." He grinned. "I think she's happy."

They made plans to meet at the Magnolia after work. Nick said he had some errands to run and had to meet a guy bringing some cattle out to his place.

"Cattle?"

"They belonged to an old rancher west of Austin. The man died and his kids don't want the cows slaughtered. I guess they considered them pets. When I was calling around to find a place to put Sunny, I heard about these cows, and, well . . . we've got all that land."

Charlotte smiled. "More rescue cows."

"I guess so. Okay, I better get out of here. I just stopped by to pick up a couple of things and say hello to you." He kissed her cheek and went to his office. He left altogether a few minutes later.

Charlotte watched him drive away, and an image popped into her mind for a brief, fleeting moment. It was an image of her and Nick at his house with their dogs, their rescue horses, and their rescue cows. And three little kids refusing to eat her eggs because they were yucky.

Charlotte couldn't help it. She grinned with delight.

And then she went in search of her pillows. She would not let him win this war.

Chapter Twenty-two

Charlotte wore a new red dress and high heels to meet Nick for dinner, and the result was deadly—he could feel his blood heating before he'd even said hello. His mind instantly wandered to the types of mind-blowing sex they might have tonight, and he wondered briefly if he could talk her into walking back into her house and taking off the dress.

"I'm starving!" she announced.

So much for his little fantasy. "You look amazing," he said appreciatively.

Ella was away from the hostess desk when they arrived, so Nick and Charlotte jotted their name on the list and went into the bar. Ella had been hostess here since before she met Luca, and even though she didn't need the job now, she kept it, working two or three nights a week. Luca had told Nick that Ella kept it because she needed her space away from him. "I mean, *why?*" Luca had asked. "I want to be with her all the time. Why doesn't she want to be with me?" He'd seemed truly perplexed.

Mateo, the bartender, appeared before them, rubbing his hands on a bar towel. "Well, look at *you,* Char-lottie. That's a sick dress."

"Thank you," she said, and dipped a curtsy.

Mateo's gaze moved between her and Nick. "So I guess the many, *many* rumors are true."

"You mean the one about me and wine?" Charlotte asked. "All true. Do you have a rosé tonight?"

"Of course I do." He started for the other end of the bar, but looked at her once more over his shoulder. "Looks like you've figured out how to get those babies after all, huh, girl?" he asked, and laughed.

Charlotte's face instantly pinkened. She laughed sheepishly and said to Nick, "Ignore him. Mateo and Ella and Mariah are really good friends, so . . ."

So, he surmised, everyone was speculating. "Ignore who?" he asked with a wink.

Charlotte had just received the glass of rosé when Ella appeared behind them and wrapped her arms around Nick, hugging him. "It's so good to see you two here. Especially you, Nick. Are you coming to Sunday dinner? Bring Charlotte again!"

"Well, that will depend on whether the Saddle-bush Sluggers beat the Fred Savages or not. If we lose, she's not invited. I won't want to see any of you."

Ella laughed. "From what I've seen, the Freds couldn't bat their way out of a paper bag. Come on, you two. I have a table for you," she said. "Hey, how's Caitlin?" Ella asked as she led them into the dining room.

"Great!" Charlotte said, and pulled out her phone. "Want to see pictures of the baby? Oh, Nick! I have some new ones to show you."

Charlotte had been sending him baby and little-kid pictures all week. He didn't really need to see more. He was a little surprised that Ella seemed so interested. He sat patiently as Charlotte scrolled through what seemed like hundreds of pictures on her phone. "Here is Liam after his bath," she said.

He'd never imagined himself sitting in a restaurant looking at baby pictures. It was bound to happen, obviously—his sister would have the first grandchild in a couple of weeks. He had friends who had children. He should have expected this, like every other human being.

"That's Noah," Charlotte said, pointing at her phone.

But it did feel odd, because for the first time, Nick realized that this could be his life. He could just picture it—Charlotte forcing everyone to look at photos of their kid. Talking about the first time the baby ate a banana or something. He could even see a baby, one that looked like Caitlin's, all squishy-faced and red. But where was he in that picture? He couldn't see himself. He didn't know how or where to put himself in that picture.

"Oh, see that? It's Hannah's one-eyed, one-armed doll," Charlotte said with a laugh. "We had to do some surgery after Rufus got hold of it."

Ella laughed, and they bent over the phone again.

Charlotte's smile was beautiful. She looked truly happy, scrolling through all the pictures she'd taken. She was in her element. She was exactly where she wanted to be. She glowed as she related some story about breaking up a fight between Caitlin's two little boys. That was the life she wanted, and all she lacked was someone to share that life with her. He remembered what she'd told him that night at Stars, Boots, and Music. *I want someone who would ride so hard to get to me.*

He understood exactly what she meant by that. She wanted someone who was all in with her, one hundred percent on board. And he . . .

He was not.

He was not.

A lump formed in his stomach. It wasn't so much a revelation as a stark acknowledgment. Nick loved Charlotte, he truly *loved* her. But he wasn't all in. There was still another part of him, a burning, determined part of him, that wanted out of here. Wanted to fly. He didn't think he could let that go.

He loved her, and because he did, he had to be honest about it.

When Ella had left them, Charlotte perused the menu, asking him what he thought of this dish or that dish. She went back and forth between a burger and salmon. "Sometimes, you just need to sink your teeth into a good, greasy burger, don't you?" Her head popped up over the menu. "Present company excluded, of course."

"Of course."

"What are you having?"

"Salad," he said.

"Ugh, I *can't* with the salad. I've eaten so much salad with you I feel like a giant head of lettuce."

"Get a cheeseburger, then," Nick suggested. He noticed he'd downed his beer pretty quickly. He needed another one. He was feeling restless.

When the waiter appeared to take their order, Charlotte ordered the salmon.

"What happened to the greasy cheeseburger?" he asked as he held up his empty beer bottle to indicate he wanted another.

She smiled and shrugged. "Seems mean to eat beef in front of you, and I don't really care. I would never want you to feel uncomfortable."

She was all in on him, Nick realized. She loved him, too. She didn't have to say it—he knew the way she looked at him, the way she was with him. How emotional she was after sex sometimes. So was he, he guessed, but the difference between him and Charlotte was that she was willing to make all the changes he needed. Perhaps that wasn't a fair comparison. Choosing fish over beef wasn't nearly as hard or as important as choosing children over none. Or a family life over a mobile life.

He couldn't stop thinking about this. He tried to will it away, to enjoy her company and think about sex, but he couldn't keep the thoughts from his head. He was being unfair to her, and he couldn't stop berating himself at having failed to see this coming. At having failed to even *think* it before her nephew was born. It hadn't seemed an issue before then—they'd been living each day and not worrying about the next. Isn't that what they'd been doing? Or had he been grossly negligent with her feelings?

Had he been kidding himself, too? Or was there a part of him that thought this could work, that he could settle for this life?

"Is there something wrong?" Charlotte suddenly asked.

"What?" He looked at her. "No, why?"

"Because I've been talking about how the Sluggers are going to crush the Freds tomorrow, and you just keep looking off like you can't hear me."

She'd been talking softball? Jesus, he was deep in the weeds of his own thoughts. "I'm sorry," he said, and reached for her hand. "It's been an odd week. I've had a lot on my mind."

"Like selling the office?"

Why did she sound almost annoyed? "It was your idea," he reminded her.

"I know, but I thought you'd do a little more analysis before just deciding to do it. I thought maybe we'd figure it out together."

Nick didn't know what to say. "It was a good idea. George and I had already talked about it, so I ran with it."

"But don't you—"

"Charlotte Bailey!"

They were both startled by the sound of a woman's voice. A slender, middle-aged woman appeared at their table dressed in a shirt with the collar turned up and pearls around her neck. The shirt was neatly tucked into a pair of capris. She dressed like Nick's mother.

"I heard your sister had her baby!" she exclaimed, and folded her arms. Half a dozen gold bangles on her wrist clanked together.

Nick knew this woman. She was a friend of his mother's and ran in the same social circles. Sarah Jenkins Cash.

"She did, Mrs. Cash. A boy! Want to see pictures?"

"I would love to!"

Charlotte reached for her phone. "You know Nick Prince, right?"

"Of course I know Nick. I've known him since he was a baby," she said with a flick of her wrist. "Oh, my, isn't this baby *adorable,*" she said as

Charlotte handed her the phone. "Isn't he just adorable, Nick?" Mrs. Cash asked, turning the phone to face him.

"Adorable," Nick agreed. Charlotte's father was right—that baby looked like a Martian.

"How is Caitlin?" Mrs. Cash asked as she scrolled through the pictures.

"She's good now, but she had some complications early in the week. So I got to play mommy."

"That must have been fun! Caitlin has the most beautiful little children, doesn't she?"

"She does. And yes, it was fun. But exhausting. I don't know how Caitlin does it."

"Well, that was good practice for you to have when your time comes. Isn't it, Nick?" Mrs. Cash asked, and raised both brows at him.

"What?"

"I'm just teasing you! You know how I like to kid around."

Nick did not know this. He hardly knew Mrs. Cash at all, in spite of her claim to have known him since birth.

Charlotte laughed, but she was shooting Nick a look as if he'd done something completely inappropriate.

"I'll leave you two to have your dinner. Please tell Caitlin how happy I am for her, will you?" Mrs. Cash asked.

"I will," Charlotte promised.

Charlotte resumed her seat and picked up her

fork. She looked straight ahead for a moment, then said, "We were talking about selling the office."

"Right," Nick said. He explained that he had decided the sooner they were out from under it, the better. That the money could go to some much-needed work at the ranch. He told her that he'd spoken to George and that George had offered them offices there at a very low rate. He told her everything . . . except the part about flight school.

He needed to tell her about that when they weren't surrounded by people and would not be interrupted. Someplace he could explain his thinking. He needed to talk to her about a lot of things. But not here.

When they finished, he paid the bill and they made their way outside to the parking lot. Charlotte didn't say much on the way home, but when he pulled into her drive, she gave him a funny little smile, like she wasn't certain what was going on. "So, hey, big guy, you want to come in? If you do, I'll show you just how much I've missed you."

Nick desperately wanted to come in, to sink between her thighs, to feel the heat between them. He had missed that desperately. But he was feeling so at odds with himself and with their relationship that he didn't see how he could. It was so unfair to her when these thoughts were rattling around in his head, trying to form into something coherent. He needed to get his head on straight first. They needed to talk about things first. "Ah . . . not tonight. I've got Sunny to tend to."

"Oh," she said, clearly taken aback. "Okay." She put her hand on the door handle, then looked at him. "Are you seriously rejecting me for a horse?"

"I would *never* reject you for a horse, baby. But the horse needs consistency right now. An old cowboy once told me you could teach any animal to drive a tractor as long as you were steady and consistent and didn't mind an animal driving your tractor. And then he said that if you can't be steady and consistent, you ought to do yourself and the animal a favor and hand them off to someone who can."

"Who was this old cowboy?" Charlotte asked dubiously.

"My grandfather."

"The one who was arrested for cattle rustling?"

He laughed. "How do you know these things? Yes, that one."

"I know these things because, unlike you, Charlie Prince talked all day long."

They got out and walked up onto her porch. She didn't make a move to unlock her door, but looked up at him, her eyes searching his. "Will I see you at work tomorrow?"

"I've got some things I've got to do at the ranch, but I'm sure I'll be in at some point."

"Okay." Her eyes narrowed slightly and she tilted her head to one side to study him. "Are you sure there is nothing wrong, Nick? You seem a little distant."

It was unnerving that she could sense his mood as well as she could. It was unnerving that he didn't have an honest answer for her yet. "I don't mean to be distant." That was not an answer, and judging by the expression on Charlotte's face, she knew it.

"Okay," she said.

He cupped her face with his hands and kissed her, lingering there, wishing that they could turn back the clock a few weeks and do things a little differently. When he lifted his head, she was still staring at him. "You're certain you don't have something you want to say."

"Charlotte," he said with a bit of a laugh.

She sighed. "Okay. Good night, Nick. I miss you."

"Me, too."

He waited until she had opened her door and stepped inside before he walked down the steps. What was he doing? Why was he acting like this? He had strong feelings for Charlotte, stronger than he'd ever had for a woman. So why was he pulling away? He could feel himself taking a giant step backward.

Worse, so could Charlotte.

Nick was worried. He didn't know how to do this, to become someone he was not because he loved her. Charlotte wanted something very specific. She had a timeline for it. And it seemed to him, the longer he stood in her way pretending at this life, the more harmful it was to her.

He just had to figure out how to get her to see that.

Chapter Twenty-three

She had sworn to herself that was not going to overanalyze it.

Oh, but she was overanalyzing it and she couldn't make herself stop. It was half past twelve, long past her bedtime, and here she was, sitting on her bed, her arms wrapped around a pillow, listening to Rufus snoring loudly on his dog bed. It must be nice to be a dog and have not a care in the world except a crippling fear of thunder.

Charlotte kept picking up her phone and scrolling through pictures of Liam and the kids, then tossing it down again to obsess about Nick. What was *up* with him? She knew him too well to not sense something was off. He was often grumpy, but this wasn't grumpy. This was different. This wasn't general disgruntlement with life. This was . . . this was him standing away from her.

It was weird. Physically, he had stood right beside her tonight. Emotionally, he had been a ghost. "Okay, Lot, too many Netflix dramas," she muttered. She picked up her phone but before she even looked at the pictures, she tossed it aside and lay back down to try to sleep.

The thing was, you couldn't spend every day with a person—just the two of you for the most part, for two whole years, and some even before that—and not know him. In the last few weeks, everything had been magical between them. *Perfect.* The sex was outstanding, the conversation better. But he was suddenly pulling away from her and she could not figure out why. What had changed since Caitlin had her baby? What had she done?

Maybe she should have thought more about where their relationship was headed in the first place. Maybe she should have broached it somehow, if only to protect herself. After all, it wasn't the first time he'd pulled away from her. But she'd really believed this was so different than one night after a Christmas party. He'd made her believe it was different. It *was* different. She didn't believe for a minute that Nick was leading her on. He wouldn't do that.

Or would he? Maybe she didn't know him as well as she thought.

"God, I'm making myself nuts," she muttered, and closed her eyes. But her sleep was fitful, and the next morning, she felt tired and a little cranky when she went into the office. Today, *she* was going to be the grump.

Nick didn't make it into the office. He texted her, told her something had come up with some of the stock and he'd be out with

Rafe all day. He did not mention that night.

The next day, Charlotte felt even grumpier, even with sufficient sleep. When Big Barb brought the mail, they chatted about the game that night—if the Sluggers won this one, they would be in the league playoffs. They hypothesized about who else might make the bracket. The Tool and Diehards, certainly.

"What about the Fred Savages?" Charlotte asked.

Big Barb laughed roundly. "Not a chance! They bat like a bunch of puppies."

In the mail were some papers that had come from Tim Mitchell's attorney. Charlotte decided to take them to George Lowe's offices over the lunch hour for something to do and to get out of the space where she was constantly reminded of Nick. She texted Keesha to tell her she was coming. At noon, she locked up the offices, stuffed a sun hat on her head, and climbed onto her blue bike.

"Hey!" Keesha said when Charlotte came in. "Ready to play tonight? You know you'll play us in the first round."

"Don't get ahead of yourself. We have to get past the Fred Savages first." Keesha's gaze met hers. They burst into simultaneous laughter.

She took the mail Charlotte had brought and put it in a basket labeled *GEORGE*. "You want to see your office? I've been cleaning it out."

"You already know which one I'll take?" Charlotte asked, surprised.

"Sure. Nick was over here a couple of days ago and we did the office thing."

That was quick. They were already assigning offices? Why was there such a rush? There was so much to do—they had offices at the Saddlebush building that needed to be cleaned out first. They had to think of off-site storage and a million other things. Didn't he know that? "Did he say when we are moving?"

"By the end of the month is what I understood."

"I can't be ready by then!"

Keesha halted her stride and looked with surprise at Charlotte. "He hasn't told you? Hey, maybe I'm wrong. I just know it's going to happen quick. I think he needs the money."

Things were tight, but they weren't *that* tight. Charlotte followed Keesha into an office down the hall. It was small, but it was very nice, with a view of the river. She wondered if she'd be able to bring Rufus to work with her like she did now. How sad it would be if she couldn't. "This is great," she said, standing at the window. "Is this my office, or Nick's?"

Keesha frowned as if she didn't understand why Charlotte was asking. "It's yours, Charlotte."

"So where is Nick's office?" Charlotte asked, looking over her shoulder at one across the hall. "He likes to yell for me a lot."

Keesha didn't answer. When Charlotte looked back at her, Keesha looked a little afraid. "You mean Rafe's office, don't you?"

"Why? Where is Rafe's office?"

Keesha pointed across the hall.

This was confusing her. There weren't so many empty offices here. "So where is Nick's office?" Keesha was staring so hard at her that Charlotte's skin prickled. *"What?"* she insisted.

"Nick doesn't have an office here."

Charlotte laughed. "Then where is he going to be?"

"Flight school?" Keesha answered uncertainly.

Well, that was ridiculous. There was no way he had made a plan to go to flight school without telling her. Charlotte wanted to tell Keesha that she'd really misunderstood something, but oddly, she couldn't make a sound. Because it felt like someone had gut punched her. She felt nauseated. Sick to her stomach. Light-headed. She wanted to sit down, and Keesha was staring at her like she thought she was going to faint. "Charlotte?"

Charlotte turned away from her friend's look of pity. She really wished she could sit down. Or at least kick something. Maybe she should just go ahead and vomit, because that felt like it was churning in her, too. So were tears, and she wanted to let them fall instead of forcing a smile. But most of all, she just wanted to kill Nick.

Wednesday 4:35 PM
Hey, Slugger, do you remember the game tonight? I'm worried something has happened because I usually have a hundred lame smack-talking messages from you by now. What was it a couple of weeks ago? That you liked the cool breeze my bat makes when I strike out? Another favorite—that there is nothing soft about your softball skills. Are you sick? Getting in some last-minute practice?

Wednesday 6:15 PM
See you on the field.

Wednesday 6:17 PM
Okay. Everything all right?

Charlotte didn't answer him. He didn't deserve an answer.

She couldn't believe she was going to show up. She couldn't believe *he* was going to show up. But she had decided somewhere in the middle of her meltdown this afternoon that she would not allow him to give her one more moment of distress. She was through obsessing about Nick Prince. She was going to play softball, and the Sluggers would annihilate the Freds, and then that was that—she was done with him. She was going to start looking for another job and get as far away from the Prince family as possible.

Nick wasn't going to make it easy, apparently. When she arrived at the field, he saw her, and for the first time since the league started, he didn't stick with the Freds to "get his game face on," which is what he said he had to do before each game. He jogged over to her side to say hello.

"Hey, Nick!" Luca said. "Ready to get your ass handed to you tonight?"

"Ready for me to put a hole in that glove at my first at bat?" Nick said, and shoved his little brother playfully.

"You shouldn't be over here," Rafe warned. "Big Barb has it in for you."

"Damn straight I do!" Big Barb shouted from where she and her husband were warming up.

Charlotte continued to put out the bats, carefully propping them against a chain-link fence.

"Hey," Nick said as he walked over, all smiles, like he hadn't horribly betrayed her, the bastard. "How are you? How is Caitlin today?"

"She's *great,*" Charlotte said. She continued to take the bats out of the bag, reminding herself each time that she could not swing one at Nick's head. Was he deliberately obtuse, or was he just incapable of taking a hint? Because he continued to stand there.

Charlotte couldn't take it. She dropped the bat

bag, pushed some curls from her face, and said, "I'm going to warm up now."

He smiled at the same time he frowned, as if he was amused by her but confused by her, too. "Okay. Are you—"

"You should do the same," she said quickly. "In fact, you taught me that. Get your game face on, right? *Always* have your game face on," she said, fluttering her fingers at his face. "Don't you need to go do that?"

Nick looked like he wanted to speak. But being Nick, he didn't. He just said, "Good luck tonight."

"Ho," she said with a loud laugh, and waved her arm at him. "You should wish *yourself* luck!"

She was loud enough to make Chase turn around and give her a look of incredulity. *"That's* your smack talk? Remember what I told you. Hit 'em where it hurts—in their lack of skill."

"Can you just worry about the snacks?" Charlotte said irritably. "Did you bring them?"

"When did softball turn into whose turn it is to bring snacks?" Chase complained as Nick retreated.

"And where's your team shirt?" Charlotte asked crossly.

"Man, save some of that anger for the field. Who stomped on your posies?" Chase called after her as she marched off to the metal bench that constituted their dugout.

"You don't even know what that means!" Charlotte shouted back at him.

She refused to look at the Fred Savages's bench when the game started. She refused to be drawn into the friendly banter between teams. She couldn't even smile at Colton, who kept looking at her like she had grown some horns. She tried not to be obvious, but she was aware that everyone was looking at her sideways by the third inning.

But her game was exceptional. She had never batted or fielded so well. When she ran, it was with a speed she had never before experienced. It was amazing what fury could do for one's athletic prowess.

Unfortunately, for once, the Fred Savages weren't pushovers. When Colton arrived on second during the seventh inning, he said, "We're playing *awesome* tonight. I mean all of us, but especially my team."

"Yeah, why is that?" Charlotte asked, miffed by their sudden show of skill.

"We've been practicing. Me and the girls, after work. I couldn't let the Sluggers beat us again," he said, and with a wink, he was off to third.

At the top of the ninth inning, the game was tied at four runs each. Chase had a hit and made it to third. Charlotte was next up. All she had to do was bat Chase in. "Focus," Rafe said, massaging her shoulders.

"Hit the damn ball, Charlotte!" Hallie shouted from the stands.

"Isn't she supposed to be on bed rest?" Charlotte asked no one in particular, and stepped up to the plate. Chase shouted at her to spread her feet farther apart at the same moment Luca suggested she put a little bend in her knees. *Men.* They could all go to hell. Charlotte ignored them. She swung so hard at the first pitch that she wrenched her back and missed. The second one floated just into the strike zone. She could see the Fred Savage outfielders talking to each other as if they were bored. They were having a proper tea out there.

She could also feel Nick's gaze on her, burning into her back. Like he knew her, and he knew she shouldn't be this out of sorts.

Like he knew anything about her at all. *Bastard.* The next pitch came, and she swung so hard that the impact of the ball onto the bat hurt her hands. But the ball flew off the bat, over the infield, and bounced between the tea party participants. Everyone started screaming at her to run. Charlotte ran. She rounded first, and headed for second. The woman on second looked frightened and, with a squeal, fell back from the bag. Charlotte made sure her foot hit the bag and flew past her, headed for third.

Nick was standing on the bag, waiting for the ball. He turned his head to look at her barreling toward him. In the few split seconds before she reached that base, he looked confused. And then looked alarmed. He turned his body to catch her, but Charlotte wasn't going to be caught. She was a *bulldozer.* She plowed into him at full speed. They both went down, her on top of him, knocking the breath from him for a moment. "What the fuck, Charlotte?" he demanded hoarsely.

Charlotte scrambled up, touched third base, and ran for home.

The Saddlebush Sluggers won the game by two runs.

The Sluggers were prepared to celebrate. Big Barb had brought beer enough for both teams, and Luca and Ella had come with chips and salsa. But Charlotte begged off, said the collision had given her a headache. She in fact did have a headache, but it had nothing to do with that collision. *That* had made her feel good.

"Charlotte! You're the captain! You have to stay!" her cousin Nora complained.

"Chase is really the captain," she said, and clapped her brother on the shoulder. "I'll celebrate when we win our league." She refused to listen to any other protests about her leaving and gathered her things, giving them a wave, and started a brisk walk to the parking lot. She wanted out of here, away from all their happy, smiling faces. Most definitely away from Nick. She still couldn't look at him.

She heard Nick call her name and kept walking. A moment later, he caught up to her, grabbing her arm, making her slow her step. "What in the hell is wrong with you?" he demanded.

"Me?"

His brows dipped. "Tell me what is wrong!"

Her shoulders sagged. She'd been angry for hours and she couldn't sustain it. She rubbed her temple a moment. "Were you going to tell me you were going to flight school?" she asked, and looked up into his storm blue eyes.

Nick's expression went from irritated to stricken. He looked like someone had told him one of his rescue cows had died. "Who told you that?"

"Does it matter?"

He seemed to ponder that for a moment, but shook his head.

So it was true. Charlotte turned her gaze from him and looked at her car. She wished she'd made it before he caught her. She wished she could have gone home and gotten her head together with a shot or two of tequila before they had this conversation.

The touch of his fingers to hers startled her. She yanked her hand away from his. "Keesha told me. She thought I knew."

"Damn it," he muttered. "I haven't seen you—"

"Don't do that, Nick. Don't make excuses. You should have told me when you didn't take an office at George's. You should have talked to me whenever you first had the *idea*. Just out of curiosity, when *did* you decide this? At what point did you decide that you were going on with your life and it didn't matter what I thought?"

"Never," he said flatly.

"Just tell me, Nick," she pleaded with him. She needed to know if he'd decided after a night of fantastic sex. Or when he was looking at her. Or the moment she went off to help her family. At what point had he decided that he was moving on without her? The thought snatched her breath away, and she made a pitiful sound of trying to gasp for air.

Nick reached for her. She pushed his hand away, but he wrapped his arms around her anyway and held her. "You knew I applied to flight school. I was very open about that."

"But you said you didn't know if you'd be accepted. You said you didn't know if you could afford it."

"Yeah," he said, and sighed. "I got the confirmation when your nephew was born."

She pushed away from him and folded her arms around her body to hold herself. "So you, what, just jumped at the chance to go without mentioning it to me? I was texting you every day."

"I didn't think a text message was the way to have the conversation. I wanted to see you in person, Charlotte, and we haven't had hardly a moment—"

"We went to dinner! I asked you if something was wrong and you said no. Is that why you're selling the office? To pay for flight school?"

"No," he said. "That had to be done. That's why you suggested it, remember? It's a drain on the ranch coffers. That happened quickly because George brought me a buyer." He took a step closer to her. "I wanted to talk to you about it. At dinner. Before then, after then. But I wanted to do it in person, without interruption. And it took me a while to figure out what it was I wanted to say. But more than anything, I wanted us to decide together where this thing between us is going."

"Then why didn't we, Nick? I didn't know. I was just enjoying this, I didn't know I was supposed to nail you down and have a conversation. Why didn't you tell me?"

"I was enjoying it, too, Charlotte. You know that I was. It's been . . . it's been amazing," he said quietly, and touched her face. "But we want different things. We've always known that. And I . . . I realized when your nephew was born that I can't be the person you want."

"What are you talking about?" she said angrily. "I didn't ask you to marry me or give me your sperm."

He drew a breath. "You want a family, and that was never more apparent to me than when I saw the way you looked at that baby. I want to fly and see the world. It's a big difference."

"What I *want*," she said bitterly, "is you."

"I want you, too, Charlotte." He looked down a moment. "I'm making a mess of this. But I want you and I have for a long time," he said, looking her in the eye again. "Unfortunately, I don't want the same life as you want."

"What are you saying, that you don't want marriage?" she asked, confused. "I don't care about—"

"I don't want kids," he said flatly.

His admission stunned her. Did people really not want kids? "Never?"

He rubbed the back of his neck. "I don't know. I . . ." He sighed, dropped his hand. "It's never been a desire of mine. I think no."

Charlotte could only stare at him. Her mind couldn't seem to put these things together. She knew he wanted to fly, of course she did. But to never have kids? *Never?* Was he saying he wanted to be alone in this world forever? Flying around with no one to come home to?

"Do you want me to stay and raise kids with you when you know it's not what I want?" he asked, sounding almost desperate. "Do you want to live a life with me gone half the time when you know that's not what you want?"

Charlotte slowly turned away from him. She needed to think. She needed to absorb this news.

"It doesn't matter what I want. You've already made the decision for me," she said, and began to walk.

"Don't walk away."

She kept walking. She had to—she was on the verge of crying. She was frustrated and hurt and angry and sad, and the tears were building and she would not, she *would not* cry in front of him.

Somehow, she managed to get to her car. She tried to open the door, but it was locked. *Shit.* She'd left her keys with the bats. So Charlotte turned her back to her car and slid down to the ground. She hated Nick. She loved Nick. She really truly loved him, and for the life of her, she didn't know why right now.

The tears started to fall, and she drew her knees up, wrapped her arms around them, hung her head, and let them fall.

"Charlotte?"

She jumped—she hadn't heard anyone approach. She looked up, wiping tears from beneath her eyes. Colton Rivers squatted down in front of her with a look of concern. "Hey, are you okay?"

Charlotte pressed her lips together. She shook her head no.

Colton eased himself into a sitting position next to her. Charlotte buried her face again. "I've got all night," Colton said softly.

Chapter Twenty-four

There was an old señor who lived near Uvalde and who Nick knew took in abandoned animals. He'd heard about him through the years, a widower with a disabled son. Nick had thought about calling him when he found Sunny in his drive, but he thought the man took only smaller animals.

Turns out, the old man had a variety of abandoned animals. Nick drove out to see him Saturday morning.

He couldn't even think of going to Dallas until he found a place for his livestock. He wouldn't ask Rafe to look after them—he'd already asked enough of his brother-in-law, and besides, Rafe had the martial arts studio and, soon, his first child. Luca had offered to take them, but Nick didn't feel right about that, either. Luca had his hands full with the conservation project, and he'd mentioned recently that he and Ella were thinking of starting a family, too.

He couldn't imagine the cows walking up to a fence in the morning and there being no one there to speak to them. He couldn't imagine Priscilla without someone to scratch her ears. He couldn't imagine Frank and Sunny in a place where they didn't have a little room to roam.

The Uvalde ranch, west of San Antonio, was tiny by Nick's standards, only about three hundred acres. The man and his son lived in an old, run-down house, but it was well kept. He had a kitchen garden, just like Charlotte's, and three dogs lazing around on a covered porch. There were two longhorns out in the field, both of them lying down. There were some Angus cattle in a fenced pasture, their heads to the ground, eating up the grass. On the other side of the house were several horses grazing in a field. He wondered how Frank and Sunny would fit in.

The old man's barn was a short walk from his house. There were chickens and goats, and a cat on top of a baling machine watching them closely.

"I got a couple of kids that come out every day to help," Mr. Rodriguez said. "Part of their community service from juvie hall." He smiled up at Nick. His face was weathered by sun and old age, but the crow's-feet around his eyes were white as snow. "It's good for them."

Nick nodded. He looked around again, tried to imagine his livestock moving here. He felt a little sick at the stomach. He didn't do much for his cows, but he felt like he was abandoning them all again. "My cattle, I've got twelve now, they like someone to talk to them in the morning."

"Yeah?" Mr. Rodriguez said. He seemed interested.

"The pig, she's pretty social," he said. Priscilla would be happy here, he decided. There were a lot of animals for her to befriend. "Got a horse who's a hundred if he's a day, practically blind, but he doesn't care where he goes. And then a mare. She's just coming out of a depression," he said, and looked at Mr. Rodriguez. "She needs some extra attention."

"My son, he loves the horses," Mr. Rodriguez said. "And I'm a talker," he added with a grin.

Nick thanked Mr. Rodriguez and said he'd be in touch, and drove back to Three Rivers.

He wasn't thinking clearly. He hadn't been sleeping well, his dreams tortured with Charlotte's face. She'd looked crushed the night of the softball game, and he had done that to her. He hated himself for it, for every blunder he'd made. He needed to talk to her and have that conversation about the two of them. He needed to tell her he loved her. The logical side of him said now wasn't a good time to say it. But the emotional side of him needed her to know.

So instead of turning left on the San Antonio highway and heading home, he turned right and drove into town.

Her car and her bike were at her house, so Nick steeled himself. The front door was open, and through the screen door he saw Rufus haul himself up and trot over some things she had on the floor to greet him, his tail wagging furiously.

"Hey, Rufus," he said. He knocked on the screen door.

Charlotte's head popped out of the hallway door. She stood motionless for a moment, then reluctantly came forward to open the door.

"Hey, gorgeous," he said.

"Okay," she said, and opened the screen door. "Let's get this over with."

That was not the greeting he was hoping for, but it was the one he expected. Rufus, on the other hand, was so happy to see him that Nick could hardly get in the door. He went down on one knee and gave Rufus a proper greeting, then stood up, brushed the dog hair from himself, and looked up.

Charlotte was on her couch, sitting cross-legged like a little Buddha. Her eyes looked dull, and her skin was patchy. He didn't know for certain, but he thought she'd been crying.

"What do you want, Nick?" She sounded resigned. Detached.

"To talk."

"A little late for talking, but whatever." She gestured to a chair.

Nick stepped around Rufus and took the seat. Apparently, she was painting more silk panels—four of them were hanging from the ceiling fan, and he had to look at her through them. She stared at him without any expression at all. No sparkling eyes. No bright smile. He couldn't stand it, and stood from the seat, pushed aside the silk panels, and went down on his haunches before her. He put his hand on her bare knee. "This is not how I wanted this to go, obviously."

"Oh no?" she asked. There was no emotion in her voice. "How did you want it to go?"

"I wanted to talk to you. I wanted to tell you that I love you, Charlotte. I love you so much."

Her eyes widened. "What the hell, Nick?"

"I do love you, isn't it obvious?"

"No! You're breaking up with me, so how can you love me at the same time? That makes no sense."

He took her hand in his. "I do, and that's why I have to talk to you about this. This isn't a fling for me. If it was, this would be easier. But I do love you, Charlotte, so much, and because I do, I can't help but consider what you want from life. And where we are. And where we are going."

"We're going nowhere, apparently."

"Come on," he said softly, and moved to sit beside her on the couch. "You knew I had applied to flight school again. You knew I wanted to go, that I have always wanted to go. You gave me that toy airplane a few years ago, remember?"

She looked away from him.

"And I know that you want kids, and a family. More than anything. You *told* me this. You gave

437

me your timeline. You said you wanted someone who would ride hard to get to you. Do you remember?"

She made a little gasp that sounded as if she were in pain. "I remember. I thought that was you."

That was a dagger to his heart. He slid his hand onto her thigh. "I did, too, baby. But it's not me, and I realized that when your nephew was born. You were so happy and it was so obvious how much you wanted that for yourself. I love you enough to want to see you with that. And even though it kills me, I love you enough to admit that I can't be the one to give you that. Do you know how easy it would be to just continue on, living in the moment?"

A lone tear slid down her face. "You should have talked to me if you were thinking these things."

"You're right. I should have."

She looked at him with tear-filled eyes. "I get what you're saying. But I don't want to lose you, Nick."

"I don't want to lose you, either. But I don't want to lead you on or stand in your way, either."

Charlotte wiped the tear away. "So we're breaking up." She wasn't asking him; she was announcing it. "I'm really going to miss Pepper and Frank and Priscilla. And the cows," she added tearfully.

He was, too. He put his arm around her, drawing her into his chest.

"I don't want to come into the office every day and have to see you."

He didn't want to come into the office and not see her. "I'll probably move to Dallas in a month or so," he said. "Why don't you take your office at George's, and I'll stay at Saddlebush until the sale closes."

She nodded. She pushed up and away from him, and stood up. She tried to smile, but she looked pained.

"Do you want to talk about it?" he asked her.

She shook her head. "Doesn't seem like there is a lot more to say, does it?"

Nick stood, too. This felt so strange. So painful. The end of the best part of his life.

Rufus thought they were all going somewhere and stood between them, his tail wagging. So Nick reached for Charlotte's hand, and together, they walked to the door.

The hardest thing he'd ever done in his life was walk out the door. He couldn't do it at first—he pulled her into his arms and kissed her. A long, sweet kiss, with so much emotion between them, so many regrets and sorrows. He questioned what he was doing. He questioned everything he had ever known. Here was a beautiful woman who wanted him, and he was walking out the door.

But eventually, he made himself do it. He

stepped through the screen door and moved toward the steps.

"Nick?"

He paused and looked back.

"I love you, too, you old grouch. I think I always will."

Well, that did it—his heart shattered. "Same," he said quietly, and carried on down the steps to his truck. He felt empty inside. Like the floodgates had opened and everything had bled out of him. Like something vital had been chopped off and discarded.

He drove almost blindly from her house, through town, past the ridiculously large Saddlebush offices. He drove to Three Rivers Ranch.

At Three Rivers, Nick walked into what seemed like an empty house. He looked in the kitchen, but the lights were off. He walked on, to the massive living room with the picture windows and view of the ranch, the river, the hills in the distance. Nick guessed this room and that view had been photographed dozens of times for magazines and house decor shows.

His mother was seated at a small writing desk. She looked startled, as if she'd seen a ghost. "I wasn't expecting you."

Nick felt a twinge of guilt. He didn't come around as often as he should because he found it so hard to be here.

"What's wrong?" she asked, standing up from the desk. "You look like you lost your best friend."

He *had* lost his best friend. Maybe his only friend outside of Colton. He and his broken heart. "It's been a day," he said.

His mother nodded. "I guess you've come to tell me you're going to fly out of here and go to that aviation school."

Nick blinked. He looked around, half expecting everyone to jump out from behind the bookcases or drapes and demand an explanation. "Does *everyone* know?" he asked incredulously.

"I don't know. George warned me. And you have that look on your face. Like you have something to say."

"Yeah." Nick sighed. He scrubbed his face with his hands and fell onto a leather couch. "Mom, I just want you to understand. This is something—"

"That you've wanted your entire life. I know, Nick." She smiled sadly and sat, too. "I can be a selfish old broad. I want my chicks around me, and especially you. You're the backbone of this family now that your dad is gone. But it's not fair to ask you to put your dreams on hold because Dad died."

"Mom, I'm not the backbone—*you* are. You always have been. *Especially* since Dad died. I haven't even been around."

"Well, you've been grieving."

"No. I've been mad," he said. "I've been mad at Dad for a long time. For dying and leaving me with this responsibility because he *knew*. He knew better than anyone that I didn't want to be a cattleman. That I wanted to go out in the world. So please don't make me out to be some sort of integral part of this ranch. I'm not. I'm a resentful, disgruntled employee."

His mother slowly smiled. "You know, sometimes, you really remind me of me. Go do what you need to do, Nick. But I will miss you so much."

He was stunned by this change in her. He sat up. "Mom, I will come home," he said earnestly. "I'm going to fly back and forth as often as I can. I need the flight hours, and I have the means to do it."

"But then what? When you get your hours, then what?"

"I'll still come home. If I can get on with an airline, I'll probably get the regional flights. I'll be home a lot."

She shook her head. "You're not going to be happy flying to Tulsa and Denver."

"It doesn't matter. I'll be flying. And there is something about every city that is worth seeing."

"I don't know about that." She took his hand and squeezed it. "You've been a good son."

"Don't go and make it sound like I'm dying."

She smiled sadly. "I want you to be happy."

None of this is what he'd expected her to say. He'd expected her to talk about responsibility to the family. "You know what, Mom? George is a good influence on you."

"Oh, stop it," she said, and leaned over to hug him. "Now you sound like your grandmother."

They talked a little more about his plans. He hadn't really made any, other than he knew he needed to get an apartment near the Dallas–Fort Worth airport, and that he planned to pay the tuition from his trust. Other than that, he'd thought about the animals. Always the animals.

When he got up to leave, his mother said, "You didn't say anything about Charlotte."

Just the mention of her name made Nick feel ill. "We broke up," he made himself say, and then glanced back at his mother. "She wants a family. She wants kids. Dogs. Easter Sundays and Halloweens, or something like that. I don't want kids. I'm not in a place where I could be a dad, and I don't think I'll ever be in that place."

His mother smiled a little. "You may change your mind about that one day."

Nick knew himself, and he shook his head.

"When will you move?"

"I figure I'll be up there by the end of September."

"That's just a few weeks," she mused.

It was a lifetime to Nick, and not for the reasons anyone would think. It was a lifetime of missing Charlotte.

Chapter Twenty-five

It was not as hard as Charlotte thought it would be to move on from Nick. Not that she didn't ache with the loss of him every day and think about him constantly. Not that she hadn't figured out that she had loved him for a lot longer than she'd ever let on or even admitted to herself. But she seemed to have picked herself up from that awful weekend and gotten back into the swing of things.

Cassie and Keesha helped her move her things out of the Saddlebush offices and into the law offices. Cassie was livid on Charlotte's behalf. "He's just an ass," she said again for the umpteenth time as they loaded books into a bookcase.

"No, he's not," Charlotte said wearily. "I mean, he's right. We don't want the same things. How long do you go on if you know that you don't want the same things?"

"That's a mature and healthy attitude," Keesha said. "But I'd still like to kick his ass."

"I hope he leaves soon. I don't want to see his face around Three Rivers," Cassie said.

"*You're* not around Three Rivers," Charlotte

said with a laugh. "You're in San Antonio most of the time."

"But still. He doesn't deserve you, Charlotte. No one does, really, but him especially."

She appreciated their concern and support, but Charlotte didn't think Nick was an ass. Maybe he should have talked to her sooner, maybe she should have asked more questions in this relationship. Whatever, she had to agree with Nick. There was a fundamental difference between them.

"So I guess we need to reactivate your dating profile," Cassie said. "I think you need some new pictures—"

"No!" Charlotte and Keesha shouted at the same time.

"I'm not getting back on the app thing, Cass," Charlotte said. "I think I need to Netflix and chill by myself for a while."

She would not listen to Cassie's arguments to the contrary.

Colton was a good man and checked in on Charlotte a couple of times. He'd been so nice to her that night in the parking lot, letting her blubber all over him. And he had shown up to the last two Slugger games before they were knocked out of the playoffs. One day, he came in to the office and stood in her doorway and asked if she wanted to get a drink sometime.

"Oh," Charlotte said. "Oh, I—"

"You don't have to answer me right away," he said quickly.

"Colton, you are the best," she said. "But I think . . . I think maybe I just need . . ." What did she need? She needed Nick. She *still* needed Nick. She worried she would always need Nick. But she smiled at Colton and said, "I just ended something and I don't know if I should."

"That's cool," he said, and held up a hand. "Just friends." He smiled, pointed at her in what she supposed was a friendly way, and left her office.

She should have dated Colton when everyone told her she should. Ah, but that Nick, she couldn't quite resist him.

As for Nick, she hadn't seen him since they broke up, but she tried hard to put everything back to normal for them. She didn't want an enemy. She didn't want to hate him. She just wanted her life back.

From: Charlotte charlotte@saddlebushco.com
To: Nick nickprince@saddlebushco.com
Subject: Finance Reports

I dropped them off at your office this morning. On your desk.

From: Nick nickprince@saddlebushco.com
To: Charlotte charlotte@saddlebushco.com
Subject: Re: Finance Reports

I know. Red folder. The white folder is the papers we need to sell the office. Way ahead of you.

From: Charlotte charlotte@saddlebushco.com
To: Nick nickprince@saddlebushco.com
Subject: Re: Finance Reports

Look at you, on board with the color scheme. Great! All knowledge seems to lie within you. ☺

From: Nick nickprince@saddlebushco.com
To: Charlotte charlotte@saddlebushco.com
Subject: Re: Finance Reports

Thanks. I see you've had the peppermint tea, too.

One day, three weeks after Nick and Charlotte had ended it, Hallie Prince went into labor. That same afternoon, Colton came by to speak to George. He appeared at Charlotte's office with a rawhide dog bone that was at least two feet long. "What is *that?*"

"Oh, this? This is a gift for Rufus."

Charlotte laughed. "I don't want to upset you, Colton, but he's kind of seeing a beagle around the corner."

"No," Colton said, and pretended to be stricken. "Can you talk to him for me?"

"I can try, but I have to warn you—he goes whichever way the wind is blowing."

Colton laughed. "I was thinking of getting a dog."

"You were?"

"Yeah, I think so. I moved into a new place. You know that new subdivision on Sam Bass Road?"

"Yes! Those are really nice houses."

"They are. And I've got a yard, so . . ." He shrugged.

"What kind of dog?"

"I don't know. What kind would you recommend?" he asked, stepping into her office.

"A rescue," Charlotte said instantly.

"Interesting. I don't know how to go about getting a rescue."

Charlotte smiled. "I think Rufus can teach you."

"You think he'll see me?"

"Maybe," Charlotte said coyly. "Maybe if you come by Saturday or Sunday, we can go to the animal shelter and let Rufus have a look."

Colton grinned. "Maybe I will," he said.

From: Charlotte charlotte@saddlebushco.com
To: Nick nickprince@saddlebushco.com
Subject: Re: Hallie's baby!

CONGRATULATIONS ON YOUR NEW NIECE! I am so happy for Hallie and Rafe! I went by to see the baby and she is so cute, Nick! And so big! Hallie said she'd pushed a nine-pound bowling ball from her vagina and didn't hit a single pin. Sorry, is that TMI? I know how squeamish you can be about stuff like that. DO YOU LOVE YOUR NIECE? I'm so glad Hallie had the baby before you left. When are you leaving, anyway? Not that I am counting the days or anything.

I'm really not. I'm more like dreading the days, to be honest. But that's a story for another time. I have to get dressed. Colton and I are going dog shopping today. He's getting a dog!

Chapter Twenty-six

Hallie's baby arrived after twenty-two hours of labor. Much to Luca's disappointment, Hallie and Rafe did not name their daughter Hannah Fontana. They named her Amelia. She had big blue newborn eyes and a little tuft of blondish red hair on her head. She looked squishy, Nick thought, like Caitlin's baby, but there was something different about her squish. Maybe because she looked a little like Hallie. Not much, really. But a little.

She was so inconceivably tiny, but everything was there, just in miniature. Tiny ears. Tiny fingers and toes. A tiny little nose and mouth. Little arms and legs that looked like they'd break if you touched them wrong.

Hallie made Nick hold her. "She's your niece! Pick her up and hold her, idiot!" Nick let that go. Hallie was still wound up from the delivery.

But Amelia was crying. "I'll drop her."

"For God's sake," his grandmother said. "If you can hold a beer bottle, you can hold a baby. And we all know you can hold a beer bottle."

So Ella put the little swaddled bundle into his arms. She didn't weigh a thing. He had one hand behind her head, his arm beneath her body. And Amelia stopped crying.

"Oh my God!" Hallie said. "You've got the touch, Nick!"

"What touch? What does that mean?"

"The baby touch," Ella said. "Some people have a calming influence on babies. You're like a baby whisperer."

His family had a good laugh at that.

When Hallie came home from the hospital, Nick drove over to see them about every other day. Hallie and Rafe had renovated Ella's old farmhouse and lived there for the time being. It was cozy and quaint, and it was the perfect place to bring their first child home, Hallie declared. And it wasn't too far from Nick's house.

He was amazed to see how the baby changed every day. Amelia was almost a new baby every time he came by.

About a month after she was born, Nick moved his livestock to Uvalde and said a tearful good-bye to them while the old señor stood by with his head bowed. The cows gathered around like he had something important to impart. Sunny and Priscilla stood by, too, waiting and watching, although he suspected Priscilla thought there might be food involved. But Frank, bless him, stood with his hindquarters to Nick. He was so old now he probably didn't know what was going on.

The next week, he locked up the Saddlebush offices—now under contract—and paid a visit to Charlotte in the office. He brought in a box of files, arranged by color.

"So this is it, huh?" she said, and stood up from her desk.

"Yeah. I'm going to fly on out of here," he said. His heart was hammering in his chest. There was so much he wanted to say, but as usual with him, words didn't come easy. Charlotte understood him so well. She smiled, her swimming pool eyes sparkling, and walked from around her desk to him. She tilted her head up and examined his face. She touched her fingers to the beard he'd grown. "I'm going to send you a care package of Just for Men to touch up the gray."

He couldn't laugh. He still couldn't speak. There was no way to say how sorry he was. Or how bereft he felt in leaving her. Or how excited he was to be embarking on this adventure after a lifetime of wanting it. He opened his mouth. Then closed it.

"It's okay," Charlotte whispered. "I know. Me, too." And she hugged him. Tight. Then kissed him lightly on the mouth. "I'm going to miss you so much, you old grouch."

"I already miss you," he said. "I've been missing you. I will always miss you."

Her eyes filled with tears, and his did, too.

Charlotte shoved his shoulder. "Get out of here. Go be a pilot or something."

That tender good-bye kiss sizzled through his heart and shot out through his veins for hours afterward.

Nick flew out the next morning with Pepper, a couple of bags with his belongings, and his laptop. Amelia was seven weeks old.

Nick loved flight school. He was learning so much, and he couldn't wait to fly bigger planes. Every weekend, he flew home. Every weekend, he couldn't wait to see Amelia.

The weeks zipped by, and Amelia was smiling. When Nick walked in the door, she gave him that little baby smile, and Nick's heart melted a little more.

"She loves you, Nick," Hallie said with wonder. "And she doesn't like men."

"No, she does not," Rafe said. "I don't know if I ought to be offended by how much she likes you. It took her weeks to warm up to me."

Nick laughed. "That's not true."

"The hell it isn't," Rafe said. "When George or Luca or my dad drops by, she cries. But not you."

Nick grinned so wide that it felt like his face might split.

On one of those weekends home, Nick was on the floor with Amelia, watching her reach for the stuffed toys hanging above her from her baby gym. "This is cool," Nick said.

"Charlotte gave it to her." Hallie was sitting on her couch, her legs tucked up under her, a new Harlan Coben book on her lap. Nick had brought it to her. He'd already read it.

Nick watched Amelia kick her legs out, over and over again. "So how is she?" he asked.

"Charlotte? She's *great*."

"You don't have to yell."

"Yes, I do. That was dumbest thing you ever did, Nick, letting her go. But it's too late now because she's dating Colton Rivers."

His gut clenched. "Good for her," he muttered.

"Mm-hmm," Hallie said, her eyes narrowing.

"Are they serious?"

Hallie suddenly tossed the book aside and came off the couch, falling onto Nick's back to hug him. "*What* are you doing?" he asked.

"I don't know, you looked so sad that I thought you needed a hug. I don't know if they are serious. Maybe. Probably. Colton is a great guy."

Colton *was* a great guy. He'd kept in touch with Nick, checking in to see how it was going in flight school, and giving him news about Three Rivers. They'd chat about flying and planes over text. They'd even gotten together for a drink a few weeks ago. Funny, Colton had failed to mention he was seeing Charlotte.

Nick hadn't talked to Charlotte. It seemed like they'd both silently but mutually agreed to go on with their lives, and the contact had dropped off.

But Lord, he thought about her every single day. She was like a little bird, flitting around his thoughts. He lived with her ghost. She was his biggest love, his biggest regret, his biggest wish.

Nick loved what he was doing, loved what he was learning. But he needed more hours. The usual path to more flying time was to get work as a flight instructor for beginning pilots. Nick had signed up to do that, but one day, Bob Ferguson, another pilot he'd become friendly with, mentioned another way for him to get some hours—flying dogs on shelter lists for euthanasia to rescue organizations in different parts of the country. It was something he could do with his own plane, and nonprofit animal rights agencies helped with the cost of fuel and maintenance if he donated his time. When he had the necessary hours and certifications, Bob said, he could fly bigger planes with bigger animals.

"Bigger animals," Nick said. "Bigger than dogs?"

"Well, sometimes we've got abused or neglected animals that need a lift. Like a herd of goats."

"Goats!" Nick laughed.

"Horses, too. Since you know about horses, it would be a good fit."

Nick realized Bob was serious. "What about cows?"

Bob laughed as if that was a joke. "Haven't heard of that, but you never know."

"I'm interested," Nick said instantly.

It didn't take long to be vetted and start flying the animal transport. He split his weekends—two flying for the organization, and two flying home. He had to see little Amelia when he could. He didn't know how it had happened, but she'd wrapped him around her tiny finger. It was amazing to him that a man could be so convinced he didn't want kids in his life and then, practically overnight, become a slave to one. He came home with toys and outfits he ordered off the internet during the week. He talked Hallie into letting him take Amelia to the dog park to see some dogs. He took the baby to the ranch under the guise of seeing Nana—his mother refused to be called grandma—but really to hold her up to the fence and guide her little hand to touch the horses.

Amelia tugged at his heartstrings, and the harder she pulled, the more he thought of how he'd thoroughly, utterly, blown it with Charlotte. He didn't dislike kids. And now he didn't feel like he didn't want them, either.

Why did he have to make it all or nothing with Charlotte? Why hadn't he even considered asking her to come to Dallas with him? They could have figured out how to hand off Saddlebush to Rafe and Hallie. But he had assumed for the both of them that he didn't want her life and she didn't want his.

He'd been a goddamn fool, that was what. And

he'd lost the only woman he'd ever really, truly loved.

In April, Charlotte turned thirty-three.

Nick came home one spring afternoon after flying six dogs from Pennsylvania to Tulsa. He liked Tulsa. It was a pretty town. He thought maybe someday he'd fly his mother up there so she could see for herself.

He went to visit Amelia, and convinced Hallie to let him take Amelia to the park. "I saw some ducks," he said. "She'd want to see the ducks."

"She's seen the ducks," Hallie said.

"Come on, Hallie."

"Fine," she said, grinning at him. "You are *such* a softy. You're like a grandpa. Let me get her dressed." Hallie went to a basket of clothes and began to dig through them. "Hey, that realty office took the big bronc-riding monstrosity down from our old office building."

"They did?'

"They didn't think bronc riders went with Hearth and Home Realty. They moved it to some-place in San Antonio. Charlotte said they took it apart and are going to put it back together, and that moving that thing cost almost as much as creating it." She laughed and shook her head.

Nick put his hand into his pocket and made a fist at the mention of Charlotte. "I guess she and Colton are going to make it official, huh?"

"What?"

"Charlotte and Colton."

Hallie stopped what she was doing. She turned her head and looked at him. "They broke up."

Nick's heart stopped beating. Just stopped. And then started again with such a violent fit that he coughed. "They . . . when?"

"Three or four months ago. You didn't know that?"

Nick could only stare at her.

"Wow!" Hallie said, delighted to impart the news. "She said he was a great guy. But between you and me, I think Colton was no challenge for her. He did whatever she wanted," Hallie said as she dressed her daughter. "Charlotte needs someone to push back. He never pushed back."

Charlotte definitely needed someone to push back. She thrived on the pushback.

Hallie finished dressing Amelia and handed her over to Nick. Amelia gurgled with delight and grabbed a fistful of the beard he'd grown in over the winter. Hallie strapped the diaper bag over his shoulder. "Back by three for her nap. Do *not* be late. The whole house is in chaos when she's off her schedule."

"Got it," Nick said, but he didn't really hear her. All he could think about was that Charlotte was not with Colton.

He strapped Amelia into his truck and drove into town. He did not drive to the river park, however, because at the intersection of Main

459

and Hope Streets, he turned toward Charlotte's house. He didn't know what he was going to say. He didn't know if this was stupid or smart. All he knew was that he had to see her.

As soon as he pulled into her drive, he remembered it was noon on a Thursday. "Idiot," he muttered, and glanced at Amelia in the back seat of his truck. "I'm talking about me, Amelia. Not you."

"Ba ba ba ba ba ba," Amelia said, and grabbed her toes.

He put the truck in reverse, and when he looked in his rearview mirror, his breath flew out of him. Charlotte was riding up the street on her bike. She was looking curiously at the truck.

He instantly turned off the truck and got out.

"Nick?"

"Hi," he said awkwardly. "Ah . . ."

She dropped her bike and stood looking at him, her long legs braced apart, her curly hair piled on top of her head. Nick didn't know what to do. But then he heard Amelia and said, "Just a minute. One minute." He hurried to the other side of the truck and got his niece out, then walked back around with her in his arms.

The moment Charlotte saw Amelia, her face burst into sunshine. "Meli!" She exclaimed. "May I hold her?"

Amelia immediately held out her arms for Charlotte. "Wow, this is a treat! Come in, come in!" she said, and she was already bouncing up the steps with Amelia, talking to her, explaining that she had a puppy who was dying to say hello.

That so-called puppy was Rufus, who launched himself at Nick with such joy that he nearly knocked him over. Amelia laughed with delight as Rufus covered Nick's hands with kisses. When the dog had sufficiently covered Nick in slobber, he allowed Nick to follow Charlotte and Amelia inside.

Amelia was on the floor, and gurgled with laughter again when Rufus had a good sniff of her.

"How the hell are you, Nicholas Nickleby?" Charlotte asked. "How is flight school? Keesha said she heard you'd be done in a couple of months. She was hoping you'd be flying her plane when she goes on vacation next month."

"Yes," he said, and tried to swallow down the croak in his throat. "I'm not flying commercial yet. I've been flying animal rescue."

"I heard!" she said. "Couldn't find a better person for that, could they? You want something to drink?"

"No. Charlotte, I—"

"I'm not going to lie. I went out to Uvalde to check on your animals. I had to see for myself that they were okay. Mr. Rodriguez and his son could not have been sweeter."

Nick was surprised. And very touched. "You did?"

"Sure," she said, looking at him with that dazzling smile. "I know that must have been hard for you. I know that—"

"I love you." The words were projectiles out of his mouth, flying like missiles at her.

Charlotte gasped. Her mouth gaped.

"I think I love you more than I did last summer. Yeah, I do. I love you, and I think about you so much, and I would give anything if we could sit in that tub and stare at Frank staring back at us, and I think about so many things like how wrong I was, and why didn't I just ask you to come with me? Why didn't I ask how we could work it out? Because I was so angry for so long, and I thought I had all the answers. But I didn't, Charlotte."

Charlotte sank onto her couch. She reached down and picked up Amelia and put her on her lap.

"I know I said I never wanted kids, but that little squirt changed that. I love her to pieces, Charlotte. I love her so much that I feel like my chest could explode with it. But mostly, I love you, and if you're not seeing anyone, and you don't hate me, I hope . . . no, actually, I'm begging you, can we try and work it out? Can we at least see what it would look like?"

She said nothing. She seemed a little shell-shocked, and he didn't blame her. He was, too.

He couldn't believe he'd just said all that, but it was like his heart had exploded all over her living room. "I have missed you so much," he said thickly. "You were right, you know. My heart's not broken—it's beating like a damn drum right now," he said, and pressed his hand to his chest. "Because I am riding hard for you, Charlotte. I am riding hard."

"Wow," Charlotte said softly. "Okay."

What did *okay* mean? He was standing there, his heart on a silver platter between them. Had he not said it the right way? Had he not made her understand how deeply etched into his soul she was?

"Meli, I'm going to tell you a story. Once upon a time, there was this Christmas party. Your uncle Nick and I had some *outrageously* good sex." She looked at Nick. "Would you agree it was outrageously good?"

He did not get where she was going, but he swallowed and nodded.

"Uncle Nick could never get over it. I used to tease him about it in so many ways. But the thing was, I finally figured out that I never got over it, either. I had always had a little bit of a crush on him, because I have a huge character flaw that makes me attracted to grouchy men, and Uncle Nick is a big grouch. And after that night, there was no turning back." She looked at Nick. "There's still no turning back. But . . ."

She swallowed. Her gaze was clear and blue, and piercing his. "But Uncle Nick broke my heart, Meli. *Twice.* The first time wasn't as bad as the second, and I'm pretty sure the second wouldn't come close to being as devastating as the third."

"Charlotte . . . there won't be a third time. I swear it."

"I'm not sure I can believe that, Nick." She stood up with Amelia, stepped over Rufus's stretched-out body, and came to stand before him. Amelia tried to grab his beard as Charlotte pressed her palm against his cheek. "We still want different things. None of that has changed."

"But it has. I was wrong about kids and family. There's not just one road to happiness. It doesn't have to be perfect. We can take different roads but end up together all the same."

But Charlotte shook her head. "Is that really true? Listen . . . you don't know how much it means to me that you came here today and said these things. But I can't take the risk again. It hurts too bad." She handed the baby to him. "I'm sorry, Nick."

"God, please don't say that, baby," he begged her. "At least think about it. I love you, Charlotte. I will always love you."

"Yeah. Same here." She smiled sadly and stepped back. "I do love you. But I can't." She folded her arms across her, as if she were holding herself together.

Nick's heart sank. He'd been filled with so much hope, but this . . . this, he should have expected. He didn't want to accept defeat, but he couldn't stand in her house and hope she'd suddenly change her mind. So he nodded, buried his face in Amelia's neck, and smelled the sweet baby-powdered scent of her, and turned to go.

He scratched Rufus behind the ears on the way out. He was walking almost blindly, his mind's eye filled with images of Charlotte and his heart drowning in regrets. When he reached his truck, he looked back. She was standing at the door with Rufus, and he could tell by her pained expression she was trying to keep from shedding tears.

He was not so lucky. He strapped Amelia into the truck, then got in the driver's seat. "Want to see some ducks, kid?" he asked.

Amelia babbled.

He drove down to the river with her, took some stale bread Hallie had given him, and held Amelia on her feet while he tossed bites to the ducks.

He felt devastated. He had to cling to the idea that she loved him. Charlotte had said it today— she loved him.

Wait . . . did that mean there was still a chance? The only way there would be a chance was if he could convince her that he'd never hurt her again. But how in the hell did he do that?

"Ba ba ba ba," Amelia chatted at the ducks.

She fell onto her bottom and started to grab handfuls of grass.

What would Charlotte do in his situation? He couldn't suppress a smile. She'd never leave him alone, that was what. She'd be blowing up his phone with pictures of Amelia . . .

Hey. He could do this the Charlotte way.

Nick smiled at Amelia.

Chapter Twenty-seven

Charlotte was finishing up some paperwork related to the lawsuit when her phone buzzed. She reached down for her bag—Rufus was lying on top of it, so she had to maneuver it out from under his uncooperative self—and dug her phone out. When she opened it, a picture appeared. It was from Nick.

"Hey, what are you doing for lunch?" Keesha asked, appearing in the doorway of Charlotte's office.

"Ah . . ." She was staring at her phone. Nick had taken a selfie.

"What is that?"

"I don't believe it, but Nick took a selfie." She turned the phone to Keesha so she could see. The picture was of Nick in the pilot seat of a plane. Behind him were five dogs, all grinning, all with their tongues hanging out.

Tuesday 8:48 AM
Look at these mutts. I'm flying them from Little Rock to Austin to a rescue organization there. One of these could be Rufus's friend.

"I didn't know you and Nick were talking," Keesha said, her eyebrows rising with each word.

"I didn't, either," Charlotte said.

Tuesday 8:50 AM
They'd all be Rufus's friend. He's a Pisces, and therefore, according to all the charts, ultra popular.

More pictures popped up. They were of Amelia.

Tuesday 8:51 AM
When I drop these guys, I'm flying on to Three Rivers. Amelia and I are available for a playdate with Liam.

"What is he saying?" Keesha asked.

"That he and Hallie's baby are available for a playdate with Liam?" Charlotte said uncertainly, and looked at Keesha.

"Oh my God, is he asking you *out?*" Keesha nearly shouted.

"No! Well, maybe. But I don't think he—"

"Charlotte, if you let him back in, he will do the same thing—"

"I know, I know," she muttered, and quickly texted back before she did something foolish.

Tuesday 8:53 AM
I'll let Caitlin know.

She thought that would be it, but it wasn't. The texts continued. Nick started sending pictures of Pepper and Amelia. Amelia petting Pepper, Amelia eating applesauce and smearing it on her face. Amelia in her bouncy chair, playing with the attached smiling suns and flowers that wobbled around on springs as she moved.

At first, Charlotte didn't answer. She didn't understand what was happening, exactly. But she loved the pictures. One afternoon, she was with Cassie and Caitlin, and took a picture of Liam, his two bottom teeth prominently displayed. She sent it to Nick.

Her phone pinged a few minutes later.

Saturday 5:14 PM
I think you should know that I have plans for Amelia and Liam. They're going to get married and run Three Rivers Ranch. I'm going to give them my ranch house and bathtub as a wedding gift.

Charlotte snorted.
"Who are you texting?" Cassie asked.
Charlotte hardly spared her a glance. "Nick."
"No, you're not," Cassie scoffed.

Saturday 5:15 PM
Meli and Liam are not going to want to live under your hermit rock out there,

even with that awesome bathtub. They are going to want to be around friends and family LIKE NORMAL PEOPLE. I'll give them my house.

Saturday 5:16 PM
Your house? Where are you going to be?

"Are you really texting Nick?" Caitlin asked as she picked up Liam.

Charlotte sent another text before she answered.

Saturday 5:17 PM
Remains to be seen ☺.

She hit send, then looked up. "Yes, I am texting Nick."

"Why?" Caitlin demanded.

"He came to see me."

Cassie gasped so loudly that Rufus's head snapped up as if he thought food was involved. "Start talking," Cassie said, pointing at her.

Charlotte did. She told her sisters about his visit to her house. His declaration of love that had sunk into her soul and taken up residence in her thoughts. She told them about the texts he'd been sending her. How she wondered about his change of heart.

Caitlin was firmly against them getting back together. Charlotte hadn't said she would, but as she talked, she realized she was really thinking about it. "A guy hurts you once, shame on you. If he hurts you twice, shame on . . ." She paused. She shook her head. "Just shame on everyone, Charlotte."

But Cassie, who had wanted to beat Nick up in the beginning, was surprisingly thoughtful about it. "I don't know, I don't think he would have come back if he didn't really mean it."

"Really?" Charlotte asked.

"A guy wouldn't come back after all that time, *with a baby,* if he didn't mean it."

"It wasn't his baby!" Caitlin insisted.

"Well, of course not. He doesn't have a baby. He had to borrow one to make a point. But you have to admit, it's a big step forward for that stick-in-the-mud."

Charlotte laughed.

"I don't know what you see in him," Cassie continued. "But if you're into a billionaire in boots—"

"*Millionaire* in boots from what I've heard," Caitlin said, as if that was something to be ashamed about.

"Comfortable in boots is more like it," Charlotte corrected them.

"My point, if I may have the floor again," Cassie said impatiently, "is if you are into the guy in boots, he is totally into you." She shrugged. "Maybe you should go for it."

"And maybe she shouldn't," Caitlin argued. "Once an ass, always an ass."

"How many times did you and Jonah break up, again?" Charlotte asked, referring to the patchwork dating history Caitlin and Jonah had experienced before getting married.

"Shut up," Caitlin said, and turned a couple of shades of pink.

At this point, Liam started crying and Caitlin's kids came nosing into the kitchen looking for more snacks, and Charlotte's sisters forgot about Nick.

But Charlotte didn't. He was trying. No one but she knew how much effort it was for a guy like him to try like this. He'd taken a *selfie* for God's sake. She couldn't figure out how he was even doing it without her to tell him how.

But he was trying.

And the texts continued to come until Charlotte felt her defenses beginning to erode. Nick Prince got an A for effort.

From: NPrince@ultimateflight.org
To: Charlotte@saddlebushco.com
Subject: Check out these donkeys

Take a look at these two donkeys I am flying to Montana tomorrow. They were rescued from a farm in Illinois and someone knit them sweaters. Who knits sweaters for donkeys?

Charlotte stared at the picture he'd taken. Yep, that was two donkeys, all right, one in a baby blue sweater, one in a pink sweater.

From: Charlotte@saddlebushco.com
To: NPrince@ultimateflight.org
Subject: Re: Check out these donkeys

Whoever knit two enormous sweaters has way too much time on his or her hands, but I am totally going to do this for Rufus. Why do donkeys need sweaters? And what is the difference between a donkey and a mule, anyway?

From: NPrince@ultimateflight.org
To: Charlotte@saddlebushco.com
Subject: Re: Check out these donkeys

One is a jackass. These two donkeys are interesting. The one in pink really wants to go to the donkey refuge and can't wait to get the hell out of dodge. The donkey in blue doesn't trust anyone and doesn't want anything to do with me or anyone else. Keeps giving me the side eye. He acts like he's got big plans that don't include anyone but him. But the donkey in pink is friendly and wants to smell everything and brays a lot. I mean, *a lot*. Like she's telling me what to do. When the day came to move them off the farm where they'd been kept, the pink donkey was the first in the trailer. She fears nothing. The blue donkey hung back. He fears everything. Wouldn't even make eye contact. But when my colleague got in the driver's seat, the blue donkey started braying and bum-rushed the trailer. Nearly killed himself trying to get in. He wasn't going to let the pink donkey get away from him. Still won't let her out of his sight.

From: Charlotte@saddlebushco.com
To: NPrince@ultimateflight.org
Subject: Re: Check out these donkeys

Wait a minute—is this a parable? If it is, I demand to know which donkey is the jackass.

From: NPrince@ultimateflight.org
To: Charlotte@saddlebushco.com
Subject: Re: Check out these donkeys

The donkey in the blue sweater is definitely the jackass.

From: Charlotte@saddlebushco.com
To: NPrince@ultimateflight.org
Subject: Re: Check out these donkeys

Figures. You have to look out for the jackasses. They will sneak up on you when you least expect it. They are stubbornly loyal, apparently.

From: NPrince@ultimateflight.org
To: Charlotte@saddlebushco.com
Subject: Re: Check out these donkeys

I hear jackasses mate for life. I don't know about the pink donkey. She may be headed for greener pastures. It's a donkey sanctuary they are headed to, so who knows what she's got in mind.

From: Charlotte@saddlebushco.com
To: NPrince@ultimateflight.org
Subject: Re: Check out these donkeys

I hear pink donkeys really want to mate for life but often get caught up with jackasses. Speaking of jackasses, when are you coming home? Mateo has a new cocktail he's very proud of. It's called Sex in the Back Seat of Your Dad's Car. He said the drink speaks for itself. Think you could handle it?

From: NPrince@ultimateflight.org
To: Charlotte@saddlebushco.com
Subject: Re: Check out these donkeys

Jackasses can handle whatever pink donkeys throw at them.

Chapter Twenty-eight

Nick was nervous. He was never nervous about anything, but he was incredibly nervous about meeting Charlotte tonight. He'd made Hallie tell him one more time that he looked okay.

"You look great! But I am so glad you shaved off that beard," Hallie said. "You look really nice, Nick. Stop being nervous. You'll say something stupid if you're uptight."

"That is my fear."

She smiled. She handed him the bouquet of wildflowers she had picked with Amelia that morning. "Please tell Charlotte that Stars, Boots, and Music is starting up next weekend and the Baileys and the Princes should get a spot by the river. Liam and Amelia love each other so we have to be together. And so do you and Charlotte."

"I don't know if she does."

"She does, trust me."

"I should really tell her that?"

"Yes!" Hallie slapped the flowers against his chest. "God, I hope you don't do anything to mess this up," she said wistfully.

"Thanks for the vote of confidence," Nick said as he went out.

He was early to the Magnolia Bar and Grill, a sure sign that his nerves had gotten the best of him. He checked himself one last time in the rearview mirror, took a breath, and got out of the truck, shut the door, and locked it. Then immediately unlocked it and grabbed the bouquet Hallie had made for him.

He started for the door, making sure his shirt was tucked in, and silently questioning his judgment for wearing new boots tonight of all nights.

"Hey."

He heard her voice, but he couldn't see her. Nick did a quick twist around before spotting Charlotte walking up from the parking lot. She was wearing a dress the same color as her eyes, and he had a wild memory of those tanned legs wrapped around him. Her crazy curly hair had gotten longer and bounced around her face. And she was smiling that dazzling, brilliant smile that had lived in his heart all these months. She was happy to see him, and Nick felt that knowledge zap through him like a cattle prod.

"Charlotte."

She walked forward and glanced down. "Were those supposed to be for me?"

Nick looked down, too. He hadn't even realized that he'd dropped the bouquet. "God. Yes." He quickly dipped down and scooped them up. "Amelia picked them."

"*Oh,*" she said, and her face lit with pleasure. She took them from him, put them to her nose, and smiled at him over the top. "You look great, Nick."

"So do you."

"I forgot how square your jaw is. I think you've gotten hotter."

He arched a brow.

"Well? I have to call it like I see it." She laughed.

He wanted to laugh, but he felt like he was on pins and needles. "Thank you for . . . for this," he said, nodding at the Magnolia.

She shifted closer. "Don't be nervous, Nicholas Nickleby."

He nodded. He swallowed.

She tilted her head to one side. "Let me ask you something. Do you still love me?"

"What?" He was surprised by the question, but his love for her flared. He nodded again. Earnestly. "I do," he said hoarsely. "Always."

Charlotte slipped her hand into his. "Good."

"Do . . . ah, do . . ."

"I'm here, aren't I?"

"Charlotte," he said, but his tongue felt thick. He wanted to tell her how much he loved her, how much he wanted this with her. He wanted to give her as many babies as she could carry and show them—his little family—the world.

She waited for him to speak.

"Charlotte," he said again, and damn it if he didn't feel dangerously close to tears.

But it turned out he didn't have to speak. Not now, anyway, because Charlotte understood. She rose up on her toes and kissed his cheek. "It's okay, Nick. It's all good. We've got a lot to talk about, like the why and the how and the when, but I promise you, it's all good. I've really missed you."

He thought he might sink to his knees with relief. He didn't know where this was going to take them. All he knew was that she was here, and he'd never been so grateful, so adoring, so in love in his life. He cleared his throat. His hand was shaking as he sank it into her curls to pull her forward and kissed her. A long hello kiss.

When he let her go, he said, "Do you want some sex in your dad's car, or whatever?"

Charlotte laughed, the sound of it like music in his heart. "*So* bad," she said, and put her arm around his waist as they began to walk to the door. "Guess what?" she asked as they moved to the door. "I've been learning to knit."

"You have?"

She nodded. "I'm knitting a blue sweater." She glanced up, the mirth dancing in her eyes. "You'll need it where we're going."

This jackass would follow her to the ends of the earth. "Where are we going?"

"Unclear," she said as they walked up the steps.

"But far. Farther than we've ever gone before."
She winked and opened the door.

Nick looked up to the blue sky overhead and closed his eyes. For the first time in his life, he realized there were other, perhaps even more satisfying ways to soar than a plane.

But far, further; this we... ... before
Sits ...cked and orgastic the ...
which looked up to... ...blue...wanderers
...lost his eyes like the ...sacred to all...
...my own ...
...rushing...

Epilogue

Cordelia was seated across from George at the Magnolia Bar and Grill. She was wearing a new blouse and the pearl necklace Charlie had given her for their twenty-fifth wedding anniversary. George had on a button-down with a sport coat. "Is this a date, George?" Cordelia asked after he ordered bourbon on the rocks for them.

"What do you want it to be, Delia?"

"I don't know about her, but *I* want it to be dinner and soon," Dolly said.

Cordelia sighed and turned her head to look at her mother-in-law. After manipulating an invitation for herself, Dolly had dressed in a Spanish skirt and cowboy boots, as if she intended to get up and perform a Mexican folkloric dance later.

"That's why I asked," George said kindly.

Cordelia looked at George and rolled her eyes.

The waiter appeared with bourbons for the three of them, then asked to take their order.

"I'll have the nachos," Dolly said.

"Lord. You'll be up all night," Cordelia warned her.

"Worth it," Dolly said with a shrug. "You only go around once, you know. Sometimes you have to sacrifice a little sleep to enjoy the ride. Which, I might add, is what everyone is saying about Nick and Charlotte. They are sacrificing sleep to enjoy the ride, if you get my meaning."

"For heaven's sake," Cordelia muttered.

"What would you like, Delia?" George asked.

"The salmon," Cordelia said, and closed her menu and handed it to the waiter.

"I'll have the same," George said.

When the waiter left, George lifted his glass. "To the sale of the Saddlebush Land and Cattle Company office building. That's a cool 1.2 million in your bucket."

"Good," Dolly said, and clinked their glasses. "I've had my eye on those gravity-free loungers for the cemetery over at Walmart. We should also toast Nick and Charlotte. Lloyd says he thinks they'll be married before the end of the year."

"Lloyd speaks?" Cordelia asked.

"Oh, he's got lots to say. He said he can tell just by the way that Nick looks at Charlotte that he's itching to get down on one knee. Just you watch."

Cordelia groaned. "Why did you invite her, again?" she asked George.

"Because he loves me, too, Delia," Dolly said, and patted her hand. "We're a boxed set."

Cordelia looked at George. He gave her a subtle wink to let her know he understood they were not a boxed set, and reached for her hand across the table. "It's a date, Delia."

Cordelia smiled. She was still getting used to the idea of dating George. She'd known him forever, but had never thought of him as a romantic partner, obviously, as she'd been married all those years. But he'd pointed out that they weren't getting any younger, and there was a spark between them. Moreover, Cordelia had to admit that Nick was right—George was good for her.

They chatted about the final sale of the office building until the food came, and then about the kids. Always the kids. Dolly was expounding on her theory that Nick and Charlotte would start a family before Luca and Ella when Cordelia became aware of someone's eyes on her. She turned to look, and her gaze met the blue-eyed gaze of Charlie Prince.

Except it wasn't Charlie, of course. It was his bastard son, Tanner Sutton. The love child Charlie had sired with Margaret Sutton Rhodes while Cordelia was busy being the perfect wife and mother. Tanner smiled tentatively, a little hopefully, and lifted his hand.

Cordelia tried to smile but she couldn't manage it. She turned away from him.

If that young man thought he could somehow be a *Prince,* that he was going to develop some sort of community on land that Charlie should *never* have given him, he was sorely mistaken.

Books are produced in the United States using U.S.-based materials	Books are printed using a revolutionary new process called THINKtech™ that lowers energy usage by 70% and increases overall quality	Books are durable and flexible because of Smyth-sewing	Paper is sourced using environmentally responsible foresting methods and the paper is acid-free

Center Point Large Print
600 Brooks Road / PO Box 1
Thorndike, ME 04986-0001 USA

(207) 568-3717

US & Canada:
1 800 929-9108
www.centerpointlargeprint.com